The Second Life of Ged Baker
Secrets of Porthcovery Grange

by

F. E. Miles

**Grosvenor House
Publishing Limited**

This book is published by
Grosvenor House Publishing Ltd
Link House
140 The Broadway, Tolworth, Surrey, KT6 7HT.
www.grosvenorhousepublishing.co.uk

This book is a work of fiction. Any resemblance to
people or events, past or present, is purely coincidental.

A CIP record for this book
is available from the British Library

Paperback ISBN 978-1-83615-302-3
eBook ISBN 978-1-83615-303-0

This book is dedicated to my inspirational friend Jessica.
Without her persistent encouragement,
it would never have been published.

And also thanks to my family and friends for their ideas,
patience and encouragement.

Prologue

October 2019

The October afternoon sun has a curious effect on the east coast of Cornwall, or so it seems to me. The dullest scene is transformed by the unique fluidity of the sunlight, which has an enriching effect on the dazzling array of autumn leaves at this time of year. It was this effect that I noticed in the garden of Porthcovrey Grange care home, the day I first visited Aunt Mary, not long after she became a resident.

I suppose it's possible that those beautiful autumn colours in that rich and oddly watery autumn sun might have been the thing that cast its spell and gave me a deep and lasting fondness for the place. It might also have been the breathtaking views visible from the bay window of the communal sitting room over Porthcovrey Bay towards the promontory of Falmouth. The millpond calm bay, ever-changing from steel-grey to the most iridescent, Mediterranean, turquoise as it reflected the sky's mood.

The truth is that it was neither of these beautiful things. It was the beauty I found *within* those walls in the residents of Porthcovery Grange.

To the average visitor coming to see an elderly relative, it appeared much like any other residential care home: with hard-wearing, scrupulously clean, red and blue paisley-patterned carpets and those high-backed, wipe-clean blue and pink padded armchairs with their familiar, uncomfortable-looking wooden armrests. I never could figure out why such places use these chairs. If I were to sit for hours in my dotage, I should hope that I may have a sufficiently padded place to rest my weary old arms while having an afternoon doze or gazing out of the window at those beautiful views lost in my memories (or lost in my lack of them should I be so afflicted).

I sat with Aunt Mary at a round coffee table in the sunny bay window. We had been served afternoon tea with scones, a dollop of strawberry jam, and lashings of locally made clotted cream. It had been a long time since I had drunk tea from china cups with matching saucers, and there was almost a sense of occasion about it.

Aunt Mary had been here three months and had settled in well. I can't imagine anyone finding it hard to get on with her. She had the staff in fits of giggles with her stories, which seemed to have had more details added and had become slightly more risqué (or perhaps I was just too young for the full-blown versions the first time she told them). As the only female engineer at RNAS Culdrose, the air base at Helston, she had earned a reputation for telling shaggy dog stories.

"I've been looking forward to seeing you, Jane," said Aunt Mary. "I know you're going to love hearing about the friends I've met here." She leaned forward, glanced left and right to make sure no one was in earshot and lowered her voice to a conspiratorial whisper. "You wouldn't believe some of the things I've heard. I was hoping you would write them down so that the fascinating people here might be remembered long after we are all pushing up the daffodils."

"Isn't it daisies, Aunt Mary?"

"Pardon, dear?"

"You said, 'pushing up daffodils'; it's pushing up daisies, isn't it?"

"Never liked the things dear, awful little weeds; I'd much rather push up a nice bunch of daffs when I'm gone, wouldn't you?"

"Um...I've never really thought about it," I said truthfully.

There were eight other residents in the lounge. She scanned her eyes around the room, then nodded towards a lady doing a crossword at a table in the corner. At least, it looked as though she was doing a crossword. She had a pen in her hand, and the newspaper was open at the crossword section, but there was no movement from the pen or the rest of her, for that matter. It was as though someone had pressed 'pause' on an invisible remote control.

"Take Miriam over there, for example," said Aunt Mary. "She's ninety-eight. We get along famously. During the war, she was drafted to make aircraft parts in the Birmingham munitions factories. Oh, don't worry that she's not moving; she has these absences where she just sits for a few minutes. It's one of the reasons she's here. I think it's some sort of mild seizure. She'll come-to in a minute."

"I must admit, I did wonder," I said.

"Anyway," Aunt Mary continued, "Miriam was a dab hand with a screwdriver. She says she enjoyed the work and did well at the factory, but I think there's more she hasn't told me yet. After the war, she married a cameraman from the BBC. They went all over the place filming wildlife in the seventies before settling down in Oxfordshire."

She paused momentarily as if in thought, so I took a sip of tea and nodded for her to continue. I loved to listen to her stories.

"Well," she said with a conspiratorial look, "The husband had an accident of some sort, and...to cut a long story short, the settlement was very generous. She sold the place in Oxford, bought a little cottage down here with the insurance money and lived here ever since. She must be local; she's got a Cornish accent." Aunt Mary took a bite of her jammy scone and continued talking through the crumbs. "She made a fortune in the '90s house-price boom and owns a few houses in the village, or at least so one of the cleaners told me." I raised my eyebrows at this, but I wasn't surprised. Aunt Mary's second career was as a journalist. She had a knack for digging up a good story and had a way about her that made other people talk. It was Aunt Mary who had sparked a keen interest in story writing for me as a child. On sunny days, we would observe people in the village and on the beach from behind mirrored sunglasses so they wouldn't know we were looking at them, creating imaginary characters using what we had observed: what they ate, how they dressed, walked, played and behaved. We spent wet or cold afternoons in her cottage if we weren't reading or baking, making up and writing stories about some of the people we had seen that week.

"Then there's Bert," she nodded towards a slim gentleman in a wheelchair watching TV on the other side of the lounge. He wore salmon pink chinos, a short-sleeved cotton shirt of a lurid pastel multi-coloured plaid, and polished tan leather slippers. He looked as if he ought to be on a golf course.

"He was in the Navy most of his life – did a tour of duty in the Falklands – claims to be the first gay serving officer in the Royal Naval Air Service."

I frowned quizzically at this -

"But surely, he would have been given a dishonourable discharge, Aunt Mary. In those days, wasn't it against the rules?"

"He couldn't come out; the consequences were too severe, but his commanding officer got him a posting at Culdrose, away from the gossip. That's how I know him. I hadn't seen him for twenty-five years before I came here. He's a real joker… had a string of boyfriends, but he never settled with anyone. His niece and her husband come every Tuesday to take him out; very sweet with him, they are." She picked up her teacup and settled herself more comfortably in her chair.

"He still has a house in Helston. He rents it out to help pay for this place… where he gets the rest of the money; I have no idea… I'll have to do some more digging."

The cynic in me wondered if the niece hoped his house might be left to her. Aunt Mary saw my expression and gave me a hard stare.

"I know what you're thinking," she said with pursed lips. "He told me he's leaving everything to a dog's home. He's barmy about Chihuahuas. His niece brings a couple when she comes, but he can't keep a dog here. Pity, a few dogs would cheer up some of the old stiffs and liven the place up."

"Stan, over there," she continued, "he's Polish – Stanislav Goldman. He was a POW but escaped before repatriation. He thought he would be gassed if he went home."

"Oh, the poor man," I murmured, "Do you think he ever went back?"

"Not as far as I know, but that's not the interesting part," she said, looking left and right and whispered, "His story is of unrequited love. He spent his twenties in Cornwall, working for a crust on farms, milking cows, picking vegetables, and cutting daffodils, depending on the season. Spent some time on that Trellassick estate… met the daughter of the lord of the manor and...well, that's a story for another day.

"I suppose this place must be expensive," I mused. "Are you managing, okay?"

"Oh, yes, Dear," Aunt Mary replied. I said I would put some of my book money away for a rainy day; it turned out there was enough for a year of thunderstorms!"

Mary had written a few books about her exploits as the first female engineer in the Royal Navy, the challenges she faced, and some of the more colourful and entertaining things she did during her service days. They were not blockbusters but were well received, especially by feminists and service personnel. Reviews usually contained phrases like 'page-turner' and 'hysterical'. One critic wrote: '*Hilarious, but not for the faint-hearted.*' A television producer loved the books and created a sitcom series based on them. Royalties still trickled into her bank account from the repeats.

She had always intended to use the proceeds to go on safari, but never seemed to get around to it. Then, when her health began to falter, she wrote more and travelled less. Now, she was wealthy enough to stay here for several years.

"More about them when I see you next time, Jane," she said, lowering her tone so that I had to lean closer. "The one I really wanted to tell you about first is young Gerald over there with Emily. Have you got a dictaphone app on that smartphone of yours?"

"Sure, why?" I said, surprised that she had asked the question.

"Because I think this is your first novel," she said simply, "and I want you to remember every detail."

I reached into the back pocket of my jeans for my phone and thumbed to the voice-memo app. Aunt Mary recorded all her interviews on a dictaphone to avoid libel or misquotes. Each tape carried a sticker penned in Aunt Mary's neat, swirly capital letters with date, time, place and interviewee. I remembered the tapes carefully filed in shoe boxes under her spare bed. She was nothing if not thorough.

The man Aunt Mary had indicated was called Gerald Baker. I had seen a glasses case on the table next to him, with the name; I thought I had heard the name before, although I heard one of the staff calling him 'Ged' when I arrived. Aunt Mary confirmed that everyone called him Ged or "Chippy."

I regarded him as he snoozed. He sat in his uncomfortable-looking, blue-padded, wooden-framed armchair by the bay window; his eyes closed, the corners of his smiling mouth twitching slightly as if dreaming. His right arm was dangling, and he held the hand of the elderly lady next to him.

Aunt Mary poured more tea and tapped her saucer with the spoon, waking me from my daydream.

"Are you recording?"

"Sorry, Aunt Mary. Tell me about him," I said as I opened the app again and tapped the red button to start recording.

"That's Emily", she said, inclining her head towards the lady whose hand Ged gently held. She was also dozing in the syrupy afternoon sun.

"How nice that a husband and wife can be together here," I said.

"Oh, they're not married," said Aunt Mary. "But Emily tells me that they are very much in love." I sat up, hooked. Aunt Mary went on, "Emily met Ged years ago when she ran a restaurant in Porthleven. He took his family for dinner there about twice a week when they came here on holiday. I may have taken you there once or twice. It's the little place by the harbour with Georgian-style bay windows on either side of the door where you can hardly ever get a seat."

I remembered the café, with its red gingham tablecloths, glass vinegar bottles, and salt and pepper shakers on every table. Sketches and paintings covered the walls, each with a small price tag. I often wondered whether they made more money selling paintings and postcards or serving customers tea, cakes, and fish and chips.

***

This is the story my Aunt Mary told me over tea and scones in that beautiful Cornish nursing home. Ged's daughter-in-law has since given me a few extra details, and the rest I made up. I've used artistic license to protect the innocent!

Warwickshire, July 1998

Ged Baker pushed the last of the bags into the boot of the Honda estate; the heavy blue picnic backpack was stuffed with juice and milk cartons. It stuck out, so he shoved it with both hands and slammed the rear door hard to make it latch. Packing the car had left him breathless and sticky. Wiping beads of sweat from his forehead with a tissue, he thought: *How on earth can two people need all this luggage?*

"Come on, Marge," he called. "I'm sure Mrs Teal will water the begonias tomorrow. Can we please just go? I want to get there before midnight." His wife, Marge, was nowhere to be seen. *Probably dead-heading geraniums*, he mused.

It was 6 pm on a sunny July evening. They were setting off for their annual fortnight's holiday with their son, his wife and the grandchildren in their holiday house in Cornwall. They always journeyed later to avoid the Bristol and Exeter rush hours. They would get coffee on the way and arrive around eleven for a quick chat and a nightcap before bed.

"Have you seen my handbag, Gerald?" called Marge from the front door as she zipped up a green diamond quilted gilet over her rose-printed blouse.

"In the boot, Marge, I just put it there," Ged called back.

"Oh, honestly, Gerald! We never put my handbag in the boot. Get it out, please. I want it in the front."

"Yes, of course; sorry, I'll get it now." He went to the back of the car, shaking his head, scolding himself for forgetting to put her bag in the front, and perplexed at how anyone could wear a gilet in this heat. He opened the tailgate, and the heavy blue backpack that he had just forced in leapt out and landed on top of his left foot.

"Bastard!" yelled Ged, hopping desperately on his right foot. He turned and sat down heavily on the tailgate, biting his left hand to stop himself from swearing any more.

"Gerald! Language, please!" scolded Marge, hurrying to the back of the car. "What on earth has happened?"

Ged's face was screwed up in agony. "It's that bloody cool pack," he growled through clenched teeth. "It's fallen on my foot. It's murder!" God knows why we have to take all that sodding wine anyway; Brian and Sarah bring loads!"

"It's my favourite Chardonnay... I'll get some frozen peas," she said, rolling her eyes and hurrying back to the house, fumbling in her gilet pocket for the key. She quickly grabbed a bag of peas from the freezer, snatched a neatly ironed and folded blue-checked tea towel from the drawer to wrap them in and jogged back to him. Ged had taken off his shoe to check the damage. He tried to remove his sock, but it hurt too much.

"Here, take these. Put your foot on the backpack; let's get this ice on it." She gingerly placed the pea and tea towel parcel on his foot.

"Aaargh!" he cried, "Get it off!"

"If you can't stand a bag of peas on it, you need to go to hospital," she said simply.

"I'm not going to A and E on a Friday evening when we have a four-and-a-half-hour journey to make. I'll put up with the peas," he mumbled grumpily.

"How did it happen anyway?" asked Marge suspiciously.

Ged didn't want to admit that it was entirely his fault for forcing the bag into the boot.

"The cool bag fell out as I was reaching for your bag," he muttered. "Can you get the handbag? The cool pack can go behind the passenger seat." Marge didn't press him on the matter. She fetched her handbag and stowed the backpack after carefully lifting his foot up onto the bumper of the car.

"Can you drive?" asked Marge tentatively.

"I'll manage," mumbled Ged and tried to stand. Just placing his foot on the ground was agony! He took a deep breath and tried to hop out of the way of the car as he brought the tailgate down again. He hopped to the driver's door and sat clumsily on the seat with both legs outside the car.

"Marge, would you get my shoe and pop it in the back, please? I left it behind the car. I'll drive in my socks." He undid the laces and took off his other shoe, tossing it in the back of the car, swung both legs in and put his seat belt on. Marge went to lock the front door, relieved that they were on their way. She was putting the key in the lock when there was a scream of pain from Ged.

"It's my clutch foot!" he cried. "There's no way I can drive." He looked at her with an expression of apology and pleading. "You'll have to drive, Marge."

Marge turned pale. She didn't like driving and positively *hated* motorways. She hadn't done a long journey in over twenty years. She took a deep breath and closed her eyes. She so wanted to be in Porthcovrey, sitting in the garden, doing a crossword with the view of the sea and a glass of white wine, the book she had been saving for the holiday. The thought of this gave her strength.

"Oh, this is typical, Gerald! I told you to get an automatic when we bought this huge thing…" She glanced around the packed car, her hands planted on her hips, closed her eyes and took another deep breath. "Alright. I'll do it," she said in a decisive tone. "But no complaining about how fast I'm going. I hate the motorway…I'm going to get something. Wait here."

"I'm not going anywhere," muttered Ged miserably.

Marge hurried back to the house. She went first to the drinks cabinet in the dining room and fetched a bottle of whisky; grabbed a small glass from the kitchen (She didn't want her husband looking like a vagrant); then opened the internal door to the garage and grabbed a pair of crutches, which were leaning behind the door. She had bought them when she twisted her ankle on the ice last winter. She took the crutches, whisky, the tumbler and her headscarf from the coat hook, then returned to the car with them all. She poured Ged a generous measure of whisky and told him to knock it back.

"Why the sudden booze-fest?"

"To help with the pain," she said. "*Plus, you might nod off and won't moan about my driving*", she thought to herself. "Swing your legs out and

3

lean on me to stand up. Don't put your foot on the floor." Ged took the crutches from her, giving her a grateful kiss. He looked into her eyes. "You are wonderful, Margie. Have I ever told you that?"

"Oh, once or twice, and less of the *'Margie'* if you don't mind. I'm not a little girl."

Ged hopped slowly round to the other side of the car on the crutches. Marge had left the door open. While he made his way around, Marge tied the autumn-leaf-patterned headscarf in a knot under her chin. The car windows would need to be left open, and she had been to the hairdresser that day to get her hair set.

They set off in silence, save for a deep breath: Marge for courage; Ged for patience.

Marge's driving always irritated Ged. He enjoyed driving, and it annoyed him when she wouldn't overtake or if she dawdled.

Ged tried to doze as they set off. He knew he would get frustrated if he kept his eyes open. Sleep wouldn't come. His foot throbbed, and he was ravenously hungry. Marge's pre-holiday diet meant that they had only eaten a bowl of leek soup that evening, not even a crust of bread with it! Marge had done well on the diet. She was slimmer than she had looked for years! She had her slinky waist back again and was wearing some of her old dresses and a few new ones she had bought, presumably as a reward for losing weight.

"Marge, indicate! We are going left here, aren't we?" he said at the end of the lane.

"There's no one to indicate to, Gerald," Marge replied, glancing in the rearview mirror. Ged sighed.

Marge took another deep breath. She would have to take a lot more deep breaths on this trip. She would rather sit through ten episodes of Star Trek than drive to Cornwall. This was going to be a very long four-and-a-half hours.

"Marge, this isn't the way we usually go to the Motorway," said Ged, trying to sound conversational.

"I want to get on at the Junction where you can only get on in one direction. It's quieter."

"Good idea. It *will* be quiet in the evening."

4

"Thank you, Gerald. Nice to have a compliment for once, she said tersely."

Marge was hardly touching sixty-five miles an hour. Ged was grinding his teeth to a stump, but the first hour or so passed without incident. As they neared Bristol, the traffic became busier. Marge gripped the wheel so tightly that her knuckles were white.

"I wish these drivers would make up their minds about which lane to use. Everybody keeps juggling around…" she babbled. "All these lorries and caravans are in the way, and I can't see past."

Oh great, here we go… Thought Ged, *she's babbling…And that means that she's not concentrating…* Subconsciously, his senses sharpened. He noticed other drivers giving her less room and passengers glaring at her as they overtook. Marge stayed in the middle lane. Ged suggested she get into the slow lane to allow the faster drivers to pass. Marge hesitated, then became boxed in as she was going so slowly.

The familiar sight of Avonmouth docks came into view, with acres and acres of parked new cars glinting in the sun, the huge loading cranes dominating the skyline. Marge yawned and fidgeted in her seat.

"If we stop for coffee, we can wait until the traffic dies down," she suggested.

"We shouldn't stop long," replied Ged. "All the trucks we've passed will overtake us, and we'll be right back where we were half an hour ago."

They agreed on a takeaway coffee. Ravenously hungry, Ged bought a sneaky chocolate bar from the shop, scoffing it before he got back to the car whilst Marge was in the queue for coffee.

Back on the Motorway, the traffic had eased. Marge sat up straighter and appeared more focused. A lifetime tea drinker, she found the coffee helped, at least at first… She *was* more alert. Her heart beat in her chest like a butterfly. Ged tried not to comment but noticed her grip on the wheel had tightened again.

"You're doing great, Marge," he said, hoping to ease her nerves.

"Don't be patronising, Gerald!" Marge said curtly, "I've had a driving licence as long as you have. I do know what I'm doing."

"Just trying to be nice. You seemed nervous."

"Oh, go to sleep," she snapped.

Ged tried to settle down. His foot throbbed. He tried another large shot of whisky. It didn't do much for the pain, but after a few minutes, he seemed to care a little less about it. Despite a desperate urge to speak, on several occasions, he managed to bite his lip until Marge almost gave a BMW a new number plate when she hesitated and then suddenly came out in front of it from between two huge vans. The driver blared his horn and flashed his headlights. Marge hadn't checked her mirrors, and Ged couldn't keep quiet.

"Your hesitation probably caused that. It's a good thing that chap has decent anchors, or we'd have been back-ended," he chided as calmly as he could.

"If I had gone earlier, a bruised foot would be the least of our problems," she retorted. "Look at him! He thinks he's driving a spaceship! He thinks that 'i' on his BMW stands for 'important'… 'idiot', more like." She was starting to shriek.

"Okay, Marge… I'm only saying that you could be a little more decisive."

"Rubbish," she interrupted. "It was that idiot going too fast. He's probably late for dinner with his mistress!"

Ged raised his eyebrows. *'Best to keep quiet, or it will get worse,'* he thought.

The situation with the BMW had shaken Marge, and she concentrated better if anything. Ged eventually dozed off as they left the motorway.

***

The car swayed as they went along twisty roads, and Ged's head lolled from side to side, which woke him. He blinked a few times, rubbing the back of his neck as he got his bearings. Marge was hunched forward, peering into the dusk.

"Why aren't you using your headlights?" Ged asked groggily.

6

"I don't know where the switch is," she admitted sheepishly. "I've never driven this car in the dark."

"Left-hand column stalk." Ged yawned.

Marge fumbled for the switch. Ged reached across and turned the lights on.

"Thank you," mumbled Marge.

"No harm done," he said. Shifting back into his seat, his face screwed up in agony.

"Jeez!" he yelped. "It's worse than ever!"

"Oh, Gerald. You gave me a shock! If it's that painful, you need to see a doctor. Maybe the hospital in Truro has an Accident and Emergency department. I think you need an X-ray."

"Oh, come on," he groaned. "It's just a bad bruise. I'll be ok in a day or so." But his tone wasn't convincing anyone.

Marge pulled into an almost empty supermarket car park and stopped near the door. She turned to Ged, a serious expression on her face.

"I'm phoning Annie," she said, "and then we can decide. Pass me my handbag." Her sister, Annie, had been a senior ICU nurse. Marge took the mobile phone their son Brian had bought her from her bag. She had only used it a few times, but she could see there was a faint signal. Ged sat back and awaited the inevitable. There was no arguing with Annie.

"Hi, Annie," said Marge brightly. "No, not yet ... Truro. Listen, I don't have time for chit-chat. Ged had something heavy fall on his foot earlier this evening: a picnic bag. He's in quite a bit of pain. Do you think we should get an X-ray?" Ged could make out Annie's voice on the other end of the call...

"Can he wriggle his toes freely without any more discomfort?"

Ged tried to wriggle his toes, knowing the answer already. For the third time that evening, he bit his hand to stop himself swearing. He shook his head vigorously.

"Okay, that's a no. Look, can you remember if there's an A and E department in Truro? Right. Near Sainsbury's... Thanks. I think I should be able to find it."

She pressed the end call button and checked her watch. Five past Ten…

"Gerald, wait here. I'll get directions."

"Okay, I promise I won't run off," he said dryly.

Marge went into the store. At the customer service counter, she explained her predicament. The assistant acted as though she was asked this kind of thing every night and seemed disappointed that Marge hadn't had anything more interesting to ask.

"Yeah, it's easy," she said, yawning. "Take the dual carriageway up the 'ill to the double roundabout and get on the a-three-ninety. Sainsbury's is about a mile up there on yer right. The roundabout for the hospital is another 'alf mile after that."

"Well, thank you…erm, Janet," said Marge, looking at the girl's badge.

"Oh, I'm not Janet; I'm Hermione. I couldn't find my Jacket, so I borrowed Janet's," she shrugged.

"Right, well, thank you, *Hermione*…I hope you find your jacket," said Marge briskly but politely.

***

Marge drove as close as she could to the Emergency Department entrance to drop Ged off and went to park the car.

Ged, half-shuffled, half-hopped to the doors on Marge's crutches. They were too short. He had to bend his left knee to avoid putting his foot on the floor; his face was pale, his mouth a tight line. A friendly-looking grey-haired nurse met him at the second doorway, "Oh dear. It looks like you've been in the wars. Let me help you," she said kindly. She took one crutch, put an arm expertly under his left elbow, guiding him into the waiting area.

Ged squinted as he entered the brightly lit, white-washed waiting area. It was almost empty, except for a blond-haired young man in a yellow and black striped rugby kit, his arm in a blood-stained bandage, and a frail-looking elderly lady in a wheelchair with curly silver hair. Next to her, a man, Ged presumed her son, stroked her hand.

"Come straight into triage, sir," said the nurse brightly. "Let's get you sorted."

"My wife is parking the car. She won't know where I am," said Ged.

"I'm sure she's a bright woman; she'll work it out. We're not a large department," she said gently. "Come and take a seat in my office."

She helped him into a plastic chair, briskly pulled across the blue-patterned plastic curtain, and went over to a chair by a computer on a small table.

Ged explained about the bag and even admitted to how it came to spring out of the car in the first place. The nurse made notes and asked for his name, address, date of birth, next of kin and so on. Then she bent down to look at his foot and asked if she could remove his sock. He said it would be fine… that is, until she attempted it, at which point, he swore and bit his hand again, which now sported a red semi-circle of tooth marks.

"I think you had better have a good curse, Mr Baker, or we'll need to treat that hand, as well. We can leave the sock on. It's likely you've cracked a bone in your foot; we'll know better after the X-ray. I'll get you a wheelchair," she said simply.

"Is that necessary?"

"If you've broken your foot, we don't want it waggling about 'til it's sorted."

She swept out and returned with a comfortable-looking, upright, padded red wheelchair with small wheels. She applied the brake and helped Ged into the chair, carefully placing his feet on the footplates. Then, she wheeled him out to the reception area, where Marge stood waiting.

"Wheelchair!" Marge said in a worried tone. "That bad?"

"You must be Mrs Baker," said the triage nurse, smiling. Mr Baker needs an X-ray. Please take a seat." She wheeled Ged to the end of a row of hard plastic chairs so that they could sit together." I'll call down to X-ray. I think you can go straight down," she said and returned to the cubicle.

"She thinks I've broken my foot," said Ged sadly. "She didn't even take my sock off, but my bad language when she tried said it all."

Marge pursed her lips; driving down was bad enough, she thought. Would she have to drive back as well?

In the X-ray suite, the radiologist helped Ged get onto the table and positioned his foot, once flat on the table, then on its side. Ged clenched his teeth and uttered an involuntary squeak each time she moved his foot.

The radiologist wheeled him into a curtained cubicle with a hospital bed and offered them a drink of water. The tea machine was broken, she explained.

"I'd rather have a Scotch," Ged whispered to Marge.

"Not sure they'd approve in here," she whispered back.

Marge got out her phone and tried to call Brian to tell him they were delayed, but there was no signal. She thought of sending a text message, but couldn't remember how. She recalled that one had to press the number buttons once, twice or three times, depending on which letters one needed, but how to get to that point, she had no idea. She thrust the phone into her bag in frustration. A young doctor entered the cubicle. "I'm Dr Tanner," she said. "Is it Mr and Mrs Baker?"

"Yes," said Marge.

She checked Ged's date of birth and full name before proceeding. "I'm afraid you've broken a small bone in your foot, Mr Baker," she said, clipping the X-ray film to a light box. The fluorescent bulb flickered into glaring life, with the grey bones on the X-ray film quite clear. "Here." She pointed with her biro. "It's the third metatarsal. There's the crack; it's not displaced, though."

"Do I need a plaster cast?"

"It'll be a boot. You'll need paracetamol to help you sleep comfortably. Ibuprofen can also reduce inflammation. I'll get a prescription made up."

Dr Tanner left the cubicle. Marge delved in her handbag for tablets, prising two white paracetamols from a blister pack, which Ged took gratefully with some water. He wondered why she hadn't given them to him earlier. Dr Tanner returned with two large grey plastic boots, which looked like spare parts for a pantomime robot. She checked Ged's size by holding the insole under his good foot. She told him to grit his teeth but pay attention while she fitted it, showing him how the thick fabric liner went on, followed by a curved panel, then the hard plastic "boot" secured with velcro straps. Ged's jaw ached from clenching his teeth.

Dr Tanner asked him to stand up on his crutches. She took one, adjusted its length with the button on the shaft, and returned it to him. She nodded, satisfied. She then took the other, adjusted it in the same way, handed it back, and he shuffled forward.

"I think you'll manage," she said. "Keep your weight off the foot and elevate it as much as possible over the next few weeks to reduce the swelling."

The triage nurse had fetched the prescription. Ged took the ibuprofen immediately.

"If you have some food with you, it's a good idea to have something. Ibuprofen can irritate your stomach," she warned. "Anyway, I hope you manage to have a good holiday in spite of this, even if you can't go hiking."

2

Back in the car, Ged sighed heavily, thinking about how much this would affect the holiday. He loved playing with the grandchildren, but what on earth would it be like with a broken foot?

He directed Marge to the road out of Truro. Marge felt more confident as she navigated the familiar roads. Ged wished the car was an automatic so that he could drive. Marge was so slow. On the plus side, the painkillers were beginning to have an effect. It was past 11 pm. His head dropped back onto the headrest, and before long, Marge noticed that he was breathing softly and deeply.

She took a swig of cold water and shook her head. There weren't many cars on the road. The bright headlights of cars that came towards her blackened the space beyond them, making it hard to make out the edge of the road. She slowed down even more in the corners because it was so difficult to see the bends. Her spirits lifted with each familiar landmark or place name. The petrol station near Carnon Downs, the college buildings near Falmouth, RNAS Culdrose with its high wire fences, and she relaxed as she saw the red lights at the top of the radio telescopes on Goonhilly Downs.

"Nearly there," she said aloud, with a sigh. A jumble of feelings washed over her: relief, exhaustion, frustration, contentment and anticipation at the thought of seeing Brian and Sarah, a cup of tea and a glass of Chardonnay that Brian would have made sure was waiting for her. "Brian!" she exclaimed out loud. "Oh, Gerald, they'll have been worried sick!"

Ged blearily blinked and snuffled awake. His foot throbbed, and his neck was stiff from the position he had been snoozing in.

"Whassamadda?" he mumbled sleepily.

"It's nearly midnight, Gerald!" she snapped.

"Oh…uh, I suppose so… um…" He said, forcing himself awake. Marge would start getting cross if he didn't say something coherent soon.

"It's not far now. They'll just think we got stuck in traffic," he said, trying to exude calm and confidence.

"Well, you should have called them when we stopped at the hospital," she snapped. "I don't know why you didn't think of it, Gerald!" Marge set her lips in a tight line. Ged could think of a perfectly good reason why he hadn't thought to phone Brian and Sarah; he had been a bit preoccupied with one thing and another. Added to which, he recalled, that although Marge appeared to have forgotten, she had tried to send a text while she was at the hospital, but seemed not to know how. Ged thought it best not to point this out as his head might take leave of his shoulders if he did.

"I'll try them now," he said quietly, pulling the phone from Marge's bag. The signal was awful, and there was no reply, only Brian's voicemail. Ged left a brief message apologising for being late, hung up, and started sending a text.

"There's no point doing that now!" snapped Marge. "It's too late now!" Ged took another quiet, deep breath.

The remainder of the journey passed quietly enough, although Ged had to remind Marge about dipping her high beams from time to time.

As they wound down the steep hill and into the fishing village of Porthcovery, Marge's mood lightened again as their favourite sight met their eyes.

The full moon shone across the rippling water of the bay from the horizon beyond the old lifeboat slipway at the far end of the village, creating a silver, shimmering path across the water. Despite the frosty atmosphere in the car a few minutes before and the events of the evening, the sight still filled them both with an inflatable feeling of joy in their chest that only our favourite places can. It was a spellbinding sight which they never tired of. It was the reason they always took their holiday during this particular fortnight each year. They knew they would be treated to the wondrous moonscape. The tension and stress began to melt away. Marge stopped at the turn of the road at the north end of the village.

"I will never tire of this," she breathed. "It's the best view in all the world."

"Certainly is, my love," Ged replied, putting his hand on hers. "I hope you don't mind me saying *'well done,'* Marge. You've never driven all the way down here before, and I know you hate motorways," he said sincerely.

"Actually, although I'm glad it's over, I am feeling rather proud of myself," she said.

Marge drove along the seafront and turned up the steep driveway of their holiday house in the centre of the village. Searing pain surged through Ged's foot as she braked hard. It was past midnight, but the lights were on in the kitchen. The door opened. Sarah's wavy, brown hair shone in the hall light, and she grinned broadly. Ged was fond of this cheerful woman, his son had married. They say men marry their mothers, but this woman couldn't be more different. Positive, easy-going, and charming. She couldn't cook to save her life, but as Brian was a chef, she didn't need to.

"At last, the intrepid duo has made it!" she said, coming out to the car in pyjamas and flip-flops. "You cut it fine; we nearly finished the Merlot! Are you getting out, Dad?"

"Here, Sarah," called Ged from the passenger seat. "Would you give me a hand?"

"Oh my God! What happened?" she cried as she went to the passenger side and saw Ged's booted foot sticking out of the car.

"It's been an eventful journey, Sarah, love. Can you pass me the crutches from the back seat and ask Brian to give Mum a hand with the luggage? We'll explain over a cup of tea, and I think I'll have a decent measure of that *'Isle of Jura'* I left here at Easter." He heaved himself out of the car and set his hands and elbows on the crutches. Navigating the steps up to the house was easier than he expected. Brian met him at the door.

"Blimey, Dad! What's happened? You never told us you'd broken your leg!"

"I didn't, and I haven't. Can you please help Mum with the cases, Brian? I'm about as useful as a chocolate teapot!"

Although he loved the evening view in Porthcovery, at this moment, the best sight was a comfy blue sofa and a large glass of his favourite malt whisky.

Sarah grabbed a whisky tumbler and some ice and poured a generous measure of Jura, handing it to Ged as he lowered himself onto the sofa. He had leaned his crutches on the door frame. One began to fall. Sarah deftly caught it with a free hand and laid the crutches carefully on the floor. "We don't want the kids waking up. I only got Jamie down at ten," she said. She went to the kitchen and put the kettle on, poured a large glass of Chardonnay for Marge, and then topped up her and Brian's Merlot glasses while Brian unloaded the car and helped his mother unpack some essentials.

With steaming mugs of tea in hand, the older couple finally breathed a mental sigh of relief and told their son and his wife the whole tale.

"It was Gerald's fault, of course," said Marge. "He put my handbag in the boot, but he knows I always have it with me in the front, then he forced that cool pack in the back, so, of course, it fell out when he opened the door to get my bag. Lucky I didn't go to get it, or it could have been me wearing a space boot and looking ridiculous!"

"Mum!" chided Sarah, "Dad's clearly in a lot of pain, don't make him feel even worse."

Ged waved his hand dismissively. "No, it's okay, Sarah," he said wearily, swallowing a mouthful of whisky. "She's right. I should have remembered about her bag, and I should have known better than to shove a bag in like that. I just wish I'd moved my feet a bit quicker when it fell."

"I assumed you had bad traffic or something," said Brian. "You must have been at the hospital for ages. I guess we lost track of the time because we got into this film."

"Actually, the hospital people were quicker than I expected," said Ged. "We were only there for about an hour. They were really efficient," he said brightly.

The Jura had now reached his foot, and the throbbing had finally subsided. Or maybe it had made its way to his brain, and he no longer cared. Either way, it was the first time since getting in the car that evening that he had actually felt reasonably comfortable. He allowed his head to tip back on the sofa and closed his eyes, glad to be there at last.

"You both look like you're ready for bed," said Sarah. "Why don't you just get changed? You can unpack in the morning."

It was usually Ged's job to unpack, and Marge took care of the food and bathroom.

"I'll unpack this time if you like, Mum," said Sarah, intending to be helpful.

"No, thank you, Sarah. You'll only put things in the wrong place." Marge replied. She had this unnerving way of putting Sarah down without even trying. Sarah owned and managed a small chain of estate agencies, but Marge treated her as though she were a dim and clueless child.

Brian shot Sarah a glance. He knew taking his mother to task about her sharpness was a waste of time. She was a leopard whose spots would not change. He drained his glass and stood up decisively.

"I'll give you a hand in the bedroom, Dad. Let's leave Mum to it, shall we?" he said, glancing at Sarah, who rolled her eyes, stuck her tongue out behind Marge's back, took a deep breath, cleared up the empty mugs and glasses, popped them all in the dishwasher and went to get ready for bed.

Brian brought the cool bag and food box into the kitchen, leaving them by the fridge. It frustrated him intensely as a chef that his Mum usually turned up at the house after he and Sarah had been there a week and rearranged the kitchen to her liking. Even if he memorised precisely how she had left it the last time they were here, she would move things to a different place. He knew she needed to feel like the queen of her castle, not the maid, to feel in control – even if it meant she couldn't find the jam in the morning.

He shared this with Ged as he helped to unpack the suitcase in their bedroom.

"Mum always does this," he complained. "Last year, I even took a photo of how she had it organised and put everything *exactly* where she had left it. She still rearranged it."

"I know, Bri," said Ged. "But you know your Mum. She's always looking for a new and better way to have things. She reorganises the kitchen at home about once every two or three months. I can hardly ever find anything. It can't do much good. If she had found the ideal

16

way to organise it, she'd have stopped reorganising it by now. I'd just let her do it if I were you. Reorganising somehow makes her feel more at home. Do me a favour, though; when we leave, will you put it back the way it was, so we don't confuse the paying guests?"

Marge and Ged had bought the house together with Brian and Sarah ten years earlier, and for most of the year, it was used as a holiday let. The profit from the lettings covered the mortgage and upkeep of the place as long as they managed to rent it out for twenty weeks each year. It was popular as it slept six people comfortably and had a superb location on the seafront. They bought or replaced something in the house each year, such as a carpet, curtains, or appliance. This delighted the guests, and their housekeepers, Gary and Jill, made sure it always looked immaculate.

The house had an English country cottage feel, although the ground floor was mainly open plan. There was a large bay window into which Ged had built a games cupboard with a deep-cushioned seat on top that could easily seat two happy holidaymakers with a good book each.

The cream curtains were patterned with pink roses, and there were matching cushions on the dark blue striped sofas. At the other end of the living area lay a shaker-style kitchen with cream door fronts and oak trimmings, a large round oak farmhouse table and a beautiful antique pine Welsh dresser with an eclectic mix of crockery.

Upstairs were two double bedrooms, with en-suite bathrooms on either side of the house, and a small room with bunk beds. All three rooms had a sea view. The main bathroom was small, but as it was only used by those in the bunk bedroom and anyone sleeping downstairs, it was enough. The property had a rental fee reflecting its fantastic location. Sarah managed the agents, although Marge made decisions on decor.

Then, there was the garden. Marge looked after that, with a bit of help from the cleaner's husband, who mowed the lawn and weeded in the weeks that the family weren't at the cottage. It was Marge's pride and joy. When the others went to the beach, she would spend hours clipping, trimming, tying up climbers, or poring over books for species of plants that would give colour at different times of the year so that

17

the garden would always look interesting, whatever the time of year. Her Granddaughter, Alice, would sometimes join her, pulling out weeds, looking for ladybirds or digging up worms.

A clove-scented, pink climbing rose arched over the front door porch, pretty alpines bloomed in the small border at the front, and a large, pink-purple lacy '*Alchemilla Mollis*' hydrangea at the corner of the house with designs on becoming an oak tree, judging by how much it grew each year, much to Marge's disapproval as she pruned it back hard when she and Ged had their October break there.

Marge kept the garden *very* neat and tidy, clipping and pruning back bushes and shrubs so hard that it was nothing short of miraculous that some of the plants ever managed to grow back. By the end of their summer fortnight, the little garden usually looked more like a corporate show stand than a Cornish country cottage garden.

Holidaymakers loved the house, as the comments in the visitors' books attested. Around a dozen regular families rented the house year after year, and the Bakers had to book the family's fortnight two years in advance.

Ged felt at his most relaxed and content in Porthcovery. The calming breath of the sea washing the shore, the friendly locals, having his family around him and, best of all, being able to sleep in late and not go to work. It wasn't that he disliked working. He had a good job, a fair and friendly boss and got on really well with his team, but this place… he had a pipe dream of living here… but he knew Marge would never go for it. She was so deeply involved back home. Treasurer of the Women's Institute, volunteer at the Oxfam shop, the village gardening society… She would hate to move. So, Ged settled for the next best option, which was coming down here for holidays and weekends. He had spent many weeks and weekends there on his own over the years when the house needed decorating or maintenance. He did most of the work on the house himself, whether it was plumbing, joinery, electrical or just painting and wallpaper. As a senior maintenance engineer at the factory, it could have been a busman's holiday, but doing work here was never a chore. He enjoyed the peace and quiet; he had got to know quite a few locals who lived in the village on those occasions and was well-known to many of them. During his "maintenance" weeks, he had helped out at some of the cafés and shops when they needed an extra pair of hands, and in return, they had offered help when he needed a lift with a heavier item or would lend him a ladder if he needed one. He had also managed to eat what he liked wherever he liked, go on long walks and read a few good books into the bargain.

Ged was fast asleep by the time Marge came to bed. Brian had helped him unpack, and he had managed to get into his pyjamas without too much discomfort, thanks, in part, to the scotch. Marge was exhausted. The feeling of pride at having driven down was replaced by annoyance that Ged's injury would impact their holiday. She liked to visit gardens, but Ged wouldn't be able to drive her to them or walk around the gardens. She'd either have to go by herself or persuade Brian or Sarah to go; neither of them was interested in gardens. It couldn't be helped. She would simply have to ask them anyway.

3

Cornwall, July 1998

"Yeah! Grandad's here!" Came a shout from the living room. Jamie, the older of the two grandchildren, was delighted whenever his grandparents arrived. At nine years old, he loved playing with his grandfather more than anyone else he could think of. They had that special unspoken connection, treasured by grandparents and grandchildren the world over. Sometimes, they could tell what each other was thinking. They liked the same food; they were both cricket-mad, loved all things small and crawly, were both bookworms and understood each other's jokes when no one else seemed to.

"And Nana too," called Sarah to her eldest, conscious that the unbridled delight of Ged's greatest fan might hurt Marge's feelings. Jamie wasn't so well-connected with Marge. She had never understood how anyone could get excited about beetles, worms and crustaceans. To Marge, the love of cricket was something of a mystery. Roald Dahl, Asterix and Spiderman left her cold. She found Jamie's line of conversation hard to grasp or get enthused about. Nevertheless, she reasoned, he was her grandson after all; he was healthy and very bright; he kept Ged busy all holiday, and she liked that he got on with his grandfather so well.

Jamie had burst into their room at eight am. He was about to leap onto the bed to embrace Ged when Marge shouted, "No, Jamie! Grandad has hurt his leg. Just give him a little hug this time. No bouncing on the bed – understand?"

Jamie was shocked to receive his first reprimand from his grandmother so early on in the holiday. Usually, it would be at breakfast when she would tell him off for eating noisily, spilling something, running or breathing too loudly. He cautiously put his arms around his grandad's shoulders and kissed him on the cheek.

"Grandad, are you ok? What happened?"

"Your silly Grandad has a footballer's injury and doesn't even play football," said Ged, hugging his grandson and pulling him onto the double bed beside him.

"I don't understand. Mum didn't tell me you had hurt yourself," he said.

"I put too many things in the boot of the car yesterday, and one of the heavy bags fell out and broke a bone in my foot," Ged said ruefully.

"When will it get better?" asked Jamie, worried.

"I'm not sure, Jamie. It still hurts a lot. The doctor said to rest it as much as possible this week, so I can't play cricket with you. I'm really sorry, I'm going to miss our games. I'm sure we can find something else to do. You and Alice enjoyed finding things in the rock pools last summer, didn't you?" Ged replied apologetically.

"Poor Grandad," said Jamie, hugging his grandfather tight.

"Stay in bed, Grandad; Alice and I can get you and Nana a cup of tea and breakfast in bed. Then you don't have to get up, so your foot can get better more quickly."

"Oh no, Jamie," said Marge, "You'll spill the tea, and we will get crumbs in the bed."

Ged gave Marge a gentle dig in the ribs with his elbow and frowned at her.

"Actually, Jamie, that's a really kind offer," he said. "If your Mum or Dad think you can manage it, I would love a cup of tea, but I'd hate you to get scalded, and if I have porridge or cereal, I promise your Nana I won't get crumbs in the bed." Marge rolled her eyes.

"Oh, very well," she conceded. "I'll have a banana and some bran flakes."

"Great!" said Jamie and bounded off to the kitchen.

"The lad was just trying to be kind, Marge; don't put him down," said Ged. "Not many kids his age would offer to make breakfast in bed for their grandparents."

"He'll only go and spill the tea; then we'll spend more time cleaning up than if we got it ourselves," she grumbled. "You indulge that boy; You're too soft on him."

21

Ged decided it was a waste of time to argue. He sighed and reached for his book on the bedside table. A few minutes later, Jamie returned with a tray laden with two half-filled mugs of tea and two bowls of bran flakes with banana.

Ged's heart sank a little. He wasn't keen on bran flakes and positively despised bananas, but he didn't want to hurt Jamie's feelings.

"Great idea to only half fill the tea mugs, Jamie!" he said.

"Oh, that was Dad's idea," admitted Jamie as he brought the cups around. He said I might spill a full mug. He said he would get some more tea in a bit."

"I'm going to have breakfast; see you later, Grandad," he said, skipping off.

Once he had disappeared, Ged asked Marge if she wanted his banana slices.

"Go on then," she said, offering her bowl. "That was a good idea of Brian's, but I could do with a bit more tea."

***

It was a beautiful day. Ged was glad it was sandals weather. He wouldn't have to face the pain of putting socks on. He looked down at his foot and got a shock. It was almost entirely purple with bruises and still quite swollen. No sandal on that foot today, just the clunky boot.

Seven-year-old Alice peeped around the door of the bedroom.

"Hi Nana, Hi Grandad," she said. Then, she saw Ged's foot. "Grandad, your foot is all big and dirty."

"Hello Alice…actually, it's not dirty. That's a big bruise. I broke a bone in my foot."

"Poor Grandad," she said and gave him a gentle hug. He lifted her onto his knee as he always did and instantly regretted it. Pain surged through the top of Ged's foot, making him want to howl and swear; instead, he clenched his teeth and smiled at his granddaughter.

"Alice, could you help me, please, sweetie?" said Ged.

"Yes, Grandad?"

"I have some crutches to help me walk. Do you think you could get them from the sofa?"

"What's clutches?"

"They're metal poles with grey plastic letter Cs at the top," he said. "They are about as tall as you."

"Okay, Grandad," said Alice, and wandered out of the room.

"I doubt you'll be getting crutches any time soon, Gerald," said Marge in a matter-of-fact tone.

"Ye of little faith." Replied Ged. "Let's see if Squirt has a bit of gumption to ask again if she's unsure."

In just a minute or two, Alice was back, beaming with the crutches in her hands.

"Is this what you wanted, Grandad?"

"Well done, Alice!" exclaimed Ged. "Yes. Those are my crutches."

"They're mine, actually," said Marge out of the corner of her mouth.

"Thank you, Alice," said Ged, leaning over to kiss her on the cheek.

"Okay, Grandad, are you coming to the beach today?"

"Definitely," said Ged, "wouldn't miss it for anything."

"And how, exactly, are you going to get down all those steps, may I ask?"

Marge had been sure that Ged would have to spend most of the week at the cottage, probably getting in her way half the time.

"I'm not sure exactly yet, but I'll work out a way," said Ged. "By hook or by crook, I'll find a way onto that beach even if it takes me half the morning."

He struggled onto his crutches, wincing and went to the bathroom to find the painkillers. This was going to be a long day, he thought to himself. He hopped to the top of the stairs. How did he get up them last night? He couldn't remember. He had been so tired he had forgotten.

"Marge!" he called. "You've used these crutches before; how do you get downstairs on them without breaking your neck?"

"It's tricky; you either put one crutch down and use the handrail, or you put both sticks on the next step down, then put all your weight on the sticks while you hop down on your good leg."

"What do I do with the other crutch if I use the rail?"

23

"You give it to me," came a reply from behind him. It was Sarah.

"Oh, thanks, Sarah, love," said Ged gratefully, "You're an angel."

"No trouble, Dad. I think you're doing great on those crutches. I guess we will just have to take each day as it comes. You must try to take it easy; let it heal."

Jamie was getting beach things together with Brian, and Alice was drawing and colouring at the breakfast table. Ged went and sat down at the table with her.

"Let's see, there… tell me about that lovely drawing. It's certainly very… very pink!

"It's a fairy princess castle," said Alice, simply. "Princess Sparkle and all her friends fly in at this window here, and they go to bed here, she pointed to a vaguely square window in a rocket-shaped section of the palace. Princess Tiffany wants a pony, but I can't draw ponies; they look weird," she said in a slightly grumpy voice. "Can you draw a pony, Grandad?"

"I'll have a go, Alice, " said Ged. I used to draw a lot when I was little. That's a long time ago now, but I'll do my best. What colour shall it be? Black, chestnut, grey, brown?"

"Light blue, please, Grandad, that's Princess Tiffany's favourite colour," said Alice, oblivious to her grandfather's raised eyebrows.

Ged took up the pencil and drew a pony trotting towards the castle. The pencil felt light in his hand. The image of a slim pony began to take shape under the pencil point. It felt odd to be drawing something that didn't have wires or pipes coming out of it or showing which way a door would swing by drawing a gap with an arc.

"Isn't he too skinny, Grandad?" said Alice. "Tiffany is quite fat; his legs might snap."

Ged was a little crestfallen.

"Oh, erm, well, that pony can be for Princess Sparkle. I'll do another one for Tiffany. I'll make it a bit sturdier, shall I?"

"Yes, please."

A short, stocky, Thelwell-style pony found its way onto the corner of the page, complete with saddle and bridle.

"Yes, Grandad. I think Tiffany will like him as long as he gets to be blue. But where are his wings?"

"Wings?" said Ged. "Nobody said anything about wings."

"You can't have a fairy pony without wings, Grandad. That would be silly."

Ged thought a purple palace with a phallic tower was pretty daft, so a wingless fairy horse didn't really strike him as a problem. However, he kept his thoughts to himself and dutifully drew some large gossamer wings on the fat pony.

"Why are the wings so big, Grandad?" asked Alice.

"I figured that a fat pony would need big wings to get it off the ground, Alice, as it would probably be a bit heavy," Ged explained.

"Oh." Came the reply.

Ged coloured the ponies in a light blue with mid-blue shading under the ears, in the nostrils, eyes, and ears, giving them both a mid-blue mane and tail. If blue had been a natural colour for horses, they would have looked quite realistic.

Although he wouldn't have liked to admit it, Ged had rather enjoyed drawing the blue ponies. In fact, although ponies were not really his thing, drawing them reminded him of how much he had enjoyed drawing as a child, especially on wet days when he couldn't play cricket or fly kites. He wished he could have done more art, but life seemed to get in the way. Anyway, he wasn't sure he was all that good at it.

"Are we going down to the beach, or what?" called Brian. He had a picnic ready and wore shades, blue shorts, a Bermuda shirt with yellow banana leaves, and red flip-flops.

Ged stiffly got to his feet and steadied himself on his crutches.

"Ready as I'll ever be," said Ged, taking a deep breath. "Although I might need my sunglasses for that shirt, Brian. Did you get dressed in the dark?" he said, grinning.

"I'll help you down the steps to the beach, Grandad," said Jamie cheerfully.

"I'd like to try on my own if I can," said Ged. "If I'm careful, I should be able to get down the steps, although I don't want to sit on the picnic blanket today. Can we take down one of those green picnic chairs with a pocket for a can of beer?"

The family trooped off to the beach, minus Marge; she was already in the garden.

The steps down to the beach were more difficult than in the house. The carpet on the stairs allowed the crutches to sink into the pile, providing grip. The gravel and sand on the worn concrete steps made them positively treacherous.

Nevertheless, with Brian's help, Ged managed to get down to the beach. Now for the really tricky part: finding a way across the pebbles.

"Okay, Dad, time for your first piggyback in 20 years!" Said Brian with a grin.

"What? You're kidding, surely?"

"I'm afraid there's no other way to get across these pebbles," said Brian, seriously, although he had a mischievous twinkle in his eye. "Come on, Dad, you can't be that heavy. You're thirteen stone, maybe?"

Brian crouched in front of Ged and told him to put his arms over his shoulders and hold tight. Ged trusted his son, but was more than a little embarrassed. Brian was strong; he went to the gym most mornings before going to the restaurant. Ged shrugged, swallowed his pride and allowed his son to give him a piggyback onto the sand.

Jamie had set up a picnic chair on the sand and started to build a Sandcastle right next to it. Ged carefully lowered himself down onto the picnic chair on his good leg. His broken foot was throbbing badly, and he needed painkillers. He felt as though everyone on the beach was looking at him. He must be crazy coming down onto the beach with a broken foot and crutches, especially this beach. It was hardly set up for people with disabilities.

"Hey, Dad," called Sarah ", you're looking a little pale… is your foot hurting?"

"I should have taken something; it's pretty painful," said Ged.

"No problem, I've got some co-codamol; here you go," she said.

"Sarah, you're amazing!" said Ged sincerely. "You think of everything. I bet you have that office of yours running like clockwork."

"I usually keep painkillers handy," she replied. "To be honest, I can't believe you made it down here, but I know Jamie and Alice are really glad you did."

"Look, Grandad!" said Jamie. I'm building St. Michael's Mount. You can put the castle on top because I built it next to your chair."

"Clever boy, Jamie, you really are a chip off the old block," said Ged. "Okay, fill me a bucket, and I'll do the castle."

Ged and Jamie managed to build their version of the famous old house on St. Michael's Mount. Alice fetched pebbles and shells, which they placed around the sandcastle, and it did look quite grand. It was a warm day and not too breezy, but Ged's foot was cold. He removed his fleece and draped it over his foot to keep it warm. Once the children had run off to find pebbles and shells to decorate the castle, Ged really wished that he hadn't filled the boot of the Honda so full. He loved playing on the beach with his grandchildren, especially when they were being imaginative.

Ged watched children playing cricket with Brian, who was quite good at it for someone who spent twelve hours a day in a restaurant kitchen. They were having a great time shouting "owzat" as loudly as they could whenever someone was out...and quite often when they weren't. Ged felt a pang of jealousy as he watched them.

"Do you want coffee or ice cream, Dad?" said Sarah. "I'm going up to the shop."

"Yes, thanks. Love. That would be nice," replied Ged. "Take my wallet; my treat; I'll have a coffee and an ice cream, please; Rum and raisin if they have it, or sherry trifle."

"Trust you," she replied. "Anything with booze in it," she said with a wink.

"That does make me sound like a bit of an old wine-o, doesn't it? Well, get clotted-cream vanilla if they don't have either," he replied in mock apology.

The little coffee and ice cream shop was owned by the Mawgan family, famous all over Cornwall for their award-winning gelato, Italian artisan-style ice cream, which they made with milk from their herd of gentle Guernsey cows. Some of the flavours were weird and wonderful, as well as the usual strawberry, chocolate and vanilla. They had other less common varieties, such as a Cornish cream tea ice cream with genuinely gooey splurges of strawberry jam, clotted cream and chunks of scone. Gill, who ran the shop, knew Ged well and made his coffee exactly how he liked it. Dark, strong and sweet with plenty of hot milk.

Sarah returned with Tracey, their friend from the Gallery shop. Ged had helped Tracey to build shelves in the shop the previous year.

"Hi, Chippy," said Tracey. "Sarah told me about your foot, you poor thing. If you need anything, just let us know. I'm going into town later if you'd like me to do any shopping for you; it would be no trouble."

"A bottle of scotch is all I need right now, and I've got a full one, thanks," said Ged sincerely. It seems to be the only thing that numbs the pain."

"Well, take it easy," said Tracey as she handed Ged his ice cream and coffee.

"Thanks for helping me carry these down, Tracey," said Sarah. "How's business after the gales last year?"

"Much better, thank goodness. The news coverage of the gales and bad weather in April made tourists stay away. I'm glad families like yours come every year, no matter what, or we wouldn't have made any money at all," she said solemnly. "Some of the other businesses weren't so lucky and folded. It's such a shame."

After his coffee and ice cream, Ged felt bloated and uncomfortable. Normally, he would've gone for a walk, but that wasn't happening today. He loved playing cricket, but occasionally shouting 'Owzat!' at Brian, Sarah, and the children just wasn't the same.

Tired from the cricket, Alice came back to the picnic blanket. She got out her drawing pad and started to draw again.

"Grandad?" said Alice uncertainly. " Can you draw me another picture? I liked the horses. Can you draw something else this time?"

"Sure," said Ged. Maybe it would take his mind off his stomach. "Anything in particular?"

"Another Fairy Castle, please," came the matter-of-fact reply.

"Let's have lunch, shall we?" said Brian cheerfully, suddenly breaking Ged's concentration. "Nice castle," said Brian, grinning.

Ged had become quite engrossed with his drawing for Alice. He had sketched a magnificent, enchanted castle, complete with a moat, drawbridge, pointed turrets and tall towers with pennant flags fluttering from the ramparts, similar to the Disney castle or Schloss Neuschwanstein. He had drawn it on a hillside surrounded by an alpine forest. It looked like something from a fairy tale.

"Look what Grandad drawed, Nana!" shouted Alice as Marge gingerly stepped across the pebbles towards them.

"It's 'drawn', dear," said Marge. "We say, Look what Grandad has *drawn*."

"Yes, but look, Nana, it's a Fairy castle. It's magic!" exclaimed Alice, unable to contain her delight.

"Mmm, very nice, dear," said Marge, barely glancing at the drawing that Alice thrust into her hand. "Where's *my* picnic chair, Brian?" said Marge irritably, handing the drawing pad back to Alice.

Brian exchanged a look with Ged and began to unload the picnic things.

"We don't usually bring them down to the beach, Mum," said Brian. We all sit on the blanket."

"Well, your father has one," she snapped.

"That's on account of his foot, isn't it?" said Sarah.

"Oh, that blasted foot!" growled Marge. "That's going to be the excuse for everything, isn't it? He'll be waited on, hand and foot, all holiday while I slave away in the garden and do everything."

"I'll do the cooking, Mum," said Brian. "And we can get Harry to prune things and do the garden this year if you like. You don't have to do anything you don't want to."

"No, I'm not having that man mess with my roses," she said vehemently. "he can mow a lawn and do a bit of weeding, but he would have the roses rambling over the rooftops, given half a chance. No, I have to do it, or it won't be done properly."

"Shall I get you a picnic chair, Mum?" said Sarah.

"Yes. If you don't mind, my back is killing me." Normally, this would be an innocent comment, but as Sarah was recovering from back surgery after a cycling accident 6 months earlier and was in constant discomfort, it was somewhat tactless.

"No, Sarah," said Brian, making eye contact with Sarah. You get the rest of the food out; I'll fetch a chair.

"Don't put yourself out, Brian dear. I'm sure I can manage on the blanket."

Sarah began to get the food out, muttering darkly under her breath. *"Oh, don't put yourself out, dear... I mean, your wife with the broken back can fetch me stuff. You're too precious..."*

"Sorry, Sarah, what did you say, dear?"

"Nothing, Mum, just checking that we have backup sandwiches for the kids. Do you want a glass of wine?"

"Have you got any soda to go in it? It is only lunchtime, after all."

"Yes, I brought a bottle of soda. Half and half, okay?"

Brian returned with a camping chair and set it up on the sand. Marge sat down heavily on it. "Thank you, that was very kind; you needn't have troubled yourself; I'd have been fine on the blanket."

Brian, Ged and Sarah all exchanged looks. Brian had prepared chicken, paprika and red onion couscous with a rocket, avocado and beetroot salad. He served everyone a portion in white pasta bowls. Sarah handed out forks and a bottle of honey, lemon, and thyme dressing, which Brian had been testing for the restaurant. "It's got a couple of secret ingredients in it. Would you all tell me what you think?

Having eaten his food in about two minutes, Ged held his bowl out for more. "Fantastic, Brian!" he said. Where do you come up with all the ideas? I'll have seconds if there is enough."

"Jamie! Alice! Come and get some lunch!" called Sarah. The children were kneeling by a rock pool. Jamie got up and ran over to the picnic blanket, flopping down on his knees beside his father. "What's that, Dad?"

"Chicken couscous," said Brian. "Want some?"

"Okay, but I don't want salad. Can I have something else for vegetables?"

"Yes, I sliced some carrots and a pepper. I think you'll like the couscous."

Jamie tried a forkful, chewed it thoughtfully and tucked it into the rest hungrily.

"Slow down, James, you'll get hiccups," Marge reprimanded.

Jamie scowled at his grandmother – he hated being called James. Brian and Sarah had named him Jamie on his birth certificate and always called him that, or occasionally, Jim. Only Nana ever called him James. It was her father's name.

"Did you see Grandad's picture, Mum?" said Jamie. "He did it for Alice."

"Yes, I did. I didn't know you could draw, Dad," said Sarah.

"I forgot, actually...I enjoyed it when I was a boy, although fairy castles weren't usually my thing," he replied with a wink.

"He's just doodling," said Marge. "He's always doodling on the newspaper around the puzzles; it's rather annoying when I come to do my word search."

"I like it," said Jamie. "Can you draw something for me this afternoon?"

"I don't have any more paper, Jamie," said Ged apologetically.

"I'll go to the shop and get you a sketch pad, Dad," suggested Sarah. "It'll be something to do while you're laid up with your foot."

"Can I get some drawing stuff, too?" said Jamie.

"Okay, come and help me choose...do you want to come, Dad?" she said to Ged.

"I'll need to use the loos anyway, so I might as well come to the Gallery shop too."

They finished the picnic with bowls of mixed berries with Chantilly cream.

"It's great to have a chef in the family," mused Ged as he wiped his finger around his bowl to get all the cream. "I mean, look at all these

31

poor families on the beach with their tuna or cheese and ham sandwiches and bags of crisps, and here we are with a Michelin star picnic! That was absolutely delicious, Brian."

"I'm not doing that *every* day, Dad. We've got lunch at the Pub tomorrow, and I booked Cornish pasties from Peggy's for Monday lunchtime."

"Yay!" cried Jamie. "Her pasties are the best in the world!"

"None better!" agreed Brian.

"Well, that's high praise from a Michelin-starred chef," said Ged.

"It's true, though, Dad," said Brian, "they're sublime—the balance of flavours and the texture of the meat. The pastry is spot on – not too thick or greasy. I wouldn't even attempt to make Cornish pasties, having eaten one of Peggy's, I'd never get close."

The children returned to their rock pool while the adults finished their exquisite picnic with peach and lime iced tea from a cool flask.

"This iced tea is very tasty, Brian, dear," said Marge enthusiastically. "One of your new creations, is it?"

Brian and Sarah exchanged glances. "Actually, Mum, I made it," said Sarah. A friend gave me the recipe. I'm glad you like it."

"Well, of course, it is a bit sweet for my palette, but it's alright after such a sweet dessert," replied Marge.

Sarah took a deep breath, closed her eyes, and finished her iced tea. "Come on, Dad, let's get up to the Gallery shop, shall we? There's a drop of vodka in that iced tea; you'll fall asleep if you have any more."

Ged got up stiffly from the chair—his foot hurt from sitting still for so long. Brian crouched down in front of him so he could get another piggyback across the pebbles.

"What on earth are you doing?" shrieked Marge. "Put your father down at once, Brian! You both look ridiculous!" she cried, looking around to see if anyone was watching; if they weren't before, her shrieks had got their attention now.

"It's the only way to get Dad across the pebbles," explained Sarah calmly.

"Can't he manage on crutches?" growled Marge through gritted teeth.

"I don't think that would be very safe, Marge," said Ged. "A piggyback is not something I would prefer, but it allowed me to get onto the beach and have a lovely morning…and I've not been getting under your feet."

"It's not a good idea; you're quite a weight, Gerald. Brian might hurt himself."

"I've carried heavier sacks of carrots, Mum," said Brian. "Dad's not fat."

"Come on, Bri; Let's get this over with, can we?" said Ged.

Brian carried his father over to the beach steps and began to climb.

"You're not carrying me all the way up the steps, are you, Brian?" exclaimed Ged.

"Mum made me think of it." I carry sacks of potatoes and carrots up and down a flight of stairs from the cold store at the restaurant. It's no different."

Brian gently set his father down at the top of the steps as Sarah passed the crutches.

"Thanks, Brian." I feel like a bit of a twit, but it's a lot less painful than hopping.

"Dad," said Brian quietly, "Mum is being much worse than usual; I'm really having to bite my tongue."

"I expect it's because I'm not much use this holiday. I promised to help her put up a trellis for her climbers and fix a few things. I'll have to do it in October. She'll relax after a few days. She did well to drive all the way here on the motorway. I think she's probably still recovering from that, too."

Brian didn't soften despite his father's explanation.

"I don't want her speaking like she has been to Sarah and the kids; she keeps putting them down and snapping. It's not on. If she doesn't relax soon, it'll spoil the holiday."

"I have an idea that might cheer her up," said Ged. "Why don't we take her to Glendurgan Gardens tomorrow? A bit of horticultural therapy might do her good."

"What about Sunday lunch at the Pub?" replied Brian. "It's booked."

"Just re-book for another time. Tell them about my leg. They'll understand. We could go in the evening instead."

"Alright, I'll go to the pub and rearrange it. Take it easy, Dad," he said, patting his father affectionately on the shoulder.

Sarah and Jamie went ahead to the Gallery shop. Ged called in at the door to Sarah. "I'm just popping up the road to the loos."

Tracy, the gallery shop owner, called out to him. "Use the one at the back of the shop Chippy. I'll have closed the shop by the time you get back from the public loo on those crutches, and that's no good for business," she said with a wink.

***

As Ged returned to the front of the shop, someone held the door for him.

"Oh goodness, Chippy, what have you done to yourself?" said the woman leaving the shop. He had been so busy looking at the crutches and the floor that he hadn't seen who held the door; it was Peggy.

'Chippy' was a nickname by which many of the Porthcovery locals had come to know Ged on account of the help he had given to some of them, doing small joinery jobs. He always had a pencil behind his ear, and his jeans were usually dusted with a fine layer of sawdust when he came down for his 'maintenance' weekends, as well as the frequent trips to the café or the pub for supper.

"Footballer's injury."

"I didn't know you played football!"

"I don't!" Ged grinned, "All the famous footballers seem to break their third metatarsal, and they make millions; I thought it might work for me."

"Don't be daft, Grandad; tell the truth," came Jamie's voice from the other side of the shop door. "It was the cool bag that you stuffed in the boot."

Peggy smiled and winked at Ged. "Oh dear, a real tourist's injury. Did you do it after you got here?"

"Before, I'm afraid, Peggy – Marge hated driving. I think she'll feel better after one of your pasties on Monday, though."

"I'll make a nice tray of brownies. She likes those. I have to go now; I was only bringing Tracy her lunch. I'll see you all on Monday".

5

The Gallery shop was delightfully cool away from the sizzling lunchtime sun. Since the gales, it had been hastily – but very nicely – fitted out with new shelves, a chic, simple grey and white paint job, and new stock. The shop didn't feel as cluttered as before.

The artist's corner was well stocked with sketch pads, watercolour boards and pads, watercolours, acrylics, brushes and pencils. Ged browsed a while, looking at paintings and sketches on the walls. Soft and watery, like the light here, they were… nice…not remarkable, just nice – they certainly captured the beauty of the area, though they didn't inspire him. Then, something caught his eye: Several small, darker, bolder prints, acrylic paintings of moonlight on the water, and night-time harbour scenes by Gilly Johns. They caught the magic of the moonscape in a way which drew him into the painting.

"What are you going to get, Grandad?" piped Jamie, startling Ged a little.

"Sorry, Jamie, I was looking at these pictures by Gilly Johns. Aren't they good?"

"I like the moon and the boats, Grandad…they aren't very realistic, though."

"Art doesn't have to be realistic all the time, Jamie," Ged murmured, gazing at each scene in turn. "Sometimes an artist is more interested in getting you to feel something. I feel calm and peaceful when I look at these. What do you feel?"

"Impatient, Grandad. I want to get the art stuff and go back to the beach. Mum said we could have an ice cream. I didn't get one earlier."

"Okay, Jamie," Ged chuckled, "let's get this done, shall we?" He handed his crutch to Jamie, reached up and took an A4 Sketch pad from the shelf, then selected a variety of sketching pencils, ranging from 4b to 2h, an eraser and a ruler.

"What's the ruler for Grandad?" said Jamie, curious as always.

"I'll show you later," Ged tapped the side of his nose with his finger and gave his grandson a wink. He paused momentarily; his eyes rested on a beautiful wooden artist's box on the display; its lid was open, showing off the contents. The box seemed to have everything: Acrylics in tubes, a twenty-pan watercolour set, a white plastic mixing palette, brushes, a set of pastel crayons and a complete set of sketching pencils.

He immediately remembered being in Crawford's artist supplies shop in the village where he grew up, staring at just such a set and wishing that his parents could afford to buy it for his birthday or that he could save up for it, but his parents always bought him a train for his train set, a cricket bat, new pads or a set of cricket stumps.

This wooden set had a sticker displaying a reduced price of eighty pounds, down from one hundred and nine. Ged took a sharp intake of breath and looked away, giving the pencils, eraser, and sketch pad to Jamie, who handed the crutch back and took them to the counter along with his chosen set of Spider-Man-themed drawing and colouring pencils, a drawing pad, an eraser, and a sharpener. Sarah paid with her card, and Tracy put them all in a paper bag.

"You can sell your pictures if they're good enough, Jamie," said Tracy, grinning.

Jamie looked up at his mum.

"Can I really sell them if they're good, Mum?"

"I guess so, Jamie, and considering some of the dodgy stuff I've seen for sale around on café walls. If you can get it framed and mounted, you can sell all sorts of scribbles. I sometimes think people bring their wallets and leave their common sense at home when they come on holiday; some tourists will buy anything."

"It's amazing what some people will buy, that's true," said Tracy. "Sometimes the cheaper stuff by locals sells well because people want an 'original' by a new artist, and some hope they can sell it for a fortune when the artist becomes famous, and their paintings are selling for millions. Imagine if you bought an etching by Picasso in a Spanish tapas bar in 1892 or found Van Gogh's childhood sketchbook. It would be worth a fortune, but back then, you wouldn't have paid tuppence."

"I could have gone through Tracy Emin's bins when we went to London, grabbed a pair of old tights and a pizza box, and I'd be quids in by now," quipped Ged.

"Tracy chuckled, "Do you think the Tate would believe me if I told them that pile of bricks at the back of my house was an early *'Carl Andre'*?"

"When I'm back on my feet, Tracy, I'll have them off you and build a barbecue at our place, said Ged. "I've been thinking of building one for years, and I keep forgetting about it. I'll do it in October and surprise the kids with it next summer."

"I've seen your brickwork, Dad. You could enter the barbecue for an abstract art competition at the Tate Modern when you've built it," joked Sarah.

"Ouch!" Tracy winced.

"Come on, let's get back to the beach," said Ged, changing the subject. He wasn't offended. Sarah was right; bricklaying wasn't his forté. "Marge will want to get back to her dahlias; we've left her babysitting Alice."

They left the shop with a cheery wave to Tracy and spotted Brian returning from the Pub.

"I've changed the booking to tomorrow evening," he said. "I'll go and tell Mum about Glendurgan; she really likes it there."

"What about the kids? They love going to Glendurgan, too," said Ged.

"Yeah, Mum, I want to go. Can Grandad come too?"

"I can get seven in the car," said Sarah. So, we can all go, but you're not going to be able to get about much on those, are you?" she said, nodding to his crutches.

"I'm not much for gardens, to be perfectly honest; I'll be fine back here, thanks." Ged was happy to have an excuse not to have to make polite conversation about differently shaped vegetables that you can't eat.

He carefully made his way back, pausing at the house and placing his hand on the garden wall for support.

"Are you coming down to the beach, Dad?" said Brian.

"Yes, but I'm not sure I can stand your mother's hard stare when you give me another piggyback. I'll manage the steps with crutches. Can you set the chair up by the sea wall on the pebbles? The tide will be coming in soon, anyway."

Brian called to his Mother, "Mum, we're back now, and we've had an idea for tomorrow. We're thinking of going to Glendurgan for the day. We'll have lunch there. I bet there are some nice plants to buy."

"I'd like that, Brian, dear, but your father can't drive, and I definitely don't want to."

"It's okay, Mum. Sarah's car is a seven-seater, so we can all go in that."

"In that case, that would be nice," said Marge, clearly relieved. "What are we going to do with your Father? It's not very practical with crutches, is it?"

"Dad's staying here; he can't get into too much trouble on a Sunday, can he?"

Marge pursed her lips. "As long as he doesn't go to the pub all afternoon," she said.

"He's hardly the type," Sarah said over her shoulder.

"Mmm," Marge responded doubtfully. Well, I'm going to go and have a cup of tea and do my crossword in the garden; what are we doing for dinner?"

"Beef casserole," said Brian. "It's in the slow cooker; we'll see you about five."

"Sounds lovely, Brian, you're so organised," crooned Marge.

"Had a good teacher, didn't I, Mum?" called Brian as she started up the beach steps.

Sarah shook her head as Brian came to fetch some of the beach paraphernalia and carry it towards the sea wall to get above the waterline as the tide crept up the beach.

"Well, I think you've put her in a better mood, Bri."

Brian kissed his wife on the tip of her shoulder.

"Let's hope it lasts; my tongue will start bleeding if I have to bite it much more. Come on, Jamie," he called. "Another round of cricket before the tide comes in?"

Sarah hovered around the picnic area and glanced at Ged. She felt bad about joining in with Alice, Jamie and Brian, as it would leave Ged on his own.

Ged read her mind… "Go on, I'll be fine. I'm going to play with my new sketchpad."

Sarah took off her flip-flops and headed over to her family. Ged picked up the paper bag from the Gallery shop and took out the sketchbook and pencil. He opened the book and immediately remembered how intimidating it used to feel in art class at school. A blank page…where to start? He twiddled the pencil in his right hand, flicking it around in a spiral as he often did when he was thinking; he stared into the middle distance, allowing his mind and gaze to wander. A cormorant was fishing off some rocks about a hundred metres from the beach. Ged had good eyesight and could make out its bright yellow eyes. The cormorant took off from the rock and dived into the water like an arrow from a bow, surfacing a few moments later. It gulped down its catch and then rested, floating on the water for a minute before taking off, flapping its wings with great, slow, languid beats. Once it had resumed its perch on the rock, it began to preen its wing feathers.

Ged began to sketch the bird with a light touch, allowing the tip of the pencil to find its place on the page naturally, not forcing the image of the bird but allowing the balance of the animal to become evident, its confidence to be felt. He didn't open the watercolour pencils but left most of the beady eye white with some accents. He held up the ruler for a moment and held it against the page, checking the ratio of the bird's beak to its overall height so that the beak was in proportion. He thought about mentioning it to Jamie, but he was having too much fun playing French cricket.

Having sketched the bird to his satisfaction, Ged began to draw the rock, allowing artistic license to take over where he felt the rock's actual form would seem odd. He added a suggestion of the sea around the rock and held up the sketch for a moment before turning the page.

The cricket game was going well. Alice was having a great time, yelling *'Owzat'* every time she bowled, whether or not it went anywhere near the stump or the batsman's leg. Ged began to sketch the scene with a light, vague touch, leaving out some details but capturing the excitement-or disappointment-on the faces of the players. In the sketch, Brian held his brimmed Warwickshire cricket hat in his right fist, wiping sweat from his brow with his forearm. Sarah was bowling at Jamie, her face concentrated but relaxed. Jamie's eyes were fixed on Sarah as he gripped the bat tightly in both hands. Alice had her fists in the air, her face already stretched in a gleeful shout.

Turning the page, Ged looked around and spotted a family building a dam to channel water from the stream that drained across the beach into a pebble-lined lagoon that they had dug out. Many little generals were attempting to take charge, shouting instructions to make this civil engineering masterpiece the best it could be.

"You need to build a wall over there, Dad, the water is getting away!" shouted a boy of about ten years old urgently.

"No!" said his little sister, "I'm creating another channel into the lagoon."

Ged's pencil slid silkily across the page, feathering the girl's hair, shading to show tensed muscles, and adding laugh lines around the father's eyes. Again, he left out details that he felt didn't add to the scene and allowed himself extra details to embellish the story of the sketch.

He turned the page and started another sketch of the dam-building scene, focusing further upstream on a group of teenage boys digging a deep trench to divert stream water to a 'temporary holding pond' as he heard one of the boys call it. Their mother was standing on the other side of the stream, taking photographs of the scene. She wore an all-in-one white swimming costume with an Aztec-patterned sarong in vibrant shades of red and orange tied at her waist. She was slim, tanned and muscular. Her bare feet were dusted with sand, and her hair was tied in a ponytail. Wisps of dark hair played around her eyes and ears as the wind disturbed them. Her sunglasses were perched on her head as she photographed her children. She reminded Ged of his mother taking photographs with her little Brownie camera while on holidays in North Wales.

By three in the afternoon, he had created around six sketches and had a small pile of screwed-up pieces of paper at his feet. He was beginning to feel more confident and was starting to enjoy himself. He noticed a group of older teenage girls in bikinis daring each other to swim in the sea; a boy with them was skimboarding impressively on the water at the edge of the sea. The girls were chasing and grabbing one another, trying to drag each other into the water. He sketched the girls, giving them bigger bosoms and slimmer thighs, exaggerating their facial expressions, giving an impression of the shrieks and shouts as the people in the sketch dared each other in the gentle waves by the shore.

A man was walking a greyhound on the far end of the beach, throwing a tennis ball, sending his dog galloping along the wet sand. Ged sketched the dog at full tilt, its front legs stretched out, and the line of his strong quadricep thigh muscles clearly showing as he kicked up the sand behind. The sketch of the dog on the page had all the speed and power of the actual dog that now sat with the ball at his feet, tongue lolling, a look of satisfaction on his face. The man flopped down on the sand and stroked his beloved dog's head and ears. Ged quickly sketched this calmer scene on the next page, capturing the contentment of both dog and owner.

He was so engrossed in sketching that he hadn't noticed his own family had stopped playing French cricket and were gathered around a rock pool with nets and a bucket. Once he spotted them, he began to draw them with their nets poised, bucket half full of water, staring intently into the pool.

He realised his right hand was beginning to ache. He put the pencil on his lap and leafed through the sketches. "Not perfect," he thought, "but not bad, I guess. The dog at least looks like a dog, I suppose."

His head began to droop, and he dozed in his chair, his head on his chest, sketchbook and pencil resting on his lap.

6

"Let's see, Grandad."

Jamie's voice awoke Ged from his dozing. He lifted his head from his chest and rubbed the back of his neck.

Jamie was leafing through the pages of the sketchbook. "Mum, Dad! Come and look; Grandad's drawings are amazing!"

Sarah and Brian looked up from packing the beach things and came over.

"Wow, Dad!" said Sarah. Her face animated as she turned the pages. "These are incredible! I had no idea you could draw like this. The expressions are amazing!" she said with a chuckle. "The life in these drawings is… well, it's palpable. I can hear them screaming in this one of the bikini girls. You've been kind to them; they're not as shapely as that in real life. I remember that lad laughing his head off when he got pulled him into the waves."

Brian looked over Sarah's shoulder. "I like the one with the man and his greyhound," he said. "The power in its hind legs – the dog was putting his feet down like ready money. The way you've got the sand being kicked up. I remember you doing drawings for me when I was a kid, but they were cartoons, like Spiderman and Donald Duck, nothing like these."

"I suppose I just drew what you asked me to draw," Ged replied.

"You should frame these and sell them in Tracy's shop, Grandad.

"Oh blimey, Jamie, no," said Ged dismissively, "I was just doodling, and anyway, Tracy sells watercolours, not sketches. No, you have them, mate."

"Really? Thanks, Grandad!"

"Dad, can you paint?" asked Brian. "Some of these could use a bit of colour."

"I learned it at school, but can't remember much of it now. I suppose if you're all out at Glendurgan tomorrow, I could get a small pallet of watercolours and a few brushes from the shop and give it a go."

"You should," said Sarah. "Let's get some before Tracy closes the shop."

By the time they had packed all the picnic things and folded the chairs, it was almost 4:30 pm. Brian insisted on giving his father another piggyback up the beach steps. As he set him down on the pavement, Tracy breezed past on her way up the road in her jogging pants.

"See you tomorrow, guys; I need to run off the massive ham sandwich Mum made me for lunch. Phil and I are supposed to be having a curry tonight."

"Oh, so the shop is closed then," said Jamie, disappointed.

"Sorry, Jamie. We're open again at ten tomorrow," she called over her shoulder.

"It's okay, Jamie; I'll go to the shop and get the brushes and things tomorrow."

"Oh," said Jamie in a rising whine, "I wanted you to have a go today, Grandad."

"It can wait, Jamie," said Sarah. "Grandad has a whole fortnight of sitting around waiting for his foot to heal. There's plenty of time."

"You can use my colouring pencils if you like, Grandad," came the shy voice of Alice from under the hood of her pink poncho.

"Thanks, Alice," said Ged. Shall I try and draw you a unicorn after dinner?"

"Ooh, yes, please, a purple one with wings and a golden horn."

"Well, you certainly know what you want, Alice," said Brian. "Do you think you can manage those specifications, Grandad?"

"As long as there is enough of Alice's purple pencil left to use," he said with a wink to Alice. "You use a lot of purple, don't you? Do you have a gold pencil?"

"Not proper gold, but there's a sort of dark yellow which will have to do," she said.

"Pragmatic, too," said Ged. "You'd do well at the factory, young lady. You should apply for a job."

"I don't like cars much, Grandad; I don't want to work there," she replied instantly.

Ged chuckled to himself at the simplicity of the way Alice's mind worked as he walked carefully with his crutches next to his

43

granddaughter… "You know, Alice, I have a feeling you'll do well whatever you decide to do. You are a woman who knows her own mind and will see that things are the way she wants them to be. You've been taking notes from Nana, I can tell."

"I don't take notes, Grandad. I hate writing," she said simply.

Sarah and Brian exchanged rueful glances at the truth of that last statement. Sarah took Alice's hand as they walked across the road to the house.

Marge was in the front garden, sitting on the bench with the newspaper on her lap. She wore a big straw hat and appeared to be doing the crossword.

The garden had been trimmed and clipped until it looked like a gardening diagram. Not a single dead flower or yellowed leaf remained; as a result, there was not a great deal of colour in it any longer—just a pleasant mixture of green shades and textures. The garden wheelie bin was full to the brim, and her tools lay on newspaper beside the bench, cleaned, sharpened and freshly oiled.

"Hi, Mum!" called Brian from the gate. There was no movement from her hat. "I think she's nodded off," he said quietly. "I'll go and make a start on dinner. I want to steam the rice and cook a few greens.

Ged leaned the crutches on the wall, placed his hand on the backrest of the bench and lowered himself carefully to sit next to his wife. She stirred but didn't wake. He leaned over, tipped up the brim of her hat and gently kissed her on the cheek. "Wake up, sleeping beauty," he said.

Marge awoke with a start. "Oh! Get off me, you fool!" she chided. Ged sat back and let out a sigh. There was a time when she would have turned to him, smiled and kissed him on the lips. What had happened to his lovely Margie, so pretty in her turquoise dress at the dance hall where they had met fifty-one years ago?

Ged gazed into the middle distance as he recalled the vision of loveliness as she danced with her friend to the jitterbug, the Waltz and …the one that made him laugh out loud…the Tango! That was when he had decided to ask her to dance.

***

"Er…wouldn't you rather dance the Tango with a gentleman?" he had called when she came near.

"Yes!" she had called back with a twinkle in her eye as her girlfriend marched her past. "Have you seen one?" She had definitely winked!

At that point, he nearly ran out of bravado but gave it another try. Standing as tall as his five-feet-nine-inches would allow, he put his left hand on his chest, bowed solemnly, then held out his right hand and looked her in the eye. She whispered something to her friend, who giggled and walked away, as Ged led this beautiful girl onto the dance floor.

Ged held her with a confidence and firmness that she had never experienced. He was silent with his directions, occasionally moving her hand to a more correct position on his rib cage. He exaggerated his head movements in perfect time to the music. Marge tried to copy his moves. There was only a minute to go. This was exhausting!

In the final move, he held her firmly so she felt she could trust him to lean back against the support of his hand, and she flung her left arm back in a flourish!

As he walked her back to the bar, he felt nine feet tall! He had the best-looking girl in the dance hall and had just given her a dancing lesson!

He ordered two cream sodas while the beautiful girl got her breath back.

"Where did you learn to dance like that?" she said.

"My mother is a dance teacher. I used to compete when I was young. I've not seen you at the dance hall before," said Ged in a matter-of-fact way. "What's your name?"

"Margie," said Marge. "Margie Cookson. My friend Flo is teaching me to dance.

"She's pretty good," said Ged, "but she can't Tango and certainly shouldn't lead. She's not tall enough."

"Well, what's your name?" said Marge.

"Ged…Gerald Baker… at your service, Ma'am…I mean, Margie," Ged said with a bow. "Thank you for the dance. I hope we meet again," he said, taking her hand and kissing it gallantly. He started to walk away, but something drew him back. Could she be the one? He may regret walking away for the rest of his life. He turned to look at her. "Would you like to dance again? The next one is a foxtrot."

"I would be honoured if you would teach me to dance the foxtrot, Mr Baker."

She already knew the basic moves, so he just corrected her foot position here, hand and finger position there, and lifted her elbow to create a more correct posture for the dance. The foxtrot they danced was relatively slow, so it was great for teaching, but that made it harder to balance.

"Pull your stomach in for balance," coached Ged calmly and confidently. "Chin up a little, that's right; try not to look at your feet, trust them to do what you want them to do and leave them to it. You'll soon know if you make a mistake."

"How?" Asked Marge

"You'll tread on my toes! Feel the music in your body, and you won't need to count."

As he wheeled her around, her skirt swirled around her knees. He felt a lightness in his chest and a tingle down his spine…

***

"Dad! Mum! Come on, it's dinner time. Are you two coming or not?" called Brian from the front door of the house, waking Ged from his daydream.

Marge folded up the paper and put the pencil in her apron pocket. "Come on, Gerald, you were half asleep; it's time for dinner; you need to wash and get the wine opened. Brian can't be expected to do everything!"

Ged's daydream shattered and dispersed like a dropped champagne glass. What had happened? He knew what… Life, kids, work, a mortgage…and Marge's father…James Cookson. Now, there was a name he would rather forget…

"Come on, Grandad, I'm hungry. Do you want some help?" said Jamie.

"Oh, thanks, Jamie," Ged replied, "I'll be fine if you could take my paper bag with the sketchbook into the house; I'll manage on the crutches. I'm getting the hang of them now."

Ged washed his hands in the kitchen sink and leaned his crutch against the worktop while he rummaged in the drawer for the corkscrew.

"It's a screw-top bottle, Dad," said Sarah. "Merlot or Rioja?"

"From the smell of that stew, Rioja…what do you think, Brian?" called Ged.

"Rioja would be perfect; it's a Spanish beef stew, actually."

Marge touched Sarah's arm gently as she passed her in the kitchen; "I'd rather have a white wine, if you don't mind, Dear," she whispered.

Sarah opened the fridge and pulled out a new bottle of white Rioja. She poured a glass for Marge, returned the bottle to the refrigerator, and expertly grabbed three red wine glasses by their stems in her other hand.

Dinner was delicious, as always, although Alice didn't like the beef. She was tired and had always been a fussy eater. Sarah took the meat off her plate and mixed the sauce into her rice. "Come on, Alice, all the meat has gone, just a little rice and sauce," she said encouragingly.

"Can I have cake if I eat this?" enquired Alice, opening the dinnertime negotiations.

"As long as you've eaten your rice and vegetables, Alice, yes, there is a pudding."

Brian kept the servings relatively small, so everyone usually had enough room in their cake stomachs for something sweet. The adults took their time over dinner, savouring each mouthful and discussing ingredients, flavours, textures, and colours. They debated amiably whether small salad potatoes would have been a more suitable accompaniment…the usual Baker dinnertime discussion.

Dessert was a deliciously light but moist Spanish *Tarta-de-Santiago* that Brian had made at home and brought with him. Made like a traditional Bakewell tart sponge with ground almonds, eggs and sugar, flavoured with Madeira. He served it with a few fresh blackberries and a drizzle of single cream. Ged had eaten Brian's Tarta-de-Santiago before and loved it.

"A toast to the chef?" said Ged with his glass raised.

"Chef!" Sarah and Jamie chimed in, raising their glasses. Marge raised her glass in appreciation, but she had been quiet all mealtime.

They decided to start a jigsaw that evening as a long walk along the seafront was out of the question due, in part, to the crutches and also on account of how full everyone felt after dinner. An old favourite was chosen – a pretty image of a thatched cottage with hollyhocks. The children cleared the table and then pulled Ged's homemade folding jigsaw board from under the sofa. Ged made it the previous summer so that the jigsaw could be stowed away under the sofa in a part-finished state, allowing the table to be set for meals. It was basically a large piece of thin plywood, covered in green baize cloth, with hinged flaps that folded over on top of the part-finished jigsaw, preventing the pieces from moving about as the board was moved.

Brian made coffee for the adults while Sarah tidied the kitchen. Ged helped the children to sort the corners and straight edges from the other jigsaw pieces. Once they had completed the edge, it was well after seven-thirty, and the children were yawning and flopping. Being by the sea always seemed to make them sleepier.

Ged took his crutches and followed the children upstairs to read a story to them. This week, he had decided to read 'Swallows and Amazons', one of his childhood favourites. Ged sat in the comfortable winged armchair between the children's beds. He gave each character in the story a unique voice and character. The book's dialogue meant that the children in Swallows and Amazons had to be terribly posh – or *'tewwibly pawsh'* as Sarah put it. At first, Jamie tittered at the hyperbolic home-counties accent that his grandfather gave the children in the story, but soon, he became too immersed in the tale to notice. He imagined the hull of the Swallow and her calico sails fluttering. He did interrupt the tale at one point to ask his grandfather what a 'Duffer' was.

When Ged heard a soft, rumbling snore from Alice's pillow, he finished the last few sentences of the paragraph he was reading to Jamie and folded the dust jacket into the page to mark his place.

Jamie turned to switch off his bedside lamp, yawning widely.

"Can I really keep those drawings, Grandad? Are you sure you don't want to sell them?" he said sleepily.

"I promise, Jamie…I'm a man of my word, and I have spoken – when I make a promise, it's never broken." Ged recited.

"Love you Grandad." murmured Jamie.

"Love you too, Jamie," said Ged. He leaned over and kissed his grandson on the forehead. He checked that Alice was properly sleeping before whispering, "Love you, Alice," and kissing her lightly on her cheek.

He took up his crutches and, with great care in the dark bedroom, sidled out, trying hard not to bump the children's beds.

The others had gathered around the dining table. The jigsaw was starting to take shape, but they were all yawning now, especially Marge. She fiddled, half-heartedly, with a jigsaw piece for the roof of the thatched cottage.

"The kids are asleep," he announced to no one in particular. "I don't think I'll be long out of bed myself. "Have you seen the painkillers, Marge? My foot is throbbing".

"Have a look in my handbag," she replied. "I went to the shop for the newspaper this morning and bought some more co-codamol and ibuprofen while I was there."

"Thanks, Love," he said gratefully. He found the tablets and hobbled to the kitchen for a glass of water. He forgot to rest the crutches in a corner. They fell with a clatter.

"For goodness' sake, Gerald!" snapped Marge. "You'll wake the children!"

"Sorry," said Ged, wishing he had stowed the crutches better, wondering how to pick them up without hurting his foot.

"Here, Dad," said Sarah, handing him the fallen crutches, "I could have got you a glass of water. All you have to do is ask."

"Thanks, Love; I didn't think to ask."

Marge crossed her arms across her chest, regarding Ged with pursed lips.

"That's your problem, Gerald Baker, you don't think!"

"Mum!" snapped Brian. "What's got into you?"

"Nothing has *'got into me,'* Brian. This broken foot is going to ruin our holiday. We're all going to be running around after him, giving him tea and sympathy, and it's his own silly fault for leaving my handbag in the boot instead of giving it to me...*and* stuffing the cool bag in the boot when it was already too full. That's the problem, you see... when *you* don't think, things like this happen, and *we* all have to suffer the consequences."

The others simply stared at her, open-mouthed.

"Oh, good grief!" she said after a short silence. "I've had a long day in the garden; I'm going to bed."

7

The following morning, Ged woke early, and as their bedroom window faced South East, he was in for a magical treat. The sun was just rising above the horizon, and the sea was bathed in a reflection of the awesome orange, pink, mauve, and violet of a Cornish sunrise. He had woken early in many other parts of the country and in France, where they used to go camping with friends, but nowhere had he ever seen a sunrise so breathtaking as in Porthcovery. He had first seen it over twenty years ago when they rented a cottage on the headland when the twins were about ten years old. It was on their first morning, and he had been utterly spellbound.

He put the boot carefully on his foot, fixing the velcro straps securely, grabbed one of his crutches and made his way carefully down the stairs. He took a couple of co-codamol from the packet he had left on the dining table the previous night by a glass of water and took them, draining the glass. Then, he spotted the paper bag from the Gallery shop near Alice's purple backpack with a unicorn picture on it. A thought struck him…He went over to the backpack and took out her pencil case. He took the backpack and his paper bag with pencils, the ruler and sketchbook and made his way over to the bay window at the front of the dining room.

Ged arranged himself as comfortably as possible on the thick, padded window seat, with two cushions behind his back. Once comfortable, he realised he was facing entirely in the wrong direction. All he could see out of the window, from this position, was a few bushes and a little bit of sea. He heaved himself up and went to sit with his back to the other wall, which allowed him to use his right leg to haul himself further onto the window seat. He used his hands to lift the clumsy boot onto the window seat. After just one day on the beach, the boot looked as if he had been wearing it for a week. He rested it against another cushion and sat leaning against the two cushions at his back. His right leg flopped sideways, providing the perfect place to rest his sketch pad.

The tide was on its way out, leaving a shimmering wet beach with sparkling rocks reflecting the morning sun protruding from the flat sand. There was a white, twin-hulled Catamaran with a small red inflatable dinghy tied up behind it, anchored in the far end of the bay near the harbour. It bobbed and swayed gently, its mast tipping from side to side rhythmically like a nautical metronome. A small, blue fisherman's boat was phut-phutting slowly across the bay on its way back from dropping crab pots.

Ged began to sketch what he could see from the window. Using a hard pencil and a light touch, his pencil strokes were feathered. A hazy scene began to form on the page, reflecting the softness of the diffused morning light. He sketched quickly, as he wanted to capture the colour if he could.

He opened Alice's pencil case, tipping the contents out on the seat beside him. He selected colours that he felt would match and sharpened the pencils to a good point. Using the side of the pencil point, he gently shaded the sky in all its magical, multi-coloured splendour. He was surprised to find the colour of the pencils so light. He couldn't persuade the shades to deepen, no matter how much pressure he applied. Then he spotted, as he was placing one of them down, stamped on the side of the pencil, the words *'watercolour pencil'*. Having never used them before, he had no idea how to use them, but he assumed they would behave differently if wet, so he put the end of one of the pencils, an orange one, in his mouth to dampen it slightly and scribbled a little bit on the edge of the page. Sure enough, a more vibrant, deep orange appeared under the pressure of the pencil. He tore the page out and practised with the orange watercolour pencil, testing out what would happen if he smudged it with a damp finger and what effects he could achieve for a given level of dampness on the pencil tip.

Once he had figured out how to get the effect he wanted to achieve, he took his original sketch and began to apply a small amount of colour to the sea, just a suggestion of colour, to reflect the colours of the sunrise he had shaded in the sky, but in a slightly deeper shade. – The actual sunrise outside had long since lost its brilliant spectrum, and the village of Porthcovery was now bathed in hazy sunlight. The purple, pink and orange shades of the sunrise sky were giving way to the azure blue of another warm summer's day.

Ged spent a few minutes applying a little more colour to the sky and then picked up a softer sketching pencil. The picture seemed... washed-out, too vague; it lacked something... but what? As he stared at the page, he twirled the pencil around the base of the thumb of his right hand, occasionally stopping, tapping the pencil against his bottom lip and glancing out of the window. The village was gradually coming to life. Some fishermen were hauling in their catch in large plastic barrels using the winch at the end of the harbour. On the deck of the catamaran, a woman was coiling ropes and making adjustments to the rigging and sails. He could see a girl pulling on a pink hooded sweater as she appeared on the deck of the boat.

'Details,' thought Ged, that's what it needed. He scanned around for more subject matter and began to sketch...a seagull on the end of the harbour wall, a fisherman using the small crane on the harbour wall to guide his barrel of fish onto the harbour, shading on the rocks on the beach, the portholes on the side of the yacht, some shading on the mast, just a few touches... don't over-do it...

He suddenly remembered a promise. He discarded the sunrise picture and turned the page. He pulled Alice's backpack onto his lap and rummaged about in it, hoping he would find some of her storybooks. Ah yes. This one would do. 'The Promised Pony.'

He quickly sketched an imagined scene of meadows and trees by a wide river. Then, using some of the illustrations in Alice's storybook and the picture on the front of the backpack as a reference, he sketched a perfectly proportioned horse drinking peacefully at the edge of the river. Finally, he gave the horse a twisted horn, like that of a Narwhal.

He took Alice's colouring pencils and began to shade the unicorn in varying depths of purple and pink: darker purple at the muzzle, around the eyes and ears, a uniform, light-ish mauve shade over its front legs, head, neck and back, with darker shading in the right places to give a 3-dimensional appearance, the deep purple shades gave way to a speckled pattern on its rump, flanks and hind legs, rather like a South American dappled Appaloosa horse. Finally, he gave the unicorn a deep pink mane and tail, then lightly shaded some suggestions of more typical colours in the landscape, the trees and the river, remembering to reflect some of the purples and pinks of the magical beast in the water.

**

"Mummy, come and look!" cried Alice. "Look what Grandad has done! He forgot last night, so he got up early and drawed me my unicorn! I love it, Grandad! It's the best Unicorn in the world! But I think you forgot something."

"Oh? What did I forget, Alice?" said Ged, putting on an air of genuine curiosity.

"His wings, Grandad. He has to be able to fly," she said in a serious 'surely you know this' voice.

"Ah… I see. In my old storybooks, it was only Pegasus who had wings. Unicorns just had a horn, but as this is *your* unicorn, if you want it to have wings, Princess Alice, then wings it shall have."

Ged took the hard pencil and sharpened it with Alice's pencil sharpener. With the lightest of touches, he sketched a pair of gossamer wings sprouting from the unicorn's back. They were almost transparent, folded back against the unicorn's flanks, with the tips almost touching the ground. He handed the picture back to Alice with a look that translated as: 'Does this meet your approval – boss?'

"Oh yes, Grandad! He's wonderful. Thank you! I'm going to call him Dazzle," said Alice. "You did everything I said… Mummy, come and look what Grandad did!" Alice grabbed the picture and ran to the stairs, as a somewhat dishevelled Sarah came padding down in a vest-top and black pyjama trousers, her normally tied-back hair tumbling over her shoulders.

"Shh, Alice, keep your voice down," she scolded, almost in a whisper. "Nana and Daddy are still asleep…Wow, that's a lovely and very…er, 'purple' horse…no, no, sorry, it's a unicorn. Did Grandad draw that for you? I hope you said thank you. She shot a glance at Ged."

"She did. Did you sleep well?"

"Mmm, not really. I think we need a new mattress for our bed. This one is just too hard. I can't get comfortable."

"Why don't you go into Helston today and see if there's something suitable at Kennerton's? Buy something decent; there's no point in being stingy. You spend a third of your life in bed, and you want to make the most of your lie-ins on holiday."

"I can't go today; we're supposed to be going to Glendurgan for the day."

"If you go to Helston for nine, you'll have about thirty minutes in the shop and can get back before ten. I can't see Marge being ready before then."

"It's Sunday, Dad; they don't open 'til ten."

"Good point; go on the way then, or perhaps make your excuses and duck out of the trip. I'm sure Brian and Mum can manage the kids. It won't be much of a holiday if you can't sleep."

"I'll have a think about it and talk to Brian," she said, yawning. "Anyway, how come you're up so early?"

"I just woke up when the sun came up and decided to come in here to watch the sunrise. It's what this window seat was built for."

"Did you get a photo? I've tried a few times to capture a good sunrise here, but I think I need a better camera."

"No, sorry, I don't even know where the camera is. Tell you what, I'll make you a cuppa. You look like you could use a bit of caffeine."

"Haven't you forgotten something?" she said, regarding Ged with slight amusement, her hands on her hips.

"What?"

"Your foot," she said simply. "You can't go serving me when you're hobbling about like an old sea dog, can you, 'Peg-Leg Pete'!"

"I'll give it a try, just this once. Come and get comfortable with these cushions here, and I'll put the kettle on. I've been sitting here since about a quarter to five this morning. If I don't move soon, I'll either seize up or grow roots."

"Go on then," said Sarah, giving in. "But you'd be careful where you stash those sticks, or they'll fall over, and your old lady will be after your blood for waking her up!"

Ged could get about in the kitchen without the aid of the crutches; leaning them carefully in the corner with the brushes and mop, he used the work surfaces to steady himself, holding his broken left foot up all the while. He found that any amount of pressure applied through it sent searing pain through his foot, numbing the toes and sole. So, he had quickly learned to keep his weight off it. He managed to get the kettle filled and find four mugs, the teapot, teabags and milk without so much as a wince. Realising he hadn't had a drink since sunrise, he filled a glass with filtered water from the jug for himself and poured another glass each for the children.

Pleased that he had managed to make tea, he was faced with a dilemma: How to carry the tea across the room without spilling it? That was not going to happen. He fetched the crutches and made his way back into the sitting room to tell Sarah that her tea was ready and ask her to bring it in. He stopped short; she was fast asleep on the window seat with his sunrise sketch on her lap. She had used the cushions to support her back and had somehow managed to find a suitable position to sleep in.

Ged hobbled over and reached past her with his right crutch, clumsily pulling the curtains closed to darken the room a little; then he looked around for something to cover her with. He heard footsteps on the stairs. Looking around, he saw Jamie tiptoeing down the stairs as he always did in the morning. Ged put a finger to his lips.

"Jamie," he whispered. "Can you get a blanket from your mum's bedroom and come and tuck her in? She's fallen asleep, and I don't want to wake her."

"Okay, Grandad," whispered Jamie and tiptoed back upstairs. He came down with a soft Tartan fleece blanket, closely followed by Alice and Brian.

"Mummy's asleep," Ged whispered to Alice.

Jamie opened out the folded fleece, carefully holding it with arms stretched out wide and draped it carefully over his sleeping mother. She stirred but didn't wake.

They trooped into the kitchen. "Let's have breakfast Al Fresco, shall we?" said Brian to the children as he carried some plates and bowls out to the little back yard.

"Does that mean breakfast outside, Daddy?" said Alice. "How exciting."

"Shall I take one of these teas in to Mum?" said Brian. "I'll tell her we're having breakfast outside. I know Sarah didn't sleep well last night. Her tossing and turning woke me twice, and I usually sleep like a dead man!"

"Great idea," said Ged. 'I'll give you a hand with breakfast."

"It's fine, Dad. Is there some more tea in the pot for me?"

"Yes," said Ged. "I'm not such a hopeless invalid. I managed to make a pot of tea."

"Yeah, but you can't carry it anywhere, can you?" jibed Brian, winking.

"Hmm, true, you have me there," said Ged, grinning. "I'll have to find a solution if I'm to survive a day on my own. Can't go a whole day without a cuppa."

"You can hop down to the Café on your crutches."

"Good suggestion. I'm nipping down to the Gallery shop to get a few things later. Oh, Brian… Sarah said she couldn't sleep because of your mattress. Can you drop in at Kennerton's furniture shop on your way to Glendurgan so she can try out a few mattresses? The sooner you get one, the better."

"Mum won't like that," said Brian doubtfully.

"I think she'd prefer it to option two."

"Which is?" asked Brian dubiously.

"Sarah can borrow my car to go to Kennerton's, and you and Mum have the children all day at Glendurgan without her," said Ged bluntly.

"Ah, well, when you put it like that, I think we'll go for option one. Sarah has ten times the patience of Mum and I put together!"

Just then, Marge appeared at the bedroom door in her dressing gown. "Any tea, Brian dear?"

"Yes, Mum," whispered Brian. "Dad just made some. Sarah's asleep in the living room. I was just about to bring you a cup."

"Oh dear," said Marge without lowering her voice. "Have you two had a quarrel?"

"No, Mum, can you keep it quiet, please?" hissed Brian. "She had an awful night's sleep on the hard mattress in our room and is more comfy on the window seat by the look of it. We're going to have breakfast on the patio while she gets some sleep. Go back to bed; I'll bring your tea in."

"Oh, I wanted to have my tea on the window seat," complained Marge.

"Marge," chided Ged, irritated. "She hasn't slept all night!"

"That's hardly my fault."

"I think we can be charitable, just this once, can't we?" said Brian, quietly but firmly, through gritted teeth. "Would you like breakfast in bed, or will you join us on the patio? We're having scrambled eggs and smoked salmon in about half an hour."

I'll have breakfast with you, but I'll do my crossword in bed. You can bring my tea into my room, dear," she said.

Brian decided against any further comment. He knew better than to challenge his mother before breakfast.

8

Sunday breakfasts had been an occasion for the Baker family for as long as Brian could remember. They liked to make it a special breakfast and always shared it as a family around the table; whether it was kippers, kedgeree, full English, or pancakes, it would always be a family affair. Ged had started the tradition when Brian was a small boy. Brian and his twin brother Edward played football or cricket on Saturday mornings throughout their childhood, so Saturday breakfast was usually rushed. Ged had typically left for work by the time the boys were up for breakfast on weekdays. He wanted to make at least one breakfast a week, a special, family one.

It was those breakfasts which had kindled Brian's love affair with cooking. As a boy, he often helped Ged to prepare Sunday breakfast, and as he got older and was able to manage the kitchen safely, Ged let him have a go at making it on his own. He liked to surprise the rest of the family with new and interesting breakfasts...Initially, not all of his creations were successful. His smoked mackerel with lemon sauce and herby peanut butter stuffing was one which particularly stuck in Ged's memory...and at the time in his throat, but Ged usually managed to help him recover the situation and make something edible, if occasionally unconventional.

On this particular Sunday morning, Brian had prepared Marge's favourite breakfast: scrambled eggs and smoked salmon served on toasted wholemeal muffins lightly buttered with hollandaise sauce.

There was a fruit salad of melon, pineapple and strawberries, orange juice and a fresh pot of Brian's favourite Jamaican blue mountain coffee.

The children didn't care much for Smoked Salmon but were happy to have the muffins buttered with hollandaise and topped with Brian's fluffy and moist scrambled eggs.

Sarah came into the kitchen, yawning and stretching as Brian served breakfast.

"Morning, Beautiful!" he said, kissing her cheek as she put her arms around his waist and kissed his neck.

"Morning, Chef, ooh, aren't I a lucky girl?" she said in a drawling, mock-upper-class accent. "Smoked salmon and scwambled eggs for bweakfast... Have we got any bubbly daaahling? One simply must have a glass of Bollinger with it."

"I'd rather have a cup of coffee, actually," said Brian, grinning.

"Fair enough. I'll pour then, shall I?" she said, back in her normal Cheshire accent.

They still had breakfast on the patio, although Marge complained that the eggs had gone cold too quickly because they were eating outside. "Why couldn't we have eaten in the house? After all, Sarah isn't sleeping in there anymore." No one commented. It wasn't worth an argument, and the others knew there were bigger fish to fry with the main discussion of the morning...the matter of the little shopping trip.

Fancy another cup of tea, Mum?" said Brian. "Or would you rather have a coffee?"

"Thank you, Brian." His mother replied, smiling sweetly.

Sarah sat at the end of the table with the two children, looking at the guidebook for Glendurgan Garden. Jamie was convinced that he could memorise the route through the maze so that they wouldn't get lost, as they usually did.

"There's an aerial shot of the maze on the leaflet," said Sarah. "If we use that when we are in the maze, we should be able to work out how to get out... if we can get to the middle, of course."

"Can I see if I can get out by memory first, though, Mum?" said Jamie.

"I know you like a challenge, Jim," said Brian, "but there's a kink in your thinking."

"Why?" Jamie replied.

"Well, if you are at the beginning or the very middle of the maze and you have the map, then you can use it, but if you've become lost, it's very hard to tell where you are on the map, and that makes the map useless because you don't know where you're starting from" explained Brian.

"Oh, well, in that case, Mum, I'll start using my memory, and you can tell me if I start to go wrong."

"Okay," said Sarah. "Well, that's if I come to Glendurgan at all, of course."

"Why would you *not* come?" asked Marge sharply.

"I have to run an errand in Helston this morning," Sarah replied. "Dad said I could borrow his car while you and Brian go off to Glendurgan with the children."

"But Mum!" exclaimed Jamie, "we always do the maze with you. It won't be as much fun without you."

"I would much prefer it if you came, Sarah; I'm not sure Brian and I would manage the children for a whole day."

Sarah glanced at Brian. Their brief exchange of looks communicated so much more than they could say out loud:

"Dig me out of this, will you?"
"You got yourself in; you can get yourself out of it."
"What if she doesn't agree to us stopping off in Helston?"
"We'll work that out if it comes to it."

"It's not a long errand, is it, Sarah?" Ged said innocently, "What if you were to stop off in Helston on the way?"

"I could drop in at the shop; they open at ten, but I'll be at least 20 minutes."

"Well, I would rather wait for you than not have you with us, wouldn't you, Mum?" said Brian, hoping to garner support from his mother.

"I smell a trap," said Marge. "What is this *errand?*"

"She's getting some furniture for our bedroom," said Brian.

"Oh? What furniture is that?" asked Marge.

"We need a new mattress."

"You've only had the one you've got for two years. Why are you buying a new one?"

"My physiotherapist suggested I get a softer mattress. We bought one for home, and I have slept much better since we've had it."

"I see, so the one I bought isn't good enough, is it?"

"Marge, it's their bedroom. If they need a new mattress, I don't see any harm in them buying one."

"It seems a bit of a waste of money, and can't it wait? Why do you need to get it today?"

"Because…" Sarah stood up, shoving her chair back so that it scraped noisily on the flagstones. She put her hands flat on the table and looked directly at Marge, her temples pulsing. She spat out her words slowly and deliberately – "Because – Marge…If I don't get a few good nights' sleep very, *very* soon, I'll get rather short-tempered, and I won't be able to tolerate people who complain about everything!"

No one said a word. Sarah pushed her chair back under the table, picked up her coffee cup and went inside for a shower. Marge finally closed her mouth. She had been doing a good likeness of a goldfish.

"Well! I say!" she said. "What was all that about?"

Ged and Brian locked eyes briefly, looked down and shook their heads.

"I need a shower, too," said Ged. "I think I'll just stick my foot out of the shower and put it on the bathroom stool."

"Better have a bath, Dad," said Brian. "Standing on one leg with the broken foot on a stool sounds uncomfortable, not to say dangerous – you'll end up with a broken neck!"

"Good point. I'll use your bathroom upstairs when you've all finished with it."

The children had been quiet since Sarah's outburst and had gone off to the jigsaw. Brian went over to see how they were getting on and to hurry them up so they could be ready to go well before ten.

"Why did Mummy shout?" said Alice uncertainly.

"I think Mummy hasn't slept very well for a few nights," said Brian, giving her a hug. "Nana gets upset when things don't go to plan. I think a nice day out at Glendurgan will make us all feel better."

"Can we take Grandma and Grandad Williams there one day? We could push Grandma around the maze in her wheelchair," said Jamie.

"Great idea, I think they'd love it," said Brian.

Sarah's Mother had a heart condition, which left her needing to use a wheelchair if they had to go any distance. They planned to come and stay in the house during the October half-term.

"Come on, let's go and get our teeth brushed. The sooner we get going, the sooner we get to Glendurgan, and we can lose you two in the maze."

They went upstairs, where Sarah was drying her hair.

"Sorry if I scared you," she said, turning off her hairdryer and hugging the children. "I don't lose my temper often, do I? I didn't sleep well, so I didn't have much left in my patience bucket. I feel better after my shower," she looked at Brian, "and I'll feel better still when I have a new mattress on the way."

"You can borrow my fluffy unicorn; It always makes me feel better when I'm cross," said Alice, seriously.

"Thanks, Alice. That's very kind of you. I might borrow it later if I'm feeling grumpy, but I think a day of getting lost in a maze with you two will cheer me up, too. How could I be grumpy after that?" she said, winking at Brian.

While the others were getting ready, Ged packed the backpack cool bag (or, as he now called it, the 'evil-foot-slaying, backpack of doom') with day-trip necessities: water bottles, apples, snacks for the journey, sun cream, and insect repellent. He also made sure the little first aid kit and an inhaler for Jamie were in there.

Sarah usually prepared this bag of essentials, which they used on every trip. He tried to imagine Sarah packing it so he could remember everything she put in. He cast his eyes around the kitchen for clues... Biscuits. She usually had chocolate-covered snack biscuits or granola bars. Yes, he thought, that should do it.

Sarah came into the kitchen looking flustered.

"Day-bag?" said Ged, handing the backpack of doom to Sarah. "Done... At least, I think so... Water, apples, snacks, insect repellent, sun cream, kitchen roll, wipes, first aid kit...er, I think I remembered everything you usually put in."

"Dad, you're a star! Thank you!" She said, giving him a peck on the cheek.

Ged waved his family off, then made his way carefully upstairs on his crutches and ran a bath. Getting in and out was awkward, but it was good to rest his boot on the edge of the bath. By the time he had dried and dressed, choosing baggy cargo shorts that easily slid over the boot, it was only ten-thirty; plenty of day to fill yet.

All the activity had made his foot throb. When had he last had some tablets? He was sure it must have been when he started sketching before five that morning, so he found ibuprofen and co-codamol and took two of each. He would have a good four hours of comfort, at least, he figured, especially now that he didn't have to go up and down stairs.

He decided to go to the Seagull café near the Gallery shop and have a coffee. He hadn't spoken to Bill and Sharon, the owners of the café, since his last maintenance trip in May. Bill would often sit and have a chat if Ged timed his visits right.

The Seagull café was a firm favourite with tourists and locals alike. Bill and Sharon kept the place spotless. The food was good, and the service was quick and reliable. The menu had remained largely unchanged for the last thirty years. They sold a small range of items for breakfast: Pancakes, toast, and a "Full Cornish" breakfast (much like a full English but with Bill's famous homemade hash-browns and without black pudding). They offered beach food at lunchtime, such as sandwiches and filled rolls, Cornish pasties, and sausage rolls. Toasted sandwiches, baguettes, and small cones of chips were available for cooler days. Cornish cream teas and cakes were available until 4:30, and the evening menu was a dependable range of affordable evening family meals: Sausages and mash, Fish, Chicken and Chips, Baked Potatoes, Lasagne, Spaghetti Bolognese or Chilli. The specials board typically offered curry, veggie or vegan options and a catch of the day.

What Ged liked best about the Seagull was their clear knowledge of what children are happy to eat (and what their parents like them to eat). Bill had a good stock of small pork or veggie sausages, nuggets, fish or veggie fingers, and calamari. He also had plenty of frozen peas, baked beans, carrots, broccoli, and …most importantly, tomato ketchup. He kept jellies in the larder, as well as ice cream, chocolate biscuits, and even rusks for the tiny ones.

Meals were served on blue and white striped 'Cornishware' crockery, and there were black and white Cornish flag placemats on all the tables – Bill was a patriotic Cornishman and considered himself English only if England were winning the rugby Six Nations championship.

During the season, holiday-makers flocked to the café, many of them several times a week. Some would book a table every night of the week and have something different each night. Bill and Sharon had a local skiffle or folk band come and play on Thursday evenings. Over winter, they held tea-time quiz nights, which were popular with locals and 'driftwood' (Bill's term for people who came to Cornwall to live permanently).

From Easter to the end of summer, Bill and Sharon employed two local teens, one to help Bill in the kitchen, cooking and washing up, and the other assisting Sharon, waiting tables, and keeping customers happy. It worked well. There were tough seasons when poor weather kept people indoors or away from the coast altogether, but steady custom from locals in the village and surrounding area allowed Bill and Sharon to make ends meet.

Bill, born in the nearby village of St Killian, began working at the café in the holidays for the previous owner as a teen and had grown to enjoy it, eventually becoming the Chef permanently. He met Sharon one summer when she got a job waiting tables. Sharon and Bill fell in step. Sharon had learned to cook and be a superb host in a pub in her home county of Wiltshire. She often came to stay with her Auntie Dorothy ('Dot' on account of her height) and Uncle George in Porthcovery during the summer holidays. That summer, she simply never went home. The following year, Bill and Sharon got married in the local church, and Bill moved into Dot's cottage with Sharon.

By the time Nora, the previous owner, decided to retire and sell up, Bill and Sharon had been running the place for Nora for eight years. As they had lived almost rent-free in Dot's cottage and worked at the café from seven in the morning until around eleven in the evening, six nights a week, they had managed to save enough for a deposit. It was not hard to convince the bank manager to offer them a mortgage on the café and the two-bedroom flat above.

To anyone but those most closely involved, no one would have noticed any change in the place when ownership passed from Nora to Sharon and Bill, but the more observant might have noticed a change on the sign from "The Seagull' to 'The Seagull Café (Licensed restaurant).

***

Ged made his way along the seafront, timing his arrival at the Seagull to coincide with Bill's coffee break. Bill and Sharon had recently joined the barista revolution and had purchased a gleaming Italian coffee machine, complete with hot steamer spouts. At first, they didn't know how to use it and wasted gallons of milk trying to create perfect frothy cappuccinos. They employed a talented seventeen-year-old local lad who had a reputation for coffee-making in Helston. He taught Bill and Sharon to make coffee, barista style, and how to create patterns in the milk froth. This involved a few winter evenings of banging metal jugs on the worktop, a bit of swearing and many more pints of milk. Still, it had been worth every minute: the café had gained a new string to its bow and an enthusiastic-though perhaps somewhat sleepless-local following... at least until Bill found a decaf that tasted like the real thing.

Ged eased himself into a chair on the outside patio by the door near the kitchen. "Service, ma'am!" he called. "Can a man get a decent cappuccino around here?"

"Certainly, sir," said Sharon, who had spotted Ged coming along the road. She set down a large mug of frothy cappuccino in front of him, complete with a fern pattern and a Cornish flag-shaped sprinkle of chocolate powder. "Would sir care for a slice of coffee and walnut or carrot cake?"

"Not today, thanks, Sharon," said Ged, "I'm watching my waistline."

"What have you done to your foot?" she asked.

"Elephant handler's injury," he said, grinning.

"Right…so…you've broken a metatarsal…and…as you're not an Elephant handler…what embarrassing happenstance led to that?" she said, pointing at his boot "You didn't get run over by one of the cars at your factory, did you?"

"Cool bag fell out of the boot when we were packing," said Ged sheepishly.

"Poor Mrs B," said Sharon. "She'll have hated the drive," she said, shaking her head sorrowfully.

"Morning, Chippy!" called Bill from the kitchen window, "I'll be out 'dreckly'. Just finishin' the soup for lunch – courgette and thyme, today."

Ged sat back as Sharon went to serve some other customers who had just asked for their bill. He cast his eye along the seafront and across the bay. The catamaran was still anchored in the middle of the bay, but the dinghy was missing from the back. They must have come in to harbour. He glanced at the couple paying their bill. He was pretty sure the woman was the one he had seen on the deck of the Yacht early that morning. She caught his eye and gave a nod towards his foot.

"I overheard about your accident," she said with a slightly Scandinavian accent – Danish, perhaps? "How awful – and on the first day of your holiday. I broke mine a few years ago. I dropped a bucket of water on my foot. I should have been more careful. I couldn't ride for weeks," she said regretfully.

"Oh, that long?" said Ged, worried about how long his recovery might take.

"Well, I couldn't get anything but a pair of pumps on for weeks. There's no way I could pull on riding boots, and I can't ride in flip-flops!" said the woman.

"No, I suppose you can't," said Ged sympathetically. Then, changing the subject to be more cheerful, he asked, "Is that your boat?"

"Yes," replied the woman. "She is called Annafried. We sailed her here from Öslo. We've only sailed in Kattegat and the Baltic until this week. We've crewed around the British Isles before, but never had our own boat. My husband, Chris, has just retired. He passed his final skipper exam last year, so here we are! We have been coming here for years, but never on our own boat. We feel very lucky, don't we, darling, she said, putting her hand on her husband's knee." Husband? Thought Ged. She looked at least 20 years younger…or was she?

"Oh, yes. I am thinking every day, I'm a very lucky man," he winked secretly at Ged and kissed his beautiful, young-looking wife on her cheek.

Ged grinned broadly at them both and held his hand out to them. Well, it's lovely to meet you both, Chris and…er?"

"Rita," said the woman, shaking Ged's hand briefly. Her hands were weather-worn. He looked at her face as they shook hands; he saw that she probably wasn't as young as she seemed.

"And you are…" said Chris.

"Ged," said Ged, shaking his offered hand, "although you might hear people calling me 'Chippy'. It's a nickname for carpenters. I sometimes do little jobs for the local shops here."

"We need a carpenter on our boat," said Rita. But I don't think that will be you this week with a broken foot… a pity."

"I wish I could help you, but I think you're right. May I ask how long it was until you could walk with your broken foot, Rita?"

"Oh, I was walking without the sticks in about ten days. I should have rested more as it was quite painful," she said.

Chris got up and slung a small rucksack over his shoulder. "Well, it is nice to meet you, Ged. I am sure we will meet again. We stay here for five days while we learn Windsurfing. We are having our lesson now. Then, on Friday, we go to Helford, and later, we sail to Fawey. We are touring the south coast for four weeks."

"Sounds lovely," said Ged. "Enjoy your lesson."

Rita and Chris walked off up the road to the harbour to the windsurfing school.

"They must be having a tough time, poor things!" said Bill sarcastically as he sat down in the chair opposite Ged with a huge mug of coffee.

"Yeah, doesn't your heart bleed?" Replied Ged sarcastically… Riding horses, a forty-foot Cat, Windsurf lessons, and three more weeks sailing the south coast…you'll have to sell a few more plates of cod and chips before you'll be doing all that, Bill."

"Pshh – yeah," sighed Bill, "but blimey...that wife of 'is... phooooeee! She's a bit of alright, in't she?"

"I 'eard that Bill Callywick!" called Sharon from the kitchen window. "You keep your buttery hands off the Danish pastry!"

"Ah, but that Danish pastry ain't quality the likes o' you, my lovely!" said Bill with a wink.

"Gerroff, you daft thing!" Sharon called back, chuckling.

"You're a lucky man too, Bill," said Ged, "I mean, look at your wife... beautiful, hard-working, tolerant..."

"Yeah, you're right there, Chippy," said Bill, "but that one, eh? Bit of an age difference, I reckon...trophy wife?"

"I dunno, Bill." Ged replied honestly, "I'm not sure they were so different in age, really. She's very pretty and looks young, but she has laugh lines around her eyes and age spots on her hands. I reckon she isn't that much younger...and they seem to have a teenage daughter. There was a teenager on the boat earlier this morning."

"Okay, detective-sergeant chippy...anyways, it weren't her hands I was lookin' at most o' the time, if you get my meanin'... good luck to em," Bill's tone suggested he had no more to say on that subject. "Anyways, young Gerald, what about you and this leg, eh? What've you been droppin' on it?"

"Cool bag," Ged said, making a face.

"'Evvy, was it then?"

"Yep. Ice packs, milk, and three bottles of white wine," replied Ged, wincing at the memory.

Bill's face screwed up in mock agony: "I think you got off lightly; how many bones you broke?"

"Just one. Third metatarsal, so they said at the hospital," said Ged simply.

"What on earth are you goin' to do all week, boy?"

"Well, I thought I'd get a load of Jigsaws and puzzle books...but I've been drawing a few pictures for Jamie and Alice. I want to have a go at a bit of painting, too."

"Oh, 'ere we go...said Bill with mock scorn. "Another tourist from up-country comes down an sees a few nice pictures on café walls an' goes all dewey-eyed; thinks 'e can be the next John Dyer," he said, with a hint of bitterness. "Happens to so many, but I never thought it would get *you*, of all people. It's the light, see... makes people think they can paint just by bein' 'ere and 'oldin a paintbrush," he went on. "Ave you seen some o' the tosh on the walls o' the galleries and cafés around 'ere? sellin' for goodness knows how much... Any old twit reckons they can paint when the light gets 'em... but you gotta know what you're doin'. An' well... even the trained 'uns don't all 'ave the eye."

Ged was astonished by this intense and passionate speech. Bill seldom spoke more than a few words; this was unprecedented.

"I didn't realise you felt so strongly about it, Bill," he said.

"All of us café owners get it in the neck with this," he began to explain, twiddling a tea towel nervously in his lap. "These rich-kid artists from Berkshire or wherever think they're the next big thing, come in your café an' ask you to put their pictures on the wall to sell... An' when you say no...an' you don' wanna say *'cos they're crap'*... they get the 'ump an' tell all their friends, an' the local press, sayin' that your café's rubbish an' nobody should ever eat there, or you get bloomin' salmonella."

"Really? That's crazy!"

"Yeah, well, that's what happened," said Bill, casting his eyes down to his feet. "So, now we 'ave to be polite, no matter how crap their stuff is an' say summat like: 'Oh, sorry Leonardo, there's quite a waitin' list of artists with pictures already waiting to be displayed in our café, but you can come back in a few months if you like.' Or some such bull-crap."

"So that's what Sharon told you to say, is it?" said Ged.

"Yeah, and my lawyer when I sued the little creep," spat Bill.

"Good grief...you sued him?"

"Had to Chippy, my lad. Got my reputation to protect 'avven I? Sued the little blighter for defamation and libel."

"Well done. Did you win?"

"We got "im on libel, but 'ee didn't 'ave any money did 'ee, so it didn't get us very far, but the judge made 'im write a full apology as an open letter in the Helston Packet an' told 'im 'ee 'ad to send it to all the other local papers too. A young journalist thought it was a good story an' got on the front page, but we didn't hear much about it from customers after. Well, it was only in the Falmouth Star an' 'elston Packet, so I'm not sure if it did any good or 'arm."

"I guess it's a bit of PR, I suppose," said Ged thoughtfully, "But I can see why budding artists aren't exactly your favourite kind of people."

"Sorry, Chippy, I din' mean you personally, like, but it really got to me, that whole incident. The court case was jus 'afore Easter, so I worried it'd affect business."

"And did it?" asked Ged

"It's 'ard to tell; business is pretty good this year, an' it could be the weather, but I get more customers in 'ere, lookin' at the paintin's and critiquin' 'em like we was a gallery. We got together with Carolyn and 'er friend Jenny to get some decent art in 'ere, by some o' their students, so the pictures in 'ere are better than they've been for years. Not many customers buy 'em, though; One of them pictures costs more than dinner!"

Ged chuckled at the thought of this. To his mind, paying more than forty pounds for a painting or picture in 1998 was absurd!

"Well, I won't darken your doors asking you to sell my etchings, Bill," said Ged in earnest as he pushed himself to stand and leaned over to get his crutches.

"No thanks, but tell you what, Chippy; bring that lovely family 'o' yours for dinner this week, 'an you can 'ave that cappuccino on the 'ouse!" Bill got up, drained his mug of coffee, and flicked the tea towel he had been fiddling with over his shoulder. "See you anon," he said, holding his hand out. "An 'ave a nice time sketchin' boats in the 'arbour, jus' like all the other daft buggers." he quipped.

"See you, Bill," said Ged, smiling and shaking his friend's hand warmly.

"Goin' already, Chippy?" called Sharon from the store room. "Come for tea soon, eh?"

"We'll come for tea this week, Sharon, I promise," called Ged and drank the rest of his coffee. "That's really nice coffee, actually," he said to himself.

9

Ged arrived at the gallery shop as a group of children ran in, wearing beachwear and jelly-bean shoes. They clearly had been at the beach as their legs and shoes were coated in a fine layer of creamy-grey sand.

The children ran straight to the ice cream freezer and slid open the top, reaching in for lollies. One boy stopped at the back of the group, holding the door open for Ged. He was about nine or ten years old, slim, tanned, with striking, deep brown eyes.

"What a nice young man you are to hold the door open when you could be getting ice cream," said Ged.

The boy met Ged's gaze. "You looked like you could do with some help," he said.

"Thank you," Ged replied. "I'm not used to these things yet; it's my second day."

"Oh," said the boy sympathetically, "What have you done?"

"Broken a bone in my foot…Elephant trod on it," said Ged with a wink.

"Really?" said the boy, fascinated. "I love elephants. Which Zoo? Or is it a safari park?"

"Oh dear, I'll come clean. I only say the elephant thing because I'm a bit embarrassed about dropping a cool bag on it," confessed Ged as he negotiated the doorway with his crutches.

"Oh, I see," said the boy, slightly disappointed but getting the joke. "Elephant accident sounds better than a cool bag."

"Well, thanks for being such a gentleman…er…"

"Danny," said the boy, shifting from foot to foot.

"Nice to meet you, Danny; I'm Ged."

"Nice to meet you…er Ged," he said uncertainly. Ged supposed that calling adults by their first names felt strange to a boy his age. Danny opened the ice cream freezer, grabbed a lolly and took it to the counter where a tall woman in a red dress was waiting.

"Come on, Dan, where've you been?"

"Holding the door open for the man on crutches. He's broken his foot," said Dan.

"Oh, that was kind, she said. "I'll have to remember to tell Mum and Dad when we get back to the beach; none of these other hooligans bothered to help, I suppose?" she commented, looking around the group of kids, presumably some of whom were her offspring, already ripping open ice cream packets before she had even finished tapping in her pin number on the card machine.

Ged smiled at her as she passed, and she smiled and nodded in acknowledgement.

"Thanks again, Danny," said Ged, and got a shy smile in return.

The shop became quiet once more as the children left. There was only Ged and a blonde teenage girl in a short-sleeved wetsuit in the corner, trying on paddling shoes.

A laminated poster above the rack of paddling shoes, showing a photograph of a weever fish with its spines pointing up, warned of the dangers of these spiky little fish and the benefits of wearing such shoes or jellybeans. Tracy, apparently as an afterthought, had also hand-written a short paragraph explaining what to do in the unfortunate event of falling victim to a weever fish sting. It announced, in a friendly font: *"Should you be unlucky enough to tread on, put your hand on or – horror-of-horrors…sit on a weever fish spine, you'll discover it is eye-crossingly painful. For relief, plunge the affected body part into the hottest water you can stand until the pain subsides – at least 15 minutes. Failing that, soaking or dabbing the wound with vinegar can offer some relief."*

A menace to paddlers on British shores, weever fish are up to three inches long, well camouflaged in the sand with spines containing a potent toxin along their back, which protrude through the sand at around the low to mid-tide mark. The sting is excruciating, and, indeed, hot water can help… the idea of peeing on such a sting comes from the fact that urine is hot and contains acid, which can help relieve the pain, though it is neither as effective nor helpful as hot water or vinegar and far more gross.

Ged cast his eye along the display of postcards; many were images of paintings by local artists. He studied the watercolours for sale on the wall above the souvenirs and swung his way, increasingly adept on his crutches, to a rack of prints stacked up on their ends. He leafed through them, trying to get an idea of how the watercolour might have been applied, but he was still none the wiser when he had been through them all. He selected around half a dozen postcards of different paintings and then crutched over to the artist's supplies display.

The beautiful wooden set caught his eye once more. It was so cleverly arranged, with a separate place for each medium: A tray of acrylics lay on a ledge that was glued and then nailed with brass panel pins to the sides of the box. Underneath was a box of pastels and a small, white plastic box of twenty half-pan watercolours, a mixing palette and a tray for your own pencils or other equipment. There was a water glass with a wide base that would help to prevent it from being knocked over and a rolled-up sheet of chamois with thin leather strips sewn down onto it, creating loops which held a dozen paintbrushes of varying shapes and sizes. A shallow drawer was partly pulled out to display its contents: A range of sketching pencils, charcoal and watercolour pencils and, Ged noticed, the lid could be used as an easel by seating a wooden peg riveted to the inside of the box into some notches cut into two securing stays attached to the lid.

The label showing the reduced price of eighty pounds explained that the display unit was the last in stock and had one or two items missing. Ged was tempted but couldn't justify such extravagance. He moved his attention to the display of individual art materials. He chose three brushes: A 'liner' for fine detail, a medium size eight brush, and a half-inch flat-shaped brush; he presumed this would be useful for getting larger areas of colour down quickly.

He didn't know which of the half-pan sets to buy, so he delayed a decision on that. Assuming he would make lots of mixing mistakes, he chose two plastic moulded pallets, a large budget pad of cheap paper to practise on and an A5 spiral bound pad of cartridge paper that claimed to be ideally suited to watercolour painting.

A lady beside him reached up to get one or two of the individual watercolour tubes. "Want some help?" she said.

"I do need a little advice if you know about watercolours," said Ged. "I haven't painted in decades. I need a decent beginner's set. Can you recommend which of these I should go for?"

"I'd suggest the Cotman twelve-colour set of half-pans. The colours mix well, and it's not too pricey, so if you decide watercolours aren't for you after all, you haven't wasted too much money." – She looked down at the things he had chosen in the basket at his feet – "The lid of the twelve-pan set is a palette, so you won't need two of those. Mmm, nice brushes. I'd get a size 6 and 12 round as well, and maybe a one-inch flat if you're doing seascapes. Do you have some rags or an old tea towel to wipe the brushes with after you've washed them?"

"I'm sure I'll find something. I assume they don't wash out well. Thanks, I really didn't have a clue what to get. What do you think of that box over there?"

"Pah! Complete waste of money!" said the woman scornfully. "Looks like it weighs a ton… Why anyone would need all those mediums at the same time is beyond me. I travel light, but I only paint in watercolour and sketch a bit, so I don't need the rest. If you ask me, things like that are for people with more money than sense."

"Oh," said Ged, feeling slightly self-conscious for coveting it… realising that the woman's view on its practical use was probably fair."

"Not that I wouldn't have the box in my studio, though," said the woman, "but I'd throw out half the stuff and fill it with my own things… nice bit of walnut."

"I see," said Ged, thinking that £80 was a lot of money to spend if you were going to throw away half the stuff and keep the box.

"Well. I must be getting along. Best of luck. Just one more thing… Don't leave your brushes in water. Wash and wipe as you go; they'll last longer."

"Thank you…er…?"

"Val – nice to meet you – and you are?

"Ged."

"Nice talking to you, Ged," she said, smiling. She turned and took her tubes of paint to the counter where Tracy was arranging silver rings in a display.

"Hi, Val," said Tracy as Val deposited her paint on the counter. How's old Potts?"

Val sighed, "I don't think he'll last long, Tracey," she said sadly. "The vet says he's too old to operate, and I think it would be cruel to try. He's on painkillers, so he's comfortable. He just sleeps on the windowsill most of the time. I'll miss him horribly, but he's almost nineteen."

"Oh, Val, I'm sorry..." said Tracy, with feeling. "I agree with you, though; it seems cruel to put animals through the pain and suffering of operations. *They* don't know why the mean humans are hurting them."

"I just wish I could capture his character when I try to paint him," said Val. "He was such a 'Boss-cat.' I've tried dozens of times, but he ends up just looking like any other old Tabby Moggy. I'm a landscape artist. I never could do humans or animals."

"You've got photos, though, surely?" said Tracy.

"Yes...but I'd love a little sketch or painting of him, though; it would feel more special, somehow."

"You're coming over for a drink tomorrow evening with Jen, aren't you?" Tracy said, hopefully. I bet, between us, we could think of someone who would do him justice."

Ged ambled to the counter a little awkwardly. He had put all his purchases in a plastic shopping basket, which was banging against his left crutch.

"I'm Sorry to hear about your cat," he said kindly. He sounds quite a character—a good mouser, is he?"

"Brilliant!" said Val. "Well, he used to be before he got ill, but I hated it! He used to eat them in the house. I kept shooing him out, but he'd find an open window and sneak back in. He even ate them on the sofa...eugh, the crunching sounds...it was disgusting!" She made a face... "I hate seeing him like this, but at least I've not had mouse entrails to clear up."

"Mmm, I can identify with that," he said. "When I was a kid, our cat used to leave stuff on the doormat. Claws, feathers, and a grey squishy bit I could never quite identify."

"Yep – delightful creatures," she said, affecting sarcasm, "but we love them... despite the unidentified grey squishy bit on the sofa."

"Well, I hope he stays out of pain," said Ged, sincerely.

"Thanks," said Val, picking up her receipt and the paint tubes. "Good luck with your watercolours...See you tomorrow, Tracey."

"Yeah, bye, Val," called Tracey after her, then turned to Ged. "This is getting serious Chippy. Has the Cornish art bug finally got you, or is this a present for the grandkids?"

"I thought I'd give it a go. I'm not exactly racking up the runs on the beach, and I can't do much with my foot like this," Ged said apologetically.

"Not a bad time to try it. Val's right about that artist box, by the way. I only bought four to see how they would sell, and all three people who bought one looked like they were absolutely loaded and wouldn't know the difference between a half pan and an oil pastel! That's the last one, and I'm discounting it. All the kids keep playing with it, and we've lost 2 of the pencils and a brush already. I might get some empty easel boxes to sell that people can fill with their own stuff.

"I almost bought it myself," confessed Ged. "Val made some good points. It would be a bit heavy to lug around. You'd have to keep it in your house, and it might look nice and pretty now, but it would look awful when half the stuff was used and there have been a few spills."

"Exactly – Let's see now," she said, examining the contents of the basket, "nice starter set of brushes; pallet... Cotrill's half pans are a good choice; I'd have recommended them too—sketch pad, mmm, practice paper; good enough for the time being. I'll throw in one of those wide-bottomed water glasses. She went to the artist's corner and reached up to get one. (Ged had often wondered why she sold large vodka shot glasses.)

"What's the damage then?" said Ged, extracting his wallet from the pocket of his baggy cargo shorts.

"Thirty-two-fifty," said Tracy after totalling the items in the till. "That sounds a lot, but the brushes are really good. The paintbrushes are hand-made; I don't sell the cheap ones as people just come back and complain. I've given you the glass for free."

"Oh, thanks, Tracey. That sounds fine," said Ged. "I figured about that much, and with the glass, I think I'm all set up for a colourful, interesting and occasionally frustrating day."

He paid with his credit card, and Tracy took a large, sturdy paper bag from under the counter and put all the items in it.

"There's only one problem now. How are you going to get it back to the house on the crutches?"

"I have a solution for that," he said, winking. "He turned around to reveal a slightly grubby, pink and purple rainbow-unicorn rucksack on his back."

"Oh, that's brilliant!" she laughed. "I love it! How come I didn't notice it before?"

"I kept it tucked in the back of my shorts and hidden under my shirt up 'til now," said Ged. "But now, I've no choice… it has to come out."

"People might think it's you that's 'coming out' if you go around wearing that."

"Ah, let 'em wonder," Ged replied. "At sixty-one, I'm brave enough to wear a pink rainbow unicorn rucksack. I've had to lengthen the straps to maximum, and I didn't ask Alice if I could borrow it. I hope she doesn't mind."

"She won't mind a bit," said Tracy, walking around the counter. She opened the zip, stuffed the paper bag into the rucksack, and zipped it up, chuckling to herself.

"Rainbow unicorn and pink are really you…. It goes nicely with your blue shirt, too."

"Thanks, Tracy," he said, giving her a sideways look and returning his wallet to the pocket of his cargo shorts.

She opened the door for him. "It's going to be an overcast day today, she said, looking skywards."

"Yep, a good day for one of your Mum's pasties," he said. "There's just enough room in this bag for a small steak one."

Peggy's pasties were much sought after by locals and tourists alike. Hikers, tourists and day-trippers who knew of her legendary pasties would call her early in the morning or the day before to reserve one to collect when they arrived in the village or take it with them to warm up later. Peggy got up early and baked enough to keep her busy until lunchtime. She rarely stayed open long after two.

Ged arrived at the bottom of the garden steps of Daisy Cottage just as Peggy was coming out with a pot of tea for an elderly couple sitting at a table in her garden. She called to Ged. "Morning, my love. Steak Pastie, is it?" Ged nodded and smiled. "You stay there while I get one. Don't come up those steps on your crutches, or you'll be back in Truro hospital before you know it.

"Thanks, Peggy," he said.

She set down the pot of tea and spoke to the older couple briefly before disappearing into her cottage again.

"Nice backpack you got there, Chippy!" came a strong-accented Cornish voice from behind Ged...It was Glyn, the pub landlord. "I 'erd about your mishap from your lad Brian. You're still comin' up for your dinner tonight, aren't you?"

"Too right, Glyn," said Ged. "Save me a portion of your glorious lasagne. I've been looking forward to it for weeks!"

"Alright, see you later then, ...unicorn boy!" he said, chuckling and grinning broadly as he strode off up the road to the pub.

Peggy came down the steps with two paper bags. "'Ere's your pasty, and I've a nice big slice of chocolate brownie in here for Mrs B... poor woman deserves a treat, having to drive all the way down 'ere from up-country, those motorways turn good drivers into loonies if you ask me."

"Could you pop the pastie and brownie in my rucksack?"

"Yes o'course – turn round then, Lovely," she said. Ged turned his back, and she giggled. "Ooh, that's a pretty one!" she said as she unzipped the backpack and stuffed the paper bags inside. "Where's the rest of 'em? ... the family, I mean."

"Glendurgan," said Ged. "I'm having a day to myself."

"Well, you enjoy yerself. I better be gettin' on. Give Mrs B my best."

"Will do," said Ged. Setting himself on his crutches, he ambled back to the house.

10

Despite his foot, Ged managed to pull the dining table over to the window seat to get some better light to try out his new watercolours.

He filled a glass of water for himself and the wide-based glass for his brushes. Having to hop everywhere made for slow progress; it was almost noon by the time he was set up. Undeterred, he sat at the dining table and dipped a medium-sized paintbrush in the water. He sucked the other end of the brush for a few moments before deciding what to do. He saw the rainbow unicorn rucksack in the corner of the window seat, and it gave him an idea.

He began to wet one of the half-pans; it was a deep crimson red, and he applied a little watercolour as a line across the page. It was light, rather wet, and washed out at first, but then he gradually worked out how to deepen the colour as he went across and down the page.

He rinsed the brush and used a ripped tea towel he had found in the kitchen drawer to dry it, squeezing the bristles gently, drawing the cloth up the brush, repeating this until he was satisfied it was clean. He did the same as before with the scarlet pan, then the orange, the yellow ochre, the yellow, the light green, mid and dark green, deep and cobalt blue. The page looked amazingly colourful, and Ged gained confidence with each colour. He had taken just one sheet of paper and laid it on a folded piece of newspaper. The colours at the top were rather wet, the paper had become wrinkled, and the newspaper underneath was now quite damp.

He laid the spectrum to dry on another dry pad of newspaper, then took another sheet and began mixing colours to see how much of each he would need, depending on the shade he wanted to achieve.

In his work in maintenance at the car factory, he was organised, methodical and systematic. He brought the same approach to watercolour, giving each colour a code such as RO for red ochre or MG for mid-green and made a note of the ratios he had used with a sketching pencil when he created a colour he was happy with: so, for the purple of the unicorn, he noted RO1 / MB2 / WH1 meaning red ochre-one, mid blue-2, white-1.

He continued experimenting with different mixtures and combinations, using all the brushes to see what effects he could achieve. He filled four pages of practice paper with splodges, strips, shading, and clouds of colour.

His stomach gave a loud gurgle. His watch confirmed that it was almost two in the afternoon. No wonder he was hungry. As he leaned back in the chair, his booted foot hit a table leg, and he grimaced. He heaved himself out of the chair, took his crutches and made his way to the kitchen. He flicked on the kettle. Deciding that he was too hungry to wait, he decided to eat his pasty cold rather than wait for it to warm in the oven.

He made a pot of tea while he ate his cold but superbly tasty steak pasty. "*Definitely better hot*," he thought. "I must ask Brian to remind me how to use the timer settings on the oven," he muttered to himself. He was then faced with a dilemma: "How do I get a cup of tea to the table without spilling it?" He mused out loud.

An idea struck him… Was there an insulated mug in any of those cupboards? he already knew…and tea from a metal flask was like drinking infused paperclips. He tried getting over to the table on one crutch…definitely too much hopping…Now what?

He scanned his eyes around the room for inspiration… That's it – do it in stages, like at the factory. He ambled around the room, pushing the coffee table to the doorway of the kitchen and placing a chair between the dining table and the coffee table. Back in the kitchen, he took the largest tea mug he could find, poured himself a mug of tea and added milk.

He slid the mug along the worktop until it was close to the doorway and left it there while he crutched to the door. Leaning back against the frame, he reached for the mug of tea and carefully lifted it onto the coffee table, sliding it as far as he could using the end of his crutch. He made his way to the other end of the coffee table and balanced on his right leg with his crutch in his left hand; he lifted the mug, twisted round and placed it on the chair. He moved beyond the chair, holding the dining table for support, leaned over and transferred the mug from the chair to the dining table, placing it on a pad of newspaper. Finally, he went to the window seat, reached across the table and pulled the piece of newspaper with the mug on it towards himself. He sat back, holding his tea mug, feeling pleased with his ingenious plan.

He smiled to himself as he stared out of the window. The tide was fully out, and there were several families on the beach, some sunbathing, and groups of kids and parents digging holes and making moats around sandcastles. One family were playing a game with pebbles, something similar to boule. Rockpool lovers were busy peering into the pools at the far end of the beach near the harbour. It was a typical, lovely Porthcovery summer's day.

Ged pushed the paints to one side and picked up his pencil. On a piece of practice paper, he sketched the pebble-boule family; there was a middle-aged woman in jeans and a deep-blue t-shirt, her auburn hair tied back in a pony; a muscular brown-haired teenage boy, a tall, broad-smiling man in his forties with greying hair at the temples and a slim blond girl of about eight. He sketched them freely and smoothly. He added a few details of their clothes but left much out. What he captured was the expressions on the faces of the players; he gave each a personality…Mum was competitive and a little serious, Dad – confident and jokey. The girl was uncertain and a little awkward. The teenage boy appeared sullen and bored, a look of resignation on his face. This was clearly family time, whether he liked it or not.

The game continued while Ged added a few waves on the sea and seashells on the beach of his sketch, even though there were none. He heard a shout and looked up. The boy's face had changed from sulky to laughing! He must have won a round. He was giving the girl a high-five as the Dad patted her on the back. Ged corrected his assumption. It was the girl who had won, and her brother was congratulating her!

He quickly sketched their faces. He would add some details later. He looked up again, and the boy had now taken his sister firmly by her forearms and was swinging her around and around. Dad had his arm around Mum, and she was smiling and pointing at the children. He captured this third scene, starting with the faces once more. He added some detail after that: The boy's arm muscles, taut as he bore the weight of his sister; the creases of his jeans as he adjusted his stance for balance; her legs, skirt and hair flying as she whirled around. He left out anything that didn't seem essential to the scene.

The family on the beach started another game, and Ged considered the three drawings on the page. He found that he liked the lack of unnecessary detail. It seemed to suit the situation as it played out. It was like a storyboard or a comic strip. Instead of a rock in the sand, there was a mere suggestion of a rock. Instead of fully forming the boy's and girl's feet, the sketch stopped at the ankles. He figured feet weren't important to the story. He took a swig of his now tepid tea and made a face. "Ugh – cold tea, I hate cold tea!" he exclaimed to no one in particular.

He decided to try adding a little colour to his family boule game scene and pulled the palette over once more. He looked out at the family, trying to decide which colours struck him as important. The boy's green shirt and blue jeans, for sure, and the girl's skirt and T-shirt were pale yellow, which blended with the sand, so he decided he would change them. After testing a denim blue blend on the edge of the newspaper until he was satisfied with it, he shaded the boy's jeans. Again, it was more a suggestion of colour than filling in the whole outline. It took him several minutes to come up with a believable sand colour for the girl's T-shirt, so he gave up and made it yellow. As for her skirt, which was the only other item he wanted to add colour to, he decided a bright orange-scarlet would bring a lively feel to the scene. There was more to shade, but he was gasping for a drink and didn't want cold tea, so he retraced his steps with the two-thirds mug of tea, using the newspaper, chair, and coffee table technique.

He managed to get the cup to the kitchen without incident, filled the kettle, and watched the birds in the tiny backyard helping themselves to the contents of the bird table. It never failed to amaze him what opportunists garden birds are. Considering no seed had been put on that table in at least three weeks, a handful of seed had them coming back in just two days!

Once he had made his tea, he repeated the process of getting it to the table. He was becoming more adept at placing the mug in just the right place so he could simply pick it up and place it. (No need to risk using the crutch to push the mug along the coffee table if he sat on the chair for a moment.) He sat down and took a quick slurp of tea, feeling pleased with the solution.

He reached for the medium brush and decided to add a suggestion of golden-yellow to the sand and the girl's hair. He had to spend a few minutes getting the balance of yellow ochre with the bright yellow, and added a tiny hint of red to deepen the tone. It still wasn't right. He frowned, stirring the now brownish colour he had created in the palette. He lifted the brush to dip it in the water and clean it. As he lifted the brush to wipe it, he noticed it was warm. To his horror, he realised what he had done. Instead of washing it in the now quite murky brush glass, he had, in fact, washed it in his tea!

"Oh, come on!" he exclaimed. He pushed himself back in his chair, grabbed one crutch to help him stand up, swung it across the table to hold in his left hand and promptly knocked the tea mug, emptying the contents straight across the set of half pans and his earlier watercolour spectrum.

"Aaagh, no!" he shouted. "You clumsy idiot, Baker!" He hopped as fast as he could to the kitchen, grabbing a hand towel, a dishcloth and a roll of kitchen paper.

Hobbling back to the table, he saw what an awful mess the tea had made. There was paint of every conceivable shade blending with the brown tea and soaking into – oh God, *please*, no – the white, embroidered tablecloth! Why, oh why, hadn't he thought to take the tablecloth off before he started? "Marge will do her nut! She'll chop me up and serve me to the sparrows."

The tablecloth was clearly the priority. He had to get it into cold water to soak, but he needed to clear the table. Ok... push the tablecloth slightly aside, leaving the bare, polished oak table, pile up the newspaper at the window end, and place all the painting things and half-finished drawings on it. Right... now, the tablecloth could be taken into the kitchen to soak with some of that stain remover in the pink tub under the sink. He turned the cold tap fully on, plunged the tablecloth into the sink and reached for the stain remover. He hobbled about, adrenaline numbing any pain. He was hot from exertion, but was aware of a slight breeze. The curtains began to flap at the window, and then he saw it... Too late. He had placed the paintbrush washing glass too close to the end of the table; the corner of the flapping curtain licked the edge of the glass, tipping it over, allowing the brown, murky liquid to spill and spread out in two or three directions across the polished surface of the table and over the edge onto the nearly-new, light, oatmeal coloured carpet...

Ged swore – loudly and vehemently. I won't repeat what he said, as some don't like that kind of language, but it was one of those situations where you might expect a man to run through his entire repertoire of expletives to see which ones might make him feel a little better. The adrenaline effect on his foot was rapidly wearing off. He threw the hand towel on the table and scrambled back to the kitchen, hopping while using the various items of furniture he had lined up to keep his left foot off the floor. He opened the cupboard under the sink, desperately longing for a bucket and something that would clean up the brush cleaning water. To his horror, he heard a diesel engine and the crunch of car tyres on the gravel driveway. A glance at his watch told him it was four-thirty... and he was in trouble.

Fortunately, the first person to appear at the door was Brian. "Oh my God! What the...?" he said, his hands up to his face. "Jeez, Dad... Mum is going to have a fit!"

"I know that!" hissed Ged. "Keep her outside and busy while I clean up."

"I'll send in the rescue crew; you'd better hope Mum doesn't see this, or you're toast." Ged glowered at Brian's back. "Hey, Mum!" said Brian cheerily, "I'll help you plant those now, and we can get them watered in. Sarah, can you go and put the kettle on?" Brian looked at Sarah meaningfully, jerking his head towards the house.

"Can we go to the beach, Dad?" called Jamie. "The tide's out, and there are rock pools."

"Great idea, Jamie. Your nets are in the yard at the back," said Brian. The side gate is open. Don't go through the house with those muddy shoes on," he said, trying to avoid the children seeing the mess inside. They'd never keep quiet.

Sarah took the picnic backpack inside. She stopped dead at the doorway, taking a sharp intake of breath. "Oh, my goodness! What on earth happened?"

"A flailing crutch, a curtain and a gust of wind," he replied tersely. "Don't tell me your Mother-in-Law will have a fit. I know that. Brian is going to keep her out there while I sort it out." He took a hop towards the kitchen and crumpled onto the chair in agony, biting his hand hard to avoid shouting out.

Sarah dropped the bag and rushed over. "When was the last time you had a painkiller, Dad?"

"Er, about ten, I think," said Ged through gritted teeth. All this rushing about after I knocked the tea over has done it for my foot. It's absolute murder!"

"Right... first, you need tablets, and then I'll help you sort this out," said Sarah. Where did you put them?"

"In the kitchen, near the kettle," he said. "I should have taken them earlier, but it wasn't hurting."

Sarah filled the kettle and fetched the tablets with a glass of water. "Right, let's get this sorted out quickly. "Sit down while I clean up the carpet. What is it? Tea or paint?"

"Both," said Ged, feeling foolish.

Sarah fetched carpet stain remover, a cloth, a bucket of warm water and a fresh hand towel. In a few minutes, she had removed the stain from the carpet and dried it with a towel.

"I'm glad we got the carpet stain guarded. It's coming off a treat!" she said.

"Thank God. It's only the tablecloth I have to worry about, then."

"What?!" You mean you were..."

"Yes," interrupted Ged. "Your idiot father-in-law forgot to take off the white, embroidered damask tablecloth before he started chucking tea and watercolours all over the place."

Sarah closed her eyes and grimaced. She tidied up the table and cleaned any splashes of paint she could see.

"Not a complete idiot," she said, returning from the kitchen. "You got it into cold water straight away. I'll take it upstairs to our bathroom and hand wash it." Then, noticing the odd placement of the furniture, she said, "I can see the plan with the tables and chairs. Was that to get your cuppa over to the main table without spilling it?" Ged nodded miserably. "Nice one," she said.

"Well, I *was* feeling rather pleased with myself, and this certainly wiped the smug look off my face," he said ruefully.

"Worse things happen at sea," she said with a wink as she replaced the furniture and went to make the tea while Ged put away his art materials and carefully laid the wet paintings on newspaper to dry.

11

Dinner at the pub was quiet. Good to his word, Glyn had made sure there was a portion of lasagne for Ged, and the rest of the family had their favourites: scampi, fish, or whitebait for dinner. Chatting about the day, the children recounted climbing a big laurel tree and getting lost in the maze at Glendurgan with their Mother. Brian stood on the hillside above the maze and tried to direct them out as best he could with hand signals. Marge wouldn't let him shout, saying it was 'uncouth'.

She had bought several plants to replace those that had perished in the February storms (or which had fallen victim to her overenthusiastic use of secateurs last autumn). The garden looked neat and pretty, but after a long day at Glendurgan, she appeared washed out and pale.

Ged's equally pale pallor was more down to pain and a gradually diminishing fear that Marge would somehow find out about the tablecloth.

"Did you order a mattress, Sarah?" he asked, suddenly remembering the trip to Helston that morning.

"Yes. It's coming tomorrow; they had one in the warehouse," said Sarah. "So, if I make sure I have too much wine tonight, I can pass out on our *'bed-rock'* tonight and get a proper night's sleep tomorrow!"

"You could sleep on the sofa," suggested Brian. "Dad slept on it for weeks while we were doing up the place."

"Yes, it's really comfy," said Ged, but use eye shades, or you'll wake up with the sun."

"It can't be *that* bad, Sarah, can it?" said Marge, the disbelief apparent in her tone.

"Since the accident, my back pain has got worse," she said.

"Can't you sue the other driver or something?" Marge replied.

"I don't want to; black ice isn't their fault. My chiropractor says if I change my gym routine, reduce the weights, and do more swimming, Pilates and yoga, it should improve," said Sarah. "I just need to get on with my life and keep fit; oh, and she told me to get a better bed."

"Well, dear, we all have our crosses to bear," said Marge dismissively. "I'm sure a night on the sofa isn't necessary."

Sarah dug her nails into her palm, closed her eyes and took a breath before speaking. "All the same – *Mum,* I'll try it tonight and see if it's more comfortable."

Ged paid for the meal, and they all walked back to the house along the seafront. Most of the day-trippers had gone home, and there were just a few people on the beach walking their dogs and a large family group having a barbecue. They had clearly brought more wine than sausages and were laughing and joking.

"Oh really?" Marge complained. "Some people don't consider how noisy and disturbing they are being."

"Come on, Mum," said Brian, "they aren't too loud. They're just having fun."

"Fun?" she spat. "Call that fun? Eating burnt sausages and staggering about, shouting? It's uncouth and common."

"Don't be a snob, Marge," Ged chastised. "I remember us having a few too many sherbets at the dance hall when we were young."

"We may have got a little merry, Gerald, but we did not shout and squawk."

There was no point arguing. He recalled a Bill Haley concert at the town hall in 1958 where Marge, as a young woman, sang along at the top of her lungs along with the rest of the audience as they made their way home, their voices fuelled with Dubonnet or Cinzano and lemonade. Instead of arguing, he tried to remind her of that night and began to sing quietly to himself, but loud enough that Marge could hear.

"One, two, three o'clock, four o'clock rock.
Five, six, seven o'clock, eight o'clock rock.
Nine, ten, eleven o'clock, twelve o'clock rock,
We're gonna rock – around – the clock tonight.
Well, put your glad rags on and join me, hon.'

We gonna have some fun when the clock strikes one.
We're gonna rock around the clock tonight,
We're gonna rock, rock, rock, 'til broad daylight,
We're gonna rock around the clock tonight," he crooned.

"Alright, Gerald, that will do," chastised Marge, slightly bashfully. "We did have our high times, but that's a long time ago, and it was different in those days; we didn't go about yelling on the beach."

"Oh, when the band strikes two, three and four,
If the band slows down, we'll yell for more,
We're gonna rock around the clock tonight,
We're gonna rock rock, rock, 'til broad daylight..."

"I admit, I did sing along and dance, but if you recall, my father was furious, wasn't he?" she said seriously. "There's a reason for that; like these – she waved her hand dismissively in the general direction of the beach... 'hoodlums' on the beach, we were young and foolish and didn't realise what a spectacle we were making of ourselves," she said as if that explained everything. Ged was quiet. He remembered, alright.

***

It was a metaphorical fork in the road... Go right or left? The tickets to the concert were Ged's gift to Marge for her twenty-first birthday. They had danced all night. Already partners in Latin and Ballroom for a year, having won a couple of local competitions, that particular night, they danced the Jitterbug, the Jive and the Lindy hop, which they had practised to perfection at his Mother's dance school. As they danced, everyone gathered around, clapping and cheering. What a night that was!

Ged had proposed to Marge that night, and she had accepted, but they hadn't asked her father. Councillor Cookson disapproved of couples dancing in public generally, deeming it *'exhibitionist'; worse* still, he deemed Latin American dances, risqué and attention-seeking, unseemly for a magistrate's daughter. He would be appalled if he knew they had been showing off their Rock & Roll skills at the Town Hall.

Should he ask straight-laced, respectable banker and magistrate James Cookson for the hand of his daughter and the girl of Ged's dreams, the beautiful Margie, knowing that if he did, it could spell the end of their dancing for good? Or should he walk away and maybe regret it for the rest of his life?

James Cookson was resolute. He had heard about the concert and had punished Marge severely. He took her favourite blue patent leather dancing shoes from her room and burned them on the coal fire in front of her. Ged had no idea of this, but when he plucked up the courage to ask him a few days after the concert for Marge's hand in marriage, Cllr Cookson had made it a solemn condition of his permission to marry that there would be no more 'cavorting and showing off'.

"A waltz at respectable parties is one thing," he had said, "but competition dancing was 'vulgar' and that filthy South American wiggling and this Rock and Roll business was unbecoming for any respectable man and wife."

Ged had swallowed hard and accepted this condition. He and Marge went to occasional tea dances once they were engaged, and they waltzed at their wedding, but without the excitement of Jive and Latin, the fire that had been lit inside them gradually dimmed. Besides, after a year or so, with twins to care for and a wife to support, Ged needed to focus on earning a living. Just before they were married, he became an apprentice furniture maker and needed to complete his apprenticeship if they were to manage.

***

The children were tired, and both fell asleep before Ged had finished the second page of the storybook. He felt like lying down under their soft duvets and joining them, but instead, he went back downstairs. Marge was doing a crossword, Brian was reading, and Sarah was nowhere to be seen. Then he remembered...she was probably trying to wash the stains out of the tablecloth... He called quietly up the stairs... "Need any help, Sarah?"

"No, I'm good, thanks, Dad; you could make a pot of tea, though. I'll be down in a bit," she replied.

After making tea, Ged went to rest on the window seat. The revellers on the beach sat around a campfire, chatting. He reached for his sketchbook and pencil. It was becoming an automatic response. He sketched a suggestion of sticks and flames; he spent more time on the faces. Unable to see them now, he imagined the expressions. He made up a story in his head that they were teasing each other about girls and love interests, and the tall slim one was the butt of the humour. Ged gave him a bashful expression, and the others he drew laughing, with mischief in their eyes.

Crab fishermen were out in the bay, hauling in the pots onto their tiny fishing boats. He reached for the binoculars that were hung on a hook by the window and took a closer look. He could see the fisherman in the nearest boat had dreadlocks and a shaggy beard. He looked young, though... thirty perhaps? Weather-beaten and swarthy. In another scene, he could have been taken for a pirate.

Ged hurriedly drew the scene he had seen through his binoculars. The muscles and sinews of the fisherman's arms as he lifted the crab pots – the bend in his back, the angle of the boat, its gunwales dipped towards the water as the man worked the side of the boat nearest to the beach.

Then he smiled mischievously and drew the same man standing on the quarterdeck of a pirate ship with a bandanna on his head, a bottle of rum in one hand and a shining cutlass in the other. He now wore ripped, striped trousers and a leather waistcoat.

"What are you chortling about?" came Sarah's voice as she set a steaming mug of tea down on the pad of newspaper on the table. "You forgot to pour it, so it's a bit stewed, I'm afraid." She peered at the sketch of the pirate. "He looks scary!"

"Well, you don't make much money hauling in crab pots," Ged said, grinning. "I decided to give him a second career."

"That's the fisherman with the dreads, isn't it?" said Sarah.

"Yes, I guessed there was more to him than meets the eye with that expensive-looking Nissan pickup truck of his," said Ged.

"You're enjoying this, aren't you?" she said.

"I am. I'd forgotten how relaxing it was just to draw."

"Huh," said Marge, "It's hardly what you'd call mind-expanding, though, is it? – Oh, that tea is disgusting; it's almost soup! You'll have to make another pot, Gerald. You know I hate it strong."

"I expand my mind enough at work," said Ged. "I want to relax on holiday."

"They say being creative is very good for mental health," said Sarah. "I was reading about it the other day in the Guardian."

"Well, of course, they would say that in a 'leftie' paper, wouldn't they?" scoffed Marge, with an air of superiority and more than a little scorn.

"It makes sense to me…I'd have thought any activity where you create something has to have a good effect on stress or depression or whatever."

"*You're* not depressed, though, are you, Gerald?" said Marge in a condescending tone. "What you lack is vocabulary, and reading good books and a quality newspaper, as well as doing crosswords and puzzles, expands your vocabulary. Stands to reason."

"I'm quite satisfied with my vocabulary, thank you," said Ged defensively. "I may not be grammar school educated, but I manage to communicate just fine."

"Well, go back to your silly doodles then," she said, waving her hand dismissively and returned to her crossword.

Ged rolled his eyes, shrugged his shoulders, then, closing his sketchbook, he yawned and heaved himself onto his crutches.

"I think I've doodled enough. Are you coming to bed, Marge? Let Sarah have the sofa tonight. You can do your crossword in bed, can't you?

"I suppose so," said Marge, sighing, "though why you can't manage one more night on a perfectly good, nearly new mattress is beyond me."

"I think we should all go to bed," said Brian, decisively. He closed his book, got up and took the cups back to the kitchen. "Night, everyone."

Sarah got ready for bed upstairs, brought a blanket down to the living room and settled down on the sofa. Surprisingly comfortable, she was asleep in minutes.

***

The weather over the next three days was glorious! Ged went to Bill and Sharon's café each morning for a coffee. He took his sketchbook and tried a few different scenes. He sketched some kids as they chose buckets and spades outside the gallery shop, A lady weeding in a nearby garden, A Tabby cat sunning itself at an open cottage window, and he sketched Bill, leaning against the doorframe of the café kitchen with his flour-dusted navy-blue apron and a huge mug of coffee.

Each day, as the café became busy, he finished his drink, packed up his rucksack and headed to the steps down to the beach. He checked where the family were, then gingerly hopped down the steps, Rainbow Unicorn bumping on his back.

He had lunch with the family and wished so much that he could join in the games of cricket and rounders or go for a swim. Brian hired Kayaks for the children one day, and they offered him a ride. He wished his foot didn't hurt so much when he put weight on it. He loved going out on the kayaks from the little windsurfing school by the harbour.

Sarah saw him gazing at the kids on the third day as they played French cricket with Brian. "How do you think the foot is healing?" she said.

"Hard to tell," said Ged. "It hurts to put any weight on it, but if I rest it, I don't need tablets."

"Sounds promising," she said. "I guess it's going to take a while. How are the sketches coming along?"

"Ok… I'm enjoying myself, actually," Ged said, a note of mild surprise in his voice.

"I like this one," said Sarah, picking up the sketch of the fisherman again. "You've given him a mischievous look; it's as if he's up to something and not just hauling in lobsters."

"Well, he is a pirate… maybe he hides his loot in the lobster pots and hauls it in later when no one is looking," said Ged with a wink.

"That reminds me," said Sarah, "isn't it about time we went to the Lobster Pot Café in Porthleven for dinner? We usually go twice while we're here; we haven't been yet, and I think Brian needs a rest from cooking."

"Mmm, great idea," said Ged. "My scampi belly is crying out for one of Emily's best. Let's go this evening, shall we?"

"I'll see what the others think. I don't think you'll get an argument out of the kids, at any rate."

12

The Lobster Pot café was well known for all the right reasons. Emily Herraty kept her establishment scrupulously clean and hired friendly and efficient staff, whom she trained well to keep customers feeling welcome, comfortable, and well-fed. She offered great-value dinners and lunches, deliciously light scones, perfectly cooked chips, and arguably the best cup of tea in the South West.

The place was delightfully old-fashioned... teardrop-shaped vinegar bottles, glass salt and pepper pots and a few carnations or chrysanthemums in a white vase placed on each red-gingham-clothed table. There were two small tables for two set in the bay windows at the front of the café, which were always reserved in the high season. Outside, the door and wooden window frames were painted dark green. The door glass of the café was a glass panel with a frosted design of a lobster, the name of the café above it and 'Porthleven' below.

Ged, Marge and the family had been coming to the Lobster Pot for evening meals every holiday since they began coming down to Cornwall, from the days when, as a couple, they stayed in a caravan at Praa Sands and had their evening meal there almost every day – to the days when they stayed in the larger caravans in Porthcovery after the twins were born; to the holidays in the rented thatched cottage on Porthcovery seafront; and even since Brian had become a well-known chef and they had bought the bigger house five years earlier. A Baker holiday wouldn't seem complete without at least two visits to Emily's Lobster Pot café.

Emily welcomed them in her usual relaxed, effusive style, noting how much the children had grown since last time – she did this even on the second visit of the week, joking that the Cornish air made them grow.

"Well now, Mr and Mrs Bakers' and ...who are these big children? They can't be Jamie and Alice! How lovely to see you all!"

"Lovely to see you too, Emily," said Ged warmly. "How's business?"

"Oh, I can't complain," replied Emily, grinning. It's been a good summer weather-wise, and that's certainly brought plenty of customers my way."

"Well, I'm glad we could get a table then."

"What have you been up to?" she asked, gesturing at the plastic boot.

"Shark attack," said Ged, winking.

"Grandad, tell the truth," said Jamie.

"A lively, cool bag and an idiot who can't pack the boot," admitted Ged sheepishly.

"Ouch," Emily winced. "Was that when you were coming down here?"

"Yes," replied Ged, "Marge had to drive all the way."

"Rather you than me, Mrs B. The last time I drove such a long way must have been about 1972. I always let Ron do the driving; I hate those motorways."

"I don't like them either," said Marge, "Too many BMW drivers who drive too fast and think the 'i' on their car stands for 'important' instead of idiot."

"Well, I hope that doesn't include Ron," Emily replied with a polite smile, "his old 320i is coming up for its 10th birthday, and he drives it very sensibly. Daft bugger polishes it to death every month. He reckons the 'i" stands for immaculate."

Marge appeared not to recognise that her pronouncement lacked tact. Ged glared at her, annoyed that she had made no apology to Emily, who had always been so kind and welcoming. The family began to arrange where to sit at the table, which Emily had indicated. Ged made sure he took a seat next to Marge. Emily gave everyone a menu card and took a drinks order.

Whilst Emily made drinks, Ged leaned over and spoke quietly to his wife.

"Marge, the BMW driver comment was a bit tactless," he scolded in a whisper, "and then not apologising when she told you they had a BMW…that was a bit rude."

"Oh, it doesn't matter now, Gerald," said Marge. "Don't make a fuss."

"She's coming back," he hissed. "You should apologise in case she was offended."

"Don't be so silly, Gerald," said Marge, speaking in a low mumble so as not to be overheard. She looked up as Emily brought the tray of drinks over. "Thank you… Oh, I didn't want ice in my lemonade," she said.

"Sorry, I'll get you a fresh one, Mrs Baker," said Emily, smiling, her tone polite and patient.

"I don't know how she does it," said Sarah quietly to Brian. "Mum was pretty rude, and Emily is so unflappable."

"There are plenty of awkward customers, and you don't get far in the hospitality business if you let the more annoying ones get to you," said Brian quietly. "Emily is just being professional… and Mum… is just being…Mum."

"I've never seen her this bad," said Sarah. "She's even worse than usual."

"I must admit," agreed Brian, "she does seem to be behaving even more Mum-ish this week. It usually means that she's worried about something that she doesn't want to talk about. I'll try and get some time on my own with her to find out what's eating her."

"What are you two whispering about?" asked Margie impatiently.

"Just trying to decide what to choose off the menu, Mum," said Brian. "It's always so hard to choose as everything is so delicious here."

"You know you're going to have Whitebait, Daddy," said Jamie, winking. "It's what you always have the first time we come. You spend ages looking at the menu and thinking about other things, and then Emily comes and asks you what you want, and you say, *'I think I'll have the Whitebait.'* It would be weird if you had anything else."

"Well, Ron does it beautifully," his Dad replied. "I've tried serving it at the restaurant, but it's never as nice. Maybe there is a secret ingredient in the seasoning, or perhaps it just tastes better because we're by the seaside."

"Probably both," said Jamie. "Everything tastes better here."

Emily came back with Marge's no-ice lemonade and took food orders. Brian did indeed order Whitebait with a wink in Jamie's direction.

Before the meal, Sarah took the children to wash their hands. On the way, they browsed the paintings, sketches and illustrations for sale on the café walls. Many of them were softly shaded beach and landscape scenes of places around the Cornish coast, nicely painted, pleasant images. There were some more abstract pieces in acrylic and a few inked line drawings of local buildings and well-known monuments. Each frame had a small white ticket tucked in the corner with a price. The prices varied widely. Perhaps some of the artists were better known than others, or perhaps they were simply trying it on and charging a higher price to see what they could get. Sarah was no art critic, but the variation in the prices surprised her. As Emily was walking past, she asked her about it.

"Emily, I'm curious; the prices of the paintings vary so widely. How did the artists decide how much to charge?"

"Well, they don't usually decide. I give 'em a bit of a hand," she replied. "You get to know how much things will fetch over the years. Some artists are new and can't justify a high price; others are a bit better known, and their pieces might be sought after by collectors or those in the know. Some of them are prints, and of course, they fetch less than originals unless the artist is famous. I buy some prints myself, and they can make a bit of a profit if the artist does well or exhibits at the Tate."

With a finger to her lips, Sarah regarded an inked line drawing of a girl flying a kite.

"Alice, do you have any of those sketches Grandad has done with you?" she said.

"No. I left them at the house," Alice replied. "Was I supposed to bring them?"

"No, it's fine; I have to do some shopping anyway," she turned to Emily. "Can I come and see you in the morning, Emily?"

"Yes. I'm doing breakfast 'til ten, then getting the lunch sitting ready. Pop over at about ten-thirty for coffee. It would be nice to catch up."

"Thanks, I'll see you then."

***

Dinner was delicious, as usual. The children both had tall ice cream sundaes with marshmallows and chocolate sauce, which they couldn't finish, as usual, and the adults finished them... as usual.

With the bill paid and a generous tip from Brian, the Baker family bid Emily and the staff a fond farewell. Then, with full stomachs, they climbed languorously into the car and made for Porthcovery.

"Did you see the pictures at the Lobster Pot today? There were some very unusual pieces, I thought," said Sarah to anyone who was listening.

"I liked the one of the big steamer," said Jamie. "It looked like it would sail off at any minute."

"I thought those scribbly ink drawings of St. Michael's Mount were good," said Ged. "I know it's a bit of a cliché subject, but I've never seen it done like that. It made it look mysterious and foreboding. How about you, Marge? Any pictures catch your eye?"

"What? ... Oh, I didn't really look at them. The new tiles in the ladies are perfectly vile, though. There was nothing wrong with the ones they had before."

"Perhaps they had some work done and had to change them. The taps used to be a bit drippy. Maybe she had a re-fit," said Sarah.

"Or she could simply have really bad taste," Marge snapped.

"Mum!" scolded Brian, "there's no need for that."

"Well, she's got awful taste," said Marge scornfully. "I mean... those dreadful red gingham tablecloths are so nineteen-sixties, and the crockery... hardly fashionable, is it? Most cafés nowadays go for the all-white look. That blue and white Cornish ware is a bit 'last century'. Come to think of it, I've no idea why we go there anymore. The menu was written in nineteen sixty-five and hasn't changed since."

"All right, Marge, that'll do. The rest of us like the food, the decor, the company – and yes – even the crockery. Cornish holidays wouldn't feel the same without tea at the Lobster Pot."

"Don't be sentimental, Gerald; they'll go bust in a year or two unless they modernise."

"Sorry, Mum, you're on to a loser if you want us to stop going to Emily's," said Brian. "Much as I love a blow-out at a four-star restaurant. If I had to choose between that and an evening meal at The Lobster Pot, I'd choose Emily's any day. It's honest, good, well-cooked food. I always feel good after a meal there."

"Fine! Gang up on me, all of you," said Marge, her voice rising. "I was just saying it could do with a bit of modernisation."

"I think she would lose business if she modernised," said Brian. "Customers know what to expect when they come here. If everyone else is doing garlic focaccia and chickpea risotto, then I think Emily will do a roaring trade in traditional Cornish seaside food. There are still plenty of people who want it. The place was full this evening. She's doing a few specials on the blackboard if you fancy something a bit more up-market."

"Ha!" scoffed Marge. "Come off it; a Sea bass fillet and a vegetarian lasagne is hardly 'upmarket'."

"No," he replied, "but rocket, artichoke and fennel salad with steamed clams sounds pretty Rick-Stein to me."

"That was twenty pounds, Brian!"

"If you want up-market food, you have to be prepared to pay up-market prices."

"Well, I'm sure you know best, dear," she said, her mock-resigned sigh was as close as she ever got to backing down – a response reserved only for Brian. Ged would have been served a stony silence if she was getting nowhere with him.

Brian sighed and closed his eyes. He remembered his Grandpapa and Grandmama. Marge had inherited much from them. Her mother's organisational talent, for one thing, which served her well, both in helping her to attain a certain social standing in their village and rarely left her out of work. She had Grandmama's green fingers, but they came with her sharpness and impatience. She had certainly inherited the academic talents and sharp eyes of her father, along with his judgemental snobbishness, which only served to make her appear superior and opinionated. Marge had friends, but now Brian came to recall them; he realised that these were often people who wanted to gain a good standing with her father as a magistrate, a good position in the parish council, or who wanted to get voted onto the Women's Institute committee. Who was she really good friends with? He realised with an inward sigh that he already knew the answer.

***

As Sarah turned into the driveway of the house, Brian looked over to his sleeping children. What talents or tendencies had they inherited? Jamie already shared Brian's impatience and intolerance of laziness or lack of attention to detail. Something of a perfectionist, Brian was not so arrogant that he didn't recognise his own tendency, which, in fact, was one of the things that made him a good chef. He saw a competitiveness in Jamie and Alice, too, that came both from him and Sarah. Were these things genetic, or did you copy your parents without realising it?

13

Sarah started early the following morning. Getting up before anyone else after a blissful night's sleep (aided by two large glasses of gin and tonic and a very comfy sofa), she asked Alice and Jamie if she could have the sketches that Ged had given them and shared her plan with them. Alice didn't want to part with the picture of the unicorn, so Sarah promised to return it, and whether it was for the sake of fairness or whether he genuinely wanted to keep it, Jamie wanted to keep one of the pictures of the dreadlock fisherman as a pirate. He had decided that his name was Peter and had persuaded Ged to add a caption of 'Pirate Pete'. She drove to Helston and stocked up on groceries, then headed for Porthleven.

She arrived at The Lobster Pot early, just after ten and managed to get a seat in the prime bay window spot as a couple was leaving. A waitress spotted her coming in and quickly cleaned and cleared the table. She ordered a Cappuccino and a slice of the fruit cake, waving to Emily, who was cleaning up at the counter.

She had bought a book to read while she waited. It was left unopened on the table as she sat back in her chair, cradling her coffee in cupped hands, gazing contentedly out of the window at the comings and goings of the harbour – shopkeepers and tourists going about their business. It was windy, and there were countless ways that people were coming up with to prevent hats and other belongings from blowing away.

One little boy of around seven had tied his spade and long fishing net to his body with a short length of rope so that he had both hands free; one held his baseball cap onto his head, and the other held a crab bucket. Sarah smiled, following his progress.

"Mrs Baker!" came the uplifting tones of the jolly café owner. "I'm intrigued. You're not usually a mornin' customer… I can't wait to find out what this is all about." I see you've ordered some of Ron's new carrot loaf. What do you think?"

"Carrot loaf? I thought this was tea loaf."

"It is, but Ron's on a bit of a health drive, so 'e's replaced most of the sugar with carrot."

Sarah took another bite to allow a more considered judgement.

"Delicious!" she said. "Cinnamon... and ginger?"

"Yes," Emily replied. "So, it goes well with coffee as well as tea. More people are drinkin' coffee these days."

"Mmm, that's true."

"Anyway, you din't come to talk about coffee an' cake. Come on... I'm all ears."

"Well, I've got some sketches from a promising new artist. I wanted to see what you thought. I think they might be good enough to frame and sell."

"I assume you've got 'em with you...Let's see 'em then."

Sarah picked up her shoulder bag and took out the envelope containing Ged's sketches. With a little trepidation, she handed it over to Emily. Should she be doing this without asking him?

Emily slid the sketches out of the envelope and turned them around. As she leafed through them, her expression was animated, and her brows lifted. Many people came and asked her to look at their artwork for display in the café. Most of it was dross, but this was genuinely interesting and unique. She smiled at the picture of the girl being spun around by her brother on the beach and chuckled at Pirate Pete.

She went through the sketches twice. Then, a third time, muttering under her breath. Sarah quietly sat and drank her coffee, occasionally looking out of the window as Porthleven life continued to provide entertainment in the street and harbour. The windy weather made yacht masts sway, ropes and fenders slapped rhythmically against hulls and masts, the percussion of a working pleasure harbour.

"Well," said Emily, sitting back in her chair. She pushed her glasses on top of her head and clasped her coffee in both hands. Regarding Sarah seriously, she said, "You've got some talent here, young Mrs Baker. I like these a lot. Have you thought about addin' colour like in the one of the family on the beach?"

"Oh, they aren't mine, Emily," said Sarah. "Ged has done them this summer. I just love them, and I think they would sell; what do you think?"

"He's quite the artist. Has he always been this good?"

"It's the first time I've ever seen him draw anything except diagrams of shelves and kitchen plans, but I think they're amazing... I'm really drawn to the people in the pictures... I feel like I know what they're thinking!"

"I agree, the characters are brilliant! So full of life!" Emily said, grinning as she glanced again at Pirate Pete. "I love the way he's caught the expression. It would normally bother me that the people aren't drawn completely – I mean, on this pirate fella, half his arm is missing – but it doesn't make him look unfinished. It makes me look more at the face and imagine the story." She fixed Sarah with a kind but steely gaze... "Oh, yes, these are really quite good... I think they *will* sell, and I'd be happy to sell them here if you'll allow me. Even as pencil sketches, this lot would go for between £20 and £40 each, I think, although you might double that with a bit of skilled watercolour."

"What?" said Sarah, shocked. "That much? It sounds a lot."

"Decent frames and mounts are going to cost around a tenner each. It's important not to undersell artwork, as some people will think they're no good if they're too cheap. You need *'headology'* when it comes to selling art," she said, tapping her temple with a forefinger. "I' bin doing it a long time."

Sarah leaned forward. She could feel butterflies in her chest. "Where would I get them framed and mounted?"

"Ah," said Emily, winking and tapping her nose secretively... "I know a man," she said, glancing towards the kitchen.

"What, Ron?" Sarah replied.

"We had a man in Helston, doin' it, but he was retirin', and he had awful rheumatism, so... Ron asked 'im 'ow to do it, and now it's become a bit of a sideline... Quite a useful one, as it turns out. You need to wear a few hats if you run a place like this," she said, gesturing around the café. "'It's alright in summer when there's plenty of tourists and the sun's shinin', but it's handy to 'ave other ways to make ends meet."

"Wow!" said Sarah, eyebrows raised. She felt her heart beating faster, and the butterflies in her stomach seemed to have called their friends over for a party. "Emily, do you believe in fate?"

"Well, I don't know about fate, dear, but the good Lord seems to have a plan for each of us. We jus' don't know what it is 'til we're doin' it," replied Emily.

"Some things just happen for a reason",… thought Sarah to herself. She looked at her coffee cup. Tears began to prick her eyes. *"Oh, pull yourself together,"* her hands said to her. *"It's not that big of a deal. People get art mounted every day."*

"How I'd suggest we work it is this:" said Emily, in a business-like tone. "We'll get 'em framed and see what they go for. I'll get some prints done of the ones I like best. For this first batch, why don't we go fifty-fifty?"

"So, whatever they sell for, you'll give us half."

"Yes. I think that will cover the cost of the frames and mounting and give us a bit of profit, too," she said.

"That sounds great, Emily. Thank you so much."

Emily slid the sketches back into the envelope, then stood up and smoothed down her apron. "Another coffee before you go? On the 'ouse this time," she offered, "I wish I could stop and chat a while, but I've got to get things ready for the lunchtime sitting."

"Oh, no, but thanks," Sarah replied. "I should get back. I've got a few cold groceries in the car. Shall I leave the pictures with you then?"

"Yes. Leave them 'ere, and I'll have a chat with Ron this evenin' to see when he can fit it in. If you all come back later in the week for your tea, I'll let you know when we can 'ave them done."

"Can I come back on my own, please, Emily?" Sarah said quietly. "I want to keep this under wraps for now."

"'Course you can, dear," said Emily, smiling. "But you'll all come and 'ave your tea 'ere again before you go 'ome won't you?"

"Yes, um, of course," said Sarah, with a note of uncertainty in her voice. "It's just that…well, I don't think Mrs Baker-senior would entirely approve of all this."

"Oh, I see," said Emily with a knowing tone. "In that case," she said, tapping the side of her nose again. "'Mum's' the word. It'll just be between you and me."

"Oh," said Sarah, suddenly remembering her promise. "The children want to keep some pictures – The Unicorn and Pirate Pete. I'll pay for Ron to frame them."

"I'll remember those," said Emily. "We'll put them to one side for you. The pirate one – I was going to get some prints done."

"Thanks again, Emily. I am so grateful," said Sarah, holding Emily's gaze for a moment. "I can't believe I'm doing this. It's quite exciting, but goodness knows what Ged will say when he finds out."

"Well, don't tell 'im then," she said with a grin. "Let this be our little secret. If the pictures sell, I'll give you a cheque, and you can surprise 'im."

"That's a good idea, Emily," said Sarah. "Although it seems a bit sneaky."

"It'll be a nice surprise for Mr Baker. 'Ee don't 'ave to tell Mrs B if 'ee don't want to."

"Yes, I think it will be a nice surprise... and if they don't sell, then he doesn't have to be disappointed either," Sarah said – mostly to herself.

"Oh, they'll sell alright," Emily remarked. "I got a feelin' for this kinda thing. Will you bring any more that he does? If he can get a bit 'o' colour 'em, they'll go for more."

"I'll try to persuade him," Sarah said, standing up and slinging her bag straps over her shoulder. "He is having a go with watercolours, but so far, all he's managed to do is ruin Marge's best tablecloth. I've been trying to get the stain out, but it won't budge."

"Bring it 'ere; I'll get my laundry people to sort it. I don't know what sorcery they do on the staff uniforms, but there's not a stain they can't get out."

"You are a wonder, Emily! If you're sure, I'll bring it later today."

"Long as it's 'ere by ten tomorrow mornin'," said Emily. "That's when they collect the dirty stuff and drop off the clean. Oh, and best leave it in whatever bucket of cold water you've got it in already, so it don't dry out."

"I will; I can't thank you enough."

"No bother," she said, waving a hand dismissively. "Gotta go now. Need to get clean dishes out ready for lunch."

"Yes, of course, thanks again. I'll see you before ten tomorrow. Bye, Emily."

Emily waved and briskly walked off to the kitchen. Sarah looked around the café, with its gingham tablecloths, blue and cream Cornishware and gallery of framed art. She noticed that a few paintings from the previous night were no longer evident. The ink sketch of St. Michael's mount was still there, but now had a yellow sticky note on the glass of the frame with 'Sold – VM' in red marker pen. She caught her breath, excited at the prospect of selling Ged's sketches secretly. Should she share her secret with Brian? Maybe she would think about that a little longer.

14

Marge came out of the bedroom in her blue gingham blouse and a pair of navy trousers. She went into the kitchen and made herself coffee. She didn't offer Ged a coffee, but he was used to that. He would make one with the hot water in the kettle, as she always filled it too full. As she walked past him on her way to the garden, she paused; the newspaper puzzles and a pen gripped in one hand, which she now placed on her hip, the other holding the coffee cup. She stared at him with an expression of mild exasperation as he mixed his colours, then washed and carefully dried a brush.

"You've been messing with those paints for days, Gerald," she sniped. "You've hardly spoken to me... You're always talking to Sarah, Brian and the grandchildren, but you seem to ignore me completely."

Ged looked up and considered his response. It was true; Ged and Marge hadn't really 'talked' much in a while. Unless they were discussing the week's plans, what was for dinner, what to buy the children for their birthdays, what colour to paint the walls or what wallpaper to buy. However, that wasn't so much a conversation as Ged making suggestions to be pooh-poohed, and Marge would decide anyway. Ged had figured that was the way of things and wasn't particularly interested in wallpaper or which colour paint he would be expected to roll on the wall. If he did particularly dislike a design or colour, all he had to do to get it vetoed was to put it forward as a suggestion, at which point Marge, whether she had liked it or not before, would instantly tell him what a silly idea it was and choose something else.

Now, Marge was chastising him for not talking to her. Inside, he panicked, groping for something appropriate to say. He decided honesty was the best policy.

"You're right; we haven't talked much lately, have we? Even on holiday. I'm usually playing with the grandchildren or doing some job on the house, and you're busy gardening. You've done a lot to the garden this year. It looks nice."

"Nice?" she said with a questioning tone. "Is that all you can say about it?"

"Er, well, I can't comment about the plants as I don't know the names, but yes. I think it looks very nice," he said. "It's neat and tidy, and I'm sure our visitors will love it. Some cottages here have overgrown gardens that you can't sit in, but not ours. We can sit in it and admire the view…as well as the garden."

"Well, that's kind of you to say so, I suppose," she said, softening a little. "What are you going to do today? Are we having lunch here or on the beach?"

"I was planning to go to the Seagull for a coffee in a bit. Do you want to join me?"

"Certainly not! I've just made a nice instant coffee," she snapped. "I can't stand those Italian coffee machines. They are everywhere, and the coffee tastes like mud. If you go to that café, you'll end up having loads of cake, Gerald. If you aren't playing football and cricket and going for walks, you're going to put on more weight."

"…And she wonders why we don't talk?" thought Ged, ruefully.

"I promise. I won't have any cake, Marge," said Ged, trying to keep the irritation out of his voice. "Bill is a friend. I like going there. And I rather like the mud they are serving from the new machine. Brian suggested we might have lunch here as the tide will be almost in by one o'clock."

"Where are they all, anyway?"

"Sarah has gone up to Helston, and Brian has taken the kids to see the goats at the farm. They've got kids too, four-legged ones… get it?"

"Very funny, Gerald," said Marge sarcastically. "I'm going to do the crossword in the garden. I'll make lunch for one o'clock, so don't be too long. And for goodness' sake, put those paints away carefully. We don't want another spill."

Ged looked up in surprise. He thought they had managed to keep that quiet.

"Yes, Gerald, I do know about the tablecloth. I saw it early this morning up in Brian and Sarah's bathroom, soaking. I couldn't have a bath as my best linen tablecloth was in it. I will be having a word with Sarah when she gets back."

"Poor Sarah," muttered Ged to himself as Marge stalked out.

"Pardon, Gerald?" said Marge, turning sharply.

"Er… I said, 'Could you close the door, dear? ' he lied. "You know, so the wind doesn't knock the water jar over."

"Hmm," muttered Marge, closing the front door with a snap.

"She's worse than ever," thought Ged as he packed up the paints and brushes. *"I wonder if there is something on her mind. We did have that little row in the car last night, but she was tetchy before that."*

Marge had always been sharp and somewhat quick-tempered. Ged had always put it down to genes. Her mother was opinionated in the extreme, and her magistrate father should be able to make quick and certain judgements, so maybe she got it from them. The girl he fell in love with would have laughed at his silly joke. She poured scorn on his hobby. Now that he was nearing retirement, surely she would be glad that he had found a pastime which wasn't too much of a drain on finances and didn't require hours of being away from the house?

He sighed and packed away the paints, pencils, brushes and sketchbook into the pink unicorn backpack. He took his crutch and hobbled into the kitchen to wash the water jar. He threw the rag he had been using on the floor in front of the washing machine. He suspected he may get reprimanded for that, but he really wanted to get off to Bill's. The cup of coffee and shortbread were calling to him. He had promised not to have cake, but Marge hadn't mentioned shortbread.

***

Sharon was clearing and wiping down tables from the breakfast customers when Ged arrived at the café. She called out to him.

"Hi, Chippy! I'm glad you've come today; there's someone I want you to meet."

"Oh?" said Ged, intrigued. "Who?"

"My friend, Caroline, she's an art teacher. I thought she could give you a few tips about your new hobby, as she just moved here. Caroline and her hubby have just bought 'Harbour View'. She'll be here soon. Sit yourself down, and I'll get you a coffee. Want anything else?"

"Thanks, Sharon; yes, I'll have a small slice of that gorgeous-looking millionaire's shortbread of yours," he said, choosing a table in the shade. The sun was intense that morning, and he wanted to avoid getting sunburnt.

Bill had heard them talking and came out, wiping his hands on his apron. He had already made himself a coffee in what looked like a small blue and white bucket with a handle. He took a swig and turned to make one for Ged.

"You're enjoying that, aren't you?" said Ged.

"I love it!" called Bill from the coffee machine. "The smell of the fresh ground coffee and the hot milk... Sharon's more of a tea girl. I think we should swap jobs."

"No thanks, Bill," called Sharon from inside the café. You can keep your sweatbox of a kitchen. I think I'd pass out if I made so much as beans on toast in there."

"But the coffee machine," he said. "You don't like the smell of coffee so much."

"Bill Callywick, if I let you make the coffee, you'd have one every time you made them for the customers, then we'd be skint, and you'd never sleep again!"

"She's right," he said to Ged as he sat down, placing the cups on the table. "I would drink that stuff 'til it came out of my ears. I'm limited to two cups a day," he said, lifting the enormous mug of steaming Cappuccino to his lips.

Ged raised his eyebrows and looked up at Bill as he took another slug of coffee. "Two cups, eh?" he said. "That's some cup you've got there, Jack – did you climb a beanstalk to find it?"

Bill grinned, seeing the joke. "These mugs were on special offer at the old mill shop. When Sharon said I could only 'ave two cups of coffee a day, I bought a couple."

"Genius!" said Ged.

"I know. Anyway, 'ow's the foot? I see you're only on one crutch today."

"Still sore but a bit better," said Ged. "If I use the walls and fence posts along the way, I can get here on one crutch without putting much weight on it. It's easier."

Sharon arrived with a slice of millionaire shortbread on a plate. The chocolate was already starting to melt in the intensity of the sun.

"I don't think you're supposed to put any weight on it at all, Chippy," she said with a concerned frown. "The bone won't knit. It'll take longer to heal. You don't want poor Marge driving home, do you?"

"Good point, Sharon. Maybe I'll go back to two," he said.

"'Ere's Caroline!" said Sharon, looking up the hill, waving enthusiastically. "Hi, Cat!"

A tanned, short, dark-haired, slim woman in paint-splattered jeans and a tie-dyed purple t-shirt was gingerly walking with a distinct limp down the steep road towards the café and didn't wave back. She appeared to be in pain.

"Oh no!" called Sharon, "What's happened, Caz? Bill, go and 'elp her."

"No problem," said Bill, getting to his feet. He trotted down the road, apron flapping. He stopped by Caroline and spoke to her for a moment; then, he placed his arm around her waist. She put her left arm over his shoulder, ...then Bill stooped down, confidently swept his left arm behind her knees, and scooped her off the ground, holding her safely in his arms. With a grin, she looked over and waved at Sharon.

"I've got your fella now, Sharon!" she called out. "My hero!" she called, laughing and feigning a fake swoon with the back of her hand theatrically touching her forehead.

Bill carried her up the steps of the café, grinning. "Dennis will be after me for this," he said. "Though I'm not sure what's worse. Me carrying his wife down the hill or the fact she's makin' such a drama out of it!"

Sharon had been quick to get her camera out and take a photo of the scene. "Hah!" she said. "Now I have proof that you're a brazen 'ussy and a 'husband-stealer!" she said, wagging her finger at her friend and grinning. She put the camera down and pulled out the white plastic chair that Bill had been sitting on, ready to help her friend into it.

Bill gently let Caroline down in front of the chair, supporting her weight while she eased herself into it.

"What have you done to yourself, Cat?" said Sharon.

"Just twisted my ankle on the way down here. Silly, really; I wasn't looking where I was going and stumbled off the kerb up by the harbour," she said, looking sheepish.

"I'll get some ice and a tea towel," said Sharon. "Get your shoe off. Oh...this is Chippy...I mean...oh my goodness! What *is* your real name?"

"Ged," said Ged, "but I'm fine with my Porthcovery name."

"Sorry, of course... Ged," said Sharon. It was her turn to look sheepish. "Um...anyway, Cat, he's the fella I was tellin' you about; maybe you could give 'im a few lessons?"

"Hi, Ged," said Caroline, offering her hand to shake. "Nice to meet you. I've heard a lot about you."

"All good, I hope?" said Ged with a wink as he shook her hand.

"Oh yes, all very good...and not just from Sharon and Bill," she said as she unzipped her bright red ankle boot. "You seem to be well-known here. Seems like you are a handy person to know."

"I'd be more handy if I hadn't busted my foot," said Ged with a grimace.

"It's your brains I'm after," she said. "My husband, Dennis, is doing most of the work. We were going over our plans for the house and could use some advice on the joinery front. I believe you've got a house down here that you've done up, and the locals call you "Chippy", so I figured you'd be able to help."

"Yes, it's the white one up there on the left with the garden bench. We bought it a few years ago. It needed a lot doing to it, but we've got it how we want it now."

"I was wondering if you could come and have a look at our cottage? Dennis and I have lots of ideas, but we might be being a bit ambitious, and we'd value the voice of experience."

"You don't hold back, do you, Cat?" said Sharon, placing down a teapot, mug and milk jug. "Hardly shook hands, and you're already asking him a favour."

"You know me, Sharon," said Caroline. "If you don't ask, you don't get... besides, Ged looks the friendly type."

Sharon laughed. "Well, you're not wrong there, Cat," she said, "but you haven't said how you can help him..."

"Of course...I forgot the main reason you asked me to come this morning." She looked at Ged. "Have you brought your pans and brushes with you?"

Bill spluttered on his coffee and guffawed... "Oh, he has a magic unicorn that takes care of 'em."

"What?" said Carolyn, perplexed.

"He means this," said Ged, holding up his pink rucksack with the unicorn on it.

"Nice!" said Caroline, smiling and reaching for the bag. "Mind if I have a look?"

"Sure," said Ged, shrugging and handing it over.

Caroline emptied the contents onto the table and muttered to herself as she went through the collection of brushes, pencils and other assorted items. "Mmm, not bad, half and one-inch flat; Liner; definitely. Size 8: ok. Size 6 and 12 round...good choice. Cotman: Mmm, good starter set. I like the little pad of watercolour paper you've got here," she said, half to herself and half to Ged. "Yeah, not bad at all. I think we can work with this."

"We?" said Ged. "Are you offering to teach me?"

"Sure, why not?" she said matter-of-factly. "I was an art teacher, you know. And as I'm asking you for your help...seems only fair I should offer something in return. Have you got any sketches?"

"One or two," he replied. "I've given the rest to the grandkids." He flipped the practice paper and showed her one of the sketches of the family he had drawn on the beach. It was another version of the one where the little girl was being spun around by her brother. Her feet were up in the air, and her long hair, crimped from being in a plait, was streaming as she spun around. Her brother's hands were gripped around her wrists. It was the expressions on their faces that Caroline was drawn to.

"This is really nice," she said. "Have you always drawn people this way?"

"I'm not sure; it's been a long time since I did any sketching. I was in my teens."

"I've not seen anything like this," she said. "There's a lot of life in them. I can imagine what the boy and girl are thinking. You've not finished them off; there are bits missing, and normally, that would bother me, but it doesn't. It's nice as a sketch, but would you like to get some colour into it?"

"Yes, I would. I remember the girl's hair was a lovely strawberry blonde and her T-shirt was a boring sand colour, but I think she could have a red skirt, which I know my granddaughter would like. I've got a style in mind, but I don't know if I can do it."

"What do you mean...style?"

"Well, it goes with the unfinishedness of the sketch," said Ged. "I don't want to colour everything – just the things I want to stand out. Maybe a muted suggestion of the sand and sea and other things."

"I can help with that," said Caroline. "Come over to the house this afternoon, and you can have a lesson in my studio. It's the only bit of the house that's finished. You'll need both your crutches, though; it's upstairs. You know where Harbour View is, don't you?"

"The one with the bay window and little balcony near the pub?" asked Ged.

"That's the one."

"Er, okay," said Ged. Things felt like they were running away with him. He hadn't asked the family if they would mind him being out that afternoon, but he couldn't see any harm in accepting her offer, and he might be able to help them with the DIY, too.

He drained his now lukewarm cappuccino, and Caroline helped him pack the unicorn bag.

"I LOVE that bag!" she said, "it's perfect for the job."

"I'm finding it very useful, actually. I'm becoming quite attached to it. I might see if my Granddaughter will let me keep it if I get her a new one," said Ged.

15

Lunch was a noisy affair, initially at least; Sarah returned with baguettes, a warm roast chicken, lettuce and avocados. Brian shredded lettuce and made tea. Jamie was making a fuss over a ball which Alice had punctured. Alice was crying and saying it was an accident and that the ball was hers in the first place. Sarah was attempting to calm them down while Marge was telling Alice not to be a cry-baby and shrieking at Jamie for not taking his shoes off and not wearing a t-shirt.

Ged entered the house to this clamour. He called to Marge so that Sarah could manage the children without her assistance.

"Marge, can you please give me a hand? I can't find my other crutch."

Marge turned sharply. "Where did you have it last?" she snapped. "Can't you see I'm busy with the children?"

"I think Sarah can manage," said Ged calmly. "My foot really hurts, though; I've only had one crutch this morning. I think the other might have fallen and ended up hidden by the valance sheet on our bed."

"Oh really, Gerald," snapped Marge. "This foot of yours has caused nothing but trouble. I really am quite fed up with all this fetching and carrying."

"I know, Marge, darling," he said apologetically. "Please – would you be a real brick and get the other one for me from our room?"

Marge sighed noisily and marched to the bedroom. Ged knew exactly where the crutch was; it had bought Sarah some time. She glanced at Ged, mouthing silently, "Thanks, Dad." She took a deep breath and put her hand on Jamie's shoulder. "Jamie, I'm going upstairs with Alice for a minute. Please put your shoes on the rack, and there's your blue T-shirt on the sofa." She took Alice by the hand and led her upstairs.

"But, Mum, she burst my ball!" protested Jamie.

"Jamie, let's calm things down and talk about this later," she said gently. "Please go and do as I ask, and we'll discuss it when we have all calmed down."

"Come on, Jamie," said Ged. "When you've put your shoes on the rack and got your t-shirt on, we can go and wash our hands together before lunch."

"Hi, Grandad," said Jamie, a brighter note in his voice. He took off his jellybean shoes and tossed them onto the shoe rack by the door. Ged hobbled to the sofa, handed him the t-shirt, and they went to the utility together.

***

"Am I supposed to eat this with my fingers, Sarah?" said Marge as Sarah placed a plate of French bread, avocado, mayonnaise, roast chicken and lettuce in front of her. "It's far too messy," she complained. Roast chicken should be eaten with a knife and fork, not fingers, and besides, the avocado and mayonnaise make it slimy."

"That's half the fun, Mum," said Brian. "It's a challenge; can you take a bite without looking like a total prat and getting avocado all over the place?"

"I would *prefer* a knife and fork, Brian," said Marge, looking at him over her glasses.

"Here, Mum, pass me your plate," he said. "I have an idea for the more well-mannered among us." Marge passed her plate, and Brian chopped all the ingredients into equal-sized pieces and mixed them with the mayonnaise, creating an avocado and chicken salad. He placed the two halved slices of baguette on the side. "Now you can scoop the chicken and avocado onto your bread in the same way you would with coleslaw. A bit more ladylike, perhaps?"

"I'd prefer potatoes and a knife and fork, but this is better than the mess Gerald is making."

Ged had avocado and mayonnaise on the end of his nose, and a piece of chicken had just squirted out of his sandwich and landed on the tablecloth. Without moving his head, which was now directly over his plate to make sure that any further dropping food landed on it, he looked up at the others as they stared at him.

"What?" he said, peering at the others as he swallowed his mouthful and scooped up the piece of fallen chicken. "It's delicious! Best sandwich ever!"

He took another bite, greedily savouring the roast chicken and avocado blend, but this time, he wiped his mouth, chin and nose with a napkin.

Alice watched him all the while… "Can I have mine like Nana, please, Mummy?"

"Of course," said Sarah. "I think I'll do the same. It looks much easier."

Silence descended over the table as everyone was now lost in their food and their thoughts. Ged was the first to speak:

"I'm going out after lunch. There's a new couple at Harbour View who want a bit of advice on their kitchen. I said I'd give them a hand."

"You're kidding," said Brian. "How are you going to help them with a busted foot?"

Ged opened his mouth to respond, but Marge was too fast for him. She had laid down her cutlery and had both her hands flat on the table. She glared at him.

"You're not seriously considering doing joinery and handyman jobs in your state, Gerald!" she cried, her voice rising in pitch as she did. "You must be mad! How are you supposed to recover to drive us home if you go around doing things like this?" Ged opened his mouth to interject, but Marge was in full flow, and nothing short of a bomb dropping was going to stop her.

"This is typical, Gerald; I'm sick and tired of it! You act the big community hero, going around doing all these little – and not so little – jobs for people all over the village, and everyone says: '*Oh, that Ged Baker, such lovely chap – can't do enough for anyone, – such an angel, 'Ooooh arrr… a saint eee be!'*" She cooed, mocking a Cornish accent… "Well, you might be the blessed Saint Chippy of Cornwall to everyone here in Porthcovery…everyone, that is, except your own family. But if you go off hammering and drilling for those London lazies, you'll not be well enough to drive us home. Hardly saintly in my book… You make yourself look like the conscientious – Mr Holier-than-thou' Baker, but you're just a self-promoting, thoughtless fool, and I am going to put my foot down this time. You are *not* going to that house, and that's final!"

"Mum!" scolded Brian. "That's a bit much, don't you think?

"No, Brian," shrieked Marge. "It needs saying. Your father is treated like some kind of humanitarian aid worker in this village, and our neighbours at home think he should be canonised, but I hardly ever see him. He comes here for a week in October nearly every year, and what does he do? – I'll tell you what… free work for free-loaders!"

"Come on, Mum," said Sarah, her tone conciliatory, "That's not fair. The whole family got a free meal at the pub last Christmas because of the work Dad did in the bar, and he's done nearly everything in this house.

Marge wasn't backing down, and now Sarah was treated to her icy glare: "No, Sarah, you don't understand. Having a saint for a husband is not easy…." she gesticulated out of the window with a pointing finger, "and that garden is a result of hours and hours of work; my work. The curtains didn't make themselves, did they?"

"You're right, you've done a lot too…in fact, we all have," said Sarah, trying to keep the peace. "Dad…are you really going to go and do work at that couple's house… On crutches? You can't possibly…" she trailed off. Ged's shoulders had slumped, and he was looking at his plate.

Ged sighed. Did they all really think he was that stupid? He closed his eyes and took a deep breath before saying anything. Then, he leaned back into his chair, both hands resting gently on the edge of the table.

"Have you all quite finished?" he said, surprisingly calmly. "First, Caroline and Dennis don't sound like they're from London. The accent sounds more like Bolton to me. Second, I'm not hammering nails and sawing timber; they just want some advice. The only tools I'm taking are my experience, my ears and my voice. Third," he said and looked directly at Marge. "Marjorie Baker, I love you. I always have, and I always will. You're an active volunteer at home with the W.I. and history group. It's something I love about you." He considered a moment, lips pursed and continued. "There are times that I help other people when I could be helping my family, but I *try* to get the balance right…and there will be times when I get it wrong. I hope I'll be able to drive home; goodness knows, I want to." …. *'I'm not sure my nerves could handle being a passenger again."* He added silently to himself, knowing that it would inflame the situation to voice it. "But if not, Sarah has offered to drive us back and take the train home."

He picked up the unicorn backpack and both crutches. Marge was doing a very good impersonation of a Carp. Her mouth was opening and shutting, but the connection to her brain seemed to have shorted out. She looked shocked …and was that a hint of embarrassment? If it was, she certainly wasn't making it public.

"Sorry, Dad," said Brian, meeting Ged's gaze, glancing at his Mother and then looking down at his plate.

"It looks like everyone misunderstood when I said 'helping,'" he said. "Now, as it's past two o'clock, I think I'll head up to Harbour Cottage. Sarah, could you give me a lift in the car, please? My foot's sore, and I don't want to walk up the hill."

"I could give you another piggy-back," said Brian with a twinkle in his eye.

"I think that might be a bit too far for my pride, Brian, even if not for your legs," replied Ged sincerely.

"Okay, I'll get the keys." Sarah said, " Do you think they'd let me have a nosey?"

"Can't see any reason why not," said Ged. "Caroline seemed pretty easygoing. Let's go; I feel a chill in here," he said, glancing at Marge, who had, by then, fetched her newspaper and was now sitting on the window seat doing the crossword.

"Mum," said Brian. "Don't you have anything to say to Dad?"

"What? …oh, bye, dear," she said.

"No, Mum…don't you think you should…" began Brian; Ged cut him off.

"It's okay, Brian," he said soothingly, "no point. Can we just go, Sarah?"

"Dad, she can't say all that and not apologise," said Brian, almost pleading.

"Let's leave it for now," replied Ged, shaking his head; his tone was calm but firm.

***

"Have you started a yoga class?" said Sarah as she buckled her seatbelt."

Ged frowned and glanced at her, baffled at the question. "No, why?"

"How did you keep your cool in the face of all... well, all that?"

"Mmm. I was a bit shocked; I know she can be a bit sharp, but she rarely... 'goes off on one' like that. I'm still trying to get my head around it."

"Well... I can't believe I'm saying this to my father-in-law, but if you ever want to talk or let off a bit of steam, you can always call Brian or me."

"Thanks, Sarah, I know you mean well, but... I don't think that would be very loyal. She is my wife, after all." ...he fell silent as Sarah pulled into the little turning space by Harbour Cottage. Then he spoke: "I must admit, she's been acting tense lately. I think she's taken this whole 'broken foot' thing a bit hard. I suppose I've never really been – well – 'incapacitated' before, and it's stressing her out a bit."

"Mmm, I don't think I can even remember you being ill, never mind *'incapacitated'* as you put it... I like that word."

"Come on," said Ged, picking up the unicorn bag, "Let's go have a nosey, shall we?"

16

Dennis met them at the door. It was already open, presumably, to deal with the paint fumes that almost made Sarah and Ged recoil. Dennis and Caroline were dressed in blue overalls, which were covered in white and grey paint splodges. There was a fresh white handprint on the right butt-cheek of Dennis's overalls that Sarah spotted as he turned to show them into the room that was clearly becoming a kitchen. Sarah nodded her head sideways towards the handprint and caught Ged's eye, raising an eyebrow. Ged grinned, stifling a laugh and coughed in an attempt to hide it.

"Sorry…couldn't resist," said Caroline, grinning at Sarah. "Dennis was up the ladder just now. 'His backside was right in my face, so I just had to plant a hand on it!"

Sarah laughed, shaking Dennis' offered hand… "I'm Sarah, Ged's daughter-in-law. Nice to meet you both."

Dennis smiled warmly. "Dennis. Nice to meet yer Sarah," he said in a strong Lancashire accent. "We've 'erd a lot about Ged… or is it 'Chippy?' Come in. I'll put' kettle on if you've time for a brew."

Caroline winked, holding up her paint-covered hand. "I won't shake."

She went to the sink and gave her hands a scrub with the nail brush and soap. "Shall I give you the grand tour while the kettle boils?"

"Yes, please," said Sarah. "I've always wondered what this place is like on the inside. Looks like you've got a lot of work to do."

"Yes, it needs loads doing. The chap who had it before us was getting on and hasn't touched it in years, so we've gutted the place."

"The kitchen looks almost done," said Ged. "Just a few more units and a worktop to go in, from the look of it."

"Yes, that's where we needed a bit of 'elp," said Caroline as she led the way upstairs. "The units don't fit. We've had a piece of granite cut to the right shape, but the wall is so uneven that we can't fit the units we bought. We only measured around where the top of the units go, and lower down, the walls aren't the same shape."

"Not unusual around here," replied Ged. "I've been in a few similar kitchens in Porthcovery. There are ways around it, but you'll need to be sure every unit is the right width and in the right place before you start cutting to make them fit; the company won't take them back if they have been cut. I think in the old days, people just had a kitchen table that they did everything on and a few shelves. They weren't so bothered whether the walls were straight then."

Caroline led them to one of three rooms upstairs. Ged went last, remembering to use both crutches on the stairs while avoiding the still-wet paint on the rail and skirting boards. The bedroom with a balcony had been made into a bright and airy art studio with a large table near the window from which you could get a great view of the harbour and headland beyond. What wall space there was had sketches of animals and floral watercolours of bluebells, harebells or lupins. Some small watercolour paintings of roses were laid out to dry on the table. They had a depth to them that seemed almost like an acrylic painting, but the softness of watercolours was unmistakable. Sarah spent a few moments studying them. They looked as if they had been done by different people. Some looked more like a rose than others; one was quite abstract.

The room also contained a small tapestry two-seat sofa, a sewing machine and two sets of shelves stacked with artist's paraphernalia. A laundry airer was draped with cloth rags of varying colours, shapes and sizes. Ged went over to it, intrigued.

"What's this going to be, Caroline?" he asked.

"It's for a rag rug wall hanging for the living room. I couldn't find all the colours I wanted in charity shops, so I've dyed some plain rags. I've been trying out tie-dyeing for my art class and getting some interesting and often dreadful results… the failures become rags for rag wreaths or rag rugs… I never waste a thing."

Sarah stepped out onto the balcony. There was enough room for a small table and two wooden slatted foldable chairs, painted blue with cheery white daisies painted on the corners of the chair backs and randomly over the tabletop.

"I love the table and chairs, Caroline. It's a fabulous view here. Was the studio the first room you finished?"

"Yep. It's why we bought the place. We got the bathroom and bedroom sorted first. We rented a caravan at the farm while we got the roof done and made it habitable as quick as we could. Once we could plug a kettle in, wash and sleep here, we moved in... we couldn't afford to wait. The studio had to be next as I had classes booked at the village hall and needed somewhere to dry my students' work. We're going top to bottom with the 'ouse. The bedroom and bathroom are basic; they aren't how we want them, but they're functional. We can have baths 'til we've finished tiling, and we've got somewhere to sleep."

Ged hopped out to the landing to take a look at the bathroom and bedroom. They were, as Caroline said, basic, a white suite in the bathroom and plastered walls with a half-finished slate tiled shower area. The floor had been laid with russet and grey-mottled slate, and the remaining tiles were stacked up by the shower. The waste trap had been fitted, and a platform had been created ready to tile the shower floor – clearly a work in progress.

The bedroom was painted in a deep matt green emulsion. Square spirals of different sizes had been stencilled with pearlescent paint around the walls to break up the matte green, and a large acrylic painting of a rock pool dominated the wall over the bed. Two rustic wrought iron sconces on either side of the bed carried a white church candle, and there was only a wooden double bed, two oak bedside drawer cabinets, a 'distressed' painted chest of drawers and an oak wardrobe in one corner. The bare floorboards had been painted a light grey, and a rag rug in varying shades of red and deep orange lay on the side of the bed near the door.

"Not bad for 'basic.'" thought Ged. The space under the bed was packed with cardboard boxes, and the two suitcases with their contents spilling out showed that Caroline and Dennis hadn't quite finished moving in.

"I'm decorating the hall and stairwell. One of my students is helping us with the bathroom, and Dennis has started on the kitchen.

The living room won't be needed 'til autumn. The studio is our living room for now."

"Brew's ready!" came a shout from Dennis in the kitchen.

"Can you bring it up here, Love?" Caroline called... I want to show Ged some watercolour tips. And I don't want 'im traipsing up and down the stairs with crutches."

They discussed the couples' plans for decor and furnishing whilst drinking their tea, and Sarah invited them to dinner one evening at the Bakers. "At least you won't have to worry about eating pot noodle for one evening," she said.

"That would be lovely, thanks, Sarah," said Caroline, "I've had enough pot noodle to last a lifetime! ...If you're sure your husband and mother-in-law won't mind, of course."

"Well, my husband certainly won't; he loves cooking for new people. He's always glad to have new stooges to try out his latest recipes."

Caroline and Dennis exchanged intrigued glances. Ged gave Sarah a look that said: *"You'd better square this with Marge, or there'll be trouble."*

"I'll check our plans for the next few days and let you know which day. Are there any evenings you won't be able to come over?" said Sarah.

"Tuesday is Caroline's class day," said Dennis. "Any day other than that will suit us... if you're sure it's ok?"

"Absolutely... it would be lovely to have you over."

Sarah turned to Ged and checked if he would need a lift home.

"I'll manage on these things," he said, lifting a crutch. "I've got my backpack, so I've nothing to carry."

"I'll be off then; see you later."

"Bye, Sarah, thanks for the lift."

Sarah took the cups downstairs and wished Dennis luck with the kitchen.

Caroline pulled out the chair at the table and gestured for Ged to sit.

"Right, let's get you sorted on a few basics," said Caroline, pulling up a stool. "I use two water jars, one for washing the brushes and the other for clean water. I keep a large rag nearby for cleaning and drying the brushes. Remind me… what's in this famous backpack of yours?"

Ged emptied the contents on the table and spread them out. Caroline looked through it all again and nodded.

"Like I said yesterday, it's a nice starter kit. What is it you want to do with watercolours?"

"Well, not a lot, really; I just thought a suggestion of colour on the sketches might liven them up a bit; I think it will spoil the unfinished effect if I add too much colour."

He opened the watercolour practice pad with a few of the drawings he had created over the last day or so. The faces were so animated that the people in the sketches almost looked as though they might walk off the page at any moment.

Taking a medium brush, she started to mix a violet palette. "Now, if you want a more vibrant colour, you're better off layering it than trying to make a thick paste that flakes off. The paper is designed to soak up the water and leave the pigment on top," she said, sketching a pansy flower on the practice paper. She took the brush and applied a small amount of violet wash to the petals of the flower. Then she sat back and watched as the cartridge paper soaked up the water and the violet dried a little darker.

"You need to be patient; don't be too hasty to add another layer until the colour has dried to its true colour," she said, "and if you're not sure whether you need another layer, go and make a cup of tea or even go to bed and come back to it." She dipped the tip of the brush once more into the violet and applied it to just three of the petals and not to the edge this time. She had brought the pansy to life with just a few strokes of the brush.

"That's so clever; how do you do that so quickly?" said Ged, impressed, as he started to try out the violet she had mixed on another piece of practice paper.

"A good teacher, years of practice, and I suppose I have an eye for colour and form," she said as she stood up and took the palette and water jars to the bathroom. "I think you're blessed with that, too. Now, all you need to do is practice. If you want to come to my class, it's on Tuesday evenings in the village hall at seven."

Ged surveyed his efforts, pleased and quietly confident that he would probably achieve the effect he wanted with a bit of patience and practice. He gathered his brushes and watercolours and bundled them into the backpack.

"Next time you're in Tracy's shop, get a pencil case or brush roll for them so they don't get damaged jiggling around in your bag. They're good brushes; it would be a shame to break the bristles."

***

Downstairs in the kitchen with another steaming mug of tea, Ged took a closer look at the walls where the couple were planning to put the kitchen units.

The house was built from local stone. There were stained oak beams overhead, with tongue-and-groove planks in between, painted white. Large, irregular blocks of stone made up the walls, and Dennis had whitewashed the stone, which had served a useful purpose for marking out where each unit was intended to go in black charcoal pencil.

Dennis had clearly had a 'bash', quite literally, at chiselling away the stone where he wanted to fit the first unit, which, unfortunately, was a set of drawers.

"Do you have a drawn-out plan?" said Ged.

"Yeah, it's 'ere," said Dennis.

"Well, as the hob and oven are in, we can use their position to work out where everything else should go. We can use the front edge of the oven and hob as a reference point. I can show you how to modify any units that are too big." Where are the units you've bought?"

Most of the units were assembled in the living room. Ged looked over the plan and spent a while helping Dennis and Caroline modify it and figure out how to fit the units. Some would have to be cut into at the back. Ged helped Dennis to mark the units up to show where they would need to be cut to allow for the protrusion of the wall without harming the strength of the unit. He would have to saw a triangular prism off the back of two of the units; then Ged explained how a piece of hardboard could be screwed to the hole that was left to stop the contents of the cupboard from getting lost behind the cabinets.

Ged helped Dennis for the next hour or so, passing screws and fixings and giving tips on how to cut and fit the units. It was much like training an apprentice at the factory. He stood back and allowed the trainee to do the work. He knew it wouldn't be much help if he took over, and anyway, on this occasion, he couldn't.

By the time the fourth unit was in place, levelled and screwed to its neighbour, it was half four, which gave Ged half an hour to get back. It had started to rain, and he didn't like the idea of using crutches in the rain.

"I don't suppose one of you could give me a lift back, could you?" asked Ged.

"Oh blimey, look at the rain!" exclaimed Dennis. "Yes, of course. I'll get my keys."

"Thanks."

"I'll 'ave to get the car from our space up the road. Wait 'ere a minute."

Ged sat on the arm of the sofa in the living room by the window. Outside, the woman who ran the gift shop by the harbour was grabbing buckets, spades, fishing nets and beach paraphernalia from her display outside the shop as the hammering rain came in waves, the wind whipping her hair about her face. He was impressed at the speed of her progress, considering she was barefoot and wearing a sarong, which flapped against her legs and should have impeded her. She deftly tied her hair back in a bun as she came out again for the body boards. The wind and rain lashed her face, yet she showed no hint of being bothered by it. In around two minutes, everything was safely in the shop. She shut and padlocked the door, flipping the little white sign on it to "Closed."

***

In the car, Ged asked what he had been reticent to ask all the time he had been at Dennis and Caroline's. "So, you two aren't of retirement age… or at least, you don't look it. What are you doing for an income? I mean, you must have had a career before you came here…"

Dennis stopped the car outside the White House. He stared into the middle distance for a while, looking as though he was trying to find the right words.

"Yeah… seems like a long time ago… I was a P.E. teacher at a private school near Manchester. Basically, it's a school for thick kids with rich parents. If the kids couldn't pass the entrance exams for the better schools, but their parents wanted them to go to a private school, that's where they went. It wasn't so well run…They couldn't afford to pay a decent wage, and I had to get another job to make ends meet. I qualified as a personal trainer and did that in the evenings and weekends. Caz was an art teacher at the school and couldn't find another teaching job, so she went back to being a dental hygienist, but she was so bored, five days a week of bad teeth and halitosis. Then, a year later, we lost our 'enry and kind of fell apart…"

"Henry?"

"Our son, 'enry; …ee was ten. It was an accident…nearly three years ago, now."

"Oh my god, Dennis, how awful. I…I'm… so sorry." Ged said quietly. "Do you mind if I ask what happened?"

"His best mate, James, said the football bounced onto the main road. 'enry reacted instinctively – bus driver didn't stand a chance… poor man," said Dennis quietly. "'Ee were in intensive care for four months. It was a living nightmare of 'ope one day and dread the next. They thought 'is brain was repairing itself, but they warned us that he might be… you know, mentally impaired, then the day before they were going to revive him, he…" Dennis' voice faltered…" he had a haemorrhage and …well, that was it."

Dennis bowed his head and gripped his hands on the steering wheel of the car, shut his eyes and breathed in deeply, slowly exhaling… a move, Ged guessed, that was well practised. A way to stop the tears flowing, he guessed… But how could anyone stop the tears after such a tragedy?

Ged could not think of what to say. There were no words that seemed appropriate. He put his hand on Dennis' shoulder, and they sat in silence for a while.

"What a total *bugger*," he said eventually.

"Yeah…" said Dennis, "about a year ago, me and Caz were at rock bottom… we 'ad to get away, you know, properly away, where no one knew us, and nobody knew about 'enry. We thought being away from people we knew might give us a rest from the tea and sympathy. We booked a little flat for a couple of weeks 'ere, and this place got under our skin. The flat was free for another two weeks, so we decided to stay a bit longer. The doc had signed Caz off for two months. She were on tablets and everythin'. She were a shadow of 'er old self… I were a bit of a mess an'all, to be honest.

"Did it help, being away from all the tea and sympathy?"

"Yeah, it did. We just walked and walked and walked… Slowly, the grief started to feel…well, a bit less… harsh, I suppose."

Ged sat in silence but nodded in agreement.

"Well, something else happened, too," said Dennis.

"Oh?"

"Yeah… we went to the Seagull for dinner quite a lot. While we was there, Caz got chatting with Sharon. They really hit it off, as they both like a bit of art. Sharon asked her to come to her art group, and she started helping some of the budding Rembrandts, and…well, something seemed to click. Her spark came back a bit. I mean, we were both still heartbroken about Henry, but she were at least doin' somethin' *positive*. She started sketching and painting again, and it seemed to be healing her somehow. Her healing rubbed off on me. "

"So, you decided to move down here?"

"Yeah, well, there were nowt keeping us there, and we just felt rubbish when we went home. My Dad's been gone for years, and my mum moved in with a fella in Manchester. Caz's Auntie 'ad left her some money in 'er will, and the rest of the family are in Cardiff. They come 'ere on holiday every year. That's what made us think of it. We'd seen this 'ouse for sale, an' it had been on the market for a bit 'cos it was in such a state. Considerin' prices round 'ere, it was good value."

"You've done a great job with it," Ged remarked.

"Well, the guys from the art club have been great. One bloke 'elped with a bit of electrical stuff as I've not got a clue about that, and there was a bloke who did the roof with me and some joinery and tiling in return for art lessons – a bit like you – except he could use a hammer and saw."

Ged looked down at the plastic boot. "Sorry, I'd have been a lot more helpful without this blasted broken foot," he said. "I love doing this sort of thing." I've done a bit for some of the locals. It's got me a few free lunches. But this is my first art lesson in payment. I'm glad Sharon got us together. When I'm down in October and my foot's healed, I'll come and give you a proper hand."

"That'd be great. I won't get much done after t'kitchen as I'm startin' teachin' in September. I got a P.E. job up at the 'igh School in Helston. New start, new faces an' all that," he said. "Anyway, it's gone five; you'll be in trouble if you don't get in."

"You're right; I had better go in for dinner," said Ged, unclipping his seatbelt and donning his backpack. It has been a genuine pleasure to meet both you and Caroline. I hope we'll see you soon. Let me know if you run into any issues. I do electrics and plumbing, joinery… anything, really… I look after maintenance at a factory, so I've got a few tricks up my sleeve."

"Sharon said you was a man of all trades…er, Ged… I'd be grateful if you didn't spread what I told yer… we 'avent told anyone 'ere about 'enry… It all just spilled out jus' then."

"Mum's the word, Dennis; I promise I won't breathe a word.

***

Dinner was quiet. Marge had gone to bed with a headache. Brian had made chilli con carne, a Baker family favourite. Ged washed his hands and poured wine. Not much was said until tortillas had been handed around to mop up the last of the delicious sauce.

Ged listened with half an ear to the day's news as Brian served Raspberry Fool. The children had spent the afternoon with Sarah, building sand castles, rock hopping and beach combing at the far end of the beach, where few people went but where there were usually interesting things washed up on the rocks.

The children were tired and yawning after dessert. They had been watching a film before dinner, and Brian said they could finish watching if they got into their pyjamas and brushed their teeth in case they fell asleep on the sofa. Brian topped the wine glasses up as the children settled down on the sofa under the big tartan blanket.

"Everything okay, Dad? Asked Brian. "You were quiet over dinner. Is your foot hurting?"

"Oh, sorry, no, the foot's fine... just thinking," he said.

"Anything in particular?"

"I'm thinking how lucky I am," said Ged, staring out of the window at the bay.

"How so?"

"I have two healthy and talented sons, a lovely daughter-in-law, two smashing grandchildren, a good wife, a decent job... and a great house here in Cornwall," he said.

"Okay, Dad. What brought on the sudden attack of sentiment?" asked Sarah. "You normally only get mushy after a whole bottle of wine, and you've only managed half a glass. You hardly touched dessert."

"I suppose when you meet people who have it harder than you, it reminds you to count your blessings," he said.

"What, you mean Dennis and Caroline? They seemed like lovely people, but... There was something about those two that I couldn't quite put my finger on," said Sarah.

"Dennis told me something, but I made a promise I wouldn't tell anyone, and I mean to keep my word. They've had a tough time and moved down here for a new start. They just want to move on. So don't be offended if I don't say, but forgive me if I'm a bit quiet this evening."

"No offence taken, Dad. If you promised, then you promised," said Brian.

Sarah cleared the table and went to wash up; Ged fetched some newspaper and spread it out on the table. He asked Sarah for two glasses of water and got his watercolours out again.

He remembered to rest his foot on a chair to make sure the swelling went down. He spent an hour or so practising blending colours and trying out the layering technique that Caroline had demonstrated. With practice, he found shades which would work for sea and sand.

He took one of the sketches of the little girl being swung around by the teenage boy on the beach. He couldn't understand why, but as he wet the brush to apply it to the sketch, he felt …nervous… he could feel his heart beating, and he had butterflies in his stomach…

"You silly old fool, Baker… it's only a little sketch," he said to himself… "You can always draw it again if it doesn't work." He practised the brush strokes on his practice paper once more until he felt more confident that he could repeat it on the sketch, and then he smoothly drew the brush across the sea in the sketch.

It looked far too washed out, so he dipped his brush in the palette once more. Sarah came over with a cup of tea.

"Looks good… Do you have to let it dry or just keep adding 'til it's right?"

"I have to let it dry a bit first. Not bone dry, but until it's changed shade a bit." He drained his wine glass and gave it to Sarah. "Put the tea over here, away from my water pots, would you? I dipped my brush in it yesterday; that's why I had the accident… By the way, what have you done with the tablecloth?"

"Ah…" she said, winking and tapping her nose. "That's my little secret. I have my contacts down here, you know."

***

Ged applied another layer of turquoise-grey-green to his sketch, and then he used grey taupe for the beach colour. He left the colours light and subtle and began to work on a blue denim shade for the boy's jeans and a scarlet for the girl's skirt. He practised layering them on the practice paper using a smaller-headed brush. He took a deep breath and applied the colours to the sketch. Even though he had mixed a good amount of water into the blue, it applied as a vibrant cobalt. He didn't need a second layer. The scarlet took two layers before he was satisfied. He added a light green for the boy's shirt and a golden colour for the girl's top.

He sipped at his tea while he waited for the sketch – now a painting – to dry.

"That looks good, Dad," said Brian, who had come over to the dining table for a peek at Ged's efforts. "Are you going to do more to it?"

"I think I'll leave it there," he said, regarding what he had done. "I like this unfinished style. My art teacher at school would have had a fit, leaving a painting unfinished, but I like the way that leaving out irrelevant stuff makes you look at the action."

"It reminds me of my old Beatrix Potter books but with less detail."

Ged recalled the set of little white books that he would read to Brian and his brother Edward, with their vibrant illustrations. Beatrix had drawn and painted all of the illustrations herself in her unique, detailed, delicate style.

He drew the scene again, this time with a few specks of sand to give the beach more texture, rocks here and there, a ribbon in the girl's hair flying out, and a suggestion of ripples on the sea. He gave the boy more muscular arms and lines, which suggested a little more strain in his neck to show that he was resisting the girl's weight as she spun. He gave the girl a laughing mouth and added loose curls to her hair as he noticed Alice's braids as she slept.

He added watercolour as before, this time altering the depth of the colour to create shadow and highlights.

The second attempt was a little better than the first, but was it as good as it could be? He sketched the scene again, adding ruffles and folds in the boy's shirt, shells, and more rocks. As a little bit of fun, he sketched a tiny lobster in the rock pool. Would anyone notice it?

This time, he was more confident and didn't practise his brush strokes on the practice paper. The sea and sand quickly took shape, but the cobalt palette had dried, and when he applied it to the sketch, it was much too dark.

He screwed up the paper, and the blue transferred to his fingers. "Drat," he muttered… "…should've waited for it to dry."

He drained his now lukewarm tea, dipped his blue-stained fingers in the brush-washing pot and wiped them on the rag. He decided he had had enough of painting for one evening. He wanted to relax and draw.

On the last four pages of his sketchbook, he tried a couple of scenes of what he could remember of the souvenir shop lady rushing in and out of the shop, gathering wetsuits, bodyboards, buckets and spades. The lady in his sketches was much more bothered by the weather than the actual shopkeeper. In one sketch, her sarong had whipped up and got tangled in the bucket handles; the spades had clattered to the floor, and her hair was flying about her face so much that she could barely have seen where she was going. In another scene, the wind was blowing so fiercely that the body-boards were being blown about like kites, and she was attempting to tame them while trying to stop all the buckets from rolling down the road.

He was enjoying himself. He drew Pirate Pete once more, but this time, he was reclining in his boat with a pasty in one hand and a can of beer in the other. He scribbled one of his favourite wise sayings as a caption below the sketch… "Give a man a fish, and he will eat for a day; Teach a man to fish, and he will sit in a boat drinking beer."

Brian carried the now fast-asleep Alice to bed and returned for Jamie, who had woken and come over to Ged. His Grandfather hugged him and planted a kiss on his brown curls. "Goodnight, Jamie. Sleep well." Jamie yawned,

"Night, Grandad… I like that one of Pirate Pete! You'll need a new pad tomorrow."

"Thanks, Jamie; I do need a new pad if I'm going to do any more," he replied. "I had better buy a bag so that Alice can have her backpack too. Would you like to come to the shop with me tomorrow?"

"Yes, please, I need new jellybean shoes. Dad said he would buy some."

"Let's go after breakfast. I'll take you and Alice for cake at the café if you like."

"Ooh, yes, please; I like Sharon's cakes. Bill is really funny…er, Grandad… "said Jamie, a little more uncertain this time. "Could we have breakfast or dinner there?"

"That would be nice – but why so timid about it?"

"Well, I'm not sure Nana would want to go."

"Don't worry about Nana; let me worry about that," said Ged as he hugged Jamie.

Ged bundled the brushes, pencils and watercolours into the backpack, making a mental note to buy a case for the brushes as Caroline suggested. Leaving the bag and the sketches on the table, he heaved himself up on his crutches and took another appraising look at what he had achieved so far with the watercolours... *"Hmm, there's a way to go yet, but it's not a bad start, I suppose,"* he mused.

17

The morning brought a soft blanket of white cloud, which seemed to flatten every surface. Ged's foot was feeling better, and he hopped to the kitchen with one crutch.

He helped Sarah to get breakfast ready and made tea to take in to Marge. Sarah carried the tray for him as he climbed back into bed and planted a kiss on Marge's forehead. "Morning, beautiful," he murmured.

"For goodness' sake, Gerald, don't be ridiculous!" scolded Marge.

"Ged sighed and sat back, stung by her rebuke, sipping his tea, and regarded Porthcovery waking up out of their bedroom window. There was always something to notice: A woman in a bright yellow raincoat walking her Dalmatian dog on the beach, throwing a tennis ball into the waves for it to swim after. Each time the dog retrieved the ball, it would bound over the waves to the woman, drop the ball, and bark twice; each time he did this, the woman would fondle his ears, and the cycle began again. After five, or was it six, times, the Dalmatian held onto the ball; the woman fondled his ears and clipped on his leash, heading for the steps leading up to the road. This woman and her attractive hound had a clear understanding.

Marge still hadn't sat up in bed for her tea as usual. She had turned over in bed, facing away from the window.

"Are you alright?" asked Ged.

"No, would you shut the curtains? I have a headache, and the light hurts my eyes."

He reached out of bed to pull the curtains across.

"Don't you want your tea?"

"No, I'd have thought that was obvious," she replied tersely. "You can fetch some headache tablets and a glass of water if you want to be useful."

Ged took another deep breath. Even when she was ill, Marge wasn't usually so brusque. Her manner and tone were bordering on rude. He drank his tea and got out of bed to dress.

"Now, if you don't mind," muttered Marge, "you can get dressed afterwards."

"Okay, Love," he said, mustering all his patience.

***

Marge didn't join them for breakfast. Ged had fetched a cool, damp cloth to place on her forehead when he took the tablets in, but she had brushed it away irritably.

"Mum still feeling poorly?" asked Sarah.

"Yes, and she's not in a good mood. I think a beach day would be best if the tide will let us, or we could take the kids to the harbour," suggested Ged.

"Let's go to Bill and Sharon's for dinner this evening, Dad," said Brian. "I've not spoken to Bill all week; I hear he has a new toy!"

"Oh yes, the new coffee machine! ... he is rather proud of it... though if he keeps drinking those buckets of coffee, I don't think he will make much profit, and he won't sleep for months! I'll book a table for six."

The family gathered everything they would need for a harbour day, including wetsuits, snorkels, and goggles for the kids. Jamie and Alice asked if they could rent a kayak. Brian agreed to rent one, and Ged would meet them at the harbour after he had been to the café.

Before they left, Ged looked in on Marge. She was asleep with the crossword on her lap. He reached over and slipped off her glasses, placing them carefully on the bedside cabinet, then made sure she was comfortable. He decided to leave a note for her. Tearing off a piece of practice paper from the pad in his bag, he took her crossword pen and printed:

'Gone to Seagull Café, then harbour. Join us there if you feel better; otherwise, we'll be back mid-afternoon. Dinner at Seagull tonight at 6. Love Ged x'.

He placed the note under her glasses so that she wouldn't miss it, took up his crutches and went to join the others. He spoke to Alice as he met them by the garden gate. "I've been using your backpack for my art things, and you haven't complained once. You're very kind to lend it to me, but I think I should let you have it back." I was going to the shop to get a new bag for my things. Would you like to come with me?"

"Yes, please, Grandad, I like that shop."

Alice skipped ahead with Brian while Jamie strolled with Ged. They arrived at the shop to find Alice with a beaming smile and a fantastically glittery purple rucksack with Disney's Little Mermaid on its front pocket in her hand. "Grandad, have you seen this? It's beautiful! I won't need my backpack if you buy me this one; you can keep it!"

"Er…that wasn't what I had in mind, actually, Alice. I was looking for something slightly less – um… pink… But let's hang on to this one in case I can't find anything." Alice handed him the mermaid rucksack. "Four pounds fifty… hmm, not bad." He already had a feeling that the shop wouldn't stock anything suitable for him and had foreseen this possibility.

"I've looked all around the shop, and I can't see anything that's really 'you', Grandad," said Alice with her hands on her hips, an earnest look on her face. "I mean, you have to have a backpack because of your crutches, and all the grown-up rucksacks are those big picnic sets with forks and spoons and plates and everything, so I think this might be the best *collusion*."

"If that's the best solution, Alice," he said, grinning and winking at Jamie. I admit, I've become quite attached to this one – he said, patting the old backpack." He made a show of looking around the shop carefully for something else, but a cursory glance told him that Alice had, indeed, checked out all the alternatives, and the only things available were large picnic sets, which were too bulky and impractical, not to mention a waste of money. Like the wooden art set, he would have to take most of the stuff out of the backpack to make it useful. He realised that a rainbow unicorn pink and purple backpack suited his requirements perfectly.

"Okay, purple sparkle mermaid rucksack it is," he said, putting his hand out for Alice to shake and seal the deal. "Anything for you, Jamie? I'll get you the jellybean shoes you need and … I've not given you both your holiday money yet…you can have five pounds each, and you don't have to buy sensible things with it, but…" he lowered his voice to a whisper and winked at Brian, who was standing nearby, "don't tell Nana."

Jamie and Alice began to whisper in earnest, nodding vigorously and giving each other a high five. Spokesman Jamie was sent to negotiate… "Actually, Grandad, we saw some bodyboards outside the shop. They're only ten pounds… can we have one between us?"

"Great idea! Go and choose one…well, that is, if you can agree on a colour." He had seen that there were only blue or green boards outside, so hopefully, there would be no arguments with Alice insisting on a pink one and Jamie refusing. He was relieved when the children returned in seconds, brandishing a bright blue bodyboard with a sweeping black motif.

He picked up a new watercolour sketchbook and paid for everything.

"Who's ready for a cake at Bill and Sharon's, you two?" said Ged as they left the shop.

"No thanks, Grandad, we want to try out the bodyboard."

"OK. I could do with a sit-down; you two go to the harbour with Dad."

Sarah had come to the café for some takeaway coffees. She was chatting with Bill when Ged and the children arrived.

"Have you been melting your credit card again?" she said, grinning at the bodyboard.

"Alice and I have come to a negotiated settlement on unicorn backpack ownership, and the children have thought of a great way to spend their holiday money."

"So I see…Wow, guys, that board looks cool!"

"Can we ride it at the harbour?" said Jamie. "I know there are no waves, but we saw some children pulling each other around on one yesterday, and it looks fun."

"Of course, the tide is going out. We'll take it on the beach later."

Ged took a table at the side of the café verandah in the shade. Bill and Sharon were serving breakfasts and morning coffees. Sharon caught Ged's eye and called,

"Cappuccino?"

"Yes, please, Sharon, but no rush," he called back.

He arranged a second chair to rest his foot on. Although it wasn't a very sunny day, it was warm. His foot felt sweaty and itchy. He removed the boot and rested his bare foot on the chair. The bruising had developed over the last few days and now sported a murky palette of deep blue, purple, and yellow, with an orange and lime green blend at the edges. It was swollen and not at all pretty. He shifted position, sliding the chair under the table, replacing his foot on it, out of sight, then leaned back into the moulded white plastic chair.

Across the little cinder lane which climbed up the hill by the Café, he spotted a large brown tabby cat sitting neatly on a cottage windowsill in the sunshine; apparently, master of all he surveyed. It seemed to regard Ged critically, as cats tend to do. After a few seconds of careful scrutiny, clearly satisfied that Ged was neither a threat nor particularly interesting, the cat closed its eyes and proceeded to wash its shoulder.

Ged unzipped the backpack and took out the sketch pad and pencil. He couldn't remember drawing animals much before, and it took a while to decide where to begin. On this cat, the place to start seemed to be the eyes, but every time he looked up and began to draw them, the cat would turn its head away or close its eyes. The cat's form took shape beneath his pencil, surprisingly naturally. He used harder pencils to gradually build up the tabby pattern of its fur and then used softer pencils with a light touch to define the deeper tabby stripes.

The cat settled down on the windowsill, tucking its nose behind a rear paw. Ged started a sketch on another page, looking up frequently to make sure he was getting the form and details: the pads of its feet, the ripped edge of an ear, the stripes on its tail. He drew the cat with its eyes shut. He wished it would wake up; this cat had such knowing eyes. He was dying to draw them, but the cat stayed stubbornly in repose. After a few minutes, he noticed its pink tongue was stuck out and decided to add that detail for comic effect.

"I didn't know you were a cat person, Chippy." Bill looked over Ged's shoulder as he passed behind his chair. He placed a large cappuccino and his own huge pint mug of coffee on the table and sat down next to him.

"Neither did I until now," Ged replied.

"Not a bad sketch of old Potts there, though it would be better if he was awake. He's got wisdom in those eyes... like he knows something we don't."

"I was thinking that too. I'll take my time over my coffee and see if he wakes up."

"Not a chance, my landlubber, 'ee sleeps for hours on that windowsill, poor old bugger. Viv is so upset. He's not too good on his legs now."

"Poor thing, maybe another day then, did you say, Val? Is she a friend of Tracy's?"

"Yeah, why d'you ask?"

"I was in the shop earlier in the week and heard her talking to Tracy about Potts. It sounded like it was on its last legs; it doesn't look too bad from here."

"Arthritis," said Bill. "Back legs keep goin' under 'im. She 'as to keep 'im inside, and 'ee don't like usin' a litter tray... Poor Val is going nuts cleanin' up after 'im."

"Tell her to try garden compost on top of the cat litter," said Ged. "A fella at work says he uses cheap compost. Says his cat likes it better than litter. Feels like it's out in the garden, I suppose."

"I'll tell 'er when I see 'er," said Bill.

"How are you? You look busy today despite this overcast weather."

"Can't complain; that nice Danish couple come 'ere for breakfast with the other Windsurfers. They meet 'ere to fuel up with a full Cornish before goin' to freeze their arses off. All mad if you ask me! Why stand on a plank waiting to fall off and get a crack on the head from a mast when you can sail a good, honest boat round the corner and go fishing?"

"Fishing, eh, Bill?" called Sharon. "Is that what you do on your boat trips round the headland? You're not very good at it, judging by how much Bass and Pollock we get for dinner service. Maybe you should take mackerel as bait rather than a few tins of Stella!"

Ged chuckled at this exchange... so his favourite Cornish saying about teaching a man to fish was accurate, after all.

"Business is good, Ged," said Sharon, "but we don't have a magic washing-up fairy, and there's a mountain of pots the size of Everest in that kitchen, so don't be long, eh Bill?"

"Right-ho, Sharon, be there drekly," he called after her.

(*'Drekly'* – for those that are not familiar with Cornish parlance, is a Cornish measure of time describing anything between – in the next 5 minutes and the next 5 months)

"That's my least favourite job after cleanin' the loo," he grumbled.

"Pity you don't have one of those speedy dishwashers they have in restaurants, Bill. We have two at the factory. They get the plates and glasses done in seconds!"

"Not enough room in that kitchen," Bill replied regretfully. "We had to put the coffee machine out 'ere as there's no room in the kitchen for it. Can't swing a cat in there."

"Mmm, I remember," said Ged, thinking of the time he had when he was fitting new taps on the sink in there. "Best go and get your apron on, or the boss will dock your pay.

Bill stood up and drained his massive cup. "What pay?" he said, winking.

Ged took a languorous slurp of Cappuccino and turned his attention to the cat once more. It was yawning and licking its lips occasionally. When the yawn was finished, his eyes opened, and Ged was able to get a better look.

Sharon swished past the table to clear the last of the breakfast tables, which were being vacated by the windsurfers, all apparently off for their lesson. "Sharon, don't tell the missus, but could I have a slice of that fab carrot cake?"

"Sure. I'll clear these tables and fetch one... and I won't tell Mrs B," she said with a grin. "That's a lovely drawing of Potts. It's a shame he's got his eyes shut – poor old thing. He's been a fantastic mouser...."

I never had a nibble in our store room with him patrolling," she said, gazing at Potts with her head on one side. "He's not got the energy any more. If Val and Jen don't get another cat, I'll 'ave to get one of my own."

"Sharon, do you have any photos of Potts that you've taken over the years?"

"Plenty. He likes posing, the big, soft tart," she said. "There's a framed one inside. I'll bring it out with your cake."

"Can I book a table for dinner tonight?"

"I think we can squeeze you in… early table so the kids can get to bed?"

"Great! Yes, six-ish or just before."

"See you at a quarter to six. I'll go get you that cake and the picture."

18

Marge was up by the time the family tumbled into the house, laughing and joking about the harbour antics of the children and their parents. Brian had given the children rides on their bodyboards in the shallow waves. He pulled the board along like a sledge. Alice had knelt on the board on all fours and spent most of the time with her eyes shut until Sarah got her to wear goggles. Jamie had pretended to be a surfer, standing up on the board with his knees bent and arms out for balance. He lasted no more than a few seconds before falling off, with Sarah shrieking, "Wipeout!" Every time, he fell off. On one occasion, Brian had tripped over and got his shirt and shorts soaked and covered in sand. He had even managed to get seaweed caught in his hair, which Sarah picked out before he got into trouble with his mother for dropping it on the carpet.

Marge looked pale. She was trimming a climbing rose around the porch with her beautifully oiled secateurs. As the family returned, she folded them and clipped the stay.

"Where on earth has everyone been?" she snapped. Looking first at Sarah, then at Ged.

"I left a note... under your glasses on the bedside cabinet," said Ged. "Did you see it?

"Well, if I had seen it, then I wouldn't have asked, would I?" she retorted.

"We've been to the Harbour and the beach, Mum," said Brian. "We thought we'd let you sleep."

"Well, you should have told me where you were going. I might have wanted to go."

"Mum, you hate it there. You are always complaining about the smell of the seaweed," continued Brian.

"That's as may be, Brian, but it's only good manners to allow me the courtesy of deciding that for myself instead of deciding it for me." Marge scolded pompously.

"Well, I'm sorry I didn't tell you, Mum." Said Brian, deciding that an apology was the better part of valour with his mother. "Did you find the chicken sandwich left out for you?"

"Of course I found it! Why on earth did you put all that revolting, slimy avocado in it? I made it quite clear that I did not like it last night, but no one listens, do they? Just do what you like; don't ask Marge; she'll just have to put up with what she's given!"

"I thought you liked the avocado, Mum. Once I made everything into a salad, you ate it, and you didn't leave any avocado. I thought it was just the presentation that you had a problem with," said Brian, more than a little taken aback at the way his mother was reprimanding him. She rarely had a cross word to say to him.

"Well, I *don't* like it. Your father can make me a plain chicken sandwich in future," she said curtly and stalked off to the little shed.

Ged, Brian and Sarah exchanged glances.

"Mummy," said Alice quietly, "Why is Nana being mean? She never tells Daddy off."

Sarah knelt down and gave Alice a hug. "I have absolutely no idea; maybe she isn't feeling very well. I think it's best if we give her plenty of space and peace and quiet. Shall we do a bit more of that jigsaw?"

"Okay," said Alice, kicking off her shoes and taking her new bag upstairs.

Ged came out of his room, holding the note he had written that morning. He went to find Brian in the kitchen. "I found this note exactly where I left it on the bedside cabinet. I put it under your Mum's glasses so she couldn't miss it. I don't get it; she must have seen the note," he said quietly to Brian.

"So why did she say she hadn't? Listen, Dad," said Brian, looking earnestly at his father, "Mum is well out of order, you know? These outbursts, being so rude to Emily at the Lobster Pot, that huge rant yesterday, and now this tongue-lashing I just had. Can you have a word with her? It's making the atmosphere tense, and the kids are starting to get scared of their Nana."

Ged didn't know what to say. Marge had been acting even more 'Marge-ish' than usual this week. He resolved to find a good time to talk with her.

The children went upstairs with Sarah for a shower; Brian washed the wetsuits and new bodyboard with the hosepipe outside.

When Alice and Jamie came downstairs, they sat at the dining table with Sarah and carried on with the Jigsaw. Ged tried to join in, but he couldn't concentrate. He needed to talk to Marge. They hadn't told her about the arrangements for the evening meal yet, and he didn't want her to insult Bill or Sharon as she had Emily.

He found her with the newspaper on her lap on the bench in the front garden. She appeared to be reading it, but as he sat down next to her, he could see that she was simply staring down at the paper with her pencil in her hand, looking like a lost child. There were dark spots on the newspaper. Tears dripped off the end of her nose, and she made no attempt to wipe them away. Ged pulled a pack of tissues from his pocket and handed one to her. At first, she angrily batted it away with her hand, but then took it, dabbed her nose, and dried her eyes.

"Hey, lovely Margie..." Ged said softly. "I know this holiday is a bit of an odd one with my foot and everything." Marge interrupted, speaking through gritted teeth:

"Odd one... You think? Well, I don't think there's much odd about it. I mean, it's not so different from other holidays – you, Brian, Sarah, and the children are having lots of fun, and I just slave away in the garden and have to put up with whatever you all want to do. I do all that work, but I'm always left out of the decisions. Sarah tells me you've booked a table at that awful café this evening. What if I don't want to go? Once again. Marjorie is the odd one out!" She sighed, tears falling onto the paper once more.

Ged realised that she did have a point. They hadn't asked her before booking the Seagull for dinner that evening. Plus, he decided that an apology was the better part of valour.

"Oh, my lovely Margie, you're right. We should include you in the decisions. You *have* worked hard in the garden, and it shows. All the holiday rental people will love it! I suppose, as you don't seem to like going to the beach or the harbour much, we just assumed you like being in the garden and doing the crossword or reading."

"I do, but I've always felt like the odd one out. I have all my life. Nobody properly liked me at school or college, except for Jean. Even my family didn't like me much, except, of course, dear Daddy; well, you remember him," she said fondly.

"Oh, I remember him alright," said Ged ruefully.

***

Marge's Father, Cllr James T. Cookson, was stricter than strict. He would be considered a control freak these days and probably off the OCD scale. It was his way or no way at all. At breakfast or dinner times, dress code, manners, and etiquette had to be observed. Their annual holiday in Scotland was always in May (he did not want his daughters even seeing anyone in a bikini, let alone wear one).

Sunday was Holy Communion at the Pentecostal church in Warwick, followed by a small cone at the local ice cream parlour and a bracing country walk. Marge's mother would have a roast dinner ready by two p.m. sharp. In the afternoon, they would read the Bible, chapters and verses dictated by Cllr Cookson.

Marge was doted on by her father. Not in a kind and empathetic way, but by educating her. He taught her to read and play the piano and even taught her to dance *'like a lady should dance,'* as he put it. A little waltz… 'none of that Latin filth.' Their connection was strongest in the garden. As a girl, she spent hours with him, tending their garden, pruning roses, watering, feeding, snipping and trimming the shrubs and, in the summer, planting neat arrangements of annuals. Time with her mother would be spent doing flower arrangements, laundry, cooking a meal, or sewing in the dining room.

Annie, on the other hand, had been considered 'A difficult child' as Marge often put it, spending most of her time with their maternal Grandmother at her flat in town. The old grandmother had explained to Ged that Marge's mother had postnatal depression after Annie's birth. She never truly bonded with her. There was no proper diagnosis or treatment. Cllr. Cookson's response was: "Buck up, Dorothy…I said we shouldn't have another one; your mother will help look after the child." Grandmama agreed to look after Annie to help her daughter get over the birth. The arrangement had ended up being much more.

Ged was wary of Cllr Cookson and felt like a schoolchild in his presence. He assumed that role whenever he went to see Marge or to take her out 'for a walk'. Cllr Cookson would regard Ged sternly over half-moon reading glasses as if determining his worth. On their first meeting, he asked him what he did for a living and how he would keep Marge if they married with such a paltry salary. Was he going to get a promotion at the upholstery firm, or would he apply for a job at Jenson's, the furniture maker?

Marge's father referred to Ged as 'Boy' to his face and as 'That Boy' when referring to him in the third person. He would tell him that his tie wasn't straight or that his shoes needed polishing and would ask him, "What sort of impression did that give other people?" On one occasion, when Ged had saved up for months to buy himself a new leather Jacket, Cllr Cookson took one look at him when he wore it for a meal at the Cookson's and declared that he looked like *one of those thugs he had just sentenced in court*. He told him to take it off and lent him a tweed sports jacket to wear for the evening. The brand-new leather jacket had to go in the bin. (Before they went home, Ged had rescued it from the bin and secreted it in the boot of his car.) No small wonder that after they were married, Ged encouraged Marge to visit her parents while he was at work and avoided visiting them himself if possible.

***

Ged shuddered at this memory. He made the grave error of trying to be conciliatory and positive: "Brian does most of the cooking, and when I'm not stuck with this silly boot, I do plenty of jobs around the place. Sarah makes sure all the laundry is done and looks after the house. With you doing the garden, we make a good team."

"What if I want to cook? No one is going to pick up the garden work, are they?"

'They wouldn't dare!' Thought Ged… "No, that's true, except for tidying up and general bits and pieces. I don't think any of us would do it as well as you."

"Well, you *would* make a mess of it. None of you knows the difference between a weed and a perennial!" she said hotly. "But no one ever offers a word of thanks for the work I do."

Ged knew better than to argue. He had accepted this last time she mentioned it. "Well, I'm thanking you now, my lovely, green-fingered Margie. You have done a wonderful job. It looks good enough for the Duke of Cornwall to take tea in."

"Oh, now I *remind* you to say thank you. You manage it. Sarah and Brian just take it for granted that it will get done," she grumbled.

"Well, judging by their garden at home, except for growing Brian's unusual herbs and vegetables, I don't think gardening is really their thing. They just have the veg garden at the back with a lawn for the kids to play on."

"Exactly!" snapped Marge. "They don't appreciate the importance of a presentable garden. So, they don't appreciate the work I have to put into it.

Ged stayed quiet for a minute or two. Any response he made was simply going to be met with more scorn. This wasn't the right time to 'Have a word with her' about her rudeness. He had to broach the subject of the evening meal, though, so he gave it his best shot.

"About this evening's dinner arrangements…" he began.

"What about them?" she said curtly.

"Well, it's booked for the family, but if you want to stay here and…"

"Stay here on my own, and you'll bring me something back?" she snapped. "Have dinner by myself, here, while you all go and have a nice, jovial family meal cooked by that awful fat slob and served by his tart of a wife at the café?"

Ged winced. Bill and Sharon were his friends, and Marge was making judgments when she barely knew them. She was her father's daughter, alright.

"Actually, I like Bill and Sharon. But I was thinking we could have a candlelit supper together here, just like we used to when the children were little. I can whip up a Spanish omelette and salad, and we could enjoy some of that white Rioja, maybe watch something on the telly, or even have a game of backgammon."

"Well, it's better than greasy chicken and chips at the café," she said, beginning to soften.

Ged loved Bill's roast chicken and dearly hoped that he would find a way to have some during their stay, but it wouldn't be tonight. He didn't like to risk the alternative possibility of Marge going to the café under duress and insulting two of the nicest people in Porthcovery.

"I'll go up to the café now and change the booking to four. Would you like me to bring back a nice coffee for you to have with your Brownie?"

"Certainly not, Gerald. I don't like coffee. I would rather have tea."

"Tea it is," said Ged.

"From our kitchen," glowered Marge.

"Right-ho," said Ged, taking another deep, calming breath.

***

Sarah and Brian helped Ged prepare supper, laying the table and making a salad whilst Ged pottered in the kitchen, making a Spanish tortilla of potatoes, ham, mushrooms, and tomatoes. He even recruited Jamie and Alice, asking them to see what herbs they could find in the garden. They returned with oregano, marjoram, and chives.

"Well, aren't you two just chips off the old block?" he said, giving them both a little hug as they each proudly put a fistful of herbs on the counter.

"I want to stay here and have tortilla, Grandad," said Jamie.

"But I'm serving it with loads of salad," he said, screwing his face up in mock disgust… "And no chips!"

"But you always make chips, Grandad."

"Not when it's just Nana and me," he said. "There are plenty of potatoes in the omelette. I only do chips as a treat for you two."

"Oh," they both said, looking at each other as if to say: "*Is he mad?*"

"Why aren't you coming to the café?" said Alice. "I thought Bill was your friend."

"He is, Alice. I like Bill and Sharon very much, but I have been to the café lots of times this week, and I haven't had a romantic meal with Nana in ages."

"Is it because Nana might be rude to Bill and Sharon like she was to Emily at the Lobster Pot, Grandad?" said Alice.

Ged spluttered as he took a sip of his tea. "Well, Alice, you really like to say it how you see it, don't you?" He took another slurp of his tea while he thought of a suitable response. "Some opinions should stay in your head as offering them can offend."

"What?"

"It means don't be rude about your Nana, young lady," said Brian, looking at her sternly. "Come on, time to go."

***

Ged lit a candle on the table and hobbled to the kitchen to fetch the tortilla. Everything else was laid on the table, so it and the wine were the only things to get.

"Dinner's ready, Marge!" he called up the stairs.

She came down the stairs in a long green dress and was wearing her pearl necklace. She wasn't quite the slender beauty that he fell in love with all those years ago, but she had lost some weight recently, and Ged was always captivated by her curves. Especially in that dress!

"You look beautiful, Marge," he said sincerely.

"Don't be ridiculous, Gerald," she scolded. "I simply thought that I should dress for dinner."

Ged mentally brushed off this minor rebuke and set the tortilla on the table.

"Could you fetch the wine from the fridge, my love?" He asked.

"Are you doing the supper or am I?" she chided.

"Everything is ready now, and I'm going to serve the tortilla. I wondered if you could get the wine, as my foot hurts from standing so long.

Marge let out an audible sigh "Oh, that blasted foot!" She grumbled. "Very well."

The tortilla was delicious—firm, easy to cut into slices, moist without being soggy, and nicely seasoned. Brian had made a honey, balsamic and lemon dressing for the salad and the white Rioja suited it perfectly. Marge offered no opinion about the food but made small talk about the weather and how she wanted to replace some roses in the garden as they were getting old. She spoke at length about a couple she had spotted who were staying in the Loft cottage and appeared to have a very nice Jaguar car; then, she asked Ged if he had spotted the Catamaran anchored in the bay.

"It could be someone famous," she conjectured. "Porthcovery seems to be becoming fashionable, what, with that famous actor – what's his name again? Something – Terris is buying a second home here."

"You mean Charlie Terris, the comedian?" inquired Ged.

"Yes, that's him. His wife writes children's books, doesn't she?"

"No idea," Ged replied. "I don't really pay attention to all that."

"Oh, honestly, Gerald, you're not in touch!"

"No, I'm not. Being an actor or a writer is a way of making a living. I respect that. But everyone needs a break. If the Queen had a place here, I'd leave her alone and let her enjoy her holiday. I expect Charlie Terris bought a place here because it's quiet and off the beaten track. He's probably hoping that he doesn't get hassled for his autograph."

Marge sighed and gave him a patronising, somewhat sympathetic look. "Really, Gerald, actors and comedians are attention-seekers! They love it when people come up and ask for their autograph or to have a picture taken with them."

"I suppose there are some 'luvvies' who can't get enough of all that," he replied. "A conceited bunch – and I wouldn't give them the time of day, but I reckon a lot of actors and comedians do that job so they can wear a mask because they don't like to show their real selves to anyone but their nearest and dearest. So, if Bob Geldof and his family were here, minding their own business at the harbour, having an ice cream, I'd probably leave them alone."

Marge shook her head. "Oh, Gerald, bless you, you're such a saint," she said sarcastically, looking down and prodding her salad.

"Thanks...I think," said Ged.

He stared out of the bay window. Marge was speculating about the couple with the new Jaguar again. Ged tuned out for a minute. 'Keeping up with the Jones's means you have to know who the Jones's are.' Ged thought to himself. And that was one of Marge's favourite activities: She had been well-coached by her parents to sort people into their proper social categories. *'High class'* and therefore, out of reach; *'Nice, decent people'*, into which category she included herself and her parents, with Ged just skimming the edge; *'Common* or *ordinary people'* – not worth bothering with and *'neer-do-wells'* whom Marge would avoid at all costs.

Ged tended to take people as he found them. He was often amused by how the car a person stepped out of somehow helped Marge to decide which category they belonged in. In his opinion, there were plenty of morons who drove shiny Mercedes and Jaguars (firmly placed in Marge's *'nice, decent people'* category), and he had encountered a good number of truly decent people who wore faded jeans and drove rusty old Fords who would be lucky to get into her *'Common as muck'* box.

When Marge had finished declaring her assumptions about the couple with the Jaguar, he told her about Rita and Chris.

"I've met the people with the Catamaran. Danish couple: Rita and Chris. I think they have a teenage daughter. They sailed the boat over here and are anchored in the bay whilst they learn to windsurf."

"Really?" said Marge, swivelling her head like a meerkat. "Their own yacht? Well, *they* mustn't be doing too badly if they can afford a boat like that."

"I suppose so," replied Ged, wishing she wasn't such an overt social climber.

"How did *you* come to meet them?" asked Marge.

"They were having breakfast at the café. It looks like they and the other windsurfers have breakfast there every morning before the lesson."

"I see," said Marge, looking thoughtful as she stared out of the window at the white, twin-hulled yacht. It positively glowed in the evening sun, gently swaying on the swell. It was anchored port-side to the coast, and there was a light on in the cabin. Ged thought of Rita and Chris having a glass of wine in their cosy galley and how lovely that must be. It was a shame Marge got seasick, or she'd be figuring out a way to get an invitation!

Ged had finished his meal. He stiffly pushed himself up from his chair. He had been standing far too long making the tortilla and needed to move. "Are you finished?" he said, looking at her half-eaten tortilla and salad. Shall I cover that for supper if you don't fancy it now?"

"You gave me too much; Gerald and I don't like Parma ham. You should use bacon."

Ged took a deep breath, saying nothing. He gathered up the cutlery and plates and held them in one hand so that the other was free for his crutch. Marge made no move to help. She sipped her wine and looked out of the window. Ged hobbled to the kitchen. His foot was throbbing; he needed painkillers and an early night, but he knew better than to break with protocol.

"Do you want pudding, Marge?" he called.

"Dessert, Gerald, please."

"Would you like *Dessert*, Marge? It's rum and raisin ice cream, your favourite."

"I suppose it will do. Are you making a cup of tea?"

"Of course," said Ged, switching on the kettle. Brian or Sarah had half-filled the kettle and placed a jug of milk and cups on a tray. He would have to ask Marge to get the tray. He didn't trust himself to manage a coffee tray in one hand.

"Marge, could you bring the tray while I get dessert?"

"Good grief, Gerald, must I do everything? You are supposed to be treating me!"

He felt his jaw tighten, but took another calming breath.

Ged had prepared two small servings of ice cream and left them in the refrigerator to soften before dinner. They were now creamy and smooth, just the way Marge had always loved ice cream. Ged took the two ramekin bowls in one hand and carried them to the table, putting them down, somewhat awkwardly, in front of Marge.

"What's that?" she asked sharply.

"Rum and Raisin Ice Cream."

"It's almost liquid! I'll need a straw to eat that, or it will be all over my dress!"

"You've always liked ice cream a bit melted, Marge."

"Don't be ridiculous, Gerald. There's a difference between soft and not even frozen!"

Ged sighed. "I'll put it back in the freezer for a few minutes if you prefer."

"No, don't bother. I'll manage, I suppose," she said, picking up her spoon.

Ged sat down and closed his eyes for a moment. This was not the romantic meal he had planned, but at least Marge wasn't insulting Bill and Sharon. *"Small mercies, Ged,"* he reminded himself, picking up his spoon.

19

"Morning, everyone!" sang Marge as she swayed into the kitchen in a powder-blue summer dress with a lilac daisy print. She had put her hair in a neat bun at the back and carried a brimmed straw hat with a blue ribbon. She looked ready for a day out at the races.

"Morning, Mum," said Brian, quizzically looking at Ged, "Where are you dressed up for?"

"What – oh, this old thing?" she said, brushing her hand dismissively against the skirt of her dress. "Well, now that I've finished in the garden for the time being, I don't have to wear my scruffs. I thought I'd join your father for a coffee at the Café this morning."

Ged nearly choked on his scrambled egg.

Brian stopped pouring water into the teapot and turned to his mother.

"Really? I thought you hated Italian coffee, Mum!" He said, exchanging glances with Ged.

"I do occasionally have a cappuccino with Annie at Marks and Spencer."

Brian and Ged gave each other a look of mild bewilderment. Marge took the teapot to the table and poured herself a cup.

"Oh, Brian, the milk bottle is on the table again! How many times must I tell you how very '*common*' that is? Put it in a jug!"

"It's just extra washing up, Mum, and I'm on holiday."

"It's manners, Brian. Gerald, would you please pass a jug from the cupboard?"

Ged sighed, got up from his chair and opened the cupboard to fetch one.

"Mum – why did you ask Dad to get it?"

"He's nearest to the cupboard," she said, taking a piece of toast from the pile on a plate in the centre of the table. "Don't we have a proper toast rack?"

"No," said Brian. "He has a broken foot! Or had you forgotten?"

"No, *Brian*, I had not *forgotten*," said Marge irritably, "But he manages to get down to the café and the gift shop well enough; I'm sure a few feet to the cupboard won't kill him."

"Brian, it's okay. I can get a jug. I'm not a total invalid."

"Sorry, Dad, I know you're not. I didn't mean – you're supposed to keep your weight off your foot, or it won't heal, and you were standing up all afternoon making that tortilla."

"That reminds me, Mum," chirped Sarah, changing the subject, "how was the tortilla? It smelled gorgeous!"

"Pardon, Sarah?" Marge looked up from her tea, apparently deep in thought.

"The tortilla Dad made for your dinner yesterday. How was it?"

"Oh – fine," was all Marge had to say.

"There's half of it still left in the fridge if you want some," said Ged.

"Thanks, I can't wait to try it," said Sarah.

Brian got the plate from the refrigerator and removed the tinfoil. The tortilla had shrunk a little, and there were droplets of condensation on the surface, but it smelled tremendous. He cut two slices and placed them in the skillet on the stove.

The children came running in from the back garden with their wetsuits on.

"That smells nice, Dad. Is that breakfast?" said Alice.

"If you like," said Brian, scooping a slice of tortilla onto a plate. Come and sit down."

She tried a small forkful of tortilla. "Mmm, this is yummy. What is it?" she said, taking a second, bigger mouthful.

"It's Grandad's Spanish omelette; it's called a tortilla. Do you remember getting the herbs for it yesterday?"

"It can't be a proper tortilla. We have those with chicken when you make far-jeepers."

"Those are flour tortillas, Alice. This is a different kind of tortilla, made with potato, onions and eggs."

"Well, whatever it is, it's scrummy! Can you make it again, Grandad?"

159

"I'll teach *you* how to make it, Alice; how about it?" said Ged brightly.

"Ok... but not now, please; I'm going on the bodyboard today."

"I tell you what, Alice. If we have a rainy day, we could do that instead of Jigsaws."

"Yes, please, Grandad. I'm a bit bored of the Jigsaw."

Sarah, Brian, Alice, and Jamie finished the Tortilla and declared it Ged's best. Marge made no comment.

"When do you usually go to the café, Gerald?" she asked.

"Around ten-ish, Love. I'll go and have a couple of tablets and brush my teeth, and we'll go soon," he said.

***

Brian came over as Ged loaded his sketching things into the Purple-Pink Unicorn bag.

"What's going on with Mum?" he said. "Yesterday, she wouldn't have gone near the Seagull with a barge pole. Now, she's dressed up like she's going to the royal garden party; she's even putting on lipstick!"

Ged smiled. "Ah, I think she's found a reason to go to the café, Brian – keeping up with the Jones's," he said, tapping the side of his nose with his finger.

"What on earth do you mean?"

"Well, I told her that the couple who own that catamaran in the bay go to the café for breakfast every day. You can see the cottage with the Jag parked outside from the café terrace, too. You can't hob-knob with the corps d'elite if you don't go to the right places. I guess she's decided it's not such a bad place after all!"

Brian rolled his eyes and let out an exasperated sigh. "She's impossible!"

"She's her father's daughter," said Ged, as if it explained everything. "Anyway, if it weren't for people like your Mum, your restaurant wouldn't be half as full, would it? As delicious as the food is, a lot of people go there to see and be seen, if you get my meaning."

"I guess you're right, but she was awful about Bill and Sharon yesterday. I hope she doesn't say anything to upset them."

"Bill and Sharon know your mother by now; they won't take offence even if she does. They've been in this game too long to let that kind of thing get to them." He glanced at Brian. "It's their customers I'd be concerned about," he said with a wince.

***

Marge sat at a table at the front of the terrace by the road. It was hot, and Ged would've preferred a spot in the shade, but he knew better than to suggest it.

"Who is this vision of loveliness you've brought today, Mr Baker? Well, if it isn't the lovely Mrs Baker!" exclaimed Bill, hurrying to clear the table next to them. "Aren't you looking delightful!" he said to Marge.

"Thank you," mumbled Marge, her cheeks flushed. Ged glared at Bill, who grinned back.

"I was worried when you two didn't come last night. Brian said you weren't feeling well," he said kindly.

"A little too much sun, perhaps; I have been working in the garden for three days," she replied. "How is business?"

"Can't complain, it's a good season so far, plenty of crab sandwiches and cups of tea gone down. We're havin' a great week 'o breakfasts. I 'ad to order more eggs yesterday an' …"

"May we have two cappuccinos?" Marge interrupted as a slim, older couple dressed in almost matching tweed jackets came up the steps of the café terrace. Ged noticed they were the couple with the Jaguar.

"Oh, er, yes, of course, you can, m'lady," he said, a little taken aback by the interruption but recovering well. "Alright, Chippy?" he said to Ged as Sharon arrived to show the other couple to a table on the covered part of the terrace. "'Ow's that foot of yours?"

"Getting there, Bill," Ged replied. "Actually, can I change my order to a pot of tea?"

"No problem, Chippy, mate. Want any of the carrot cake this mornin'?"

Marge gave Ged a sharp look.

"Looks lovely, Bill, but I'll pass," said Ged.

"Oh, well, you'll 'ave to try it one 'o these days," he said, winking. "I think you'll love it!"

Ged, inwardly grateful to his old friend for covering up, pulled up a chair to rest his booted foot on as Bill went off to get the drinks.

A group of people in wetsuits rolled down to their waists, walked up the lane, and stomped up the café steps, chatting amiably. Rita spotted Ged immediately.

"Hi, Ged. Nice to see you again. How's your foot?" she said in her tinkly Danish voice.

"Hi Rita, hallo Chris, it's good, thanks. Breakfast before windsurfing again?"

"Yah, but I think we have to wait today, or maybe we go on Kayaks this morning; there's no wind. No good windsurfing with no wind, hey?"

"Oh, that's a shame," said Ged sympathetically. "Kayaks are good for looking at the wildlife, though."

Marge reached discreetly under the table and tapped Ged on the knee. She gave him a slightly annoyed look and then smiled much too sweetly. He didn't get the hint.

"Aren't you going to introduce us, Gerald?" she said through a toothy, thin smile.

"Oh! I'm so sorry. How rude of me… Rita, allow me to introduce my wife, Marge," he said politely.

Marge shook Rita's offered hand: "Mar-jor-ie – Bay-ker!" said Marge slowly and rather too loudly in that condescending manner that some people employ upon meeting a foreigner. It's as though they think foreignness makes them either hard of hearing or rather stupid. Rita wasn't sure if Marge was a little deaf herself, and responded in kind.

"Pleased – to – meet – you!" she said slowly and clearly, with a little more volume than necessary. "This – is – my – husband, Chris."

Chris politely shook Marge's hand, smiled and nodded. He didn't want to play this game and pretended he couldn't speak English.

"Your husband as quite a talent Mar – jor – ie," said Rita.

"Really, and what talent might that be?"

"The pictures – his drawings are very good, yes?"

"Oh, yes, I believe he has been drawing this week. I think the grandchildren like his little cartoons. Erm, is that your yacht?" she said, nodding towards the catamaran.

"Yes, we sailed over from Denmark. We are hoping to sail around the south coast of England. But it's so lovely here, we don't want to leave."

"That's certainly why we bought *our* house here. Porthcovery is lovely, and we wouldn't want to go anywhere else, so we bought a place here, didn't we, Gerald?" Ged smiled in agreement.

"Oh! You have a second home here? How lovely! Which house?"

"It's the white one just up there on the left with the bay window and the wooden porch." She indicated the direction. "Chi Gwynn; It means 'The White House' in Cornish."

"The one with roses over the doorway? That is a beautiful place. I like the garden. Aren't you lucky to have that window to sit in?"

"We like it," said Marge with an overtly charming smile.

"Well, we need to find a table," said Rita. "We have breakfast here before we go out on the water. Good to see you again, Ged, or should I call you 'Chippy'?

"You can call me Chippy if you like," said Ged with a smile.

"Later, Chippy," said Chris, in his pronounced Danish accent, winking as he passed.

Sharon brought their drinks over with a pot of brown and white sugar lumps and milk for the tea.

"Nice to see you, Mrs Baker," she said.

"And you, Sharon, how is your Aunt?"

"Er… still dead, as far as I know."

"Oh, yes, of course, so sad," stumbled Marge.

"It's okay; you can't be expected to remember everythin'. How are you enjoying this wonderful weather, then, eh?"

"It's been very nice. I've been out in the garden every day."

"So I see… It's looking very tidy! First time here this week, though. Are you feeling better? Sarah and Brian said you weren't feeling so good last night."

"Much better, thank you," said Marge, reaching for the teapot.

"Are you pouring for me?" said Ged.

"Sorry, Gerald?"

"The teapot, I'm the tea, yours is the cappuccino, isn't it?"

"Oh, I'm sure I ordered tea, Gerald. I don't like coffee! Honestly, Sharon, I think my husband is going a little doo-lally."

"Er," said Sharon, not sure what to say.

"Don't worry, Sharon – my mistake," said Ged, coming to the rescue. "I love it. I'll have the cappuccino. As my dear wife said, she doesn't like coffee." He poured the tea and pulled the cappuccino to his side of the table. "I'm a bit peckish, actually," He continued, glancing at Marge. "I think I *will* have some of that super healthy carrot cake when you have a minute, please, Sharon."

"Will do Chippy. Anything for you, Mrs Baker?"

Marge glanced at the tweed-clad couple who were tucking into a slice each. "I'll have a slice, too, thank you."

Sharon nodded and went over to take breakfast orders from the windsurfing group before going into the kitchen.

Marge said nothing to Ged about the coffee mix-up, and Ged felt it best not to mention it. He picked up his backpack from the floor and started to undo the zip.

"What on earth are you doing?" hissed Marge. "For goodness' sake, put it away!"

"Why? I fancied doing a bit of sketching."

"It's a child's pink and purple rucksack," she said menacingly through gritted teeth… "With a Unicorn on it, that's why!"

Ged took a deep breath and sighed quietly. "If I make sure no one sees the bag, is it ok with you if I sketch? The cat I've been trying to draw is on the windowsill, and it's got its eyes open for once." Ged gestured to the window of Val's cottage.

"Eugh, what an awful cat. It looks evil!" exclaimed Marge.

"The mice here are inclined to agree, but Bill, Val and Sharon think the world of him."

"If you must, but it's rather unsociable. We are supposed to be here together."

"Okay, I won't sketch; what would you like to talk about?"

"I don't know, the house, the garden, our plans for the rest of the week, I suppose."

Ged groaned inwardly. Plans. Always a dangerous subject: Best to agree if he liked the idea and keep very quiet if he didn't. Generally, Ged liked Marge's ideas, but when they were bad, they were awful, not to mention expensive. This time, she wanted to change the curtains and cushions in the living room and get some new games and jigsaws, all pretty harmless and didn't sound too costly, thank goodness. Ged's attention was momentarily caught by Potts, who had jumped onto a windowsill of his cottage and was staring directly at him.

"Are you listening, Gerald?"

"What? Oh, yes, new jigsaws; maybe we can go to the shop down the road and see if they have any?"

"No, not that. I said, I think I recognise the couple from the loft," she said, leaning closer to him and speaking in a low voice. "She is an actress; I think she's in one of the soap operas, or is she off Radio Four?"

"Pretty difficult to recognise someone off the radio, isn't it?" quipped Ged.

"Not if you read the Radio Times magazine, Gerald."

"Well, please don't bother them. I'm sure they just want to have a quiet holiday. They aren't speaking loudly to make sure everyone pays them attention, so I don't think they are the attention-seeking type."

The couple were chatting quietly at their table, picking up the last forkfuls of cake. Sharon brought over Ged and Marge's slices.

"Sharon, dear," said Marge quietly as Sharon put the plates on the table," I don't have my glasses. Is that lady an actor, or is she the woman who does Gardeners' Question Time?"

"It's Hilary Stott, off Radio 4's foodie show. I listen every week. She's really nice, actually. Not like these attention-seeking luvvies you get down 'ere sometimes. She and her hubby like to come here and have a quiet week, you know, away from the showbiz. I'm pretty flattered, actually..." She seemed to be waiting for a response from Marge, and when none was forthcoming, Ged stepped in.

"Flattered? How come?"

"She asked if she could have the recipe!"

"Wow! Praise, indeed, coming from someone in her profession," said Ged, impressed. "And, not that I'm a well-known food critic or anything, but I agree. Your cakes are amazing!"

"Why, thank you, kind sir," said Sharon, with a mock curtsey.

"I mean it, Sharon. Why else do you think people come back here day after day of their holidays and year after year?"

"Aww, well, as long as you all like it, I'm happy," she said.

Marge paid little attention to this exchange but continued to glance over at Hillary and Mr. Scott as they picked over the remaining crumbs of their cake. Marge picked up her fork and tried a little. It was certainly moist, but – ginger, oh dear – she hated ginger! Well, if Hillary Stott liked it, Marge was damned if she wasn't going to eat it.

She took a sip of her tea and tried a little more of the cake, glancing over at Hilary. Ged watched her out of the corner of his eye: Tiny bite, sip of tea, glance at Hillary – has she noticed we are having the same thing? Bite, sip, glance, and so it went on. Ged picked up his slice with his fingers and munched happily on it. It went beautifully with his coffee.

"Ah, Apricots," mused Ged. "That's why it works with coffee. Sharon, you are clever!"

"Pardon, Gerald?"

"Apricots," he said, as if it explained everything. Seeing the blank look on Marge's face, he realised it didn't, so he expanded: "There are chopped apricots in this. It makes it moist, and Apricots go well with coffee. Even on their own, do you want to try a bit of mine?"

"Alright," said Marge reluctantly, accepting the cup from Ged. She took another small piece of cake with her fork and then a sip of coffee. Her eyes bulged – no sugar! The coffee tasted awful. Then, as the apricot and dark brown sugary sweetness blended with the bitter coffee, it transformed the taste. She chewed and swallowed, nodding.

"Yes, of course, Apricots!" she said, loudly and in a slightly more southern accent than her usual one, glancing over to Hillary to see if she had noticed. "They go nicely with coffee. I've always found, haven't you?" Hillary smiled politely and glanced at her husband.

Inwardly rolling his eyes, Ged couldn't think of a suitable reply and simply took another bite of carrot cake.

Rita, Chris, and their wetsuit-clad classmates were scraping their chairs back and making their way out. They slapped down the steps in their beach shoes.

"Hey, Chippy," said Rita as she passed, "if you draw any nice pictures of the village, or the harbour, or maybe, even… our boat, I would love to buy one."

"You can have one if you like it; I don't sell anything. They're just doodles, really."

"You should. From what I saw the other day in your sketchbook, they are better than the paintings on the walls of this café."

Ged's cheeks flushed. "Thanks, Rita. That's very kind."

"Not at all. See you tomorrow," she said cheerfully and waved as she jogged off in pursuit of the others.

"Come on, Marge," he said, draining his coffee cup, "if you've finished your cake, let's go to the shop and see if we can find some new jigsaws and games, shall we?"

20

When Marge and Ged returned to the house, Brian had prepared a prawn salad for lunch. Marge went to change out of her dress while Ged helped to prepare the table ready for lunch. Brian took the opportunity to speak to Ged while his mother was out of earshot.

"Well – how did it go at the café, Dad?" he asked.

"Not too bad, I suppose. At least she didn't insult Bill and Sharon. She was too busy trying to impress Hilary Scott off the radio!"

"Hilary Scott, the food critic? She's scary!" said Brian.

"She's been nice to you so far," noted Sarah, "she gave you a good review last month."

"Yeah, but boy, if she decides she doesn't like you, it can be disastrous!"

"Maybe Sharon can put in a good word. Hilary likes her cakes," said Ged.

"The woman has taste! They're gorgeous! She's a cake legend!"

"Have you tried the carrot cake?" asked Ged.

"Had it last night, warm with clotted cream and vanilla ice cream. It was heavenly!"

"What was Mum up to?" said Sarah, "She hates coffee and doesn't think much of Bill and Sharon."

"Likes to rub shoulders with the right people," said Ged quietly. "If that's where they go for breakfast, then that's where she wants to be. If they drink coffee, her curiosity for coffee, even if not her taste for it, is rekindled; if they like carrot cake, she'll try it. If you want to climb socially, you need to be in the same places as those who put the ladders up. It's how she was brought up."

"Hmm, it's just so… obvious. It makes me cringe," mused Brian. "Where has she got to, anyway? I'm starving!"

Sarah went to look for Marge and called the children in for lunch. Alice and Jamie came running in, and Sarah appeared in the kitchen doorway, a quizzical look on her face. "Mum says she's not hungry. She's doing her crossword on the window seat."

"Well, we did have a slice of that carrot cake, I suppose," said Ged "but I'm always hungry for Brian's food. How, on earth, I'm not the size of a house by now, I have no idea."

***

Marge didn't go back to the café that week, but she did go out on more 'Shopping trips' past the café and the loft house. She never brought anything back, but seemed thoughtful.

Ged had coffee at the Seagull each morning, chatting with Bill or Sharon and sketching anything that caught his eye. He was thoroughly enjoying himself. He spotted Potts twice more, once with his eyes open. Ged had never considered himself a 'cat person,' but he considered this one an exception. It had such 'presence'. Most cats have a tendency to put on an air that they own the place. This one clearly *did* own the village but obviously felt no need to prove it. Some cats flirt and rub against your legs for attention; others look at you as though they would like to kill you quite soon. Potts was above any of that.

His eyes were bright amber rather than the usual yellow-green, and when he looked at you, he seemed to see into your very soul. Ged decided to do a montage of different expressions; then, he did some more cartoon-style sketches. Potts stalking a bird on a rooftop, sharpening his claws on a car tyre, climbing in through an upstairs window with something furry in his mouth and in one cartoon, he was closing a refrigerator door with his tail.

Ged put his pencil down and regarded the montage, his head cocked to one side. Sharon placed a slice of brownie in front of him. "This one's on the house," she said, stepping behind Ged's shoulder to get a better look at the sketches. She chuckled. "Ha! That's brilliant, Chippy! It's old Potts, isn't it?"

"Thanks, Sharon," said Ged through a mouthful of delicious brownie. "Yep, I've taken a shine to the old fellow."

"They look just like him. Oh, that one of him sneaking in through that window; I can't count how many times I've seen him do that! It drives Val up the wall! D'you know what makes these good…?"

"No…"

"It's Potts in every sketch. There are plenty of people who can draw a Tabby cat, but what you've done is captured the essence of Potts in every single one."

"Have I?"

"Yeah… It's him every time. Are you going to add colour?"

"Maybe, I'm not very skilled with a paintbrush yet. I managed to spill paint water all over a white tablecloth earlier in the week. I'm hoping Emily's cleaners have got it out. Sarah is going to the Lobster Pot in Porthleven to pick it up this afternoon."

"I haven't seen Emily for months!" said Sharon. "I'll have to go over there and have a catch-up. You know, she went to school with my aunt. It was Emily who said me and Bill should buy this place, and we've tried to model what we do on how she runs the Lobster Pot. I really like how she does things."

"It's a good example to follow. We love eating there *and* here.

"Works for us," Sharon replied. "Hey, Chippy, have you thought about using watercolour pencils. They might be better for the fine stuff. I think you can blend them a bit with a damp finger and get deeper colours if you wet 'em. I saw a lady using them yesterday."

"I did use one or two of Alice's watercolour pencils. I think Marge will be happier with me using them, too, as I can't spill them! I'll see if Tracy has a set at the Gallery shop; I've already commandeered Alice's bag; I'm not going to start nicking her pencils as well."

"I'm sure she won't mind," said Sharon. "Look at me chatting away; I've got customers waiting… better get on. See you later."

"Thanks for the brownie, Sharon."

"You're welcome!" she called over her shoulder as she disappeared into the kitchen.

Ged packed his pencils and sketchpad away in the unicorn backpack and pushed himself up onto his single crutch. His foot was feeling much better, and he could manage with one crutch most of the time. He carefully negotiated the rough stone steps of the café and headed for the Gallery shop.

170

Tracey was arranging t-shirts on a rail. She greeted Ged as he entered, accidentally banging his crutch against the door.

"Hey, Chippy."

"Hi, Tracey. Do you have any watercolour pencils?"

"I think I have some Cottman ones. Did you have a look near the paints and pastels?"

"I must admit, I didn't look yet; I thought asking would be quicker."

She put down the T-shirts and went to fetch the pencils for Ged. "You know, Chippy, you're an unusual fella, if you don't mind me saying," she said, putting them on the counter.

"What makes you say that? -Oh, thanks for getting the pencils, Tracey."

"No bother," she said, with a dismissive wave of her hand. "Most blokes spend ten minutes looking around the shop for what they want, grumbling and mumbling to themselves when they can't find it and then leave without asking. You'd think they were buying something illegal, but usually, they're just not looking properly. Then they send the missus in later, who just comes straight to the counter and asks."

"I do most of my shopping at the timber merchant, and you have to ask for everything there. I guess I'm used to it. Saves time anyway."

Tracey smiled at this. "Is that everything?" she said.

"I think I had better get another sketch pad and some of that smooth watercolour paper. I've done nothing but draw all week!"

"Yeah, Sharon was telling me you're a bit of a natural, it seems. She's dead impressed – and it takes quite a lot to impress her, y'know."

Ged flushed pink. He had thought Sharon was being kind, but perhaps she really meant what she had said earlier. He paid for his goods and stuffed the paper bag into his backpack.

"And that's got tongues wagging, too. Mum loves your bag; she says it suits you!"

"Eh?"

"It's cheerful! Hey, see you later. Chippy. I'd best finish putting these t-shirts out before the lunchtime rush."

"Okay, Bye, Tracey."

***

Ged put on the backpack and ambled up the lane to the harbour to join Brian and Sarah. He paused by the sea wall, looking out across the bay. It was gloriously sunny. The tide was halfway out. The sun glistened on the wet sand and rocks, making them sparkle like gems. Families were on the beach with buckets, spades, nets and the paraphernalia of beach life.

He noticed a boy of about ten in white shorts and a red Welsh rugby shirt crouched by a large rock pool. He was so immersed that he barely moved. An older boy in cut-off jeans and a Black t-shirt was rock-hopping over to where the rock-pooler crouched, the muscles on his slim, muscular calves visibly tensing as he balanced on each rock, nimble and agile as a mountain goat. He didn't use his arms to help his balance. He had a bag of crisps in one hand and casually ate them as he went.

Ged was beginning to automatically view quite ordinary situations with an artist's eye. His increasing eye for detail, picking up every shadow and highlight: The shape of the older boy's feet on the rocks, his toes splaying naturally as he stepped on each one, The look of fixed concentration on the younger boy's face, the Fleur de Lys on his red rugby shirt, the set of his jaw as he stared into the pool; the way his shorts creased at the hip as he crouched.

The older boy stood over the pool, casting a shadow. The younger one waved him away crossly as a crisp fell into the water. The older boy poured the remainder of his crisps into the pool. Red shirt boy scooped up the crisps and a double handful of water and threw it at the older one, who laughed and sprang away over the rocks back to a family gathered around a green, tartan picnic blanket with red-shirt boy in hot pursuit, scooping up wet sand and throwing it at the older boy. A slim, dark-haired woman shouted at him to stop, but it was too late. The boy's aim was less than accurate – a blob of wet sand landed on her white blouse. The boy stopped in his tracks, holding a sand-covered hand to his mouth as he realised what he had done. Then

172

came the realisation that his hands were covered in sand. He bent over, trying to spit sand and wipe his lips with his forearms, which were almost as sand-covered as his lips. An expression of panic came over his face. The dark-haired woman was bent double, laughing at this instant karma.

Another dark-haired woman in a yellow vest top and jean shorts walked over to him with a large bottle of water and helped him to wash the sand off his hands and face. His head was down, and he was clearly crying. The woman scooped up the boy and held him close, burying her face in his hair. After she had put him down, they went for a walk along the beach, towards the rock pools, holding hands. The boy's head was still bowed, and his shoulders jerked as he sobbed. The shoulder movements slowed gradually as they arrived at the big rock pool. He crouched once more by the pool, where Ged could just see a few crisps still floating.

***

Ged finally tore his eyes away from the scene and walked up to the harbour to join Brian, Sarah and the children. Sarah had bought Cornish pasties from Peggy's and had one ready for him with a fresh mug of tea from the little ice cream parlour by the harbour. The children ran to greet their grandad with pasty-crumb smiles and ketchup-stained hugs.

Ged sat down on the sun-warmed stone harbour wall seat, took off his backpack and unwrapped his still-warm pasty. He took a large, satisfying bite, closing his eyes and allowing the aroma of the onion, pepper, herbs and skirt beef to fill his senses before beginning to chew the first mouthful. There really was no better thing to eat. No lasagne nor expensive restaurant meal would ever replace the sheer bliss of a decent Cornish pasty and a steaming mug of tea on the warm harbour wall of Porthcovery.

"Everything okay, Dad?"

Ged chewed and swallowed his mouthful. "Couldn't be better, Sarah, love… what could be better than a cup of tea and one of Peggy's pasties right here on the harbour?"

"I know what you mean," said Brian, with feeling. "I tried re-creating these at home once. I didn't even get close. I'm glad, too, in a way. There are some culinary secrets that aren't meant to travel."

"Home tomorrow then?" said Sarah. "I wish we didn't have to leave."

"Me too," said Ged. "Are you sure you don't mind driving Sarah? I know Marge will be very grateful not to be."

"Sure, Dad, really. I've got a book to read on the train home."

"Well, if you're sure."

"Dad..." said Sarah, rolling her eyes. "I wouldn't have offered otherwise."

"I know, Sarah, love, it's just that it's a lot of hassle."

Sarah leaned over and spoke quietly to Ged so the children couldn't eavesdrop: "Actually, I'm looking forward to a few hours of alone time with my book; I'll take the slow train rather than the express."

Ged tapped the side of his nose with his finger and winked at her... "Nice plan. I suppose you don't get much time to read and just be on your own, even on holiday."

"Exactly. I love Jamie and Alice, you know I do, but it's a long time since I had a few hours to myself."

"Well, I probably don't have to warn you, but I will anyway: You know Mum and I are dreadful backseat passengers. We'll do our best to keep quiet, though."

"Oh, so that's where Brian gets it from. He's a total pain in the neck when we go anywhere if I'm driving! ...Sarah, why haven't you indicated? – Aren't you braking a bit late, Sarah? Speed up, or we'll never get there – why don't you overtake? Blah, blah, blah. To be honest, I find it's best just to ignore it."

"Probably best; no point arguing."

"My thoughts entirely. How's the Pasty?"

"Bliss. And the tea was like icing on the cake! My stomach is a very happy one."

Jamie came over holding a sea urchin shell he had found in the harbour. It's purple and mauve colours pock-marked with a perfectly symmetrical pattern of tiny, raised bumps with a hole in each, like a row of miniature, well-ordered volcanoes. There wasn't a single blemish anywhere on the shell. "Look what I found!" He handed the shell to his mother as she held her hand out. She peered at it, turning it over in her fingers.

"What a great find, Jamie! Was it in the big pool at the bottom of the ladder? Seems to be a good place for finding treasure."

"Yeah, there's loads in there. Alice found lots of shells, and there's a starfish too!"

Ged was getting his sketch pad and pencils out of the unicorn backpack.

"Have you done any more drawings, Grandad?"

"Plenty, Jamie."

"Can I have a look?"

Jamie sat next to his mother. Ged handed him the sketchbook, which he placed carefully on his knee. Leafing through the pages, he paused at the montage of Potts.

"You've been busy," said Sarah, glancing over her son's shoulder.

"I've really got into it. I had forgotten how much I enjoyed drawing. I had a few tries sketching the catamaran and one or two different parts of the village. I've become a bit obsessed with Val's cat. I've done loads of him today; they are becoming quite cartoon-like."

"Mum, these are brilliant!" said Jamie. "Grandad, I love that cat – he looks funny!"

"Yes, he is quite a character."

"I'm going back to Dad now. See you later."

Sarah sat in silence, leafing through the sketches slowly, orienting the page depending on how Ged had drawn the subject. She stopped at the catamaran, tilting her head.

"Was there really someone at the wheel when you drew this?" she said.

"No. I used a bit of artistic licence; I thought Rita would like that."

"Who's Rita?"

"The woman who owns the boat. She asked if I would let her have a sketch of the boat or the village or whatever, so I did this one. I'd like to add some colour to this and some of the others this afternoon."

"Not again! I'm getting the tablecloth from Emily's this afternoon."

"Don't worry, I've bought watercolour pencils so I won't make a mess. I'm going to leave painting until my foot is better. Who knew a broken foot would make it hard to paint?"

Sarah continued to leaf through the book, her face animated. All the drawings had that unfinished quality, which somehow created a focus for the attention. There would be a foot missing in one sketch, or an arm would end at the elbow. The sketches only showed what was needed to tell the story and no more. Sarah made a brief snort of a laugh as she came across a sketch of the old loft cottage with the Jaguar parked in front of it. It was done in more of a rough cartoon style. The lady getting out of the passenger seat was wearing a baseball cap and dark glasses and was shielding her face with the lapel of her jacket like a film star trying to avoid being recognised. She chuckled as she came to the montage of Potts. "I see what you mean about the cat. Did you see him doing all this?"

"Some of it. Others are based on what I heard Val and Sharon saying about him."

"Can I keep a few?"

"Sure, they're just sketching practice, you know, trying out different ideas. I'm doing plenty. You can have them all as far as I'm concerned… oh, except the one of the Catamaran and the cat antics. I want to get some colour on those this afternoon."

Sarah carefully tore the pages from the spiral and slid them into her shoulder bag. "Look, I need to get going if I'm going to pick up the tablecloth from Emily," she said. "I'll see if Brian is ready to go back to the cottage with the kids. They can go to the beach this afternoon if it stays like this." She got up and walked over to the edge of the harbour, peering around the fishing boats now stranded on the sand and seaweed. She soon spotted Brian and the children crouching on their haunches by the deep pool at the corner of the harbour. She walked to the ladder which led down to it. "I need to get over to Porthleven, Brian," she called. "Can you manage most of the stuff? Is there anything you want me to take back to the house?"

"I'll come up and get the buckets and spades. The kids and I are going to wade and rock-hop to the beach from here. If you could carry the beach bag with the towels to the steps near the house, I'll meet you there."

Brian climbed the ladder up to the harbour wall and came over to where Ged was sitting. Ged had turned to a new page of his sketchbook and was roughly sketching the scene of the two boys by the rock pool.

"Do you want a piggyback down to the beach again, Dad?" asked Brian with a wink.

"Not flippin' likely, Brian; it's more than my pride can stand! I'm going back to the house to see your Mum; then I might get some colour on my sketches. Shall we go to the pub for tea tonight? We'll be packing, won't we?"

"Nah...it's leftover surprise tonight."

"Leftover surprise?"

"Yeah, like that TV programme, ready, steady, cook – I have to try and create a half-decent meal out of whatever is left in the kitchen without spoiling tomorrow's breakfast. It will be as much of a surprise to me as it is to you."

21

"Daddy's done lots of little bowls. There's all sorts of things!" said Alice.

"Yes, he cheated!"

"How did he cheat?"

"The challenge is to make a *meal* out of leftovers while leaving enough for breakfast tomorrow. What Daddy has done is served *'leftovers in little bowls'.*" Said Sarah, grinning.

"Spanish Tapas!" Brian corrected in a gently defensive tone, "See. Patatas- bravas, Pan-tumaca, croquettes, garlic prawns, a few olives, a little paella with some sausages and a small tortilla, and a salad. Come on, we could be in Mallorca!"

"Well done, Bri, but strictly speaking, it is kinda cheating," said Ged, with a wink as he hobbled in on his crutch.

"Okay, smarty-pants, what would you two have done?"

"Same thing, probably!" said Ged, but not this well."

"I'd have done beans on toast and dumped the leftovers in the middle for everyone to pick at," admitted Sarah, who hated cooking. "I'll tell Mum it's ready, shall I?"

"I'll pour her a Chardonnay. I'm not sure how she's going to react to this," said Ged.

"Actually, she helped me, so she knows what's coming," said Brian cheerfully.

"Which ones did she cook? I'll be careful to compliment the right dish."

"The pan-tumaca, the olives and the prawns. To be fair to her, the flavour of the tomato is really nice on the pan-tumaca."

***

The Spanish tapas were a success. Everyone found something they liked, and Marge was pleased but a little bashful. The dish they all fought over the most was her delicious pan-tumaca, a simple dish of toasted slices of French bread with olive oil, garlic and grated tomato. Marge had added a few herbs and a little paprika. She was quiet for most of the meal and picked at her own food.

"Is everyone packed and ready to go yet?? she said.

"I'm not even halfway through!" said Sarah.

"Well, I suppose that's to be expected, isn't it, Sarah, dear," said Marge in her most condescending tone. "You know, you should try to be more organised. Come up from the beach a little earlier next time, perhaps."

Sarah took a breath and clenched her fist, digging her nails into her palms.

"Kids, help me clear the table," she said quietly when dinner was finished. "Then let's go and pack our things." She stuffed a last morsel into her mouth and began to clear the table. The children had long finished dinner and had shared out the last of the ice cream between them before helping clear things away.

"Do we *have* to go home tomorrow, Mum?" said Jamie. "Can't we stay all day and go in the evening?"

"I am leaving early, Jamie, to take Nana and Grandad back home, but Dad might let you go on the beach for a little while in the morning... Brian? Do you think that would be okay? The kids are more likely to snooze in the car after some sea air and a Pasty."

"Good call," said Brian. "But no swimming. I don't want to put wet stuff in the car."

"Do you want any help packing, Sarah? said Ged, "or shall we just clean up in the kitchen and let you two pack? You've got four to pack for and all that beach equipment."

"Oh, that's staying here, Dad; we'll never get it in the car. There's room in the shed for the bodyboard," said Brian. "Would you be ok with the kitchen, Mum and Dad? I want to give Sarah a hand."

"Oh, very well," sighed Marge. "But I don't see why my being organised has to be rewarded with more work."

"Come on, Marge, it's only fair... Brian did the meal."

"With my help!" Marge's tone was beginning to rise...

"Yes, and the Pan-tumaca was delicious, but he has cooked for us a lot this week…"

"And what about Sarah? What has she done all week?"

"Cleaned the bathrooms, done the shopping, swept, kept the place tidy… plus… she's driving us home tomorrow."

"Oh, very well. I'll do the dishwasher, and you can do the pans and other things."

"Sure. Thanks for dinner, Bri – and Marge. It was delicious! We must do tapas again."

"Yeah… It's given me a few ideas for the restaurant. There are quite a few things you can cook pretty quickly and use left-over ingredients safely. It might reduce the waste."

"So, what will you put on the menu? Left-over surprise?"

"No, it will be a blackboard special… I'll create different tapas from the ingredients we didn't use at lunchtime and serve it up as Tapas for afternoon tea or as a starter in the evening… tapas are getting fashionable…it might catch on!"

***

With the packing complete and the children in bed, Sarah flopped down on the sofa next to Brian with a glass of wine for each of them. Marge and Ged had gone to bed. "Are you going to be ok driving those two home?" asked Brian.

"No, but if I can ignore the kids when they are whining in the back on the school run, I can probably ignore your mother."

"Don't bet on it," said Brian, ruefully.

"I will keep thinking of how nice it will be on the train with my headphones on and my music playing while I read my book or stare out of the window. It'll be like my old university trips, except without the swotting."

"And if she really gets out of hand…?"

"Oh, that's easy; I'll pull over and tell her she can drive!"

Brian laughed, clinking glasses with Sarah. "Good call!"

"What about you? How will you cope with our two all the way up the M4?"

"Well, I like your plan of beach or harbour and a Pasty. I called Peggy and ordered some for everyone. If you three don't have yours, you can always warm them up for tea when you get to Warwick or eat yours cold on the train. In fact, I'm glad we are staying tomorrow; they are holding a regatta at the harbour. I saw them putting up stalls and bunting this afternoon. It should be interesting for the kids, and there are games they can join in with."

"Oh, I wish I was staying now. Maybe you'd better have towels and swimming stuff. You can always put them in a carrier bag if they get wet, and they can change in the loos."

"Yeah, we'll have lunch at the harbour, and I've got those story tapes for the journey. I'll put one of those on in the car and pray they fall asleep."

"Sounds like you're sorted."

"Took a leaf out of your book, Wonder-momma!" He leaned over and put both of his tanned arms around her, kissing her on the lips. His skin, scented with sandalwood, was soft. He had shaved and used the aftershave Sarah had bought him for Christmas. She loved that smell. "I'm going to miss you."

"I'll be home by ten or eleven tomorrow night, Bri…"

"Yeah, but that journey… just me and the kids, all the way to Haringey.. that's going to feel like an eternity without you… Well, unless I can knock them out with the pasty."

Sarah gulped the last of her wine and stood up. "Coming upstairs?"

"Could you come on the sofa…?"

"Eugh. Bri, don't be gross! Your parents will end up walking in on us. Now, that could make for an awkward journey. Come on"

"Yeah, okay, better to come upstairs. He winked and placed both glasses on the table.

***

They lay side by side, catching their breath, smiling, giggling, and kissing. "It's been a while since we did that, Mrs B," said Brian.

"Only 4 days!"

"No, not since we did it… I mean, since we did that…"

"Oh, that, yeah, it's been a while. We must do more of that kind of thing more often. It has to be good for you. Must be the wine; what was it?"

"I think it was the Caballier that Ed bought us," said Brian

Ah, that… It's good stuff. Well, it certainly warmed you up."

"What? Speak for yourself… maybe it was the tapas setting off some Mediterranean passion bomb inside us."

"Yeah, your Mum's Pan-tumaca made us frisky… oh, she'd love to hear that!"

Brian collapsed back onto the pillow, laughing.

"Come on, we'd better get some sleep; we are both in for a long, long day tomorrow."

***

Sarah woke at six a.m., feeling way too hot. The reason for her heated state was immediately apparent. A much-too-big-to-share-a-bed, gangly and sweaty Jamie was snoring contentedly next to her. She didn't remember him coming into the room during the night; she assumed he must have just slid into the bed when she was deeply asleep.

She stroked his hair, running her fingers through his floppy fringe, wondering why he might have come in, hoping it was a bad dream and not that he was ill… that would make leaving much harder.

"Morning, sleepy-head," she said quietly to her firstborn.

"Morning, Mum," he yawned. He rolled over and put his arms around her neck. "Do you have to go with Nana and Grandad?"

"Yes, my love, poor Grandad can't drive; in fact, it would be illegal if he did… and Nana …well…let's just say that it's better if I drive them home. Nana doesn't like driving, and she likes motorways even less."

"I could come with you. I could play car games with Grandad; he knows lots of them."

"I'm sure he does. All the ones Dad taught you were from Grandad. Anyway, Dad has a fun day in store for you two. What's the weather like?"

"Looks sunny…why, what are we doing?"

"There's going to be a regatta at the harbour, and Dad's taking you."

"What's a regatta?"

"Well, local people will have races in different sorts of boats, I think, that's the main thing… but they also have other games to join in and others you can watch…I remember seeing one game where they put a big telegraph pole so it sticks out over the harbour when the tide is in, and then two people have to sit on the pole over the water and try and make each other fall in. They used to whack each other with cushions, but I think they use something else these days."

"But don't you want to come and see that?"

"Of course I do, but I also want to help Nana and Grandad."

"Why?"

"Because Jamie… they need our help, and that's what families do. We help each other. Anyway, I'll be home before you know it and tomorrow, you can tell me all about the regatta. Will you look after my camera and take lots of pictures?"

"What, your proper camera?"

"Yes, why not… as long as you promise to look after it and give it to Dad when you aren't using it. After breakfast, I'll give you a little lesson on how to take good pictures."

"Okay…er… Mum?"

"Yes, Jamie…"

"Will you be home by bedtime?"

"No. I'll be back by around eleven. It will be a bit like when we go out, and Auntie Annie puts you to bed… I'll have my mobile phone. Shall I give you all a ring before bedtime so we can say night-night?"

"I suppose so," said Jamie sulkily.

Sarah drew him to her and gave him a long, lingering kiss on his forehead. "I love you, Jamie Baker… I love you to the moon and back; round the earth three times and once round the sun."

"Love you too, Mum."

"Good morning, big munchkin!" said Brian brightly, ruffling his son's hair and glancing at Sarah; he had heard the whole conversation. "Ready for the regatta?"

"I don't want to go to the regatta. I want to go with Mum, but she said I can't."

"Well, I want you to come to the regatta. It wouldn't be fair if Alice and I had all the fun. Let's go and see what's in the fridge for breakfast, and... shall we have a pasty for lunch?"

"From Peggy's"

"Where else would we get a decent Cornish pasty? Other people sell them, but they wouldn't allow you to put ketchup on it."

"Really?" said Jamie, for whom tomato ketchup was the elixir of life and the saviour of all things edible or inedible.

"Really." Said Brian. "I once went to a pasty shop at the Lizard where the shop assistants would get the sack if the owner saw them giving ketchup to customers... the local grocers sold gallons of it... and brown sauce... to those tourists who like a bit of sauce on their pasty. You'd see people hiding on the coast path, sneaking ketchup or brown sauce onto their pasty, apparently worried that Nora might catch them and whip the pasty out of their hands!"

"Is that true, Mum?"

Sarah looked briefly at Brian, remembering it well. "Yes, it is, Jamie. One of those tourists was me. I brought the sauce in a brown paper bag so Nora wouldn't find out."

***

The drive back to Warwick was relatively uneventful. Sarah drove rather too sedately for Ged's liking, but Marge appeared to approve. She only complained when Sarah asked if they could make a pit stop, and she didn't like the service station.

"This one is where all the camper vans and caravans go!" she moaned as they turned off into one of the service areas. There were, indeed, several mobile homes and caravans parked up in their designated parking area. As it was midday, the inhabitants were busy getting tables and chairs out, having picnics, and chatting with one another like old friends. There was an air of comfortable camaraderie.

Ged's developing artist's eye soaked up the detail. Caravanners wandered from van to van, offering a plate of something here and handing over a mug of tea there. A middle-aged couple were helping a frail-looking, long-bearded VW camper owner to change a wheel on his bright-orange and grey-patched van. The wheel arch and the driver's door had patches of sanded grey filler. The van looked as though it had had an interesting life. There were numerous dents on the bodywork and a multitude of stickers on the windows. A round white "Campaign for Nuclear Disarmament" sticker took pride of place on the centre window, and a yellow smiling face was right next to it. The driver's quarter glass sported a Cuban flag sticker. Clearly too old and frail to be changing a wheel, the man brought the couple a steaming mug of tea as they wound down the jack which was holding the wheel off the ground.

"They look like nice people, actually," observed Ged.

"Lefties, commies and gypsies," snapped Marge, scornfully... "Just look at them, in their pinnies, with their ham sandwiches... good grief! That one still has her curlers in!"

There was indeed a lady in a lilac headscarf, with curlers in her hair, outside one of the more modern caravans. She wore a full pinafore-style apron with pink and purple flowers and was pouring tea from a large blue teapot into matching beakers on a picnic table. At the same time, her husband, in full uniform of brown slacks and a white vest, lit his pipe, regarding the other caravans and camper vans with a discerning eye. They had an air of gentle and unassuming pride. Ged drank in the scene in moments, wishing he could get out his sketch pad and capture it. He had a compulsion these days to sketch any scene that piqued his interest.

"Dad, you're staring," said Sarah and pulled on his arm. "Can we get going, please? I really need to use the loo."

"Sorry, Love."

They trooped into the services building. "Shall we have lunch here?" inquired Ged.

"Well, if you *want* salmonella, this place is *perfect*, but I personally prefer not to have near-fatal food poisoning, and we will go to Gordano, as usual, if you don't mind."

Sarah shot Ged a warning glance that said, "Whether you mind or not, don't push your luck."

At the Gordano service area near Bristol, Marge still complained, moaning that standards were slipping. She picked at her chicken pie and ate less than half of her food.

"Are you alright, Mum...?"

"Perfectly fine, thank you, Sarah."

"But you've hardly touched your lunch."

"It's lukewarm, and there's far too much pastry. This place is going to the dogs. We will have to find one of those nice little country pubs we used to stop in future, Gerald."

"What, you mean go the long route?"

"Why not? These service stations are awful places, full of school parties, caravanners and football teams. This food is like the food they used to dish up after the match at Edward's Rugby club – mass-produced, nearly cold and second-rate."

***

"Thanks for driving us home, Sarah," said Ged gratefully, hugging his daughter-in-law in the hall after she had carried their bags inside.

"What are you going to do about work?" asked Sarah, gesturing at Ged's booted foot as she made a cup of tea for the three of them.

"I already called Peter on Mum's new mobile phone last week. He said one of the lads would pick me up on Monday, and I suppose we can work it out from there. I'll have to see the occupational health people, of course. I expect they'll give me some desk work or put me on light duties for a few weeks. I'll be bored witless!"

"Well, don't overdo it, Dad, or it won't heal. Elevate your foot to stop it from swelling and do whatever the doc tells you."

"Okay, Bossy-boots! It is feeling better today, but I expect that's because I've not been walking around."

22

Warwick, September 1998

Ged picked up the receiver of the trim phone...

"Hi, Sarah. How are you?"

"Dad, you need to sit down for this."

"Why do I need to sit down? Are Brian and the kids okay?"

"Yes, they're fine. Trust me, you'll be glad you sat down for this news…" Ged put his wine glass on the hall table and sat on the chair beside it. "Okay, I'm sitting down…"

"Promise?"

"Yes, I promise; good grief, what is it?"

"Well…I know I should have asked you first, but I showed your sketches to Emily at the Lobster Pot in the summer, and… um… to cut a long story short, she said they would probably sell quite well in the café. To be perfectly honest, Dad, she loved them! Ron framed them, and she did prints as she reckoned some of them would sell several times over, and if they did, the originals would be worth more… We agreed to go fifty-fifty on the takings to pay for the frames and prints with a bit of profit for her and Ron…Anyway, this morning, she called me to say they did even better than she expected, and she sold rather a lot… twenty-five to be exact and at an average of around forty pounds, that means they've made… I can't believe this… A thousand pounds altogether… so she's sending a cheque for five hundred pounds!"

As he listened, Ged frowned at first, trying to process the information. The furrowed brow softened, and his expression became a mixture of bewilderment and surprise. When he finally spoke, he was incredulous. "A…a thousand pounds? You're kidding…!" Then, his tone became suspicious. "Just a minute... I remember giving you the sketches, but when did you go to the Lobster Pot?"

"Do you remember I asked Emily if she could send that posh tablecloth of Mum's to her laundry company to be professionally cleaned?"

"Oh, that bloody tablecloth!"

"She didn't let me pay for the tablecloth either. The laundry company didn't charge her extra. When I went to pick it up, I took her the sketches you gave me at the harbour, and she was delighted. She says she's had to get more printed."

"Prints? So, she's selling more of them?"

"She said they are still selling at a rate of about two or three a week, and she put the prices up a bit for the popular ones."

"Well, I'm gobsmacked...so that's five hundred each? Well, that's amazing, Sarah... who'd have thought my doodles would be sold for actual money?"

"They aren't doodles, Dad; you're really talented, and I think this proves it. Maybe you should go professional – get an agent or something. You definitely need to do some more drawings, and Emily says if they had a bit of colour, they would sell even better. That one of the pirate... She says she sold five of that one alone!"

Oh, I don't know, Sarah... I don't really have the time. Do you mean Pete the Pirate? Well, I don't mind doing one for Jamie...and another winged unicorn for Alice, but as for more stuff to sell...I'd need to have a think about it."

"Give it some thought. If you went professional, you could give up the factory job and maybe do something you really love!"

"I like it at the factory...well, most of the time, as long as that annoying personnel bloke leaves me alone. Listen, Sarah, I just had a thought...put the money in the cottage account for now. We could give it to the Lifeboats or something...and don't be daft... I can't make a living from drawing! If I gave up my job, Marge would have a fit!"

"I have to go now. Alice has 'Brownies' tonight, and I have to take her. Give some thought to doing some more drawings, won't you?

"I just draw for fun, Sarah, when the inspiration hits me, but, on the other hand, it's nice to know other people like them. Thanks for phoning and letting me know. We'll speak soon. Give my love to the kids and Brian."

He put the phone down, picked up his glass of wine and drank it in one go. He still couldn't believe what he had just heard.

When the phone rang, Ged and Marge had just finished dinner. He went back to the kitchen to wash the dishes. "Where on earth have you been, Gerald?" chided Marge when he went back into the kitchen and poured himself another steadying glass of Chardonnay. "Who was that on the telephone?" she demanded.

"It was Sarah," said Ged as he started to fill the sink, watching the soap bubbles rise up the sides... he felt like there were bubbles in his stomach and chest... he still couldn't believe that people had bought his drawings.

"Well...?"

"Well, what?"

What did Sarah want? Good grief, Gerald. I think you've had a bit too much wine..."

"Sorry Marge... Sarah just told me something very odd...and quite...well... exciting..."

"Really?"

Ged related everything that Sarah had just told him... including the fact that Emily had got the drawings framed and made prints and had, so far, sold twenty-five of them for around forty pounds each.

"How dare she?!"

"Sorry?" said Ged, confused by the question.

"How dare she get that woman to clean my damask tablecloth! That was a gift from my mother! I would have been perfectly capable of getting it clean. It's probably ruined! I will have a word with Sarah."

"Seriously, Marge? ... Is that all you have to say? Sarah helped me out of a pickle. It was my fault the tablecloth got paint on it... and it's kind of Emily to help... besides, aren't you a bit... well...don't you have any thoughts on the drawings?"

"I suppose when people go on holiday, they bring their wallets with them and leave their brains at home! I mean... who, in their right mind, would pay forty pounds for one of your silly doodles... forty pounds, for goodness' sake." She scoffed. "Tourists will buy any old tat as a souvenir. I suppose it's better than a silly beach ball or a fridge magnet, but ...forty pounds... really." She tailed off. "Just a moment... You said twenty-five drawings were sold?"

"Yes," replied Ged, still feeling rather stung.

"But... that's a thousand pounds, Gerald!

"I know... five hundred pounds each."

"What?"

"Five hundred for us and five hundred for Emily and Mike at the Lobster Pot. They got the prints done, framed them all, and sold the drawings. It seems fair."

"Seems like Emily knows a mug when she sees one... Nice little earner, I'm sure."

Ged took a deep breath and sighed. How had his lovely Marge turned into this bitter and twisted woman?

"I'm thinking of giving the money to the lifeboats..." he said, immediately regretting it.

"FIVE – HUNDRED – POUNDS?" growled Marge, menacingly, between gritted teeth... to CHARITY?

"Why not?" I've always wanted to make a big donation. I mean, it's all very well putting a fiver in a pot twice a year, but that equipment doesn't come cheap, and those guys risk their lives and their bodies for no pay whatsoever. I always thought it would be nice if I ever had a little extra to give it to them."

"Gerald, five hundred pounds would buy the new three-piece suite, for which, may I remind you, we have been saving up for six months."

Ged sighed again, resignedly, remembering their somewhat threadbare sofa and armchair and the new suite they had seen in the furniture store in town for four hundred and eighty pounds... maybe, with luck, it would be in the sale by now."

"Okay, Marge, he replied with a sigh as he dried his hands. "You can have a three-piece suite... and a new haircut, too, if you want... but any more money that comes in for those drawings is going to the lifeboats," said Ged decisively.

"I'll call the furniture shop in the morning," said Marge, and left the kitchen without a backward glance.

23

Warwick, October 1998

"Gerald!"

It was a few weeks after the news from Sarah. The cheque had arrived in the post the following week from Emily. Ged was preparing a packed lunch after breakfast.

"GERALD!" shrieked Marge from the downstairs bathroom.

He was used to Marge making a fuss about something most days and was inclined to ignore her shouts and utterances at this time in the morning, but this was different. There was a definite note of fear and panic in her voice."GERAAALD!"

"Coming!" he called as he went to the little bathroom built in under the stairs.

"GERALD! I can't see anything!"

"What? Has the light bulb gone? Open the door a crack, let some light in."

Marge started to sob uncontrollably... "I can't," she wailed. I haven't finished. There's no more toilet paper, and I can't see to get it from the cupboard. Everything is blurred... PLEASE, Gerald... I'm scared!"

"Okay, Marge... try to stay calm. Take a deep breath. I can unlock it from here with a coin. I'm going to get one. Just take a few deep breaths."

"Hurry, Gerald," She sobbed. He fetched a penny from the pile of change by his car keys and fitted it into the slot in the brass bathroom lock. It was stiff, but with practised tradesman's fingers, he managed to turn it, and the lock clicked. He turned the handle and opened the door a little to save Marge's blushes... she would not be happy for him to walk in while she was on the loo. The light was on. It was a dim light, but it was definitely on.

"Marge...?"

"Oh, Gerald! I can't see...I can't see! What's happening? I'm scared, Gerald! I'm blind!" Ged knelt in front of her and put his arms around her as best he could in the cramped space.

"It's going to be ok," ... he tried to speak soothingly, though his heart was beating loudly in his ears and his mind was racing. As she sobbed into his shoulder, she gripped her arms around his neck, and his shirt was soon wet with tears and no small amount of snot.

Earlier that week, she had told him that her vision was a little blurred, and he had persuaded her to make an appointment with the optician. She was supposed to be going that morning.

"Tell me what happened ... you came downstairs while I was making breakfast. Could you see then?"

Yes... well, I was still seeing things a little blurry, but I hadn't got my glasses on... then I went to the loo, and it was a bit... well, erm... difficult, and I closed my eyes as I... well, you know... tried ... a bit harder...to go to the loo and when I opened them it was... well like it is now...Oh Gerald, Gerald, I'm blind, I'm blind... please, no... I can't go blind," she had begun to shake. She was going into shock. Ged knew he had to take charge...

"Marge," he said firmly, "We need to get a doctor or an ambulance. If I help you, do you think you can stand up and move?"

"But I haven't finished in the toilet..." She sobbed.

"Okay, here's some toilet paper. Shall I leave the room while you finish up?"

"No! ... Please don't leave me!" she said, through the first lot of tissue that she was using to wipe her face from the crying.

Gerald stayed in the cramped little room, trying to avert his eyes as she sorted herself out... "It's going to be alright," he said as soothingly as he could. "Whatever happens, it's going to be ok.... We'll always be okay. I'm here now, and I won't leave unless you want me to."

"Oh, Gerald... I hate this."

"I know, Love... I think you're clean now... come on, let's get you up and out of here."

She managed to pull her knickers up; Ged helped her to wash her hands and guided her into the living room. She was still whimpering... She walked slowly and with great care, reaching out for walls and door frames. Ged got her to the sofa and fetched a box of tissues. He sat down with her on the new navy-blue velour sofa. She leaned into him, grasping his shirt and bursting into a renewed fit of sobbing.

Ged handed her another two or three tissues and took her face in his hands. "Let's have a look..." Ged took a good, long look at her eyes. They looked normal to him... her usual hazel-green, almond-shaped beautiful eyes, those long, brown lashes. The pupils were large, but the living room curtains were half-closed, so there was nothing unusual there.

"Oh, Gerald!" ...she sobbed convulsively, gasping for breath; Gerald... blind...I mean, really blind!" She managed to take a gasp of breath before continuing, her voice becoming strained. "My garden, my roses, dahlias, busy-lizzies, begonias... what if I never see them again? I can't cook... I won't be able... to DO anything."

"Now, Marge... you have to try to get a grip. Firstly, this may be temporary. It may go as quickly as it came. Secondly, there are millions of blind people around the world who were born that way... they've never seen a rose in their lives. Mrs Arnold does OK. She has her guide dog, and she has that lovely house on the corner. She keeps it clean and tidy... with a bit of help."

"Oh, no!" cried Marge... "Dogs! I hate dogs. The food smells, their breath smells, they slobber everywhere... Oh, and the dog dirt... in my garden! No Gerald. I can't have a guide dog!" she wailed.

"Right...You need to take some deep breaths. I'm going to phone the doctor. I'll get you a glass of water and put the kettle on."

"Oh... tea! I'll never make another cup of tea! I'll scald myself!" She shrieked.

Ged, now in the hallway, placed his hand on the wall, closed his eyes and took a deep, calming breath. Shouting back would only make her more agitated. He could feel his heart rate going up. Which must be nothing compared to hers, he thought.

"Try to take deep breaths..." he called from the kitchen. "I'm calling the doctors now."

193

It took an age to get through, in which time, Ged had made a pot of tea and poured Marge a glass of water. Eventually, Sue Birchley answered. Ged was so glad it was Sue on the desk. She knew Marge from the Women's Institute, and her kids went to school with Brian and Edward. "Oh, Sue, thank goodness! It's Ged Baker here… yes, Marge's Ged… Marge has just suddenly lost her sight. She's terrified… are any of her usual doctors in today?"

"Oh my God! When was this?"

"Just now… about twenty minutes ago, although she says her vision has been a bit blurred for a while. She was due at the optician today. Unfortunately, she was on the loo when it suddenly got worse."

"She must be terrified! Give me a second. I'll have to put you on hold. Dr Oldfield is in now. I'll check his schedule and have a word."

"OK… but please be quick… she's frantic!"

"Quick as I can, Ged, I promise."

***

The morning went by in a blur. Dr Oldfield was in surgery all morning and asked a locum GP, Doctor Lowe, to come out. He asked Marge and Ged a long list of questions…First came questions looking for symptoms of a stroke, facial problems. Can you lift both arms and hold them up? No issues there. Speech… well, certainly no issues in that department! Then a great many others… Had she had any vision problems recently, any history of glaucoma, cataracts, vision defects in her family, any headaches recently…absences, seizures…the list went on and on.

Ged told them she had a few headaches on holiday and a couple of times when he had expected her to see things that she hadn't seen, like the note he left her on the bedside table. He remembered the times he had found her staring into space… were they absences? He wasn't sure but mentioned them anyway, much to Marge's annoyance.

An ambulance had already been called. It arrived whilst Dr Lowe was still asking his questions. He had a chat with the paramedics and explained what he had gathered so far. The crew brought in a narrow wheelchair. They checked a few details after greeting Ged and checking that Marge could speak. Then, the apparently more senior of the two spoke directly to Marge.

"Okay, Mrs Baker," he said. My name is Tom, and I have Becky here with me. I'm a doctor from the ambulance service. Are you ok if I call you Marjorie?"

"Yes, I suppose so," said Marge. Her nose was blocked from crying. She sounded nasal and bunged up.

"I can call you Mrs Baker if you prefer."

"Yes, please."

"Am I going blind?" Marge asked the Paramedic.

"It's too soon to say, Mrs Baker, but with such a sudden loss of sight, it's possible it could be temporary. Let's get you to the Royal and see if we can get some tests done. Now, your husband needs to get some things together before we go. Night clothes, dressing gown, wash bag, towel, anything else you might need… You may be in the hospital for a few days. While he does that, I'm going to check a few things and ask you some questions. I'm sorry if Dr Lowe has already asked these questions, but it's important that we get as much information as we can. Mr Baker, can you stay while we ask the questions? Then I'll need you to get an overnight bag sorted while I do her observations."

Tom asked an even longer list of questions, to which most of the answers were 'No,' 'Don't think so,' or 'Not as far as we know.'

Then he asked about mood swings… "Mr Baker. Have you noticed any recent changes in behaviour or even what you might describe as personality changes?"

Ged didn't know what to say… he didn't want to upset Marge, and he thought she would fly off the handle if he said what he really thought, so, using Marge's blindness to his advantage, he nodded vigorously and simply said "Yes" in what he hoped was a matter of fact and calm enough voice. He signed, with a sideways look towards the hall, that he would rather tell Tom about that in private.

"Becky, can you do Mrs Baker's obs now… I just need BP, heart, sats and temperature for now," he said to the other paramedic. "Alright, if I pop outside for a moment, Mrs Baker. You'll be safe here with Dr Lowe and Becky." It wasn't a question, and he didn't wait for an answer. Ged and Tom went to the kitchen to talk in private.

"So, changes in behaviour, maybe personality?" he said to Ged, seriously.

"Yes, definitely. The whole family have noticed." Ged felt a wave of relief in telling someone. "She's been speaking really rudely to all the family and to people we've known for years." I mean, Marge has always been…a bit… judgemental, if I'm being honest… but nothing like this. She usually keeps her opinions to herself if she doesn't like a place or finds people annoying, but on our holiday in Cornwall with our son and his family, she was having a go at everyone. All of a sudden, she seems so incredibly unreasonable. Short-tempered … er…she has no…" he fumbled for the right word… 'filter'. If you know what I mean."

"Yes, I see what you're saying, I think. Has she been sleeping longer than usual or at unusual times of the day?"

"Yes. She keeps falling asleep in the afternoon when she does the crossword… come to think of it, she never did that before… oh, and I kept finding her sitting there and just staring into space."

"Any headaches?"

"No more than usual. Have we missed something? Is it a brain haemorrhage, tumour?"

"Impossible to say at this stage, Mr Baker… there will need to be tests done in the hospital before we can be sure," he said. "Do you work?"

"Oh no! What time is it? It's almost ten! I'm on a ten-six shift today! I'll have to ring in. Sorry, can you excuse me?"

"Of course… You might want to warn your boss that it could be a few days unless there's someone else that can be with Mrs Baker whilst you're at work. She'll be very disorientated and may need someone to take her to all the scans and so on." Tom explained.

"Yes, right… good point. I think I'll phone her sister. She used to be a nurse. I'm sure she would be able to come over for a few days… I've got so much on at work… I was off work for 4 weeks, and I'm still catching up. It's a really busy time… If I take any more time off, they have to put me on discipline."

"In the circumstances, Mr Baker, only the hardest-hearted boss would stop you from being with your wife at such a distressing time, surely."

"I'll call him now; I won't be long."

Ged picked up the phone in the hall and called his boss. "Pete... Yeah, it's me. Look, I'm not going to be able to come in today. It's Marge. She has suddenly lost her sight...no, nothing – diddly-squat. We have an ambulance here now, and she has to go to the hospital for tests. Thanks, Pete. Look, I know this leaves you in the proverbial, but there's no way I'll be in today; I'll try to call you from the hospital later and keep you informed. I may be able to come in tomorrow... OK... yeah, sure, but we've got that press to strip down this week and next... If I don't come in, it won't be commissioned or safety-checked and ready for production a week on Monday. I know, but...Well, I guess we could bring him in... Look, can I call you later when things have calmed down a bit... sure... thanks. Look, can you do me a favour and square things with Bob Small? You know what he can be like... I've already had 4 weeks off with the foot and everything...thanks." Ged hung up and went back to the living room.

"Everything ok with work, Mr Baker?" said Tom.

"Yeah. My boss is a great bloke; he suggested we get a contractor that we know to cover my work. I'll call back later when we've got a better idea of what's going on."

"Good. So, Mrs Baker. We would like to get you in the ambulance now if you're alright with that. Looks like you've had a cup of tea. Have you had anything to eat this morning?"

"Er... yes, I had toast and marmalade for breakfast and a banana."

"Right. That's good. It might be wise not to have anything more to eat, but you may want to bring that packed lunch to the hospital, Mr Baker. You could be in for a long day. Bring some change for the coffee machine, too." Ged was impressed.

"Tom, you think of everything; I wouldn't have thought of that," he said, with feeling.

"Just know what it's like having to wait around in the hospital. Bring a book or a newspaper for something to read, maybe. Oh, sorry, Mrs Baker, that was insensitive of me."

"I wouldn't have thought you wait around very long, do you, most days?" said Ged.

"Not as a rule, we don't, but my daughter had Lymphoma a few years ago, and trust me, that calls for a lot of hanging about in the hospital."

"Is she ok now?"

"She's been in remission for 6 months."

"Thank goodness…How old is she?"

"She'll be twelve next week."

"My God… I have no idea how tough that must be," said Ged with feeling. He thought of Brian and Edward at twelve years old, just starting high school, answering back, eating too many sweets, and now, all grown up. He felt so fortunate and ached with sympathy for Tom and his family.

"It's been tough… I can't lie. This job helps. It's odd; I don't often talk about it with my patients. Do you have kids?"

"Yes, twin boys… Well, they're thirty-five now," said Ged.

"We need to get Mrs Baker to the hospital. Do you want to go in the ambulance?"

"I better had. I don't think I'll be safe to drive. I can always get a taxi home."

Marge had gone quiet. She still sobbed occasionally. Ged hardly got a word out of her the whole way to the hospital, but she let him hold her hand.

24

Ged was glad of Tom's advice. The day was a chaotic and confusing mess of a day. Marge had X-rays, a CT Scan and an MRI. After the MRI, she had a terrible headache. They were taken to a hospital ward overlooking the "Friends of the Royal" gardens. Ged wished that she could have seen it. She would have loved the display of bedding plants and the well-tended rose bushes. Marge looked pale and drawn. Consumed with self-pity, she listed all the things she could no longer do if she were blind. Ged tried to placate and reassure her as best he could and attempted to pass the time by reading some newspaper articles to her and reading out the crossword clues, but this only served to upset her even more.

Marge fell asleep in the afternoon, and Ged took the opportunity to make a few phone calls. First, he called Annie. He explained the events of the morning and the tests they had done at the hospital. Annie went quiet at first... she asked Ged a few questions about the mood swings and agreed that the last few times she had seen Marge, she had seemed more irritable, and her opinions were even less filtered than usual, but also that she was getting some facts mixed up. She agreed to come over straight away. "I'll clear my diary... such as it is... for the next week. I can stay in the spare room."

"That would be brilliant, Annie! Thank you... have you any idea what it might be?"

"I have some ideas, but I don't want to jump to conclusions...It could be something relatively fixable, but we should see what the consultant says. It might be some kind of tumour on the brain. It could be something else, but from what you've said, it seems likely."

"What – a brain tumour?"

"Mmm. Could be more than one. Look, don't panic... they're often very treatable. She may get her sight back. Don't tell her, though; I don't want to give her false hope. Look, Ged, I think it may be best if you go back to work if you can focus. It'll take your mind off things, and you won't be doing Marge any harm... I can sit with her over the next few days. I know what to expect. It can be a slow process."

"Annie, you are a complete angel."

"That's what they call us nurses, Ged, but you wouldn't say that to hear the language in the staff canteen!" For the first time in a while, Ged laughed. "Anyway... How's your foot?"

"Really good, thanks. The boot certainly put me out of action in Porthcovery, but I managed to find ways of amusing myself and mostly staying out of trouble."

"So I heard...Brian told me about the sketches you did, Alice showed me the unicorn...Very nice! Can you walk okay now?

"Yes, but it hurts a bit in the morning... Hey, the pips are going on the payphone. What time do you think you'll be here?"

"I can be there at tea-time tonight if I get the four-o-five. Shall I come to the Royal?"

"Yes, please, Annie. Ward 3A. See you then...and Annie... Thanks."

The phone clicked. Ged sighed. Thank God for Annie!

***

He called Sarah next... he knew it would be a waste of time trying to call Brian at the restaurant. The staff could never get him to come to the phone, but Sarah would probably be in her office.

"Hi, Dad... how come you aren't at work?"

"Bad news, Sarah, love... it's Marge."

"Oh no... what's happened... is she ill? ... or is she being sued by some disgruntled restaurant owner?"

"She seems to have gone... blind... I mean, really blind... Woke up this morning, and she can't see a thing!"

"What?"

"Yep. She's in a terrible state. We had an ambulance and everything. We're at the Royal now. She's had loads of tests. We're waiting for the consultant."

"Well, what is it? Some sort of stroke? Did she have a headache?"

"No… she says she can just see blurs and dark patches. They've done a lot of tests. Annie thinks it might be a brain tumour, but it's too soon to say. Can you let Brian know, but don't say anything to the kids just yet."

"Sure, no problem, Dad and… give Mum our love…Oh, poor Mum." She said, with feeling. "Give us another call when you've got more information. Why aren't you using your mobile phone? These calls are going to cost a fortune!"

"I forgot about it, to be honest. Marge has only had it a few months, and I've not really used it. I'll call you later; I'm running out of change, and the pips are going."

Ged thought about calling Edward. Ed and Marge had a huge argument the last time he came to stay, and he stormed out, vowing never to come again. He had spoken to Brian on the phone and on visits to London, and Ged had called him a couple of times since, but he had not forgiven her.

The problem for Marge was that Ed had never got married. He had had long-term girlfriends, but none of them turned into a wife. Then, he committed the cardinal sin of moving in with one of them, Karen. Three years older than Ed and had been married before for a short time. The argument became heated when he told Marge that they were having a baby. Marge insisted that Edward should 'make an honest woman out of her.' Ed said that neither he nor his girlfriend wanted to get married as neither was religious, and they didn't really need to prove to anyone else that they loved each other. Plus, marriage hadn't been a great experience for Karen. Marge, being Marge, did not accept that and told him that he was immoral and reckless and said she didn't want her grandchild to be a bastard. As if this weren't bad enough, she suggested his girlfriend should have an abortion if they weren't going to marry.

Needless to say, the rest of the family didn't share this point of view, but no amount of persuasion on the part of Brian or Ged made any difference. She tried forbidding Ged from speaking to Edward until he 'saw sense,' which Ged ignored. He called him when Marge wasn't around, either when she was at the gardening club or on WI evenings. She had even tried to stop Ed from going to the house in Porthcovery. Ged told Sarah to make sure that Edward and his new family were always allowed a fortnight of their choice.

For the time being, he chickened out of making the call to Edward. He only had thirty pence anyway and thought a two-minute conversation was not the best way to break this news to Marge's estranged son.

Back in the ward, Marge was still sound asleep. Ged took a seat in the padded wooden armchair next to her bed. He stared out of the window unseeingly. He fidgeted; he felt agitated… had he missed some early symptoms? Those outbursts in Porthcovery were worse than anything he could remember from Marge, though they did remind him of her father. Ged had thought it was a sign of getting older, or perhaps it was the wrong time of the month. Despite having been through the menopause, he knew that her moods still had a monthly pattern. Now he realised it must have been something else.

He took out the book he had brought with him and tried to settle to read. The chair was hard and uncomfortable, and he couldn't get into the book. He tried doing the crossword in the newspaper; it was the quick one, but he couldn't concentrate and only managed four clues.

Marge woke with a start…" Gerald! Where are you? Why is everything so …Oh, no! It wasn't a dream…" She began to cry again.

"Hey, hey, Margie…," Ged stood up, putting his hand on her arm. "I'm here. You're in the Royal Infirmary," he said gently. "We're just waiting for the results of the scans. I've spoken to Annie… she's on her way."

"Annie? Oh, good," she sniffed. "When will she be here?" she blew her nose noisily with a tissue that Ged pressed into her hand.

"Tea time. She thinks the blindness might be temporary… there is hope, my love."

"Is there anything to drink?"

"I got you a Tea, but it's gone a bit cold."

"Why can't I have a hot one? The last two you gave me were stone cold, too."

"The man with the tea trolley came around half an hour ago while you were asleep, but earlier, I was worried if you can't see what you're doing, you might spill it and scald yourself."

"I hardly think that's likely. Get me a hot one, Gerald."

"Okay, I'll see what I can do." He made to leave the ward, but a nurse stopped him.

"I'll get Mrs Baker some water. I'm sorry, Mrs Baker. If you need an operation, you shouldn't have anything to eat or drink except for a little water. The consultant has asked me to take you to one of the private rooms along the corridor. He's doing his rounds now.

***

The private room also looked out over the hospital gardens. The nurse helped Marge into an armchair, and Ged sat on a visitor's chair next to her, holding her hand. The consultant neurologist, Mr Tanduklar, arrived and explained the test results. He had a soft, rather melodic way of speaking. A strong Indian accent that was oddly calming, bordering on soporific, which was somewhat frustrating as the subject matter was so demanding of one's attention.

"So, Mr and Mrs Baker. We have the results of the scans that Mrs Baker had today. It's complex, but I will try to be as clear as possible. First: vision problems. You have a mass that has formed around the optic nerve, which is likely causing vision problems. We believe this is operable, and we will know more about it when we can take it out and have a look at it. There is a reasonably good chance you may get some improvement in your sight, but I must stress I cannot guarantee anything."

"Er, okay, so she could get her sight back?" said Ged, brightening slightly.

"It is a possibility. However, other masses have been identified in the scans, which are more concerning. They are all relatively small, which explains why you may not have had obvious symptoms, and they are mostly based in the frontal part of the brain. They can cause all sorts of symptoms which are not always obvious."

"Such as?" said Marge, quietly.

"Well, a variety of things: cognition problems and logic; memory impairment and that kind of thing; sudden changes in behaviour; personality disorders; changes in temperament; anxiety, depression, the list is extensive."

"I see. And is it, you know, er, cancer or could it be something else?" she said tersely.

"I cannot say for certain until we have operated and analysed the masses that we can remove, but it looks like it could be malignancies or possibly even metastases. In my experience, masses distributed throughout the brain in this way are usually not good news. I could be wrong, of course. There are other areas we want to take a closer look at. There seems to be a mass by the pituitary gland at the front," he pointed to his brow. "These are usually benign, but with the presence of other masses elsewhere, I am concerned that we should try to remove this if possible."

Ged was reeling. So many all over the brain. He squeezed Marge's hand, which she snatched away, folding her arms tightly across her midriff.

"Finally, Mr and Mrs Baker," said Mr Tandulkar, "with the smaller masses in the frontal area, it could be very difficult to remove those, and if we find cancerous or pre-cancerous cells in the other areas that we are investigating, I recommend treatment with chemotherapy as soon as possible to reduce the size of these rather than attempting a physical removal."

"No, no, absolutely not!" snapped Marge without hesitation. "I don't want chemotherapy. Can't you just take them all out in an operation? I'll lose all my hair and be sick all the time."

"I'm sorry, Mrs Baker," said Mr Tandulkar, shaking his head sadly, "but some of the masses are likely to be inoperable, and it could do you harm to attempt it. With your permission, we will operate tomorrow morning and remove what we can safely; then, once we have the lab results, the oncology team here at the Royal will have a case meeting to discuss the most suitable options for treatment."

"But what if I don't want chemotherapy? Doesn't my opinion count for anything?" Marge's voice was rising, and Ged could see a familiar flush of pink on her neck and chest. Tears were brimming at the corners of her sightless eyes.

"Yes, of course, Mrs Baker," said Mr Tandulkar earnestly. "We will tell you what we believe are the best options for you, and then you and your family can decide how you wish to proceed." He respectfully regarded Marge as if she could see him throughout.

"Right… and I can have an operation tomorrow, which might get my sight back?"

"It is a possibility, yes, but as I say, Mrs Baker, I can't…"

"Yes, yes, you can't guarantee anything, hedge your bets, cover your back… I understand. I may be blind, but I'm not a fool," Marge snapped.

"Marge-" Ged interjected, "I'm sure Mr Tandulkar will do whatever he can to get your sight back and give you the best possible care."

"When will I know if I have my sight back?" said Marge, ignoring Ged.

"If we operate tomorrow morning – so, Tuesday- then you'll be under heavy sedation for a day or two. We should know, maybe Thursday or Friday."

"Have you done many of these operations?" asked Ged politely.

"Quite a number actually, Mr Baker. This is my area of specialism. I must stress to you that this operation is not without risks. Ideally, we do the procedure under a local anaesthetic to reduce the risks; Mrs Baker will be sedated but awake during the procedure. Even with my experience and these scans, we don't know what we are dealing with until we have results from the lab."

"I see," said Ged.

"Hedging your bets again," grumbled Marge.

"Another thing I must stress, Mr and Mrs Baker, is that these lesions are spread over an extensive area of the brain. We may need to investigate further to see if these are metastases which have spread from somewhere else in the body.

"So, you mean these could be – secondaries?" Said Ged, remembering the term from a guy at work whose mother had passed from breast cancer secondaries the previous year.

205

"But I haven't had cancer," said Marge.

"It's not for certain, but it would be wise to investigate. Some cancers are not obvious, Mrs Baker and can initially be asymptomatic. Many patients later attribute seemingly minor symptoms that they have experienced to the primary tumour. This investigation is, of course, only necessary *if* the masses are found to be malignant. And either way, if they are, chemotherapy is the best way to give you more time."

"More time?" said Ged.

"More than you would have if you choose not to have it."

"But only if it's cancer."

"Indeed."

"And it might not be…" Ged realised he was beginning to babble, clutching at straws.

Mr Tandulkar paused for a moment or two, looking down and allowing Ged's question to hover in the air. He took the subject back to more concrete matters.

"We will let you know this afternoon what time the operation is going to be. I'd like to get started as early as possible. Have you had anything to eat or drink today, Mrs Baker?"

"Only two cups of cold tea and this water," grumbled Marge.

"And toast at breakfast, Marge," Ged interjected.

"Good. No more to eat and just a little water today. Get as much rest as possible, Mrs Baker. I will ask Sister to get you a sedative to calm you and give you a good night's sleep."

"Can I have something too?" said Ged, only half joking.

"I'm afraid you'll have to talk to your GP about that, Mr Baker," he replied, regarding Ged over his half-moon spectacles. "Under the circumstances, I'm sure something for anxiety would be helpful. I realise this has not been an easy discussion for you both. Do you have any further questions?"

Ged nodded his head vigorously, looking at the consultant with pleading eyes. He gestured out of the room with a sideways look. The consultant gave a small nod of agreement.

"No. I don't think so," said Marge.

"Then I will see you in the morning, Mrs Baker – Mr Baker?"

"Thank you, Doctor," said Ged, standing up. "Marge. I promise I won't be long. I need the toilet, but I'll be back soon, OK?"

"Oh, very well," said Marge in an exasperated tone.

Outside in the corridor, Mr Tandulkar was waiting for him.

"Er, Mr Tandulkar, if I do have some questions, how can I get hold of you?"

"Leave a message with my secretary," he said, reaching into his top pocket and handing Ged a business card. "She or I will call you back. You have questions now?"

"Yes. Well, I suppose the obvious one is: How long has she got?"

"Ah, Mr Baker. This is always impossible to answer accurately. It depends on what we are dealing with. Tell me, have you noticed changes in your wife's behaviour recently?"

"Yes, very recently. We were on holiday in Cornwall. Marge is – well, she can be quite, oh, how can I put it? Blunt, to the point and somewhat judgemental, but this was a whole new level of rude. She was totally unreasonable, upsetting lots of people and behaving quite erratically. I mean, I may not have noticed it until the holiday. She does find it a little stressful, staying with my son and the grandkids; we're so used to being just the two of us, you see."

"Yes, of course, but this was more than normal?"

"Yes. A lot more, and there was something else."

"Go on."

"Well, we had some disagreements about what we could see. I left a note right under her glasses one morning, and she said she didn't even notice it."

"Mmm?"

"And then a few times, it's never happened before; I found her in the garden; she looked like she was doing the crossword. Her eyes were open, but her pen wasn't moving, and she was just sort of staring into space like she was in a trance."

"Hmm, how recently have you noticed these changes?"

"Only in the last three or four months."

"Thank you, Mr Baker. That is most helpful. Now, I think you are someone who can accept straight talking, yes?"

"Definitely."

207

Mr Tandulkar took a deep breath and sighed. "Mr Baker, it is my belief that your wife is very ill. I have little doubt that we are dealing with some kind of tumours; they may be benign, but in my professional experience, I would say these are not. The tests after the operation will tell us how aggressive it is. If they are malignant and she decides not to have chemotherapy and the changes in behaviour are as sudden as you say, then she may have another three to six months, possibly a little more."

"Oh my," a shake entered Ged's voice, "so… so little time?"

"I do not believe in beating about the bushes, as they say, Mr Baker."

"No, no, I – I understand and if she does have chemotherapy?"

"Well, of course, there are no guarantees. Chemotherapy can slow down the growth of some tumours and reduce others. It could buy her a few months, but as your wife said, there is a cost. These are aggressive treatments, Mr Baker, and they can have strong side effects. We will do the surgery and see what we are dealing with, but I have been doing this for over fifteen years, Mr Baker, and I think these are aggressive gliomas, most likely astrocytomas, from the way they seem to have spread around the brain. They are more common in men, but they sometimes occur in women of her age."

"Right."

"Forgive me for asking, Mr Baker, does Mrs Baker have a medical power of attorney?"

Ged was taken aback. "We …er, I don't think so. Why do you ask?"

"For now, Mrs Baker seems to be able to make decisions for herself, but it may be prudent to arrange power of attorney, or the next few months could be complicated. A power of attorney would help you to make decisions for your wife if she is not able to make them for herself."

"Is that likely to happen?"

"If these gliomas are aggressive, as I suspect, then, quite soon, your wife may not be able to make sound judgements and decisions in her own best interests. A power of attorney would allow you or a member of the family to make decisions on her behalf."

Ged's gaze dropped to the floor as his eyes welled with tears. Mr Tandulkar laid a steady hand on Ged's shoulder and looked at him with such feeling and total understanding. It was oddly reassuring. "I know this is very difficult, and there is much to consider, but it is something I would urge you to think about."

"Thank you, Mr Tandulkar." Ged's voice was shaking, "Erm… by the way, you aren't any relation, are you?"

"Sorry?"

"Well, to *'the'* Tendulkar."

Mr Tandulkar smiled. "What to the second-greatest cricketer of all time? I don't know. I have been asked many times, but family research in my part of Pakistan is not easy, especially now that my grandparents and my father have passed, and my Mother, unfortunately, has dementia. Maybe we are distant cousins."

"I'm sorry about your Mother," said Ged, quietly.

"Thank you, Mr Baker; I am sorry to be so blunt about your wife's condition. We will see what we have after the procedure. Maybe it is better news."

"It's okay, I appreciate your candidness." Mr Tandulkar shook Ged's offered hand slowly and deliberately. The gentle firmness of his handshake gave Ged the tiniest glow of comfort."

***

"Hello, you two!"

"Annie!" Ged hugged his sister-in-law tightly.

"Marge, Annie's here, Love," said Ged, turning to his wife.

"I'm not deaf, Gerald. Half of the patients in the hospital can hear you both! Keep it down, please; shouting is so uncouth," scolded Marge.

"Put a sock in it, Marjorie. I'm just pleased to see you!" chided Annie, winking at Ged.

"Well, I wish I could say the same, I'm sure," said Marge.

"Try not to worry. These things can usually be removed, and you'll get some, if not all, of your sight back. So, when's the operation?"

"First thing tomorrow," said Ged, "Nine am. The surgeon wanted to get it done early."

"Hmm, they normally do. Then they can get out on the golf course in the afternoon! I'll stop here with Marge. You go and get a cuppa and some fresh air." She said in a matronly, business-like manner. "We'll get a takeaway after visiting hours. Do you have your car here?"

"No. I came in the Ambulance. Do you have any change? I've run out, and I need to make a phone call. I'll get us both a coffee."

"Here, take my purse. I'll have a tea if you're going to the café or a coffee if it's from one of those infernal machines."

Ged went off to call Pete. Calls to the family would have to wait until he got home.

When he returned, Annie was holding Marge's hand. Her sightless eyes were red and puffy, her nose pink; she grasped a tissue in her other hand. Ged and Annie exchanged looks. They sat in silence, sipping their coffees, trying not to make a sound in case Marge heard them and became upset that she wasn't getting one.

"I think you should see if you can get some sleep, Marjorie," said Annie, patting her sister's hand, "I'll be here first thing in the morning. It's late, and you need your beauty sleep. I'll see if the ward Sister can give you a sleeping tablet." She went to the nurse's desk to ask, but there was no one around. There was no need, anyway. When she returned, Marge's head was slumped on her chest. She was already beginning to breathe deeply.

"I think they gave her something just before you came." Whispered Ged, "But let's make her comfortable."

Annie rearranged the pillows and the rake of the bed and kissed her sister on the forehead, "Night, night, Sis… Love you."

Ged walked around the bed and kissed his wife on the cheek. "Sleep well, my Love."

25

Annie ordered a takeaway from the tandoori restaurant in the village using the hospital payphone and then asked the taxi driver to stop at the restaurant on the way home.

Whilst Annie got plates, cutlery, glasses and a bottle of Chardonnay from the fridge, Ged grabbed a pad and pen and sat at the table to make a list of the calls he would have to make and things he could think of that needed to be done. Annie, with her wealth of nursing experience, was a great help. She took the emotion out of it, making the tasks almost matter-of-fact. There would be time for softer discussion once the wine had its effect.

After dinner, Ged called Sarah and Brian. He filled him in on the details, pointing out that the diagnosis wasn't definite but that Mr Tandulkar had prepared him for the worst.

"Three months?" was all that Brian could say. "Three months?"

"Well, that's only if it's one of the types of tumours that he suspects."

"Oh, Dad."

"I know, Son, it's a lot to process. Let's not tell the kids until we know for sure."

"Does Edward know?"

"No. I'm calling him next."

"Jeez."

"Yep. Not going to be easy. I think I'll have another glass of wine before I attempt it."

"Good luck with that, Dad."

"Cheers, Bri – and chin up."

"Yeah. Love you, Dad."

"I love you too, Son."

Annie replenished Ged's glass. He watched the clear, liquid sunshine, with its familiar, imperceptibly green tinge swaying within it, wondering if he should really be drinking three glasses on a Monday night. Annie read his mind: "It'll help you sleep," she said.

"I guess so; I'm not looking forward to calling Ed," he said. "I'll sleep better when that's over."

Ged dialled the number. There was no answer for some time, then a female voice.

"Hello?"

"Hi...Karen? It's Ged – Edwards' Dad, how's Little Bump?"

"Hi, Ged. Little Bump isn't so little these days. I think I'm giving birth to the Karate Kid; he or she has been beating the hell out of my insides for the last hour or two, and I'm having a rest. How are you?"

"I'm, um... Could I have a word with Ed, please?"

"He's in the kitchen, making a curry. Can he call back later?"

"Actually, if it's okay, Karen, I'd just like a quick word. I've had a long day, and I might pass out if I wait 'til after you two – I should say three – have had your dinner."

"Is everything OK?" Karen's tone hinted that she knew it wasn't.

"Not really, Karen. I'm afraid Ed's Mum has been taken ill. I know Ed and his mother aren't really speaking at the moment, but I just thought... I thought Ed would want to know."

"Wait a sec. I'll get him."

Ged took a few gulps of the Chardonnay. Its sharpness was refreshing. He could feel himself becoming bolder but also more fuzzy-headed. He placed the glass on the wooden coffee table and tried to think of how to say what he wanted to Ed.

"Dad?"

"Hi, Son, almost time to be a Dad. The baby's due soon, isn't it?"

"Yes. I'm doing all the housework and cooking now. Karen is like a beached whale...Ow! Sorry, Love, I didn't mean it like that; you're still blooming and gorgeous!"

"Ed."

"What is it, Dad? You sound terrible."

"It's Mum."

"What's up now? Have they kicked her out of the W.I. for being too right-wing?" Ged would have normally chuckled at Ed's sarcastic comment, but it stung like a wasp.

212

"Now, don't be rude, Edward. She's…" Ged checked himself, almost holding his breath. When he continued, his voice was trembling. The words seemed to stick in his throat as if they didn't want to come out of his mouth for fear of making them more real. "She…she's in the Royal Infirmary. They are going to operate tomorrow, but, but…" The words had now gathered into a lump in Ged's throat, and he could no longer speak. Fuelled by exhaustion and half a bottle of wine, the emotion welled up inside him. His shoulders shook, and he sobbed silently into his fist, trying to gather the strength to speak again.

"Dad?" Ed's voice was full of concern. "Dad… What is it? What's up with Mum?" Annie took the receiver from Ged. She kissed him on the forehead, squeezed his other hand, and handed him his wine glass. She spoke to Ed.

"Hi, Ed. It's Auntie Annie."

"Hi, Auntie Annie. Where's Dad?"

"He's finding it a bit difficult to speak. I'm afraid Mum may be very ill. If the surgeon's hunch – and mine, are right, it could be terminal. I'm sorry, Ed; I wish we could be calling with better news. It's a tricky time for you and Karen with such a happy occasion looming."

"What is it? I mean, what's wrong?"

"She's been having visual difficulties, and they got much worse this morning. She can't see a thing now. They think it's multiple brain tumours. The specialist is going to remove what he can tomorrow morning, and we'll know more after the lab results. From the look of the scan and the way she's been behaving recently – and so suddenly, too – it seems likely."

"Oh, dear God… we've not talked for months. She hates me; she won't even talk to me. Did you know she refused even to meet Karen?"

"Yes. She told me what she said to you a few months ago. It's something my dear sister and I don't agree on. For all we know, it's possible that it could have been the tumours that caused her to react so strongly, so bluntly. I know she has some old-fashioned views, but she does love you and Brian very much, and I am sure meeting Karen would have changed her mind. I wonder if we've missed some subtle signs these past few months."

"Should I come up there?"

"Not yet. Mum will be sedated for a couple of days after the op. We'll know more by Thursday. We just thought we should tell you what we know so far. You have other priorities at the moment. Karen is due in a week or so, isn't she?"

"Actually, she was due last Friday and judging from the hammering she's getting from the baby, I think it's trying to break out now!"

"Oh, Ed, the timing couldn't be worse, could it? "I'd better go. Give Karen my love.

"Sure and – thanks, Auntie Annie. Had I better say bye to Dad?"

"You could if he was awake. He's passed out on the sofa. A long day at the hospital, a chicken madras and a half bottle of Chardonnay have finally done him in."

"Will you give him my love – and tell him…I'm sorry."

"What on earth for?" asked Annie, incredulously.

"I don't know… Maybe if Mum and I hadn't argued. I walked out; I could've…"

"You have not done anything wrong, Edward Baker. There is nothing to be sorry for. Now go and look after your darling girl and your precious package, and *try* not to worry too much. It won't do any good to anyone."

"Okay, thanks, Auntie Annie. Love you lots."

"Love you too – and so does your Mum, even if she doesn't say it very often."

Annie went upstairs and fetched a pillow and quilt for Ged. She removed his shoes and socks, slid the pillow under his head and covered him with the quilt. The snoring Ged didn't even stir. She went back to the kitchen, tidied away the remnants of their curry, washed the plates, grabbed her holdall and took herself and the last glass of wine upstairs.

As always, the spare room was perfectly made up and ready for a guest: A clean duvet and bed cover on the double bed with fluffy towels folded on the chair. Marge was so organised. Annie thought of her cottage in rural Oxfordshire: an ancient sandstone terrace, Its garden rampant with perennials and climbers and an inside to match: a hodgepodge of books, magazines and brochures, un-matched furniture, her beloved but threadbare sofa covered in throws and half a dozen patchwork cushions, her hand-made woollen rug; a long-wished-for make-it-yourself gift for her fortieth birthday from Marge and Ged. There were so many pictures that there was hardly a clear space on the walls. Looking around at this perfect, tidy, but somewhat sterile room: with pink rose print curtains and matching duvet cover, a polished pine dressing table, a cream and pink rug placed on the stripped and varnished floorboard, a built-in, white-painted closet and wooden chest of toys. Reminded Annie why she never invited her sister to stay; Marge would disapprove of her entire house, let alone the spare room!

Annie dressed into her pyjamas, climbed into bed with her book, and took a sip of her wine. She noticed a multi-picture photo frame on the wall. There was an image of Ged, with Alice as a toddler sitting on his knee; a family photo of Brian, Sarah and Jamie with baby Alice in Sarah's arms; Brian in his white Chef's garb; One of Ged and Marge at their 30th wedding anniversary celebration at the restaurant in London. Marge wore a smart royal-blue dress and had her white, leather 'going-out' handbag on her lap, hands placed over the clasp like a duchess. Her smile was an image of contentment, and was that – pride? Ged had his arm around her shoulders and was grinning broadly as if someone had just cracked a joke. Another photo showed Edward and his brother in cricket whites in their twenties. Lastly, she alighted on a picture of herself and Marge by a lovely, gnarled oak tree. She tried to recall when it was taken. Judging by the outfit Annie was wearing and the length of her hair, it must have been at least thirty years ago. Oh, that shirt! It was Marge's favourite! Their grandmother had given it to Annie, and Marge had been jealous, but Marge could never have worn it. She was about two sizes smaller. Tiny blue flowers printed on cream cotton with a scalloped collar. Annie winced. Part of it was now serving as a duster under the sink in her kitchen.

She recalled the bedroom she once shared with Marge in their childhood home in Warwick. They shared the room until Annie was around nine years old. Marge was constantly trying to get Annie to

Tidy up, as she called it. Actually, Annie's side of the room was reasonably tidy, just not quite so pink and perfect as her sister's. For her ninth birthday, Annie begged her mother not to buy her anything but to allow them to have separate rooms. She was happy to have the tiny room at the front of the house that her mother called her 'sewing room'. Annie thought this was an odd name for a tiny seven-foot square room containing a narrow single bed, a chest of drawers and over one hundred old books on pine shelves. Granted, it was the room where their mother kept an old hand-crank sewing machine, but she rarely used it. She preferred to hand-sew their dresses, or her own mother, Granny Marchbanks, would make something on her treadle machine.

Annie made the little bedroom a sanctuary of art and literature. She increased the number of shelves to hold even more books, found pocket-money priced prints and even hung the lids of her favourite biscuit tins on the wall, which sported reproductions of Monet, Turner, Van Gogh and Gauguin. Marge despaired of Annie's 'clutter.' The bedroom they once shared became one of pink bedspreads, white lace curtains and a pink rug on which she practised dance stretches. She had bought a hat stand from an antique shop, on which she had hung a few scarves and a treasured satin Kimono-style dressing gown that Annie often got into trouble for trying on.

"I wonder…" said Annie aloud. She got out of bed, placing the wine on the bedside cabinet and opened the door of the white louvred door wardrobe. There were two of Ged's suits and a few plastic-covered evening dresses. Annie gently moved them aside, and there it was, hanging on the rail, squashed into the side of the wardrobe. The turquoise-blue Kimono with its pink cherry blossom embroidery. A little creased, but still as beautiful as Annie remembered…Feeling a little sheepish, even looking around towards the door in case anyone was watching, she lifted the coat hanger with the Kimono gown out of the wardrobe. Discarding the hanger on the bed, she pulled its satin sleeves over her bare arms and luxuriously shrugged her shoulders into its familiar silkiness. She looked at herself in the mirror, swishing from side to side, remembering how, as a girl, she had imagined herself to be a famous actress in her boudoir in a grand mansion, a long, black cigarette holder in one hand and her latest script in the other…The image was shattered by the memory of sharp admonishment from Marge or perhaps their mother upon being discovered that she should 'put the kimono back where she had found it.'

"But you're not here now, are you…?" she said to the mirror. "I could wear it all night, and you'd never know." She twirled this way and that, walking around the room, picking up her glass of wine, taking a sip and flopping onto the bed with her book in her hand… living the fantasy. She suddenly felt ridiculous… she chuckled to herself, took off the old dressing gown and stowed it away once more on its hanger in the wardrobe, drained her glass and went to brush her teeth.

***

The familiar ring of the trim-phone awoke Ged. He rubbed his eyes and looked around. Why was he in the living room? His head felt fuzzy… 'Oh, the wine…' he thought grimly as he picked up the receiver and looked at his watch… 5 am? "Hello?" he croaked.

"Dad?"

"Brian?"

"It's Ed! You never could tell the difference! … Look, I'm sorry for calling so early, but I thought you wouldn't mind… in the circumstances."

"You're a Dad, aren't you!"

"Yes! Oh, Dad…she's so gorgeous!"

"A little girl, then? Is Karen OK?"

"She's a bit shell-shocked… and sore… they had to use forceps, and she got really panicky. She's exhausted! Oh, but Dad, the baby… she's so beautiful! I mean, she wasn't at first… she looked like something from an alien movie, but she's all cleaned up now… come on, Sweetie, are you going to say 'Hi' to your Grandad? … Sorry, she's not very talkative. Karen fed her about twenty minutes ago, and she's drunk."

Ged chuckled. "What time was she born?"

217

"About half past midnight… it was all a bit quick. We had dinner after I spoke to you, and then, when Karen tried to stand up, it just happened! I went a bit nuts… I phoned Brian, and he told me what to do. Well, reminded me. I've been to all the antenatal classes, so I did know, but when it happened, I panicked and went blank."

"Sounds like the curry did the trick! Did you put lots of lentils and spinach in it?"

"Ha-ha! How did you know?"

"Brian used it on Sarah when Jamie was a bit slow."

"Brian must have given Karen the recipe. She was pretty fed up of waiting."

"So, have you thought of a name?"

"We like 'Laura.' It wasn't on the list, but while we were in the recovery room, she had been cleaned up, and she just kind of looked like a 'Laura. '"

"Any middle names?"

"I thought of 'Dorothy, ' like Grandmama, but it doesn't really go, does it… Laura Dorothy Baker… bit of a mouthful."

"Hmm, doesn't sound right, and Marjorie doesn't sound very good with Laura either. What about Anne or Annie?"

"Laura, Anne Baker…Yeah! That sounds brilliant! I'll see what Karen thinks."

Ged could hear Karen in the background. *"I love it! That's a great idea!"*

"Everything okay with the little one? Got all her fingers and toes and everything?"

"Yeah, everything seems fine. She got into feeding quickly, too. The lady in the next bed is having an awful time getting her baby to latch on…Hey, I guess you want to get back to bed. How are you now? Look, Dad, I'm so sorry about Mum. I feel like it's partly my fault or something. I feel guilty for fighting with her."

"Don't be ridiculous. You didn't do anything wrong. Your mum and I are completely at odds on this one. Maybe the way she reacted was somehow connected with these tumours. The docs said they can cause personality changes and mood swings."

"Well, maybe, but I still feel awful. I want to make it up with Mum before…well…"

"I know, Son; bring Laura and Karen over once Mum has recovered from her operation. Let's just take it one day at a time. But you have NOT done anything wrong. You have a lovely lady and a beautiful daughter to take care of. You're a Dad! Isn't that brilliant?"

"Yeah, it's very, very cool…and a bit scary, to be honest."

"Oh, I remember that feeling. I was terrified when you two came along. Your Mum being pregnant was one thing; finding out she was having twins was terrifying! I only had that job at the upholsterer, and I had no idea how I was going to make ends meet. It's what got me looking for other jobs… but oh, you two were so beautiful! Lots of jet-black silky hair. You were such a wriggler… couldn't keep still." We could tell you apart better then than when you were toddlers!"

"I guess I should let you get back to bed."

"Not sure I would be able to sleep now. I'm so pleased for you both, Ed. I'll tell Annie as soon as she wakes up; she'll be thrilled."

"I've got to go. Laura is taking after her Dad…she's wriggling even more than she did inside her mum!"

"Okay, give Karen my love…and congratulations to you both."

***

Annie came down to breakfast with a fuzzy head. Ged had taken her a cup of tea earlier and left it by her bed. There was a fresh pot of coffee on the table, buttered toast, and he was cooking scrambled eggs at the stove.

"Alka-Seltzer with a scrambled egg chaser, ma'am?"

She sat down at the kitchen table. "Perfect. Maybe we shouldn't have shared a whole bottle of wine with the curry… Perhaps if I was twenty or thirty years younger, but not now."

"Same, but I do have some very good news amidst all this awfulness."

"Oh?"

"Yes, Great Auntie Annie."

"What?"

"You're a Great Auntie again!"

"What? Ed and Karen…?"

"Little girl, just after midnight."

"That's great! How big?"

"Sorry, I forgot to ask… but you are going to love the name."

"Really?"

"Laura – Anne."

"Really?"

"Well, Anne sounded nice with 'Laura', and Ed's always been fond of his Auntie Annie."

Annie couldn't help smiling, then laughing out loud, then crying a little. She grabbed some kitchen roll and blew her nose… she pulled herself together after a minute.

"How lovely…is Karen OK?"

"Ed says she's pretty sore."

"Ouch. I always thought giving birth was a bad idea. I'd rather borrow your kids."

Ged smiled and placed a fizzing glass of hangover relief before her, then turned his attention to plating up the scrambled eggs and mushrooms.

***

When Annie and Ged arrived at the hospital that morning, Marge was sitting up in bed with headphones on. Her eyes were open and staring straight ahead. It was unnerving. She looked as though she was focusing on the patient in the opposite bed. Fortunately, that lady was fast asleep.

Annie went off to find a coffee machine, and Ged sat down in the chair beside Marge. "Hello, darling Margie." She made no response. He could hear the music beat from the headphones: Tch, tch, tch… and a high-pitched whine which sounded like nails being scraped down a chalkboard.

He gently laid his hand on hers. She yelped and tore the headphones off her head.

"Who's that? She shrieked. Are we going to theatre now, nurse?"

"Oh, I startled you… I'm sorry, it's me. Good morning, beautiful."

"You gave me an awful shock, Gerald. You could have said something before grabbing my arm like that!"

"I…" Ged was about to say something in response… then he remembered what the doctor had said about the tumours, causing her to be more reactive, and he held his tongue.

"Annie and I thought we would come and see you before you go down for your operation. We'll come and see you this afternoon when it's all done."

"Well, I'm not sure what good it will do, you being here. Shouldn't you be at work?"

"Pete has allowed me some time off. I will go in later this morning. He asked me to send his and Rebecca's love."

"Where's Annie?"

"Getting coffee."

"Oh, for goodness' sake! I can't have anything. Surely, she, of all people, knows that!"

Annie was standing at the end of the bed with two plastic cups in a cardboard holder. "Morning, Marge! Don't get your hopes up. The coffees are for Ged and me."

The ward sister came in. "Hi, Marge. I'm Janice; I'm going to clean your hand and give you a little injection. It might help you feel a little more relaxed, and we will take you down in about ten minutes."

"As I don't know you, Nurse Janice…I would prefer it if you call me Mrs Baker." Chided Marge.

Janice hardly flinched and took this reprimand in her stride… "Of course, Mrs Baker… Scratch coming up."

"Ouch! That was more than a scratch!"

"Yes, it can sting a little."

Ged and Annie exchanged a glance as they sipped their coffees.

Mr Tandulkar arrived in the ward as Janice finished sticking a dressing over the cannula to hold it in place.

Morning, Mr Baker, Mrs Baker…and …er…

"Annie Cookson, Doctor. Nice to meet you."

"Likewise, Mrs Cookson." He said, shaking her hand.

"It's Miss, actually," said Marge from the bed.

"My apologies, Miss Cookson... Mrs Baker, we will take you down to surgery soon. The sedative should help you to relax a little. We will be in there for about an hour. We are likely to be sedating you for a while afterwards, so it may be tomorrow before you can chat to Miss Cookson here and your husband."

"We'll leave you to it; we'll be in the way, here. See you later, Marge," said Annie, brightly.

Ged kissed Marge on the forehead. "See you this evening, beautiful," he whispered. Marge had tears in her sightless eyes; her complexion was like wax, and she clasped her hands tightly on her lap. "Chin up, my girl... you can do this."

"I don't think I can, Gerald. I'm really frightened."

"I know,' he said, embracing her. She held on to him tighter than she had done for years and sobbed quietly into his shoulder. "It would be strange if you weren't. You're in good hands." He moved to allow the nurse to get around the side of the bed. He kissed Marge on the cheek and squeezed her free hand firmly.

Annie and Ged walked away, down sterile and busy corridors to a chaotic symphony of electronic beeps, crockery clinking, curtains being drawn around beds, a phone ringing for ages without answer, a squeaking trolley wheel; plastic clogs slopping on the floor behind them; his shoes, creaking as he walked... he felt...actually, he didn't know what he felt... it was as though he weren't in his real body but observing this whole scene from above.

26

Ged was glad to get back to work. After a chat over coffee with Peter, he threw himself into his work, helping one of the engineers to strip down a huge press used for making the side panels of cars. It required complete concentration to do everything in the correct order and ensure he and his colleagues were safe. Focusing on this helped keep his mind off what was happening at the Infirmary. There was no point staying at home with Annie. They both agreed that they would get on each other's nerves one way or another as they worried.

As Ged had asked the previous day. Pete hadn't told any of his colleagues about the situation with Marge. Their conversation maintained its usual level, about half an inch above the gutter: They spent the morning making inappropriate jokes about a woman in the Accounts department with a large bottom, debating how she managed to get into her tiny car and how much butter might be required in the event of needing a quick getaway. The conversation moved on to an Indian restaurant that had opened in town. Martin, who liked to think he had his ear to the ground, claimed that it wasn't really new at all, but the people who ran the Raj, which was previously called the Mumtaz, had probably gone bust again and had to refinance for, what must be the third time. He reckoned the rent was cheaper at the new premises, and it was definitely the same people because he recognised the same big brass bowl that they used for free Bombay mix in the waiting area.

"I expect you recognised some of the pieces of Bombay mix in there, too. Nobody eats that stuff," said Dave.

"There's peanuts and dried noodles that have probably been there since they opened the Ganges... they'll be forming a union soon," quipped Ged. He enjoyed having this kind of half-witted banter with the lads. As long as it didn't stop them from doing their job, it helped to pass the time.

"Someone told me if you tease the waiters or don't give a good tip, they spit on the Bombay mix," said Martin in his usual, conspiratorial mutter.

"Give-over, Mart…" called Dave from the other side of the huge press, rolling his eyes at Martin's cynicism, "That's an urban myth… anyway, the health and safety bods would spot that one, and they have to be checked every year, don't they?"

"Actually," said Ged, a café owner in Porthleven, did tell me once that she sacked a waitress for spitting on a customer's dinner… She overheard them gossiping about her Dad and decided to take out a bit of quiet revenge."

"You're kidding!" called Dave. "I'll never go to a restaurant again!"

"No joke… apparently the customer saw it too, so the owner had no choice but to sack her… Mind you, she didn't like the customer either and said she'd have put an extra sprinkle of Tabasco on their dinner in the kitchen… she didn't want them coming in and bad-mouthing people. The waitress's Dad was a friend of hers… She got the waitress a job with a food supplier. She ended up working in the Council's health and safety department in the end."

"Ha! That's ironic, considering…"

The workday passed much in this way, and with the press stripped down and parts carefully laid out on a tarpaulin sheet to check over for damage, Ged felt a sense of satisfaction that he often got from jobs like this.

***

Back home, Ged showered and changed into a pair of buff-coloured chinos and a white polo shirt, gathered up the car keys and chivvied Annie out of the house. She had kept busy, too: She had mowed the lawn and tidied the garden. As Marge kept the flowerbeds so regimentally prim, the Autumn leaves made it look messy – not in a good way as they did in Annies rambling shamble of a garden – but in a 'muddy shoes left on a freshly mopped hallway' kind of a way so, surprising herself, Annie had tidied them up and put them in bags to mulch.

They drove to the hospital in near silence, both lost in thought, both wondering what they would find when they got there. Ged parked up, and Annie bought a parking ticket to put on the dashboard. The low evening sun streamed through the coppice of trees that grew by the hospital; the colours of the leaves were uncountable. Ged never failed to be spellbound by the beauty of autumn decay. He decided, as they had arrived a bit too early for visiting time, to walk the long way around through the hospital gardens. It saved a long trudge along disinfectant-scented corridors. Dried leaves swirled about their feet in the breeze, and a hint of newly mown grass wafted across the hospital grounds. One of the garden volunteers waged war on the leaves in the rose beds with a narrow rake. The leaves were being blown out of the bags he had stuffed them in as he worked between the bushes. No point doing that job on a windy day,… mused Ged as he passed the old gent, now bent double, attempting to gather the unruly leaves between his gloved hands.

Ged did a double-take as he passed the man. He was their neighbour.

"George…? George Malik? I didn't know you worked here."

"Oh, good afternoon, Mr Baker," his Indian accent soft but obvious… "Yes, I've volunteered here since I'm retiring from the factory. It keeps me out of mischief, you know. I like the gardens here. The roses are very nice indeed. I wish this wind would give over… clearing these leaves is like pushing water uphill!"

"Well, you've certainly got it looking lovely, Mr Malik," said Annie. "There's no sign of blackspot on these roses."

"Keep it tidy," said George. "That stops the blackspot. And it's not too damp here, so we don't suffer much."

"Well, it looks great, George. We'd better go, or Marge will tell me off for being late."

"Mrs Baker is ill?" George inquired.

"Yes… she had an operation today. We should find out more this evening."

"Oh dear, do give her my regards. She is an excellent gardener, your wife. Your garden always looks very nice."

"Thanks, George. I'll pass that on. See you again."

As they walked into the ward, the sister waved them over to her desk. "Mr Baker?"

"Yes."

"Your wife has been moved to ICU following her operation. She may be there for a couple of days. Do you want to take her things home in the meantime?"

"Um… yes, I suppose that would be a good idea. Was she supposed to go into intensive care after the operation? I thought she would be back on the ward."

"Some cases do go to ICU. The doctor probably wants to keep her sedated, I expect."

"Right… can we visit her?"

"Yes, of course. Do you know how to get there?"

"I do," said Annie. "Come on, Ged, let's get Marge's bag and go now." Her tone was clipped and matter-of-fact. Ged could sense her tension.

They bundled Marge's things into the bag. Annie set off at a brisk pace up the corridor, leading Ged through a maze of stairwells and corridors to the intensive care suite. There was a lounge with sofas and vending machines for snacks and hot drinks where they had to wait before they could be admitted. Annie didn't say a word but paced the room, fiddling with her bead necklace. Ged got them both a coffee from the machine, more to pass the time than any real thirst, though he realised his mouth was dry.

"They should have a bar here…it would help calm the nerves," he said.

"Mmm"

"Do you want sugar in yours, Annie?"

"Eh? Oh … yes, ok, thanks."

"Try not to worry, Annie; I'm sure they know what they're doing."

"Hmm… Yes, I suppose so." She sat down on the very edge of the sofa, cradling her coffee in both hands… "Ged, it's not a good sign that she's come in here… it suggests the operation didn't go too well or that Marge didn't cope well with the procedure."

"Let's see what the doc says, shall we?"

The door at the far end of the waiting room opened, and a young nurse with short-cropped blond hair came in. "Can I help you? Who have you come to see?"

"Marjorie Baker," said Ged.

"Okay. I'm Jo... I'm her nurse... She's still asleep, of course, but feel free to come in. Can you wear the shoe covers, please? Have you been in an ICU before?"

"I have," said Annie. "I used to work here."

"Oh right... that's good."

"I haven't... been in ICU before, I mean," said Ged.

"Ok.... Is it Mr Baker?"

"Yes"

"Well, Mr Baker, so that it doesn't come as too much of a shock, there are a lot of machines here making different noises, and it can be a bit unnerving for relatives coming in here. I'm sure...er..."

"Annie Cookson."

"Right... I'm sure Mrs Cookson, here, can tell you what the equipment does, but if you would like a quick tour, I'll be glad to explain."

"It's 'Miss' Cookson, actually, but you can call me Annie...And it's been a while since I was here, so you might need to give me the full tour, too."

Jo led the way to Marge's 'room' as Jo called it... A more alien environment Ged had never seen. Marge lay fast asleep with some kind of breathing apparatus over her nose and mouth. There were tubes everywhere, emanating from under the covers and from a cannula in her left hand. A complicated heart monitor was reading a heart trace, blood oxygen saturation, blood pressure and another reading that Ged couldn't remember after Jo had done 'the tour'. Marge's strawberry-blond hair was brushed back off her face in a way that she would not have approved of if she were awake. Jo explained what the machines did while Annie nodded, not interrupting once and seeming to fully understand everything. Ged, meanwhile, barely heard a word; he was so taken aback by the machinery and tubes apparently keeping his wife alive.

"So," continued Jo in a level and business-like tone, "she's doing okay now… she's been through a lot in surgery and had to be heavily sedated to help her recover. I think the consultant is doing his rounds soon. He will explain. I'm sorry I can't give you more information. Can I get you a cup of tea or anything?"

"No thanks," replied Annie, raising her cup. When will the consultant be here?"

"He usually pops in around six," said the nurse, looking at her watch, so you should only have a few minutes to wait.

"Okay, thanks."

Jo took a clipboard that was hooked onto the end of the bed and went around the machines, checking read-outs. She took Marge's temperature with an ear thermometer and made notes on the forms. After returning the clipboard to its proper place, she twisted a tap on the drip and checked Marge's cannula.

"Well, I hope the consultant turns up soon," said Annie, pulling at her necklace again. She had fiddled with it so much that the skin on her neck was beginning to redden.

Ged stroked Marge's hair into a more 'Marge' style and kissed her gently on her forehead, being careful not to disturb any of the equipment. Her skin felt warm and soft. He pulled up a plastic chair and sat, sipping his coffee, mesmerised by the heart trace on the screen. It was regular and strangely comforting.

"Mr Baker? Miss Cookson? …er, Annie," Jo put her head around the door of the room. Can you come to the relative's lounge? Mr Tandulkar thought it would be best to talk there."

Annie and Ged followed her back to the lounge, where Mr Tandulkar was waiting.

"Good afternoon, Mr Baker and Miss Cookson."

"Good afternoon, Mr Tandulkar," replied Annie briskly, shaking his offered hand… "I take it things didn't go so well in theatre…"

"I'm afraid you're right. Jo tells me you worked in the ICU, so you will be familiar with situations like these… Mr Baker, your wife became quite distressed in the operating theatre. It's best in these procedures if the patient is awake but lightly sedated so that we can observe responses; however, once we were in the operating theatre, your wife became… How can I say…? Er, somewhat resistant to the care of some of the staff in theatre."

"Oh no…what did she do?" Groaned Annie.

"Patient confidentiality forbids me to go into detail… She took a dislike to one of my theatre nurses and was a little…uncooperative. She tried to leave the theatre at one point."

"Oh, good grief! Marge, you silly girl," said Annie, rolling her eyes and shaking her head in disbelief.

***

Mr Tendulkar did not give Annie and Ged the full story… he wasn't sure they would believe him if he did…

Marge was wheeled into the operating theatre. The nurse who was to be monitoring her vital signs smiled kindly at her. Putting his hand on hers, he introduced himself, attempting to reassure her.

"Hello, Mrs Baker, Love… I'm Vinnie… I'm yer theatre nurse today," he said in his natural Liverpool accent…

"WHAT?!" Marge shouted as though she were audibly as well as visually impaired…

"Vinnie…That's me, and I'll be looking after you during your operation. Now don't be scared, Marjorie… Mr Tendulkar is really brilliant…he'll have you sorted in no time…Marjorie, ooh, you know, that's me Mam's name!"

"It's Mrs Baker to you, and I am *not* having some scouse fairy nursing *me*, thank you very much!"

The whole theatre team recoiled in surprise at her outburst… they had seen people become angry before in these situations and were ready to deal with it, but it never failed to amaze them what some patients could come out with.

"MRS BAKER…" said the senior theatre nurse…in a commanding and school-matronly voice. "Nurse Gregory is an extremely competent nurse… However," she snapped, "IF you prefer, I take his place, that can be arranged… We do not tolerate insults in theatre, though, Mrs Baker. If you have opinions about the ethnic origin or sexual orientation of my staff, please keep them to yourself." Marge

229

grumbled in agreement, looking sheepish. The school-ma'am approach worked. Sister Francis changed places with Nurse Gregory and winked at him as they passed.

Mr Tendulkar explained what he was doing at every stage of the procedure. Marge had been given a local anaesthetic to numb any pain from the cutting and earplugs to reduce the noise. Nurse Gregory began to shave her hair at the back. Marge started to whimper...

"Mrs Baker...? said Sister Frances...Would you like us to pause the procedure?"

"No... she said miserably, but if you find cancer... I ... I don't want that chemotherapy... I really don't want to be bald ... I would die of shame."

"We won't give you any chemotherapy today, Mr Tendulkar replied... I'm going to make a little cut; you won't feel anything, but after that, there will be some noise.. it might sound a bit like a dentist's drill."

He began to use the cutter to carefully cut into her skull when Marge suddenly pressed herself up off the theatre gurney, which was at a raked angle and took a couple of purposeful strides towards where she presumably thought the door was."

The theatre staff acted as one. Another nurse helped Sister Frances guide Marge back to the gurney, and Vinnie held a swab tightly against the back of her bleeding scalp.

Mr Tendulkar took charge. "Okay, Mrs Baker... we don't have to continue. We can stop now and tidy you up, or we can carry on if you promise not to try to walk out. We can give you a general anaesthetic and continue, but as I mentioned to you yesterday, there is more risk to important parts of your brain that control speech and vision. It is essential that we keep you safe, and you are clearly distressed. Would you like me to stop now and close the wound?"

"No... please... give me a general, she said in a slightly slurred but definite voice... Put me to sleep! I'm too scared to do this, but I want you to help me see again... PLEASE!"

***

Mr Tendulkar gave a diplomatic version of events.

"Of course, moving around theatre once the procedure had begun was not safe. Mrs Baker decided she would prefer a general anaesthetic over halting the procedure."

"I bet that was a bit stressful for the team," said Ged.

"We have experienced this kind of situation before. It is not unusual in these cases. Tumours in certain parts of the brain can make patients impulsive. Doing the procedure under general anaesthetic makes it a little more difficult. However, we were able to remove most of the tumour affecting her optic nerve."

"So, do you think she will be able to see?"

"I am optimistic. But, these tumours are usually a secondary metastasis of a primary cancer. A CT scan was done to find out where the likely primary may be."

"So, it's definitely cancer?" said Ged quietly.

Mr Tandulkar gently nodded. "I'm afraid there is no doubt, Mr Baker. We believe we have found the primary." He produced a set of black-and-white images from the buff file under his arm. "As you can see from this image, there are two masses... In the pancreas and the stomach," he indicated with the tip of his red and silver Parker ballpoint pen. "Unfortunately, it appears to be an aggressive cancer, and to remove it is likely to be unhelpful as it has already metastasised. It is likely that Mrs Baker would not survive surgery. Your wife is a very sick lady, Mr Baker. I'm very sorry."

Ged felt as though he had attempted to swallow a golf ball ...and failed.

"Will she be revived from ICU?" asked Annie in a brisk, professional tone.

"Yes, as long as she continues to show positive signs of recovery from the operation. We will keep her sedated for a couple of days to help her to recover and minimise her stress. She will be on analgesics and sedatives while she remains in hospital. She was very distressed in theatre, even though she had been given a strong sedative."

"So, have you any idea how long...?" Annie's voice was calm and measured, as though she was asking how long the tread on her tyres would last.

"As you know, that is a question we are often asked. It is difficult to say, but I would say not long. Maybe three months."

"Can chemo do anything to help?"

"Chemotherapy may slow the growth of the tumours, but her cancer is already quite advanced, and as Mrs Baker has said, there are side effects. I'm not convinced of the clinical value in her case. The Oncology team will discuss it, of course. Analgesics and good palliative treatments and care may offer a better quality of life."

"She…she said no Chemotherapy…" mumbled Ged. "She was quite clear about that."

"Well, she might feel differently after the operation." Tears were welling up in Annie's eyes. She crossly brushed them away with her sleeve.

"Mrs Baker was clear that she does not want Chemotherapy. She is very concerned about the side effects."

Ged sat in an armchair in the lounge. His elbows rested on his knees, his forehead resting in cupped hands. The numbness returned. *"Now what?"* He thought… *"Once she's recovered from the operation when she's out of hospital… what next… back home…? Hospice…?"*

Ged looked up. "Can I ask something?" His voice was barely a whisper.

"Of course," said Mr Tandulkar.

"How come she didn't show any symptoms of the other tumours?"

Mr Tandulkar took a deep breath. "Our experience is quite variable. Sometimes, patients put symptoms down to other things, such as old age, indigestion, or tummy trouble. Perhaps your wife has taken indigestion remedies or simply ignored the symptoms. Has she had a reduced appetite over recent months?"

"She didn't eat much on holiday… and she's had me on a diet lately, as hers has been going so well… so our portions have been smaller."

"So, perhaps she has seemed largely asymptomatic. It makes sense, based on the locations and size of the masses. They may not have caused much discomfort."

"If only we had spotted something," sighed Ged, shaking his head and staring at his shoes.

"Mr Baker," Mr Tandulkar said with fervent compassion, "you must not hold yourself responsible. It is not unusual for cancer patients to be asymptomatic or ignore symptoms for many months before something is detected, let alone a family member being aware."

"That's true," said Annie, putting her hand on his knee. "I've heard that more times than I care to remember."

Mr Tandulkar nodded his head, handed the copy of the scan to Annie and put his pen in his breast pocket. "I you have questions later, please call my secretary, and I will be glad to answer."

"Yes. I'm sure you have done everything you can," said Annie.

"Um…" croaked Ged, "Yes, thanks for explaining…er… everything."

"It has been a pleasure to meet you both… I wish it were in… more pleasant circumstances," said Mr Tandulkar gently.

"Thank you," said Annie, meeting his gaze. She sat by Ged, her arm around his shoulders. Ged held his head in his hands once more as Mr Tandulkar left the lounge.

They sat in silence for several minutes…

"I'll drive home," said Annie.

"Um… yes… I'm not up to it…" Ged took a deep breath. Can you give me a minute or two with Marge first?"

"Of course," she said, squeezing his hand.

Ged went back to Marge's bedside. Once again, he stroked her hair… she looked so… beautiful. Her skin was like porcelain…there were fewer wrinkles visible. The corners of her lips were curved into a slight smile, which was something he hadn't seen for a long time. Had she been hiding something? Had she been in pain but not said anything? She *had* lost weight, and she had eaten like a bird recently… but she would have noticed something… surely?

He bent down to kiss her forehead, then spoke quietly by her ear, "I love you, Marjorie Baker. My *Dancing Queen*." He left the room without looking back. He found the ICU, with its unnatural beeps, clicks, hisses, screens, tubes and wires, deeply disturbing.

***

As the front door opened, Ged was met with the delicious smell of a beef stew that Annie had prepared in the slow cooker earlier that day. He hadn't eaten since his meagre cheese sandwich and apple at work seven hours ago. They sat in silence, neither being able to put their feelings into words, both picking at their stew, nor really having an appetite. Annie busied herself, clearing plates and beginning to wash the dishes. Ged went to phone Brian and Edward.

He dialled their numbers, but there was no answer from either. He couldn't leave a voice message telling them their mother had only months left to live, so he just said, "It's Dad... er...give me a call when you're back... don't worry how late it is."

He returned to the kitchen... Annie was hunched over the sink; her shoulders were shaking, and her hands were braced on the sink top. Tears splashed into the bubbles. Ged turned off the taps and put his arm around her shoulders. He grabbed a towel and handed it to her, then guided her into the living room. They sat side by side on the sofa, where she collapsed into his arms, weeping uncontrollably, occasionally gasping for breath. He couldn't remember the inscrutable Annie ever crying over anything – happy *or* sad. She was always so... in control. He said nothing but held her in his arms, allowing the storm to pass.

As Annie regained composure, she sat up and accepted the box of tissues he offered. His eyes were red, too. He wept for her grief as much as his own.

"I'm sorry, Ged... I...I never cry... " she sniffed... "I seem to have saved my tears up for this moment... I'm not so upset that Marge is...dying..." she blew her nose and frowned. "I'm upset that she's been so difficult, living; I wish we could have been closer, you know... happier sisters; I wish she would have let me get close... let me in... but she shut everyone out. She could have been happier if she would just... loosen up."

"Annie... you can't change people... your parents ... well, they put so much expectation on her. They were so strict. It's hardly surprising that she could be a bit ...well...stiff."

"It's not that... she always resented me, somehow. I was such good friends with Granny... we were so close. She was jealous... she never got close to anyone!"

"She got close to me," said Ged. "Well, as close as Marge could get to anyone."

"How do you put up with it all these years?"

"Chardonnay," he said simply.

"Chardonnay?"

"Yep… I pour her a glass at dinner. Once she has relaxed a little, she and I become happy old marrieds, watching a whodunnit on the TV or 'Come Dancing', speculating about who should win. When your Dad died, we thought about dancing again, but it wouldn't have been the same. Lately, though, the wine hasn't had its usual effect. I was worried we were growing apart. Now I know it was the cancer."

"Maybe I should have met her at the pub instead of Marks and Spencer for a coffee; perhaps we would have got on better?"

Ged paused and put a hand on hers. "Come on… I'll make us a cup of tea… I think we could both do with one and then perhaps a scotch?"

"I'll pass on the scotch… but I do need a cup of tea. Then… I think I'll go for a walk. I could use some fresh air.

"If the boys call back before we've finished our tea, I'll come with you if you like."

***

Brian asked all the usual questions … Ged tried to answer as best he could….

"About three months, but they're not certain… Probably not; it wouldn't be a good quality of life…she would likely not survive the operation… They'll bring her around in the next day or so…Doc says she might not have spotted the symptoms, never mind us missing them… don't blame yourself, Son…Yes, OK…

"Are they coming up for the weekend?" whispered Annie.

He nodded. "Okay, Bri, Annie is staying over, so I don't know where you'll all sleep."

"I'll sleep on the sofa," said Annie. "The spare room is set up for them anyway."

"Did you hear that, Bri?"

"Yes... Friday night then," said Ged. "Let's have fish and chips. You'll have to think of how to explain things to Alice and Jamie...they can come too... Well, if that's what you want to do. I'm sure they'll have a good time at Margot and Ben's. Probably best... Bye... Love to Sarah and the kids...and ... Brian...I love you, Son...and so does your Mum."

He replaced the receiver, took a deep breath and downed the remainder of his tea.

"Can we go for that walk now?" he said.

"Not waiting for Ed?"

"He's got enough on his plate...being a new Dad..."

"Are you taking the day off tomorrow?"

"Yes... Pete said if it was bad news to take leave... he'll sort things with personnel."

"Good bloke."

"He is. I'm lucky to have a boss like him."

Annie put on her coat. "Come on, let's get out of here." She had picked up an empty ice cream tub, which she held up. "We can pick blackberries."

27

The following two days for Marge were a blurred confusion of tubes and wires, doctors, nurses and hospital moves. Marge was brought out of her deep sedation but was kept on a drip and strong tranquilisers to keep her calm. She was moved back to the main ward late on Friday evening. Annie and Ged made sure that there were flowers and all her get-well cards waiting for her in the ward. They arrived at morning visiting time on Saturday as she was finishing her breakfast. She scowled at them both. "Did you get these roses, Gerald?" she said in a surprisingly brisk tone for someone on a heavy dose of sedation.

"Yes, Marge Love, I hoped they would cheer you up a bit."

"Well, I suppose they would if they were going to last. You should have gone to the florist, Gerald...not the supermarket. They're drooping already."

"Oh, shut up, Marjorie, and be grateful!" snapped Annie. "Ged did go to the florist. They've been on the table for a day, and the heat makes them droop. They were beautiful buds when he brought them."

"Brian's sunflowers haven't drooped!" she shot back.

"That's because they're silk!"

"What? But they look real!"

"Well, you've got some of your sight back, but not all of it, I see." Came a familiar voice from behind them... it was Ed. He was carrying his new daughter.

"Ed... Son! ... how brilliant!" exclaimed Ged, spinning around to greet his Son and new Granddaughter. "I didn't know you were coming... You should have let me know!"

"I only decided this morning, and I couldn't get hold of you, so I thought we'd just turn up... thought you'd like to see your new Granddaughter."

"Where's Karen?" mouthed Ged silently to Ed.

"She's just around the corner... we borrowed a wheelchair... she's still pretty sore. We thought we'd gauge how Mum is first and what her reaction might be."

"Edward? Is that you?" said Marge in a sharp tone.

"Yes, Mum. It's me, and I've brought someone to meet you."

"Oh, not that slut you've shacked up with!"

"Marge... that's enough. If you don't have anything nice to say, don't say anything," said Ged, more firmly than he had intended.

Ed walked over to the bed in silence and gave his little bundle to Marge. Instinctively, she cradled the baby, supporting her head and bouncing her gently. The baby gurgled and cooed; she was sleepy.

"Karen has just fed her, so she's a bit boozy."

"Edward... she's beautiful!" breathed Marge. "Just like you... all that black hair!... When was she born?"

"It was the day you came into hospital, Mum. It was all a bit sudden. She was a week overdue, so I did Brian's trick – spinach and lentil curry, and she couldn't wait to get out!"

"Can't say I blame her!" said Ged. "I hate spinach... and lentils!"

"How much did she weigh?" said Marge.

"Eight pounds two ounces... she's got a big head though... and Karen is really sore..."

"Well, now you have a baby, Edward, you'll have to..."

"Mum," Ed interrupted. "I don't want to fall out over this anymore... Karen and I are not married, and we aren't going to get married any time soon. We love each other very much and may still not be married when we are a retired, old couple, getting meals on wheels and falling asleep in front of the telly. We aren't religious, and Karen has had a terrible experience of coerced marriage, so I would never put any pressure on her. I love you, Mum, but I love Karen too, and I won't have her hurt."

"Shameful... the child will get called a Basta..."

"Marge... No!" said Ged firmly. "You mustn't say that. Things are different nowadays. Lots of kids have parents who aren't married, and there are plenty of children in an unhappy shotgun marriage or unhappy because their parents got divorced. Karen is a lovely girl. Give her a chance and love your little granddaughter."

Marge pursed her lips. The baby gurgled and stirred. She looked at the tiny little face and brushed her fingers gently on the baby's cheek. "What have you called her?"

"Laura." Ed glanced at Annie. "We both thought it suited her."

"Hello, Laura… I'm Nana…" Tears rolled down her cheeks. "Aren't you beautiful?" The baby started to wriggle in Marge's arms. Marge looked up at Ed. "A fidget, just like you… Here, let your Dad hold her; she's getting too wriggly."

Ed picked up baby Laura and turned to offer her to Ged to hold. "All in good time; I think she needs her Mum. It's not much fun being the parcel in a game of pass the parcel."

Ged wheeled Karen closer to the bed, and Ed gently passed Laura to her.

"Is it okay if I feed her?" said Karen. "She didn't have much before we came."

"Of course, if she's hungry, feed her," said Annie, returning with some cups of tea.

"You know her middle name, Auntie Annie?" whispered Ed to his aunt. In reply, she hugged him.

"What was that, Edward?"

"Just thanking Auntie Annie for the tea."

"That is for the patients; you know Anne… not hordes of visitors! Where's mine?"

"Here," said Annie, dumping the teacup on the table so firmly that a little sloshed out."

"Clumsy! Look what you've done."

"I'll clean it up…so, how's the sight, Grumpy knickers?"

"There's still haziness at the edge. They said it's as good as I'm likely to get."

"Have you seen the hospital garden from this window, Marge?" said Ged to make small talk. "I wanted to tell you about it when we came in, but I was worried I'd upset you if you couldn't see," said Ged brightly. "George Malik is a volunteer gardener here."

"Looks like it could use an expert eye. Those roses are too tall and drawn. They need pruning, and there are leaves everywhere." She replied with scorn. "What can you expect? He probably wants to let it grow like a jungle so he feels at home!"

"Pardon?"

"Well, where he comes from, they have jungles, don't they?"

"Wolverhampton? Not as far as I know," said Ged.

"You know what I mean, Gerald – wherever he *'originally'* came from.

"I don't believe there's a jungle in Karachi either, Marge."

"Mum, you just can't say things like that. It's really racist!" said Ed.

"I think we should let you get some sleep." Ged interjected. "Ed, do you and Karen want to meet us downstairs at the café? Then we can decide what to do for lunch. I need to have a chat with your Mum."

"Okay. See you down there."

"Shall I stay?" said Annie.

"Don't mind. I just think some quiet time with fewer people would be good. Mr Tendulkar is doing his rounds."

***

Mr Tendulkar greeted Ged with a smile. He addressed Mage directly:

"Good morning, Mrs Baker... how are we feeling today?"

"I have a headache, and I feel very woozy."

"The headache is to be expected, but we will try to keep the pain under control. If you need extra pain relief, just ask the ward staff. The sedatives may make you feel woozy, but we need to keep you as calm as possible so you can heal. Do you feel able to have a little talk?"

"Alright..."

"Mrs Baker, do you remember what I told you yesterday about what we have found?"

"There's some cancer in my stomach and my...er pancreas... Is that right?"

"Yes... "

"So, when is the operation to remove them?

After a slight hesitation, Mr Tendulkar said, "I'm afraid we cannot operate, Mrs Baker."

240

"Why not?"

"It has already spread to other areas, and your body is trying to fight it off, but we believe you would be unlikely to survive surgery."

"Well, I'm absolutely NOT having Chemotherapy."

"I respect your wishes, Mrs Baker. You understand the … consequences?"

"Yes," she said simply. "I'm going to die soon." She clenched her jaw and clasped her fingers tightly. Her knuckles were almost white.

"I'm very sorry, Mrs Baker…" he paused a moment, "Would you like me to arrange to have the palliative care team come and speak with you and Mr Baker?"

"When can I go home?" Marge said. Her voice was clipped and businesslike.

"It would be sensible for you to remain here for a few more days while your head wound heals, and we can make sure your pain medication is suitable."

"I see."

"I'll ask the palliative care team to make an appointment. They are very helpful. We have a telephone number for you, Mr Baker, so they will call to arrange something."

"Thanks, Mr Tandulkar," Annie said and put out her hand to shake. Ged followed suit but said nothing. His throat, again, was too tight to speak.

***

Over a pleasant lunch in the surprisingly well-stocked hospital Café, Ged and Annie took the opportunity, while Ed and Brian were together, to talk about lasting powers of attorney. It felt poor taste to discuss it, but he had spoken to a solicitor in town who had explained how messy things can get if you didn't have one – he didn't want to have to go to Court of Protection to apply for permission to be deputy attorney. Brian and Sarah nodded in agreement. They explained that one of Brian's chefs had struggled when his father's end-of-life care had turned out to be both expensive and stressful.

"It cost him and his wife all the money they had saved for their house deposit to pay for it. The stress almost cost them their marriage, too," said Brian.

Between them, they completed all the forms over the next few days. Marge was surprisingly pragmatic about the whole affair and agreed that it was the proper thing to do.

***

Marge came home after another week in hospital. Ged and Annie had been busy making sure the house was clean and tidy, but they were sure there would be lots of things for Marge to complain about, so they hatched a plan. They left a few things deliberately untidy or unfinished; that way, they wouldn't feel so harshly treated when Marge spotted them. A pile of laundry left in front of the washing machine, some dishes on the drainer and magazines left on the sitting room table. They thought that should do it. Annie had moved back into the spare room as Sarah and Brian only stayed two nights.

Marge complained bitterly all the way home in the car about how dirty it was... "It looks like you've been keeping animals in it, Gerald! Have you actually taken it to the garage to get it vacuumed?" she chided.

"Sorry, Marge, I've been a bit ... preoccupied with one thing and another. I'll get it done this afternoon if you like."

As soon as she walked in through the front door, Annie greeted her sister with a peck on the cheek. "Fancy a cuppa?" she said in as chirpy a voice as she could muster.

"Yes, please, Anne. Have you bought any teacakes?"

"Er – no, did you want them?"

"I always have a teacake around this time in the morning."

"Do you, now? Well, they certainly looked after you in the hospital. There's toast or a biscuit as we've got those, but there are no teacakes here, I'm afraid."

"Gerald. Go to the corner shop and get some, would you?" They're the ones with Sultanas and raisins in them. They might have cinnamon as well."

Ged exchanged glances with Annie but picked up the car keys and started for the door. "Was there anything else you'd like me to get?"

"What are we having for dinner this evening?" she asked.

"I made Boeuf Bourguignon with rice for tonight, and I thought we might plan what we'd like to have for the rest of the week so we can go to the supermarket and stock up the fridge and the freezer."

"Oh, very well, do we have to have rice? I'd prefer a jacket potato and beans."

"You could get potatoes and green beans at the shop in that case, Ged," said Annie.

***

Ged came back with the closest thing he could find to teacakes.

"Hot cross buns?" Marge shrieked. "Honestly, Gerald, can't you tell the difference between a teacake and a hot-cross bun? You might as well have bought a loaf of bread. I suppose it will have to do. Now, don't burn them under the grill like you usually do."

... And so, it went on. Although they sat down and planned a menu for every meal on every day of the week and took Marge with them to the supermarket, Ged and Annie were run ragged, popping to the shops to get extra of this or that, adding more milk in her tea, or making a fresh one when they put too much in it; fetching her a coffee when it was insisted on and making a cup of tea when she reprimanded them and claimed that it was what she had asked for in the first place. The central heating was too hot, then too cold; a door was open, and she could feel a draft. It was too stuffy or too cool...

They knew that this was her gliomas talking, but all the same, underneath the illness was Marge, with her high standards and contrariness. When she fell asleep after lunch on Thursday afternoon, Ged and Annie went for a walk. They had gone separately up until then, usually when they were about to say something unpleasant to Marge or scream. Marge was capable of making a drink, and they desperately needed a break to allow them to talk.

"Look, Annie," said Ged, "this is crazy. Both of us waiting on her, hand and foot, isn't doing us any good, and it's not doing her any good either."

"I know what you mean; she's acting like a spoiled child! When are those palliative care people coming? I want some advice from them about respite and carers. I'd like to go home, but I want to hear what they have to say, and I feel awful leaving you – with this."

"It's tomorrow morning. I haven't plucked up the courage to tell Marge yet," he said. "It might be better if you did go home after that. Not that I want you to, he added hastily; your company has been brilliant, but I think both of us waiting on her makes her even more demanding than if there was just one. She's got worse since the operation – I mean, she seems to be able to see, but she forgets what she said a minute ago. It's like dementia."

"I'm afraid that's to be expected, Ged. That's how it affects a lot of patients. I just hope it makes her sleep a lot, too. It usually does."

***

The palliative care social worker, Cathy, was the most colourful person Ged had ever met. Bright red Doc Marten boots below multi-colour striped cotton trousers and a dark green jacket over a deep pink polo neck top with a string of large yellow beads around her neck. Her bright, kind face was framed by a shock of frizzy, long grey hair topped with a bright magenta beret. Her persona was as bright as her outfit. Friendly and warm, she chatted with Marge about her likes, dislikes, and preferences for care possibilities. Ged even heard Marge laugh at something Cathy said about a care home with twenty cats which would curl up on residents' laps and sleep all day or allow them to stroke them. She signposted several services, Macmillan nurses, a local hospice that they may need to use in time and a charity called Marie Curie, which specialised in palliative respite care for cancer patients to offer family members a break. She asked if any of the other members of the family or friends could help out.

Ged felt he should continue working. With all the time off he had for his broken foot and the week he had taken more time off to care for Marge, he felt he was taking advantage... Besides, work did help to take his mind off things.

They decided to look at a local nursing home called 'The Hollies', which offered daycare. Marge was initially reluctant but felt that it was morally wrong for Ged to have any more time off, and the idea of a rota of different friends and family in the house each day just sounded stressful. Cathy was very complimentary about The Hollies. "They have lots to do if you're up for it and quiet areas if you're not. I'll arrange a visit, and you could go for a trial day to see if you like it."

Marge looked at the brochure and sighed. "So, this is what it has come to... a life of service in the community, and we still have to pay a fortune for care."

"You may be able to get some help with the cost. I'll look into it," said Cathy.

***

Daycare was a success. Every weekday, Ged dropped Marge off at The Hollies before work and picked her up once he had made dinner or once he had placed a cottage pie or casserole in the oven to warm up that had been brought over by a kind neighbour. Ged looked after Marge full-time at the weekends; she complained on Saturday mornings that she had to stay at home as "The tea is better there, and there's nothing to do at home except gardening, and I'm too tired for that."

She spent weekends giving Ged instruction after instruction: "Mow the lawn, Gerald; Cut the hedge, Gerald; Those windows need cleaning; Do the bathrooms before Sarah and Brian get here," she said, the Saturday of their impending arrival. "Are you making that French stew ...again?" Why can't we have spaghetti like at The Hollies?"

Marge had lost more weight. Weak and frail, even her admonishments lacked their usual ferocity. Ged didn't have the heart to complain. Marge had done so much over all the years of their marriage, keeping the house clean and tidy, making most of the meals, tending the garden... all that while volunteering at the Oxfam shop and helping with Community events.

Although he was tired, when Ged finally got to bed, he found it took a long time to get to sleep. It was as though he were trapped in a bad dream but dreading waking up …as he knew what waking up would mean and didn't want to think about it.

He confessed this to Brian that Saturday afternoon while Marge was playing Ludo with the children and Sarah. Ged couldn't remember her ever playing Ludo… but at least it gave him and Brian time to talk. They sat with cups of coffee at the kitchen table.

"Dad, maybe you could take something to help with the worry and the sleep. I mean, it doesn't have to be sleeping tablets; you could look at a herbal remedy. Sarah's mum takes something for anxiety. I could ask her."

"Marge's doctor said his wife takes something called ashwagandha. I wrote it down, but I don't know how much to take."

"I'll ask Sarah's Mum," he said. Then, fixing Ged with a steely gaze, he said: "You need a proper break, Dad. You work all day and all evening, then she has you running around like a crazy thing all weekend… you're burning out. I should know; I'm a chef!"

"You're right, but what can I do? I'd feel guilty if I didn't stay."

"Remember what they say on the plane, Dad: Put your own mask on before helping others. You're no good to Mum if you burn out. You'll both end up in that nursing home if you carry on like this."

"What can we do? I can't afford to send her there overnight. I'm saving up for that eventuality."

"I talked to Auntie Annie last night. She said she could come and look after Mum while you get away for a weekend. Go and see Ed, Karen and the baby, or stay with us – you could even stay at Annie's place while she's here. Her cottage is lovely, and you can go for walks. I think it would do you good."

"As much as I love little Laura, I'm not sure it will be very restful at Ed's place or yours, but if Annie is serious about her offer of swapping with me for a weekend, I'll go and stay at her place for a couple of days, though she'll need all her patience to look after your Mum."

28

London, September 1998

Mike Adamson stared out of the office window overlooking a dreary and wet Hamilton Street. He was tired and jaded. Rain fell relentlessly, and the broken gutter two floors up was noisily splattering on the stone sill outside. Wasn't it about time they got that thing fixed?

Although he was busy with deadlines galore, he was bored. He used to enjoy his job at Barker-Mead Literary Agency. An art critic in a former life, he loved to get involved in finding illustrators for their small pool of children's authors, matching the story to the illustrator's style, and bringing stories to life. Humourising terrible fiends was a favourite tactic, making a scary book accessible to more anxious readers and conveying a ridiculous side of evil characters, which allowed the publisher to sell more copies. His childhood had been terrifying. Some stories gave him nightmares, so he loved to turn that fear on its head and help kids to enjoy stories without being so afraid. Good illustrators could give a character more depth or suggest a side to their personality that the narrative could not or only hinted at.

Lately, it had felt as if he was going through the motions. The agency had a small, regular, and reliable pool of illustrators, some of whom were in great demand. He had spent that afternoon poring over six new artists' portfolios. They were okay as far as it went, and maybe some of his authors would accept one of them, but they didn't have that spark he was looking for. They would invariably copy the scribbled style of Tony Ross or Quentin Blake or the clean, bold, characterful style of Axel Sheffler. He hadn't seen anything like Michael Foreman's dreamy soft watercolours recently, but he couldn't help feeling as if he had seen the illustrations in the portfolios somewhere before.

The phone on his desk trilled, snapping him out of his trance. Wearily, he picked up the receiver. Which deadline was Julian going to be chasing this time? He wondered.

"Do you have a minute, Mike?" said Julian, his home-counties accent clear and crisp.

"Sure, Julian, anything in particular you want to talk about?"

"I ... er, wanted to speak with you before you leave today if it's convenient. There are...erm, a few developments I need to discuss."

Mike folded his laptop, put on his tweed jacket and straightened his tie. He clicked the button on his slim, silver ballpoint and slid it carefully into his inside pocket. It was almost four-thirty. His desk was immaculate, not a coffee ring or crumb of sandwich to be seen.

Julian's office was on the second floor; Mike took the stairs two at a time.

***

"Take a seat," said Julian. Mike looked around and picked up a pile of folders off the plastic chair opposite Julian's desk in the scruffy office and placed them on the big oak shelves nearby, already groaning with poorly stacked manuscripts, large box files and a variety of hard-back novels and children's books leaning at a variety of angles, "I... I don't know how to tell you this."

"What?"

Julian fiddled with his plastic biro, rolling it back and forth between his fingers. The last time he saw this was when the firm lost the Elisabeth Blandford libel case.

"Things aren't good," he said to his pen. "Financially, I mean."

"Er, how bad is bad?"

"How long have you been with us, Mike?"

"Long enough to know this isn't an annual appraisal, Julian. What's going on?"

Julian took a deep breath and held it for a moment, regarding every inch of his desk, the floor and the bookshelves before finally meeting Mike's gaze. His brow was furrowed, his hair ruffled, sticking up at odd angles, and he fiddled nervously with his biro.

"It's like this, Mike: The bank is putting pressure on us to pay up. Quite frankly, the partnership is on a knife edge."

"What about Lance Mead? Surely, he can get some help from the family?"

"He already did. They have been paying your wages for the last three months. Lance and I haven't taken a salary at all for the last two."

"Oh my God! Why didn't you tell us earlier?"

"We were talking to another financier, and we thought we were going to get a film deal for Bill Greening's Dark Wizard's trilogy, but the legal stuff is costing a fortune and taking ages. We need to get an illustrator for Jenny Halshaw quickly. We only just got her latest book sorted for the Christmas deadline, and she's fallen out of love with Jane Urquhart; well, you can't really have a children's picture book without pictures, can you?

"It's a nightmare, Julian. Jenny is my top priority, but it's harder to please her than it used to be. The more success she's had, the more choosy she's been. I only have a handful of illustrators still working. They can't keep up with demand, and most of them aren't good with deadlines!"

"Mike, we need a result or two. If we can give the bank confidence that we're getting somewhere with our big names, I think we can persuade them to give us more time, at least until we can sort the film deal."

"Believe me, I'm trying. Jenny hates the artists I've suggested; she says none of them capture her characters. I think even if I got Quentin Blake, she'd say no. I reviewed some portfolios today, but they're just not into her genre." He sighed and shook his head sadly. "Since Jane and I split up, I seem to have lost my mojo."

"Look, Mike, you've had a tough year. If you don't mind me saying, I think you're better off without Jane in the long run. Listen, why don't you get away from the coal face for a bit, go somewhere, blow the cobwebs away."

"I was going to ask if I can have the week after next off. I'm due some holiday, and there's no urgent stuff to attend to, well, except for finding a bloody illustrator for Jenny Halshaw. Jenny says it can wait, but the publishers are getting very impatient."

"Take all the time you need. You can have next week as well if you want. Beth and I can hold the fort, and you've got your mobile, so we'll call you if we get any new portfolios."

"OK. It'll be good to get away; give me space to think."

"Yeah," said Julian, looking down and twiddling his pen again.

"See you in a couple of weeks then, Jules."

Julian rose from his chair and walked around the desk, hand outstretched. He shook Mike warmly by the hand and gave his shoulder a friendly pat. Being ten years his Junior made that seem a little odd, but it was well meant, Mike figured.

***

Twenty-four hours later, Mike was making up a fire at Auntie Doreen's cottage in Porthleven. The ritual of crisscrossing the kindling and holding a match to the screwed-up newspaper marked the boundary between life and holiday. The familiar sight of Truro's spired Cathedral an hour ago had already melted some of the creases on his brow; even finding a parking space for his mother's old, green VW Golf hadn't phased him. It was now parked fifty yards down the street and might well stay there all week for all he knew.

The kindling began to crackle. Mike sat cross-legged on the hearth rug and placed two more sticks on top, watching the juvenile flames lick around them, blackening the bark.

He unpacked, arranging shaving things and toiletries in the bathroom cabinet, went to the kitchen and heated a frozen pizza that he had bought on the way. A bottle of Merlot, which Auntie Doreen had left in the kitchen, was a satisfying accompaniment. He considered turning on the TV but decided that the first week, at least, needed to be a genuine respite week… no TV, no radio. He wanted to forget the real world, its disasters, politics and pointless celebrity. Plus, he reasoned, if he didn't switch on the TV, there was no danger of seeing Jane's beautiful face staring earnestly back at him, reporting from outside some actor's home, or trying to get a *'brief word'* with one of them over the clamour of fans lining a red carpet of a recent premiere. This had to be a week of no work, no reality TV and definitely, *no* Jane.

From the bookshelves in the living room, he took down a hard-backed copy of '*The Colour of Magic*', gave his glasses a polish on the edge of his t-shirt, placed another two logs on the fire and replenished his wine glass. If there was a good way of forgetting about the real world, it was to sit by a crackling fire with a glass of something or other and get immersed in the fantasy world of his favourite authors.

***

After a generous bowl of porridge and a cup of tea, Mike pulled on his hiking boots and went for a walk. He had holidayed in the windswept fishing port of Porthleven since childhood, and he layered up against the elements with a fleece, his hiking jacket, hat and scarf. Despite the sunny weather, the wind along this part of the coast could give the hardiest of ramblers a nasty earache. He took a familiar route, following the river, heading east across the country, then took a path around Loe pool, pausing to watch the ducks and the gulls diving under the water and hunting for morsels in the mud. He walked with a brisk stride along the flat Porthleven sands, the wind stinging his face, until he reached the harbour. As he slowed his pace, walking up the harbour street, the relative calm of the village seemed to contrast with the fierce wind battering at the coast. Ropes slapped rhythmically against metal masts of boats moored in the harbour, a multifarious collection of wind-chimes ringing out their slaps, pings and metallic tings in the breeze. He reached the café in time for an early lunch, managing to bag his favourite table in the window. Emily greeted him like an old friend.

"Michael! How lovely to see you. How long has it been?"

"Oh, at least a year, Emily. The café looks great. You've had a few things done, I see."

"Oh yes, the new sign on the window, and we finally had to replace the door, a lick of paint for the window, and did we have the big coffee machine when you were here last?"

"You did, but I think I'll have a mug of tea. Can I book for dinner tonight, too?"

"Of course, just you, is it? Or is the other half joining you? I saw her on TV last night."

The smile slipped from Mike's face. He paused for a moment, conflicted, but decided to put it behind him as quickly as he could.

"We're not together anymore. She had a better offer from one of the producers."

"Oh," said Emily, crestfallen. "I'm sorry to hear that, Michael. Well, it's 'er that's missin' out. She don't know a good thing when she's onto it." Emily gave him a motherly squeeze of the hand. He had known her for… how long? He couldn't remember. As a young man, he worked at the Lobster Pot in the holidays while staying with Auntie Doreen. Emily had given him his first taste of a full day's work. The holidays positively flew by when he waited tables and prepared food with Ron in the busy Café.

He ordered a full Cornish breakfast and walked around the café as he waited, enjoying his first love: Art. The walls were crowded with paintings and sketches. He paused at a sketch of a large tabby cat creeping in through an open window. It wasn't just a cat. It had something about it – a *'pussonality'*. Another sketch depicted a fisherman like none that Mike had ever seen, dressed as a stereotypical pirate; the lobster pot he was hauling onto his boat appeared to have something other than lobsters in it. There were other sketches in a similar style: scenes of families playing on the beach, friends around a campfire, and a boy staring into a rock pool.

Mike was transfixed, not so much by the artistic technique but by the expressions on the faces of the characters and how, although the sketches were technically unfinished, they were nonetheless 'complete'. Part of the fisherman's boat was missing, but it didn't matter. In the beach party sketch, a person's feet were missing. The artist seemed to have decided that the feet were not needed to tell the story, an artistic 'Chekov's gun. Mike realised that his pulse had quickened. He felt a lightness in his stomach.

Emily appeared from the kitchen, carrying two plates.

"Lunch is served, Mr Adamson," she announced with a mock curtsey before placing the delicious-looking breakfast plate on his table.

"Emily," he said, with an excited catch in his breath and gesturing towards the framed images on the wall, "These sketches by G Baker, are they a new artist?"

"Give me a sec while I take this bill to a customer, and I'll tell you about him. I knew you'd like 'em."

29

Oxfordshire, late October 1998

Ged drove to Annie's cottage, Badger's Holt, on a cool October evening after dinner with Annie and Marge. It only took him thirty-five minutes. A charming little semi-detached cottage built in the traditional sand-coloured local stone, nestled by a small coppice on the outskirts of a Cotswold Village. Its dark oak and stained-glass front door stood beneath a wooden powder-blue-painted open porch with bench seats on either side, over which a pink climbing rose ran rampant, along with a tangle of honeysuckle. Annie had left a light on in the tiny vestibule beyond the front door. Ged hung up his coat and pushed off his shoes. The vestibule opened directly into a small living room. There was a bottle of red wine on the table with a note:

"Ged

Make yourself at home. Milk in fridge, fresh bread in big stoneware pot near the toaster, beef stroganoff for one in freezer for a dinner. Big ginger cat might visit. He isn't mine, but there's cat food on the side in the kitchen if he pesters.

Can recommend the pub in the village. Indian (Red Fort) in Chipping Norton is good, too.

Enjoy and above all, relax!

Love

Annie"

Annie had made up a fire in the grate in her tiny sitting room. Ged put a match to the paper fire-lighter and soon had a chattering, dancing little fire to sit in front of and a large glass of the red wine Annie had left for him in his hand. She had even left out nuts and crisps to munch on.

He nibbled on crisps and sipped his wine. Annie really was the best! He felt immediately at home. He took the remote control and switched on her little TV set, surfing around the channels and selecting a natural history documentary with David Attenborough's calming, earnest tone soothing him.

He awoke on the sofa. A news programme was talking to itself on the TV. He couldn't remember the last time he had actually fallen asleep in front of the TV. It felt indulgent.

Groggily, he stumped upstairs, changed into pyjamas, brushed his teeth and climbed into the freshly made bed. Dreading another night of lost sleep, he pulled up the patchwork quilt and switched off the bedside lamp.

***

Ged was woken by a knock at the door. He checked his watch – nine o'clock. How had he been able to sleep so well? It must have been the wine.

He dragged on his dressing gown and padded downstairs to the front door, where the visitor was knocking again. It was a postman.

"Hi," said Ged uncertainly. "Erm, Miss Cookson is away. I'm house-sitting for her," he said, expecting to get handed a package.

"Yes, I know, she told me," said the postman. "I'm just calling to say if there's anything you need; my wife Jean and I will be around all weekend. I'm Oliver – next door," he gestured with his thumb to indicate which way. Thistle cottage; the end one – that's us. Just knock or call if you need anything. Here's our number…" he handed Ged the note he had brought. It was written on the back of an old Christmas card.

"Right…well… thank you, Oliver," said Ged, yawning. "Do excuse me; I had a bit of a lie-in. Erm… that's really kind of you. It looks like Annie's neighbours are as nice as she is!"

"She's been telling me about her sister… your wife, isn't it…? I'm so sorry. It must be a tough time for you."

"You could say that… but I think a bit of Cotswold air and peace and quiet might just be what I need. I've had the first good night's sleep I've had in ages."

"Well, that's good. We won't impose… if you just want to get some peace and quiet, we will leave you alone…but if you fancy a bit of company… and a bit of fun, you can join us at the Rising Sun this evening. Annie's on our pub team, so you'll be sitting in for her. It starts at eight. Get there by seven-thirty if you want to get a drink first. It's all on the note. Don't feel pressured, though. The invitation's there if you fancy coming along."

"Thanks, Oliver. I'll give it some thought. I've just woken up, and I haven't decided what I'm doing yet. It sounds interesting, though. I don't think I've ever done a pub quiz."

"Oh, it's not hard or anything… usually a bit of a laugh, just trivia, music, sport, that kind of thing. Anyway, must dash…'got to do my round. Hope to see you later… but like I say… no pressure."

***

After a quick breakfast of tea and toast with Annie's delicious homemade blackberry jam, Ged dressed into a pair of jeans and a warm, brushed-cotton, blue plaid-patterned shirt. He pulled on his fleece-lined walking jacket and laced up his walking boots, picked up the now somewhat scuffed, pink unicorn backpack containing his sketching and watercolour things and set out to find a nice walking route.

He started by walking into the delightful, picture postcard village, with its creamy-Cotswold stone houses and shops, many of which had traditional Thatched roofs. A river sauntered through the centre of the village over which a stone bridge arched. The leaves around the village were in full, glorious, fiery autumn colour. Fifty yards or so up from the bridge stood a weeping beech tree. It reminded Ged of a waterfall, its leaves dripping off its branches, leaving a vibrant, deep-orange pool on the tarmac of the tiny village parking area.

He spotted the Rising Sun Inn as he walked up the hill and out of the village. Quite unlike the other buildings in the village, it was a small tavern, Georgian style, built in red brick with a slate roof, heavy stone lintels and leaded windows. There were troughs of flowers and ivy under every window. It looked like an inviting and cosy sort of place.

A black billboard on the wall by the front door of the pub advertised in beautifully brushed white letters that evening's pub quiz.

He walked on up the hill. The road roughly followed the river, and where it diverged, a path led off to the right to a gravel riverside footpath. Willows drooped over little sandy beaches which formed at meanders in the river and dipped their slender leaves in the water, making the thin branches drag in the direction of the flow. Hazel, beech and ash trees stretched their roots towards the water. The path was always in view of the wide and slow-flowing river, and Ged saw the dark shadows of trout treading water by the riverbank and recalled lazy afternoons with his Mum, learning to 'tickle' the trout, waiting with his hand under the water until trout came by and stroking their bellies.

Despite the bright sunshine that morning, the wind was bitingly cold. Ged zipped his jacket up as far as it would go and buried his hands in his pockets for warmth. The sound of the wind in the leaves above his head and the babbling of the water over the rocks in the river soothed him. He realised he hadn't thought about Marge since he had set off. Feeling a pang of guilt, he reasoned that as he had rarely been to Annie's home since she moved here, all his attention was taken up making sure he didn't get lost…now that he was walking along the river, that was pretty unlikely. Besides, his foot was beginning to ache. When he put his boots on that morning, he had almost forgotten the broken bone a few months before. He peered ahead, up the river through the trees, looking for somewhere to sit and rest.

There were no benches or even an old fallen tree to rest on further upriver, as far as he could tell. He decided to cut his losses and walk back the way he had come. No sooner had he set off back up the path than he saw a meander in the river with a willow tree arching over the river. One of the larger roots of the tree was exposed and quite dry enough to allow him to sit awhile. As he sat on the gnarled root of the old tree, he noticed that the trees on the other side of the river were spaced more thinly than the footpath side and allowed a view of a broad floodplain which had some kind of highland cattle grazing. Stocky, with long, shaggy, chestnut-brown coats, short necks and insanely long and twisted grey horns. He began to sketch the beasts but found that, though he had caught their form quite accurately, because of their oddly short neck and stocky legs under the massive body, it appeared that he had simply sketched them rather inexpertly and drawn a highland terrier with a cow's head. He decided to concentrate on sketching the head with those fabulous horns. Some of the cows had one horn pointing forward and one pointing back – almost as though they were screwed on and that one had come loose, or perhaps, he mused, they were antennae, and each one was tuned in to a different TV channel.

His butt had begun to ache from sitting on the hard and bumpy tree root, so he decided to make his way back to the village and see if he could find somewhere to get lunch.

***

Hattie's Café was a charming little place on the town square. It had floral-printed curtains and white-painted sash windows, and there were tubs of bright flowers by the door even though it was late September. Inside, various items of copper hardware adorned the wall, and a large oak Welsh dresser dominated the room. There was enough seating for around twenty customers, but unfortunately, there didn't seem to be any tables free. Ged didn't want to sit outside in that cold wind. He decided to ask if they did a takeaway service. A stout woman with curly, brown hair in an alarmingly bright pink apron with a teapot pattern print who stood behind the counter told him that they did take away food but said if he didn't mind sharing, he could sit at a table in the window where there was a spare seat at one of two tables-for-two. Ged said that he didn't mind, and the lady went to speak to the man sitting at the table with a free seat. He nodded, and Ged gratefully took his seat with a quiet sigh. It was the first decent walk he had done since he had broken his foot, and he figured that it was a bit too much, too soon. Or it could be that his old walking boots were pressing on the newly healed bone.

He bent down and loosened the laces on his left foot, wriggling his toes, flexing his foot up and down and winced.

"Hurt yourself, have you?" said pink-apron lady as she came over with a pad to take his order. Ged noticed the distinct accent of Oxfordshire, which Annie had.

"I broke my foot this summer, and it's not quite ready for these old walking boots."

"Oh dear. Well, hopefully, a nice cup of something and some cake will take your mind off it," she said, pen poised. "Now, what can I get you?"

Ged ordered a mug of tea and a bacon sandwich.

The man sat on the other side of the table, looked over his newspaper, and regarded Ged. "I recommend the carrot cake if you have room after your sandwich."

"Thanks. I'll give it a try," said Ged, bending down to re-tie his laces more loosely.

The man went back to his paper while Ged rummaged in the backpack for his sketchpad.

"Love the bag!" said Pink-Apron as she placed a small tray with a pot of tea, cup and saucer, a jug of milk and a bowl of sugar cubes on the table in front of him. "Sorry, no mugs left. I hope a pot of tea is okay. I won't charge extra," she said with a wink.

Ged chuckled. "Oh, my unicorn bag... My granddaughter gave it to me, and I've become quite attached to it." He ordered a slice of carrot cake as the man had recommended.

The man peered over his paper, first in interest at Ged's backpack and then turned to Pink-Apron. "Hattie, could I have a slice and a Cappuccino, please?"

"Course you can, Jed. Will bring it over in a jiffy."

Ged pricked his ears... as Hattie said this. "Well, how about that?"

"Pardon?" said the other man...

"I'm Ged, too. Well, most people call me Ged... except my wife."

"My friends all call me Jed, and so does my wife... unless I do something she's not happy about. Then I get 'Jeremy.' So, I know I'm in trouble."

Ged thought about this for a moment. Marge wasn't happy about what he did most of the time, so he supposed calling him 'Gerald' figured. "Nice to meet you... er, Jed."

"Likewise, Ged," said the man, smiling and added: "Hattie likes to wind me up by calling me Jeremy or even Gerald sometimes; she's my Sister-in-Law." He went back to his paper and began to shake and fold it until he had the crossword on a small pad that would fit easily on his side of the table. He felt around in his pockets for a while, patting and delving into each one.

"If you need a pencil, I have a few in here," offered Ged.

"Thanks... It looks like I've managed to come without one."

Ged handed a sharp one to him.

He looked out of the café window at the village square. A young woman in a knee-length, green, woollen coat and a matching deep-russet bobble hat and scarf was trying to put her child in a stroller in the little parking area. Her scarf impeded her as it was whipped around by the wind, and the child was wriggling. She grabbed the scarf and attempted to toss it over her shoulder, but it was blown back and flapped in front of the child's face as she tried to do up the complicated buckle. Ged remembered needing a third arm when he took Jamie and Alice anywhere in the stroller. You needed two hands to hold the buckle parts together and another to actually fasten it, let alone trying to keep the child from grabbing the straps, your clothes or smearing jam on your sleeves. He felt the woman's pain as she gave up, stood upright and removed the offending scarf, stuffing it in the basket under the stroller. The child took the opportunity to attempt an escape. The woman checked his progress with a strategically placed foot and then held her hand out. The child held on to her left hand whilst she walked up the street, pushing the empty stroller with her right.

Ged watched all of this with mild amusement and admiration at the common sense of the woman and made a mental note of the colours. As the woman and her charge disappeared out of sight, he turned to a clean page in his A4 sketchbook and started to sketch. Quickly and lightly, he allowed the pencil point to tell the story. He formed the shape of the woman crouching and the scarf flapping about her head; he drew the child's legs up high, kicking in excitement. He drew the woman's left hand, grabbing for the scarf, whilst her right hand held on to the buckle. He only made a suggestion of the buggy and the woman's coat and a basic form of the river and trees in the background.

His sandwich arrived, and he thanked Hattie. He took two sachets of brown sauce from the pot in the centre of the table. He was quite hungry, and the bacon sandwich smelled amazing, but he also wanted to capture another scene whilst it was fresh in his mind.

At the bottom of the page, he quickly scribbled a suggestion of the woman walking away up the road towards the pub with the child's hand in hers and her other hand deftly controlling the buggy. On the right of the page, he did a rough sketch of her standing up and tying her scarf whilst the child held on to her coat pocket, retelling the story with a little artistic license.

"Your tea will get cold," said the other Jed.

Ged looked up from his sketch. "Yes, I should have something; I'm starving!" He laid down the sketchbook and pencil and poured himself a lukewarm, slightly stewed cup of tea. He was used to tea like this; after fetching and carrying out Marge's orders, he often got back to a mug of tepid tea with a teabag that had been sitting in it for ages. He shrugged and took a large gulp, then he bit open and squeezed the contents of the sachets on his sandwich, picked it up in both hands and took a satisfying bite. Utterly delicious…this was just what he needed.

"Tall batter…" muttered the other Jed. "Tall batter…"

"Sorry?" said Ged through a mouthful of sandwich."

"It's one of these clues… Tall batter dips his fingers in the lake. Six letters."

"Willow," said Ged after swallowing the sandwich. "Cricket bats are made of willow, and they dip the ends of their branches in water. They're usually pretty tall."

"Brilliant!" Said the other Jed. Yes, that fits. The word coming down from it is 'Warsaw.' I couldn't decide between that and Krakow. Thanks."

"You're welcome," said Ged through another mouthful. "I don't do the crossword, but the wife does, and I usually get two or three clues on a good day."

"Well, you're pretty quick… You should come to the pub quiz at the Rising Sun this evening; there's usually a cryptic round."

"I've been invited this morning by a neighbour of the house I'm staying in… I think he said his name was 'Oliver'."

"Ah, up near Badgers Holt?"

"Yes, that's where I'm staying."

"What? Annie's place?"

"Yes. She's my Sister-in-Law. You know her?"

"Known her for years! She comes to my wife's stitch and bitch club."

Ged spluttered. "Her … what?"

"Sewing… they do patchwork, quilting and gossip for a few hours every Thursday."

"Stitch and bitch… okay, I get it."

"She comes to our place quite often. We have a cheese and wine supper every couple of months, and she always comes. Usually brings a decent claret… that's the kind of guest I like having over."

"Ha…That's Annie, alright. Never comes empty-handed."

"Yep…." Then Jed's expression changed to a more serious one. "So… it must be your wife who's …ill, then? …I'm sorry… must be tough. I guess you're here for a bit of respite."

Ged hesitated. Not sure he wanted to talk about it. "Yes," he said simply.

"Well, if you're here for respite, we won't get onto that subject, shall we? I see you're an artist. What kind of stuff do you do?"

"Oh, I wouldn't say I'm an artist. I just enjoy sketching a bit. I started when I broke my foot this summer and couldn't do much on our holiday. I used to draw a lot when I was young, and it's surprising how… well, how easy it feels. It's quite addictive… I've tried to learn to use watercolours to make the sketches more interesting, but I need a bit more spare time to get the hang of it. Maybe it's something I'll do when I retire."

"My wife goes to a painting class on Mondays. I went along a few times when I retired. We thought it was something we could do together, but I'm a waste of a piece of paper, to be honest…"

"Oh, what do you do instead?"

"Wood is my medium. I restore old furniture and make things in my workshop. It keeps me out of trouble."

Ged finished his bacon sandwich and drained his tea cup. He looked around for Hattie to get a coffee to go with his carrot cake.

"She'll be out in a minute," said the other Jed, guessing what he was looking for.

A woman came to the window. Slim, with sleek, wavy, grey hair and bright eyes. She wore a tweed jacket with a warm-red pashmina around her shoulders. She waved at the other Jed. He stood up, refolded his newspaper and returned the pencil. "I need to go. Barbara is finished at the hairdresser, and I promised to take her to the garden centre. 'See you at the quiz tonight?" He asked, hopefully.

"I think I will come to the quiz. It will give me something different to do."

"Good. See you later then."

"Nice to meet you... Jed," said Ged, standing up and offering his hand.

The other Jed shook it warmly, smiling broadly. "Likewise, Ged... Goodness, that sounds odd."

Ged chuckled and sat down as the café door opened with a tinkle of the little antique bell, which hung from a large, round metal coil. Hattie appeared at the sound of the bell but looked disappointed that it wasn't another customer. Most of the other tables were now empty, save for two ladies near the counter.

"Er... Hattie? Could I get a coffee, please? I should pay, too."

"Yes, of course, dear." She said, switching on her smile. She really did have a most charming face when she smiled. "Cappuccino? Latte? Flat White...?"

"Cappuccino, please."

"Certainly. Be right with you... You and Jed hit it off, didn't you? Nice fella; I'm glad Barbara married him."

"Yes. Barbara's your sister, is she? Everyone here seems very friendly."

"Oh, we're mostly okay here...Yes, Barbara's my sister. I suppose Jed told you.

"Do you live here, as well as running the café?"

"I've lived above the café all my life. The only way I'll leave here is in a wooden box. I'll get you that coffee; it goes nicely with the carrot cake."

Ged nodded in agreement. Hattie picked up the tray with the teapot, cup and plate and bustled off to make his coffee. Ged gazed out of the window at the village square. Once more, he picked up his pencil and began to sketch the bridge over the river. It was the kind of scene you might find in a jigsaw, he thought to himself. A quintessential Cotswold scene: river trees, village square, low humpback bridge and thatched or stone-slated terraced cottages along the road with tiny front gardens and low, creamy Cotswold stone walls with climbing shrubs and ivy tumbling over them. One of the cottages on the other side of the square from the café had a well-established, ancient-looking, pink climbing rose over the door that stretched the entire length of the terrace, sharing its pretty blooms with the neighbouring houses.

A large black and white cat sat washing its shoulder on the stone wall of the cottage. Ged had become quite fond of cats since he had spent so much time studying old Potts. They weren't the malevolent and self-centered creatures he had always thought them to be. They were full of character and mischief and possessed a self-assured confidence, which he supposed could easily be mistaken for arrogance or conceitedness.

As he sketched, the scene came to life beneath his pencil. Even in simple monotone graphite, there was life and energy in the drawing. He left out details that didn't seem important but caught the bend of the trees, the ripple of the water in the river, the curve of the bridge, and the turn of the cat's neck as it bent its head to lick its shoulder. A suggestion of thatched roof was enough to give the scene its Cotswold credentials.

He turned the page and began to sketch the cat in more detail. It had ceased washing its shoulder and was now peering about, observing the comings and goings of the square. It was still a blustery day, and a crisp packet tumbled along the pavement, along the row of terraced cottages. The crisp packet jumped and whirled along the pavement. The cat watched it intently. As it danced past the gate, the cat lowered its head, raised its haunches and did the classic bum-wiggle for a few moments before pouncing. Clearly a young cat with plenty of spring in its pounce. It subdued the errant crisp packet and chewed at the corner of it for a little while, but as it didn't put up much of a fight, the cat soon lost interest and began to lick its shoulder again.

Hattie brought Ged's coffee and a handwritten bill. Ged thanked her and continued sketching.

"Oh, isn't that lovely!" she said. "Those pictures of young Tabitha are wonderful! You've got her washing her shoulder again, look... She's always doing that. My mum used to say it helps them think... Maybe they've got a few extra brain cells in their shoulder. Aren't you clever? I wish I could draw."

"Thanks," said Ged, blushing a little.

"You know, I bet Angela would love to see a picture of her Tabitha. I don't suppose you could do a copy for her, could you... Oh, listen to me... How cheeky!"

"Not at all, Hattie. She can have this." He tore the page from his sketchbook. I can always do another one.

Ged dawdled over his coffee and tried re-sketching Tabitha, subduing the Crisp packet. He found that it came quite naturally to him, even though Tabitha was now sunning herself on the pavement, and the crisp packet had long since made its escape in the breeze.

30

Ged thoroughly enjoyed himself at the Pub Quiz. The Rising Sun pub was packed that evening, and the atmosphere was friendly and raucous. He didn't answer many questions in the first few rounds, discovering just how little he knew about music, or parlour games (the subject of the first and second round) and was entirely clueless on the celebrity pictures round. He regained a little dignity on general-knowledge round as he got lucky with a few of the questions. A question on the geography of Cornwall, another on the history of Warwick Castle, and he surprised his teammates, Mark, Jed, number two and their wives by answering a complicated question about the Argentine Tango. He enjoyed a delicious home-made curry at the interval and several glasses of red wine, chatting amiably with Annie's friends about dancing and what they thought of the 'Strictly Come Dancing' judges. The others were fascinated with Ged's angle on the matter as he actually knew what he was talking about.

Back at Badgers Holt, in Annie's cosy guest room, he passed out as soon as his head touched the pillow. He had missed the red light flashing on Annie's answering machine. (Not that he would have touched it anyway, as he wouldn't consider any messages being for him).

***

He was woken by the phone ringing downstairs in the little hallway. It stopped after only three rings. Assuming someone had got the wrong number, he rolled over to go back to sleep. The phone rang again. Three rings and stopped and then once again. Ged began to realise that this was some kind of code that the call was for him.

He padded downstairs in his pyjamas and waited by the telephone. Sure enough, it started to ring. He picked up the receiver.

"Hello?"

"About time!" It was Sarah's voice. "I've been trying to get hold of you since last night. Where on earth were you?"

"Oh, hi, Sarah. Good trick with the three rings. I was invited to the local pub quiz by some of Annie's friends. It was fun, actually. Everything okay?"

"More than okay, actually. Did you answer many questions?"

"Not many at first, but I redeemed myself on the general knowledge round at the end. Annie's friends are really nice."

"I've met one or two of them. Did you meet a guy called Jed?"

"Yes. By accident at lunch yesterday. It was weird, calling him Jed all the time. Anyway, surely, you're not calling to check up on me, to what do I owe the honour?"

You're not going to believe this, Dad."

"Go on – you seem to be in the habit of giving me surprises."

"Well, Emily from the Lobster Pot called yesterday, and I could hardly believe it myself when she told me…"

"What, she's sold more sketches?"

"Yes, one or two, but one in particular to a very interesting customer, and he wants to get in touch with you."

"Whatever for?"

"He's a publishing agent, and he wants to know if you might be interested in doing a few more sketches for a children's book."

"What? You must be kidding."

"No. Really, he has been trying for months to find an illustrator for this author's latest book, and he thinks your sketches would be a good fit."

"That's hilarious – my holiday doodles… in a book?"

"I called him. His name is Mike Adamson. He works for a literary agency in London, and he is dead serious. He saw your sketches of that tabby cat, and he really wants to show the author, but he wanted to ask your permission first."

"Er… well, he can show her the sketch. I mean, he owns it now."

"No, Dad. You aren't following me. If she likes it, they will want you to illustrate the book. He said they'll want at least twenty or more final images for the book. It's a kid's novel with pictures on every page or two."

"Oh."

"Yes – oh."

"But I can't get into this now! It's ridiculous. I have a full-time Job. Besides, when I'm not working, I'm running around after Marge. I'd never have the time."

"I did explain about how things are right now. Would you agree to meet up with him, at least?"

Ged took a very deep breath and tried to process what he had just heard. "Give me some time to digest this, Sarah. It's a lot to take in."

"Okay, Dad. I understand. But do give it some serious thought. Your drawings really are incredible, and this proves it. Have a nice day at Auntie Annie's. Have a safe journey."

"Alright, Love. Thanks for calling."

"Thanks for picking up. You can delete the answerphone message. It was me last night."

***

Ged's head was reeling. It was already feeling a little fuzzy, thanks to the beer and the glass of wine he had had the previous evening. He pottered around Annie's kitchen, trying to remember where everything was as he made himself tea and toast. He tried to get his head around the absurdity of the situation. Granted, he could draw reasonably well, but there was no colour, so he was surprised that anyone would want to pay for them, let alone use them as illustrations in a book. To Ged, they were just doodles, a way of passing the time on holiday or when he had time to himself.

The more he thought about it, the more excited he became. Could he really earn a living from drawing? He had really enjoyed himself at the café the previous day, sketching Tabitha, the little piebald cat.

"Don't be daft, Baker," he said to himself, shaking his head. "You couldn't make anywhere near the amount of money you need to live on from drawing, and even if you did get a few hundred quid for twenty sketches, you couldn't rely on the income."

Later on, as he sat on the sofa with his mug of tea and a slice of toast and Marmalade, he spotted his unicorn backpack lying on the floor of the hall. He fetched it and pulled out the sketchbook, leafing through the pages, perusing the last of the sketches he had done in Cornwall and the few he had done the previous day, all there except, of course, the one he had given to Hattie for Tabitha's owner.

"You could do this part-time, though. Maybe not give up the day job but do this for fun and a bit of holiday money," he mused… "or for charity."

He tried to view the sketches with a critical eye. He imagined Marge as his critic, as she would have been before her illness, when she blended diplomacy with her more critical tendency. It helped him to critique them more honestly. The cat's face was well formed, and her tail was true to her, but the legs seemed too short in one of the sketches. The river looked dull in the sketch of the mother and child, and it seemed rushed and scribbly, but the movement of the scarf and the woman's expression was interesting. Ged chuckled as he recalled the child's determination not to go into the buggy and the mother's pragmatism. The Horned cattle really did look like Scottish terriers with a cow's head.

Doing this reminded him that there was another thing that made this virtually impossible just now: Marge – she was so frail. Ged had to do almost all of the housework when he wasn't at work. When he wasn't doing housework, he was doing little errands to keep her happy. He knew it was making her spoiled, but if she really had so little time left, he felt that was a small price to pay. He had a feeling there would be tougher times ahead for her if the tumours in her head and pancreas got worse. His eyes began to brim with tears. His lovely Marge. His dancing queen. He was so glad that he had managed to stay patient these last six months as she became more demanding and critical. He had no regrets.

***

Annie had prepared a chicken curry for dinner when Ged got home on the Sunday evening. Ged's shock at Marge's frailty redoubled after being away for the weekend. In his mind, Marge was still his slim, pretty sixty-one-year-old wife. She had aged ten years. Her eyes had become sunken with deep grey shadows. She seemed to have lost even more weight than he recalled from the Friday when he left for the Cotswolds.

Marge picked at her curry, staring at the table like a lost child. Annie and Ged chatted about the weekend. Annie was delighted that he had met her friends and gone to the pub quiz.

"Oliver and Jane are great neighbours," she said. "Did you meet Marmalade?"

"I assume that's the ginger cat in your note," replied Ged.

"Yes. He's their cat, but I think he prefers my place. Probably because he knows he'll get some fuss. Oliver and Jane are out most of the day."

"Well, he didn't stick around. Maybe he was scared as I'm not you."

"Maybe. And how about Jed and Barbara? I've known Barbara for years. We met when I was at the cottage hospital. She volunteers there. They're a really nice couple."

"Yes, they all seem really friendly. It's a lovely village."

"I know. I'm very lucky to live there."

Marge muttered something unintelligible.

"What is it, Marge?" said Ged, placing his hand on hers. She was staring at the plate; she had hardly had three mouthfuls of her curry. "Come on, eat up; your dinner is going cold."

"I'm not hungry," she said quietly.

Ged exchanged a glance with Annie. The look she returned gave him the distinct impression that they needed to find some time to talk, but preferably not in front of Marge.

"Let's get the washing up done and make a brew," suggested Ged. "Do you want to go in the sitting room whilst Annie and I wash up, Marge?"

"So that you two can talk about how horrible I am?" she hissed.

"No, Love. You can stay in here if you prefer."

"Well, I'm going in the sitting room. You can bring me a cup of tea in there."

"Okay. Be there in a bit."

***

No sooner had Marge departed than Annie let out an enormous sigh.

"Oh, Ged, am I glad you're back? She's been impossible!"

"Hang on, Annie. I said we weren't going to talk about her. I know you want to talk about the weekend, and I want to hear it, too, but I want to keep my word to Marge. I'll wash up and then make a cuppa. Will you dry?"

"I'll go read my book after we've done the kitchen. We can talk later. Are you okay with me going home first thing tomorrow? Can you drive me to the station?

"Sure. Tomorrow morning, first thing, after I drop Marge off at The Hollies."

"Grrr, The Hollies. -You'd think it was the Hilton, the way she goes on about it."

"Ah, yes. We can't make tea like them, serve food as nice, or butter a decent teacake. Am I right?"

"Nor do we have playing cards that are as good, and even the TV they have is better."

"Okay, when I'm done with the washing up. I'll make a cuppa, and you can take it up. Want another glass of wine?" Ged placed a hand on Annie's shoulder.

"Better not," said Annie. "I'll have one later when Marge drops off."

Ged took tea to Marge and sat with her. She had her feet up on the sofa and was playing patience with a deck of cards on a lap tray. Her hands looked skinny and more wrinkled than he remembered, but he noticed something else, too. Her nails had been French-manicured.

"Who did your nails?"

"I had it done at Angela's," said Marge.

"You and Annie?"

"Well, I think she had her feet done, and I got a French manicure."

"That sounds nice. Did Annie treat you to it?"

"Well, I wouldn't call it a treat; we have put her up all weekend."

"Marge, she let me stay at her place and came over to be with you and help out. It's lovely of her to treat you to a manicure. It sounds like a proper girls' day out."

"It was alright. Annie doesn't know where things go, and I don't like her cooking."

"You don't like mine, either."

"Well, some of it is alright. She puts too little salt in everything."

"You can always add more if you want it."

Marge's face screwed up in pain, and she grasped at her stomach. Her face paled.

"You're in pain," he said. "Have you been taking the tablets regularly?"

"Annie won't give them to me. I have to keep asking and asking."

"Okay, back in a minute. I'll get some of that rapid painkiller the doctor gave us."

Ged trotted quickly to the kitchen to find the bottle of liquid morphine that the doctor had prescribed for these occasions. It wasn't in the cupboard where he had left it, so he scaled the stairs to ask Annie. He knocked on the bedroom door.

"Annie?"

"Come in, Ged. Everything ok?

"No. I can't find the Oramorph."

"Don't worry, I hid it. She kept asking for more when she had already had some, and then she tried to dose herself. The amount she tried to take would have floored a horse! It's on my bedside cabinet. Here you are."

"Has she been in much pain?"

"Yes. If you give that to her, make sure you take her to bed. It dulls the pain and sends her off to sleep."

Ged took the bottle and went downstairs to prepare a dose for Marge. As he passed the sitting room, she cried out in pain.

"Coming, Marge!" He hurried to the kitchen and filled a dosing syringe, returning to the sitting room with it.

"Oh, Gerald! My tummy hurts, and my head is splitting! Make it go away!"

Ged placed his hand behind her shoulder to support her and brought the dosing syringe to her lips.

"Come on, take this. It will help with the pain."

Marge allowed him to place the dosing syringe in her mouth and plunge the clear liquid into her mouth. She screwed her face up in disgust.

"Eugh! It tastes horrible!"

"I know. Have some tea to take the taste away."

"Eugh, no, it's gone cold."

"Wine?"

"You're not supposed to mix alcohol and painkillers, Gerald; you know that."

"They do at The Hollies, so if it's good enough for them, it's good enough for me."

"They certainly do not."

"Ask Mrs Jennings. She worked there and said it's a great way to hide the awful taste of this stuff, he said, gesturing with the empty syringe."

He passed her the half wine glass of Chardonnay.

He sat with her, stroking her hair until her face began to relax.

"Right. Come on, dancing queen, let's get you to bed."

"But I wanted to watch television."

"Not a chance, young lady, it's past your bedtime," said Ged with a wink.

"My head feels fuzzy."

"I know, Love."

He helped her up and put an arm around her waist. She was so light he simply picked her up and carried her.

***

Marge soon dropped off to sleep with Ged stroking her hair. Once she was asleep, Annie and Ged had a chance to catch up. Ged got out clean glasses.

273

"Red, White, or would you prefer something a bit stronger?"

"Red, please," said Annie."

"I think I'll join you."

He took the open bottle of Merlot on the counter and half-filled their glasses.

"So, what gives?" he said as he passed Annie her wine.

"Well, it started out okay. Friday night, she moaned incessantly about you going away, but I managed to ignore it."

"Okay, feeling guilty, now."

"Sorry, Ged. Just telling you the facts."

"It's okay", he replied, "hardly surprising."

"Then, Saturday morning, I thought if I kept her busy, she would complain less."

"Good plan."

"So, I thought, but she didn't like the garden centre we went to for a cuppa and cake, apparently it was expensive and too noisy. She was rude to a waitress and made her cry."

"Oh dear."

"Things went better when I took her for a manicure."

"I noticed her nails. They're lovely!"

"Hmm, well, she was awful to the girl who did her nails at first, so the older lady doing my feet swapped over with her and ignored her the whole time. I don't know how she did it; she just calmly sat there and did the nails, said 'mm' at the right places and ' sorry Mrs Baker, I'll do that again." then, would you credit it, whilst her first coat of varnish was drying, she went round the back of Marge's chair and started giving her a head massage!"

"Really? How did that go?"

"Very well, actually. Marge calmed right down. She almost dropped off."

"Clever stuff. We'll have to get her to come and give us lessons."

"Maybe. Lunch was a disaster! We went to the café at Marks and Spencer. I thought she knew it well, so she would like it. She moaned about everything. I know it's the tumours talking, and I kept my mouth shut, but I felt sorry for the staff. I didn't know what to say."

"It was like that on holiday. I should have explained."

"You know, I've looked after hundreds of patients who behave like Marge, but it's so much harder to handle it when it's someone you know and love."

"Teachers say the same," said Ged. "They can handle the annoying behaviour of teenagers and kids in the classroom, but their own kids drive them nuts."

"Yes, I guess it's just a job. I never appreciated that 'til I had to look after my sister."

"Well, thanks for trying, Annie. What did you do today?"

"I took her to Compton Verney. We were okay walking around the gallery, although she continuously whined that it was too draughty or too hot and then upset someone in the café. I apologised to the lady, but she was really offended. Quite honestly, I don't blame her!"

"What on earth did she say?"

"She told her she sounded like a chimpanzee and to get back to the Jungle!"

"You're kidding!"

"Guide's Honour," said Annie, putting three fingers up in salute."

"Poor woman."

"To be fair, the woman did have an annoying laugh, but to say that, well, it's so racist."

"What?"

"The woman was Asian."

"Good grief! If I need another respite weekend, we'll pay for her to stay at the Hollies."

"Can you afford it?"

"We have some savings. It can't hurt to get a price. I expect she'll love it."

***

Things got back to some kind of normality over the following weeks, although Marge was now waking up in the middle of the night. Her headaches and belly pains were more frequent. Ged was exhausted, and it had been noticed at work. Peter took Ged to one side after the morning start of shift meeting one Monday.

"Ged. I know things must be tough at home."

"Yep. It's pretty bad, I have to admit. Marge is going downhill, but I don't want to stop work, Pete. It's keeping me sane."

"Well, I think you need some help. Take a look at these inspection reports with me. Look, there's no date on them, and you forgot to complete the safety compliance section."

"Oh shit, Pete, I'm sorry."

"It's okay, Ged, I get it," said Pete gently. "But these presses are safety critical. We need to get you doing something that isn't safety-related."

Ged hung his head. Pete was right; Ged was usually so careful. He was a team leader and trained other people to do this. He knew it was fatigue, but he didn't want to stop working. He needed the distraction and the normality.

"Look, mate, I've been thinking… Do you remember John Murray from the Assembly shop maintenance team? He needs development, and I'd like to see his work first-hand. I've spoken to his boss, Vic Marston, about seconding him to our shift in Press and weld, and we could find different duties for you for … well, for a while, you know, see how things go. I spoke to Bob Small, and he's happy to look at a couple of areas where your skills would be welcomed. Engineering stores could use someone with your experience."

"You're right. Look, I'm really sorry, Pete. I messed up. I made a serious mistake. I guess if Kev Flynn will have me, I can't do too much damage in stores."

"It's not permanent, Ged. When things are…"

"Over," Ged interjected. "Let's not sugar-coat this, Pete," Ged replied, steel in his gaze. "Marge is going to die; it's not going to be pretty. I'll need some time afterwards to get my head around stuff, and then I guess I'll need to move on."

"I'm sorry, Mate."

"Hardly your fault."

"You know I don't mean that. I'm truly sorry that you're having to deal with all this. Maybe some time off to care for Marge could be arranged."

"No. Please – I think I'll go nuts if I don't have a bit of normality to come to each day. Stores work doesn't fill me with enthusiasm, but Kev is a good bloke. We've known each other for years. It's better than slogging away in my state of mind and making a mistake that could hurt someone."

"Okay," said Pete. "I've already spoken to Kev, and he's keen to help out. I'll talk to Bob Small in H.R. and get it arranged; then, will you work with John Murray for the rest of the week? He can do the work under your expert eye, you can show him the ropes, there's a second pair of eyes for the paperwork, so you can be confident everything is safe, and it would ease John into the work here in the press shop."

As Ged shut the car door after his shift, he paused before setting off, staring ahead, his fingers gripping the steering wheel. He didn't like the idea of working in the stores very much, but the guys there were good people, and one or two of them knew his situation. They had been diplomatic but sympathetic, too. Kevin's brother had passed away a few years earlier from lung cancer, so he understood how tough things could be.

Ged had worked hard to become a team leader in maintenance. He knew Pete's decision was right, but what if he couldn't sort himself out after Marge was gone? What if he made another mistake and someone got hurt? He felt heat rising in his chest, and tears pricked his eyes; he leaned forward against his seatbelt. Head drooped, his shoulders heaved and shook.

31

Marge woke in pain every night for the rest of that week. Ged had to keep a drink of blackcurrant cordial by the bed to wash the liquid morphine down. The morphine wasn't really taking the pain away. It just seemed to stupefy her to the point where she simply didn't care.

Dr Oldfield made a house call. He felt around her midriff. She winced wherever he pressed. He took her blood pressure and asked a few questions. She couldn't remember waking up at night, so Dr Oldfield addressed a few follow-up questions to Ged, who explained that she was asking for Oramorph at least twice a day and at least once most nights. He wrote out a prescription for a stronger dose and gestured to Ged to follow him out. Ged put on his coat and walked with Dr Oldfield to his car.

"Now, Ged, you know this isn't a good sign, obviously." Said Dr Oldfield in a low voice. "Things are moving faster than we might have expected. I think the cancer may have spread to her liver. She's looking thin, and her skin is yellowing. I've included a powder on that prescription to be stirred into her tea, coffee and any other drinks or soup she might have. It's tasteless, but it adds calories."

"Okay, how much do I use?"

"A teaspoon with every drink and meal. Try to get her to eat a little and often. When her stomach is filling and she digests, I expect it causes her more pain."

"Yes, that's the pattern I've seen," Ged replied. "Dr Oldfield, in your opinion…"

"Now, Ged, you're going to ask me the impossible question – how long has she got?"

"I just hate seeing her suffer like this."

"I know. I see it far too often in my line of work. It could be a few weeks or a couple of months. Everyone is different. For Marge, it looks like weeks. Have you been in touch with the hospice, or are you making other arrangements?"

"Oh, er, well, I guess we thought it would be the Hollies or nothing. Would you recommend something different?"

"Well, the Hollies are great in the nursing home, but they won't be cheap, and you can't guarantee they will have a bed, so you need a plan B. I'd suggest looking at the cottage hospital or St Bart's Hospice. See if they have beds available and ask at the Hollies."

"Would we have to fund it ourselves, or could we get help with the cost?"

"It depends on your income, but I wouldn't bank on it. You're looking at around £800 a week and more if she needs constant nursing."

"That's a lot, but we do have a few thousand in an ISA. Perhaps I can use that…"

"If I were a betting man, Ged, and I'm not, it may not come to that. I think she may have to go to hospital. She's getting jaundiced, and I suspect we need to do something about that, or her body will poison itself."

***

Dr Oldfield referred Marge to a specialist at the hospital. Her skin had yellowed even more over the weekend, and even with the higher dose of painkillers, she needed the morphine after meals and appeared to have lost even more weight.

Brian came to stay on Sunday, and as Monday was his day off, he went to the hospital with his parents. The specialist examined Marge and quickly concluded the same as Dr Oldfield. He agreed that it was likely that the cancer had spread to the liver and suggested that he put a stent to help drain the bile away, as this would reduce the Jaundice. He warned Marge that the procedure wouldn't be pleasant, but she would be heavily sedated, and they would give her painkillers to help with the discomfort. It wouldn't take long, and she could see her family straight afterwards.

Ged and Brian stayed with Marge and tried to keep her occupied with a crossword. She drifted in and out of lucidity, partly, Ged guessed, because the painkillers were so strong and maybe the sedatives were having an effect.

An orderly came to take Marge down to the treatment room. Ged and Brian went with her but had to leave once she was taken in. They were asked to return in around 45 minutes.

They went down to the café. Ged paced, nervously cleaning his nails with a penknife.

"Dad?" said Brian. "I got you a Coffee. Come and sit down."

"Thanks, Son."

"So, Dr Oldfield reckoned it could be weeks rather than Months?"

"Yeah, I know. Bit of a blow."

"I suppose…"

"You suppose?"

"If you had a dog in this much pain, you'd put it out of his misery, wouldn't you?"

"I guess so, but this is your mother, Brian."

"I know, and I love her, but she's a shadow of who she was. She's like a skeleton. She's so frail. Do you know what's weird?"

"No."

"I miss her stroppiness!"

"Funny, but I know what you mean… the fight has gone out of her. She doesn't have the energy to complain."

"She wasn't always like that, Dad."

"I know, Bri. I had become used to it, immune to it. I still think of her as my beautiful, super-organised, dinner-party-planning, dancing queen." His head drooped, and he could feel a lump in his throat. Brian reached across the table and squeezed his father's hand.

"Do you remember when she marched over to the recreation ground and told Ben Jameson to wash his mouth out with soap and water and give me back my cricket bat that he nicked? She was fierce! Ben was so scared. We were friends for years after that."

"No…you never told me about that… neither did she."

"Oh yeah. If anyone picked on me, she'd hunt them down and give them a piece of her mind. She did that with Ed, too, although he didn't get picked on much. I remember she called up that girlfriend of his and called her a harlot when Ed found out that she'd two-timed him."

"Oh, I remember that, alright. The girl's father came to remonstrate with us for bullying his daughter. She did have a bit of a reputation, though. I think she went through most of the boys in your year by the time she left school," said Ged, a smile creasing the corners of his eyes.

"I have to say, Dad, I'm impressed with Mum. She's got some guts, refusing Chemo."

"From what I hear, she's got her head screwed on. It might have given her more time, but time for what? Throwing up as well as being in excruciating pain and spaced out of her tree on painkillers? Not able to do the garden or go to the WI? Not to mention losing her hair.... I think she made the right decision, though it's awful to see her like this."

***

When Ged and Brian returned to the recovery area to see Marge, a nurse met them at the door. She was red-eyed and flustered. She checked their names and told them that the procedure was not quite complete. She quickly led them to a consultation room.

"The specialist will be here in a minute. Can I get you anything? Water?

"No thanks. Is everything ok?"

"I'll let Mr Norris tell you about it."

"Oh no, not another operating theatre drama."

The nurse looked at the floor and took a tissue from the box on the desk, wiping her nose before screwing up the tissue and washing her hands.

"Are you sure *you* wouldn't like a cup of tea or anything?" offered Brian gently. "I'll be okay."

The specialist breezed into the room and quickly shut the door. He offered his hand to Brian and Ged, who shook it politely.

"I gather everything didn't go smoothly, Mr Norris," said Ged.

"I'm afraid not, Mr Baker," said the specialist. "I must be brief, as I am due in theatre. Even though Mrs Baker was heavily sedated, she did not cope well with the procedure, and we have not been able to place the stent. She has had to go into emergency surgery."

"Oh no. What did she do?"

"Well, when we asked her to swallow during this procedure, she tried to leave, but it was quite uncomfortable."

"Oh, good grief! Not again."

"This has happened before?"

"Yes, in brain surgery. She tried to leave the operating theatre, and I think she was abusive to one of the staff." Replied Ged.

"I see. When Nurse Lucas tried to prevent her from leaving, she received a couple of scratches for her efforts and some verbal abuse. This does happen from time to time, but I think it's the first time for Nurse Lucas." Mr Norris placed a reassuring hand on the nurse's shoulder and smiled kindly.

"Oh no!" said Ged, turning to the nurse. "That must have been awful for you."

"I'm sorry," she said, her voice barely above a whisper, "I just wanted her to stay on the treatment bed. It can be really painful to move, so I tried to get her to stay still until we could take the tube out."

"It's the brain tumours… they make her aggressive."

"Mr Baker. I must go to theatre. The stent will be surgically placed. You can see Mrs Baker when she returns to the ward. Perhaps go for an early lunch and come back later."

***

Brian called Sarah to tell her what had happened.

"Not again!" she said when he relayed what they had been told.

"I'll stay over with Dad. I don't know how Mum will be when she's out of theatre."

"Will you ask Dad if he will meet with the agent?" said Sarah.

"Okay, which day and where?"

"He said he would be happy to come to Warwick, considering Dad's circumstances, and he said any day this or next week. I guess we had better see how Mum is first."

"You know Dad is still going to work, right?"

"Yes, and maybe you should talk to him about that too. He's burning the candle at both ends and, in the middle, Bri. He will end up in hospital too."

***

Marge had been taken to intensive care once again to recover from her operation. Ged and Brian didn't stay long but managed to speak to the doctor about her operation. He told them it had gone as well as could be expected, but in attempting to leave the treatment room whilst they were attempting to place the stent, she had managed to damage part of her oesophagus, which they had repaired and then placed the stent surgically. She would need time to recover from this and was heavily sedated as a result. They had taken some cells from the liver, pancreas and bile duct for analysis, and the results would be available in a day or two.

Brian drove to the house with Ged. They made small talk about the weather and food. There didn't seem to be much point in going to work, and Brian decided to have dinner with his father before heading home to London. Ged wasn't very hungry, but there was a chicken breast in the fridge, so he cooked up Fajitas for the two of them.

"Dad," said Brian, tentatively, "do you remember the publishing agent Sarah told you about?"

"Mmm."

"Well, he was wondering if you would like to meet up sometime soon. He wants to talk to you about doing some illustrations for a book."

"I did think about it, but it's out of the question. I don't have the headspace for it."

"Well… I just thought it might help you to take your mind off things and relax a bit. Annie says you left some sketches of a cat at her place that you drew while you were down there, and she said her friend Hattie wants to buy them."Ged sighed. "If it gets you off my back, I'll meet him. I don't want to do it now. Maybe when I retire, I'll take a business card, and that's it. I don't want you lot putting pressure on me, okay?"

"Sorry, Dad. Message received and understood."

"Maybe if you or Annie or Ed were to stay with Mum, then I would feel ok meeting with him on a Saturday."

"I'll ask Sarah. It wouldn't surprise me if he would be okay with a Saturday. From what Sarah said, he's single and doesn't seem to have much of a life outside art and books."

"Well, that's not a bad thing if he's a publishing agent."

32

Marge remained in intensive care for the remainder of the week. She was kept sedated as the doctor felt that she needed to heal properly. Ged visited after work each day on his way home. He would buy a coffee from the visitor's lounge, then sit and hold her hand, even though she was largely unresponsive. Each time he felt numb, this body lying in front of him wasn't Margie. His lovely girl was replaced by this...body.

After a long and oftentimes boring day working in stores, he would find himself daydreaming about things they had done together: The day he first danced with her at the town hall, dancing on the pier at Brighton on their first holiday as a married couple; the day they bought the house in Cornwall; the twins' birth... he couldn't think of a day when he had loved her more than that day. One particularly long daydream, he recalled, was a holiday in North Wales. He remembered a lovely day, sunny and warm. They had found a beach which was perfect for building sandcastles. After fish and chips for lunch, Marge spent the entire afternoon building a sandcastle with Ed, decorating it with pebbles and shells. Brian and Ged dug a huge hole as deep as they could until they hit rock. When they looked up from their labours, Ged and Brian found Marge gazing at the castle with her hands on her hips, grinning broadly while Ed added another row of pebbles around the base of the castle. When the tide rolled in and destroyed the castle, Ed cried inconsolably, and Marge hugged him until the sobs died away. When she finally uncurled from her embrace of the six-year-old Edward, her face was as tear-stained as his. They didn't have a camera that day, and she hadn't been able to capture their creation.

Ged smiled as the recollection played in his mind. He stood up to leave, kissed Marge on the forehead, and rearranged her hair as she would have preferred, and then he whispered in her ear. "It was a truly splendid sandcastle."

Annie came over twice during the week. On the first occasion, she handed Ged a small pot of grey-green capsules.

"Valerian. My neighbour has anxiety and says she swears by it. She told me it's the one thing that gets her sleeping. She says you have to take one a day, and in three or four days, you'll be sleeping better."

"Okay, thanks, Annie, I'll give it a try. It's just herbal, right? If it doesn't do any good, it won't do any harm."

Annie stayed over a few times, but each evening, when Ged returned to an empty house, he was rarely enthused to cook and would often make a simple omelette or cheese on toast, then sit in front of the TV with his glass of red wine. On the Thursday evening, the TV was getting on his nerves. He needed to do something different. He spotted his unicorn backpack on the floor by the sofa. He picked it up and decided to see if he could draw the sandcastle scene from memory.

Once again, as before, he found that his pencil glided over the paper and almost translated his thoughts into the image. It may not have been exactly as it happened, but the sketch was exactly how he remembered it. The long stretch of sand with an estuary emptying shallowly into the sea, a couple of children paddling in it with nets, and in the foreground, a magnificent sandcastle, covered in shells and pebbles in concentric rings, a seaweed moat surrounded the castle and a boy on the lap of his mother who sat on a sand dune embracing her child as the sea lapped at the edge of their sandcastle walls.

The sketch covered the entire page of his sketchbook and was by far the most complex picture he had drawn thus far. This time, the style was not unfinished like most of the previous sketches; this image had every detail Ged could remember. Each arm ended in four fingers and a thumb; each leg finished in a foot, complete with toenails. Even the children paddling in the river in the background were finished and complete. When he looked at his watch to check the time, he was astonished! It was past midnight. He had been drawing for nearly three hours. He regarded the sketch critically, his head tipped to one side. He would have to ask Brian if he had remembered it correctly, but actually, he was pretty pleased with his efforts—time for bed.

***

The café that Sarah had chosen for Ged's meeting with Mike was the garden centre on the outskirts of town. Mike thought it was a great idea. There was plenty of free parking, the café was huge, and he needed a few things for his tiny garden. He decided to get there early to shop.

As usual in garden centres, Mike lost himself completely in his imagination of what he would buy if he did have a large garden, as it was not so far away from Christmas. He wandered up and down, checking out the various ivies, conifers and other plants. He bought a hanging basket with pretty violets for his mother as a Christmas present. He eventually found himself in the car park of the garden centre loading his mother's car with quite a variety of things: bird seed for his feeder, three different varieties of ivy for the manger by his back door, a bag of orchid compost, three bowls of white hyacinths, one for him and two more Christmas presents for relatives, a new pair of secateurs and some plant food. He surprised himself at this uncharacteristic extravagance. He decided it must be the Christmas spirit getting the better of him.

Sarah had come with Ged as it had been she who had arranged the meeting. She had spoken with Mike the previous week at his office in London and showed him some of the sketches Ged had done for the children. Mike had been really impressed. He said he had never seen a style like this before, and although most of them lacked colour, there were plenty of Children's short stories and novels for which his sketches would be ideal.

She had bought coffee and slices of cake for them both and found a table with armchairs in the corner of the café by a huge potted olive tree. She spotted Mike Adamson in his tweed jacket as he came into the café, peering around, looking for them. She waved tentatively and smiled. Mike grinned broadly, waved back and walked over to the table.

"Hello, Mrs Baker, how lovely to see you," he said as Sarah and Ged stood to greet him. He warmly shook Sarah by the hand and turned to Ged.

"You must be Gerald Baker," he said, politely offering his hand for Ged to shake. Ged did so and nodded as his mouth was still full of tea bread. He swallowed as quickly as it would allow and gestured for Mike to sit with them.

"I'm going to get a coffee. Would you like another one?" Mike said.

"No thanks," said Ged, "I've barely started this one. He drew his wallet out of his inside coat pocket. "Sarah, why don't you get Mr Adamson a coffee and perhaps a cake? I can heartily recommend this Tea bread."

"Sure," said Sarah. "What'll it be, Mr Adamson, Cappuccino, Americano?"

"Cappuccino, please, and both of you, please feel free to call me Mike. I will have a slice of that cake; it looks delicious."

"Okay, back in a minute. I'll leave you two to get to know each other."

Mike sat down opposite Ged.

"It's great to meet you, Mr Baker," said Mike. "I know circumstances are extremely difficult, so I'm honoured that you agreed to meet me."

"You're welcome," said Ged, taking a gulp of his coffee. "You can call me Ged."

"I have to say, Ged," began Mike, "first of all, if you don't mind me saying, you have a real talent in your drawing."

"Er, thank you. It's very nice of you to say so, but this all seems like a lot of fuss over a few holiday sketches," Ged replied.

"Far from it. I have been an art critic, in one guise or another, for over fifteen years. I am paid to know talent when I see it. I rarely buy art, but I bought one of *your* sketches from Emily's in Porthleven."

"I'd have given it to you for nothing," said Ged. "Did you know that Sarah asked Emily to sell them without telling me?"

"Yes. She did mention it, and I believe she feels rather bashful about it. I think she knows it was wrong to do it without telling you, though I suspect if she had asked your permission, you would most likely have said 'no,' and we would not be sitting here right now."

Sarah returned, carrying Mike's coffee and cake. She set it down in front of him and sat down, nervously glancing at Ged. She overheard the last part of the conversation.

"Almost certainly," said Ged decisively, with a glance in Sarah's direction. "I was simply drawing to pass the time because I had broken my foot and couldn't walk or play with my grandchildren."

"Well, I'm glad you did – draw, I mean, not break your foot. Listen, I want to show you something." He opened his leather satchel and pulled out a framed picture of Potts creeping in through an upstairs window and two thin paperback books. "These are two Jenny Halshaw books published last year. I wanted to show you the kind of thing we are looking for."

"Now, Mr Adamson, I mean, Mike," Ged interjected, I don't want to be rude, but this really isn't a good time for me to be getting into anything. I have a lot on my plate, and I need to focus on looking after my wife. You see, she really is very sick."

"Yes. Sarah explained everything, so I really don't want to put any pressure on you to do anything now. I simply wanted to take this opportunity to meet you. I don't know how much longer I'll have this job, and I wouldn't want to leave it without at least meeting you... even if nothing comes of it. The agency I work for has... how can I put it? ... hit a rough patch financially, and Jenny Halshaw, plus a couple of others, is just about all that is keeping us afloat. Jenny brings out a new book about twice a year, and the kids simply gobble them up! I think if we published four a year, they wouldn't get tired of her. She can't write them fast enough!"

Mike handed over the book, and Ged leafed through it. Every few pages, there was a small black and white illustration scribbled in a rapid ink style.

"These are great; why can't *this* illustrator do her books?" asked Ged.

"Well, to be honest, we tried, but Hubbard is in such demand that he is now the bottleneck in the process. According to his agent, he already has a huge stack of commissions, and I doubt that even if he agreed, he would be able to do them for at least another six months. There's a real shortage of decent illustrative artists like you around."

"I see." He turned the book over, "This Jake Hubbard fellow... He makes a decent living out of illustration, does he?"

"Definitely! He has a nice big house on the Kent coast now with a studio in his garden, and now he is so well known he can command a very respectable fee for commissions. Some of his better-known original panels fetch thousands. His agent tends to ask for an up-front retainer to illustrate a book. For lesser-known authors, publishers usually pay a one-off fee. For better-known authors, their agent will negotiate a royalty, which can trickle in for years.

"Do you really think I could give up my job and become an illustrator?"

"Look… Ged, I don't have a crystal ball, but I have a pretty reliable instinct. It's not often I come across an artist that I am prepared to go and meet where they live, let alone on a Saturday. Artists usually bang on my door in London, asking me to look at their portfolios. It may sound big-headed, but my being here is a testament to how good you are. Authors like Jenny Halshaw would love to get illustrations like these in their books," he said, gesturing to the framed picture of Potts. "Publishers would be falling over themselves to get an illustrator like you. It's not just that the cat looks like a cat; it's because it is clearly the *same* cat in every sketch. You've caught his character. Sarah showed me another few drawings of a black and white cat. She said you were quick, too, which is a great advantage. Publishers love it when you can create illustrations quickly."

"I see."

"As for giving up your job, well, no. Most illustrators who are lucky enough to have a job would probably start illustrating in their spare time. I realise you don't have much of that at present, but maybe one day, in the future…?"

"Well, Mike," said Ged. "I am flattered by the compliment and that you've come all this way, but I need to focus on my wife. We may have very little time, and I still have a full-time job. You'll have to find someone else for the time being."

"I understand. And I certainly don't want to put any pressure on you at a time like this. I'm glad we met. Maybe in the future, our paths will cross again." He reached into his leather bag once more and brought out a business card, which he handed to Ged." Keep my card.

It's my personal mobile number, so even if Barker-Mead does go under, I might go freelance or get a position at another agency, and I could still put you forward as an illustrator."

"Thank you," said Ged, popping the card into his wallet – more out of courtesy than out of any intention to ever look at it again. Ged pushed the books across the table towards Mike: "You had best put these away. I'll end up getting coffee on them."

"Actually, I brought them for Sarah. When I met her last week, I said I would try to get some signed copies for your grandchildren."

"Oh, that's lovely," said Sarah. "Thank you, Mike," Sarah said, opening the flap at the front of the first book. It had a picture of a horse on the front. The inscription read:

"To Alice, I hope you enjoy reading this book as much as I enjoyed writing it. Your friend, Jenny Halshaw."

Sarah took the second book, entitled "Wild at Heart" A red fox stood proudly on a huge fallen dustbin on the cover of the book. *"To Jamie, A love of reading lasts a lifetime. I love to read as much as I love to write. Your friend, Jenny Halshaw."*

"These inscriptions are lovely. Jenny really took her time over them. Thank you, Mike."

"You're welcome. I had a long lunch with Jenny when I was down in Cornwall, so she had a bit more time than when she's doing signings at bookshops and festivals," said Mike.

"You were in Cornwall recently, then?" Asked Ged.

"Yes, just a few weeks ago. When I saw your work, I just had to talk to you, and Emily managed to put me in touch."

"Mike, may I ask something?" said Ged. "Your face is familiar. You don't originally come from London, do you? I'm trying to place where we might have met."

"I grew up in the Cotswolds, but my parents moved to London in my teens. We went on holidays to my Auntie Doreen's in Porthleven, and I worked for Emily at the Lobster Pot every summer holiday from when I was about sixteen."

"That must be where I have seen you. I bet you've served me a few lasagnas or portions of scampi; you're a good deal younger than I am. I would imagine the twins might even remember you."

"The Twins?" said Mike.

"My husband, Brian, has a twin brother, Edward," said Sarah. "Marge and Ged took them to the Lobster Pot for tea when they were kids. It was Emily's café that was one of Brian's inspirations to become a chef."

"What a small world!" exclaimed Mike. "I'm sure I would have served you back in the day. I was rather shy back then."

"Wait a minute," said Ged, "does Emily call you *Michael*?"

"Oh yes. She likes my full name. She hates the short name, Mike."

"Then I do remember you!" said Ged. "Or at least, I remember Emily calling your name."

"Yes, I've known Emily for years. She and my Auntie Doreen go way back."

"It's my favourite place to eat down there," said Ged. "Ron makes the best scampi in Cornwall."

"I couldn't agree more," said Mike. "Sarah said you have a house in Porthcovery."

"Yes. We were lucky. We got it in the eighties when houses were more affordable down there. My Grandmother passed away and left me some money, and Sarah and Bri officially own a stake in it, too. We could afford a decent deposit, and the lettings pay the mortgage plus a bit left over for maintenance."

"You're lucky. Auntie Doreen used to take us to Porthcovery for days out. The sun seems to shine there more than anywhere, and the ice cream from the loft is fantastic! I remember jumping in the harbour and fishing there once with my Dad." Mike's voice took on a wistful tone. "Those were halcyon days."

"We love Porthcovery," said Ged. "We rented a caravan there for a few years and then a cottage for another two when the boys were teens. When Sarah and Brian married, and the four of us started going twice a year, we realised it might cost less overall if we owned a place and rented it out, so we bought Chy Gwyn."

"You're lucky to have bought then. Properties there cost a small fortune now."

"Absolutely," agreed Sarah. "The house has doubled in value since we bought it."

"I love Cornwall, especially Porthcovery. I think I'd happily live there all the time if only I didn't have to earn a crust," said Ged, half to himself.

"Mmm, I know what you mean," said Mike, draining his coffee cup. "Maybe I'll retire down there and rent a room at Auntie Doreen's or the flat above the Lobster Pot." He picked up his framed sketch of Potts and placed it back in his satchel. "Well, I should be going. I borrowed my Mother's car to get up here; I'd better get it back to her."

"Well, thank you for coming all this way, Mike, said Ged, standing and offering his hand to Mike. "It has been good to meet you. I'm sorry if it's been a waste of time."

Mike stood and shook Ged's hand, smiling warmly, "Far from it, Ged. I have enjoyed meeting and talking with you immensely. It has been a privilege to meet the artist of a piece I now own. I only wish it could have been in better times. The next few months are going to be tough for you, I fear."

Ged nodded and shook his hand in return. "I hope you have a safe journey and find another artist for your Jenny's books."

"Thank you."

Sarah walked with Mike to the door of the café. "Mike, do you really think Dad has what it takes to be an illustrator?"

"Mrs Baker, he definitely has the artistic talent, but one also needs the desire to do it, and without that, there is no practical way forward. Perhaps in the future, when all this… *awfulness* is over, he may reconsider. Just keep my card. I fear when he took it, he only did so out of courtesy." Mike gave her another business card and shook her hand warmly before walking to his car.

33

Early the following week, Ed came to visit. Marge had been brought out of her deep sedation and could now sit up with support, but walking was very painful; her legs were so thin and emaciated that she simply couldn't support her own weight. Ged, Ed, and Brian met briefly with Mr Tandulkar, who said he felt the nursing home would give her the best quality of life possible for the remainder of her time. She was, in his professional opinion, hanging on to life by a thread, and they should prepare themselves for the worst in the next few weeks. She was still not eating well, but the staff at the Hollies were marvellous, and they appeared to be keeping her pain under control.

A week after she was transferred, Brian came up to Warwick for the whole weekend with Sarah and the children. Ed joined them on Sunday with Karen. Annie stayed over, too, sleeping on the sofa. They each took turns to visit Marge, who hardly spoke at all as it was still uncomfortable to speak, but she would answer their comments or questions with a weak squeeze of her hand, a blink of her eyes or, more commonly, a frown and a shake of her head.

Ged had been signed off work on the advice of Dr Oldfield. The situation had taken its toll on his concentration, and he found that he could barely function at work. Thanks to the Valerian, he did seem to be sleeping a little better, but he felt like he was in a bad dream that he didn't dare wake up from. He fell into a numb stupor. He often had to ask people to repeat themselves as he wasn't listening properly. As Sarah and Brian were packing to leave, the phone rang. Brian answered. A serious look came over his face as he listened.

"I see. Well, thank you – er Helen. Thank you for telling us. Yes, that's right, the funeral directors are Pringle and Mason. My wife has already spoken to them. I'll tell Dad. Thank you for looking after her… No. I don't think I would like to see her, but I will ask Dad and my brother. One of us will call if we want to."

Brian replaced the receiver and went to find Ged, who was cradling baby Laura in his arms in the sitting room.

"Dad..."

Ged knew immediately.

"I don't want to see her." He said simply.

"Me neither," said Edward. "I want to remember her like this," he said, gesturing to Brian and Sarah's wedding photograph on the shelf where Marge stood proudly in her lilac suit and pillbox hat with its little net over her eyes. "She really was a beautiful woman, wasn't she, Dad?" he said simply, embracing his Father in a bear hug as his body shook with sobs.

***

Sarah, Ed and Karen made a good team, helping Ged to plan the funeral and carry out administration. Ged was grateful for their help. The red tape and account changes, speaking to the bank, utility companies and insurance companies, sapped him of what little emotional strength he had left, but having their help and, often, their company made it more bearable.

The funeral was held at the local crematorium, with a reception at the Community Centre where Marge had spent so much time with the Women's Institute and the flower club. Neighbours, WI members, and flower club ladies swelled what might have been a meagre turn-out as there were so few relatives. Marge had only two cousins who came with their families, but Ged hardly knew them. Ged's elderly Aunt Sophie came to support him and held court with the children as it was months since she had last seen them. She was in her early nineties but still had her wits about her and enjoyed the attention of the children. Sarah decided not to mind that Aunt Sophie had brought the children a huge bag of sweets and bought them copious amounts of lemonade from the bar for the entire duration of the wake.

Ged made small talk with neighbours and friends, but most of the conversations simply seemed to float over his head. He barely remembered who he had spoken to. Thankfully, Karen had bought a condolence book, which meant that at least he could read the messages in his own time later on.

Aunt Sophie came back to the house after the reception. Brian had prepared a delicious supper of Beef stroganoff, which made the house smell cosy and inviting. Ged sat in a corner of the sitting room with his Aunt. It was several months since he had visited her, as caring for Marge had consumed so much of his time.

Aunt Sophie regarded him over her half-moon glasses.

"My dear Ged. You look exhausted, my boy. This has been a terrible strain on you," she said, putting her delicate bony hand on his arm.

"It's the toughest thing I've ever had to get through, Aunt Soph. I suppose I thought Marge and I would go much in the same way Mum and Dad did. You know, a bit of an illness and then – poof! It's been heartbreaking to see Marge waste away like this."

"I know, dear," she said sympathetically, giving his arm a gentle squeeze. "In time, the painful memories fade, and you will remember the good times more readily than the bad."

"I already have. I keep thinking of how we got together, dancing, the holidays we had together, the twins being born, and I've thought a lot about her parents, too."

"Really? What about them? I could never stand either of them. He was as stiff as a board, and her... well, she was about the biggest snob I ever met!"

"It was spending time with Annie that got me thinking. Annie spent most of her time with her grandmother. She virtually brought Annie up – I think it's what her parents wanted. Marge spent more time with her parents. It shows why Annie and Marge were such different people. It was Marge's friend who got her into dancing, or we never would have met."

"And her silly father, who ruined it all by forbidding her to dance! I remember that, alright. Your Mother was devastated. She always said you two would have made champions!"

"Really? She never told me that," said Ged, astonished at this revelation."

"You were so much in love. I don't think she felt it would have made any difference, either to you wanting to marry Marge or to Councillor Cookson allowing you to compete. So, she let it lie."

"Wow! She was probably right. I fell head over heels for Marge. She was a real catch."

"Mmm," mumbled Aunt Sophie.

"You never liked her much, did you?" said Ged, with a serious look at Aunt Sophie.

"We didn't have a great deal in common. I think she saw your favourite Auntie as a bit of a threat. I suppose I was a bit hard on her in the early days. But you loved her, she loved you, and that was enough for me."

Ged looked at his hands, deep in thought.

"People never really got to know the real Marge like I did. I think she used to wear a bit of a spiky suit of armour. But she didn't wear it when we were on our own together."

"I suspect you're right. I often misjudged her and didn't tell her so. Which I regret."

"Thanks, Aunt Soph."

"Now to you, dear boy... Sarah tells me you are drawing again..."

"Again?" said Ged, perplexed.

Aunt Sophie reached down into her battered tapestry bag and pulled from it a framed picture of a horse. The animal was a dappled grey, cantering across a wide meadow. Its mane and tail flying out behind it. There were a few trees in the picture, but they were mere suggestions and not fully formed. The horse, however, was very detailed. The dapples on its hindquarters had been carefully shaded, and the sketch had such depth. At the bottom of the drawing was a pencilled inscription: 'G Baker 11 3/4'.

"Oh my! I had completely forgotten about this. And you kept it all these years?"

"Certainly. When you came to my house in the holidays, if it rained, we would draw together, don't you remember?"

"I do remember now. Uncle David would bring us tea and biscuits while we sketched."

"Do you remember, we practised with greaseproof paper as we had no tracing paper, and then you spent all your pocket money on art things at that lovely shop in the village and got some proper tracing paper?"

"Oh, Crawfords, yes, I remember that place very well. One side of the shop was all varnish and gloss paints, and the good side was filled with shelves and shelves of stuff for arts and crafts. I was thinking of it in summer when I bought a few sketching things at a shop in Porthcovery."

"I used to go out with Tom Crawford in my teens. Your Grandad was a friend of his until then," she said with a wink.

"You're kidding!"

"Oh no. It would never have worked out. Tom Crawford's mother had ideas above her station and didn't want just anybody marrying her darling Thomas. She scuppered our tryst and blocked us at every turn."

"Huh… I know the feeling."

"Mmm, James Cookson, you mean?"

"He tried everything to persuade Marge to break up with me, and I don't think he even liked giving her away at our wedding."

"Well, he had no choice, did he?"

"No. We were too much in love."

"Pish," scoffed Aunt Sophie. "That's not why he had no choice."

"What do you mean?"

"The man had no choice because I threatened to tell his wife about his little secret."

"What little secret?"

"Let's just say he had a bit of a past that would have got him into choppy waters."

"Oh, come on, Aunt Sophie, how do you know?"

"Because Uncle David told me about it when he heard that James Cookson was being so difficult about letting you two get married."

"Well, you're going to have to tell me now."

"I promised I would never tell you as long as Cookson was alive, but when he died, I thought it would be too hard for Marge to accept, so I decided to keep quiet about it."

"Well, Marge isn't here now, so go on…"

"James Cookson was what one would now call … let's see now, a transvestite, I think. He was an entertainer in the war. Uncle David had a pal who was in the Navy during the war, and he saw a funny drag act called Jemima Puddleduck. He recognised "Jemima" at the time and never let on it was James Cookson. He ended up in front of the Magistrates for some traffic offence years ago, and as soon as Councillor Cookson clapped eyes on him, this friend winked at him. Councillor Cookson must have realised he knew his alter ego and let him off on some technicality or other."

"Unbelievable! He was so – so straight-laced! I bet his wife didn't know."

"Well, I doubt it, as he was terrified when I had a meeting with him in a coffee shop and asked him if his wife was familiar with Jemima Puddleduck. I told him I would tell her about it if he didn't get out of yours and Marge's way and let you marry."

"Good grief! I don't know what to say, Aunt Sophie."

"You could say thank you."

"OK …Thank you, but I wish you had told me. There are so many ways I could have used that information."

"I know, that's why I couldn't tell you. I wouldn't want to be disrespectful to him or drag his family's name through the mud. It wouldn't just hurt him; it would hurt his wife, Annie… and Marge, too. It would have ruined your marriage, and then Cookson would have got what he wanted. I did let him think you knew at first, but he must have realised over the years that you didn't, or you'd have used it to get him to allow you to dance."

Ged's brow furrowed, his neck and cheeks flushed. His hands were balled so tightly into fists that his knuckles were white. How dare James Cookson stop Marge from doing Latin on account of it being risqué and attention-seeking when he used to slap on too much makeup and a dress and entertain the troops as the lovely "Jemima" …

"He must have been one ugly drag queen!" he growled, rather louder than he intended.

"Definitely," agreed Aunt Sophie. "He was no oil painting as a fella; what on earth he would have looked like as a *'lady'*," goodness knows."

"How dare he stop us dancing. I resented him then, but I *detest* him now."

"Try not to be too hard on him, dear. Back then, people wanted to hide this sort of thing and would often create a persona that was the opposite of who they really were, as it puts people off the scent. I mean, who would ever have believed a rumour that the respectable magistrate Councillor James Cookson, of all people, was a cross-dresser, let alone a drag queen? No one would have believed it of such a straight-laced, stuffy old goat."

"Hmm, I guess not," said Ged, reluctantly.

"Anyway, dear boy, he was protecting his family. As richly deserved as the embarrassment might have been for him, how do you think Marge would have felt if it were her own sweet Ged who outed him? Can you imagine the upset to his wife and to Annie?"

"I wonder if Annie knows?" Mused Ged.

"It wouldn't surprise me if she does. Wasn't she brought up by her grandmama?"

"Yes. I think her mother's post-natal depression lasted years. Annie told me she spent most of her time at her grandmama's house, and Marge was jealous."

"Well, if her grandmama knew, she might have told her, I suppose. I wouldn't bring it up, though."

"Perhaps not. Annie didn't have a very good relationship with her parents… and she's so unflappable, I'm not sure she'd mind one bit if her Dad was a drag artiste."

"Anyway, Ged, back to important matters," said Sophie. "What are you going to do about the agent?"

"Now, don't you start… Sarah and Brian have been trying to get me to do this illustrating thing, but I'm not doing it. I've got a well-paid, steady job at the factory."

"As you wish, but you're not getting any younger. You're only three or so years away from retirement, aren't you?"

"What of it?"

"Well, you'll have something to do in retirement, I suppose. And it could be a nice little earner, but if you don't want to do it, that's fine."

Ged was silent for a while. Everyone else seemed to think he should do this, so why did he feel so against it?

"Marge hated my drawings," he said.

"Marge was dismissive of many things, dear. Especially things she couldn't do herself."

"Sorry?"

"Well, there were a lot of things she was good at. She was a very knowledgeable gardener and plantswoman; she knew the Latin names of every single bush in your garden… and mine, for that matter. She was a good cook and a great host, and she could sing like an angel, but if there was one thing I think she couldn't abide, it was something she wished she could do but for one reason or another found difficult."

34

Early December 1998

The two weeks after the funeral were more draining on Ged's dwindling emotional resources. Sarah, Karen, and Ed couldn't do all the administration— it had to be Ged, as he was a joint account holder in each one. Seemingly endless rafts of phone calls with the bank, Building Society, several insurance companies, utilities, and telephone companies. Every conversation involved a request for the death certificate. In one discussion, a home insurance company asked to speak to the main account holder, even though he had just told them she had died!

In a vain attempt to cheer himself up, he decided to go into town. It would soon be Christmas, and he spent a day in the two department stores in town, looking for gifts for his children, grandchildren, Pete and his neighbours. He managed to find a suitable gift of matching thermos cups for Pete and his wife, who were keen hikers, but nothing else inspired him. His heart wasn't really in it.

That evening, for no reason in particular, he wandered around their immaculate home. Every room was arranged by Marge, planned to perfection, her style, her colours. In every room, he saw her, and he ached not to.

As he sat once more in front of the TV, the Christmas aftershave commercials, the news, a Murder Mystery Drama he had seen many times before, all simply washed over him. He spotted his unicorn backpack leaning against the wall, and it gave him an idea. He had another week of bereavement leave left, and then it would be the Christmas factory shut down. He really didn't feel like celebrating Christmas. He called Ed.

"Hi, Son; how are Karen and little Laura?"

"Both fast asleep. More importantly, how are you?"

"I have to be honest, Ed. I'm not great. I need to get away. I've had an idea. I'm going to go down to Porthcovery."

"But it's Christmas soon, Dad. I was thinking of giving you a hand getting presents sorted. I know you and Mum did that together, and I thought maybe you'd like some help."

"I went shopping the other day, and nothing really caught my eye. I'll get them in Cornwall. I'm just letting you all know."

"I guess a change of scene might do you good. Look. Will you take your mobile phone with you and keep it charged in case we want to get in touch?"

"OK. I'm going to call Brian and Annie to let them know."

"Alright, Dad. What about Aunt Sophie?"

"Yes. Good idea. I'll tell her, too."

Everyone thought getting away to Porthcovery was a great idea. A change of scene and less phone calls from banks and others would help. Sarah, Ed and Karen offered to take care of any further administration, and Ed would drop by the house midweek to pick up the post and check the answering machine.

Ged took Pete and Emma's Christmas gift to his home the evening before he left for Cornwall. When Ged called to arrange it, Pete insisted Ged should stay for dinner.

"Actually, I'd like that. We haven't had much chance to talk since... well, you know."

When the time came for him to go to Pete's house, he really didn't feel up to it, but he stopped himself from calling Pete and cancelling the arrangement. Pete had been good to him, and he wanted to thank him.

"Come in, Ged. Emma has been badgering me to invite you to dinner for months," said Pete. "I hope you've brought an appetite; she's made a lamb curry, which we never would have managed between the two of us."

Ged enjoyed a lovely meal with Pete and Emma. It was so nice to talk shop and have something different to think about instead of Christmas presents and executor business. Emma was a great cook.

As she dished up their meal, Pete got a bottle of beer for Ged, and they chatted a while about work and how well John Murray was getting to grips with the big presses. They talked about their kids and grandkids and what they might do when they retired.

"What do we do it for, eh, Ged?" said Pete, taking a slug of beer. "I mean, why do we keep chasing the money when all we really need is food on the table and a roof over our heads? You can't buy your health with it, and you can't take it with you when you go."

"Yeah, life can be a bit of a sausage machine sometimes," Ged mused.

Emma could get anyone laughing. She had a way of looking at life that could bring humour to even the saddest of situations. She even saw the funny side of the situation with the insurance call centre worker asking to speak to the deceased customer.

"Maybe you could have a seance?" she suggested with a twinkle in her eye, then she ruffled her hair to make it look messy, grasped Ged and Pete's hands and tipped her head back, closing her eyes. Putting on an affected dreamy voice, she said, "Is there anybody *there*? It's Miranda, the medium from the hapless insurance company. I need to speak to the account holder... Is there anybody *there*? Beyond the *veil*. Give us a *sign*", she cooed. Ged and Pete sniggered.

Ged thoroughly enjoyed his evening, which was a big deal. He hadn't really enjoyed himself since the pub quiz in the Cotswolds. He thanked Emma for the meal and gave her a hug and kiss goodbye. As he shook Pete's hand warmly, he said, "We should do this more often, shouldn't we?"

"Definitely, mate, you should come over more often."

"My place next time," called Ged as he waved goodbye.

***

Ged decided to take his time on the journey to Cornwall, stopping more frequently than he would have done with Marge; he went for a burger lunch in the Midlands, which Marge would never have allowed and had a relaxed early evening meal at a pub in a Devon village. That way, he reasoned, he wouldn't have to make a meal when he got to Porthcovery. He could just put his feet up and relax with a scotch.

As he wound his way along the dark Cornish lanes that evening, he noticed many houses decorated with Christmas lights. He had never been there in winter, so he had no idea how seriously Cornish folk take Christmas lights. The sight that met his eyes as he turned the corner at the north end of Porthcovery was truly wondrous! A huge frame of bulbs depicting a gold crown with '1998' emblazoned below it was tied to the fence. As he turned onto the beach road, there was a long garland of multi-coloured lights fixed to regular wooden posts all along the sea wall, stretching from one end of the village to the other. Ged drove along the seafront road, high above the beach, and turned up the driveway of the white house, which looked rather drab compared to many of the other houses, which had Christmas lights around every doorway, window and many had decorations in the garden at the front of the houses. He couldn't wait to check out this amazing festival of lights.

He got out of the car and zipped up his coat against the biting December chill. He had no gloves handy, so he rammed his hands in his pockets and walked down to the sea wall. Leaning against the wall, he looked along the bay. The tide was in, and the lights reflected in the ripples on the calm sea, doubling the splendour. He counted at least ten other frames of lights dotted around the harbour, houses and other buildings in the village.

He dearly wanted to share this with Alice and Jamie. Would Brian and Sarah come to Cornwall after Christmas or for New Year? He had brought the mobile phone with him but still didn't like using it, so he walked to the phone box, now dwarfed by an enormous twelve-metre Christmas tree garlanded with so many lights; it looked like an explosion in a department store Christmas aisle. Having fed enough coins into the slot to make sure he didn't get cut off, he dialled Brian and Sarah's number and got through to an answering machine. He left a message to say he had arrived, and would they try calling him on the mobile phone later on as he had an idea about Christmas. After leaving the message, he walked back to the house and unloaded his suitcase, backpack and the evil cool bag of doom, which had sat innocently in the passenger footwell all the way down. Once he had emptied its contents into the fridge, he turned on the electric fire in the living room with its not-at-all-realistic flickering flames', pulled the phone charging cable from his suitcase, plugged it in to make sure it had charged and settled himself on the wide window seat with his mug of tea and a large measure of Jura on ice.

The coloured light garlands swayed in the breeze, sending a rainbow of brightly coloured twinkling ripples on the sea. He took the binoculars hung up on the wall nearby and trained them on the old lifeboat station at the other end of the bay. Trying to make out the Christmas light images which had been put up there. One was a sailing boat, and the other was a candle. He now understood why they often had bookings in the New Year and December. He was glad they had no bookings this year.

He was startled by the tuneful tone of his mobile phone. He unplugged the charger, pressed the green button and tentatively held it to his face. It seemed so tiny; he couldn't see how he could listen and speak at the same time. He said, "Hello?" Rather too close to the microphone, then put the other end to his ear.

"Hi, Dad," said Sarah. You don't have to speak so close to the microphone. It will pick up your voice if you hold it to your ear."

"Oh," said Ged, "sorry, did I deafen you?"

"Only a bit," Sarah replied. "You said you had an idea."

"Yes. I've never been here at Christmas. Did you know about the Christmas lights?"

"No, why?"

"The lights here are incredible! They're like Blackpool illuminations but less gaudy. Alice and Jamie would love it!" I imagine Brian will need to cover Christmas Day, but instead of coming to Warwick on Boxing Day, why not spend a week here instead?"

"What, in Cornwall?"

"Why not?"

"I can't actually think of a reason why not, Dad. I don't know why we've never thought of it before. I'll be spending Christmas Eve and Christmas Day with Mum and Dad as usual, but we could come to Cornwall afterwards. What about Ed?"

"It might be a squeeze, but I'm sure we could work it out. I could sleep on the sofa, and he and Karen could sleep in our bedroom. There's a travel cot here.'

"I'll speak to Brian and Ed," said Sarah. "Then I'll call you tomorrow."

"Okay."

"And Dad, for what it's worth, I think it's a great idea."

"Thanks, Sarah. Speak soon. I need a lesson on using this mobile phone as well."

**

Ged started his Porthcovery Christmas shopping at the souvenir shop near the harbour. He found a pair of earrings and long pashmina scarves for Annie, Sarah and Karen and an extra pashmina for Aunt Sophie. There were thick woollen jumpers and t-shirts for Brian and Ed and a purple hooded cardigan with a unicorn on it for Alice. For Jamie, he found a red hooded sweater, a trio of card games, a Where's Wally book and a puzzle book. This shop had been a revelation. He had only ever bought postcards and sunglasses there before. He recognised the shopkeeper as one of the men who fished from the little harbour.

"Have I seen you down in the harbour, hauling in a catch or two? You must be kept pretty busy running this place as well as fishing."

"You need more than one way to make a livin' 'ere," said the man, smiling. "My wife runs the shop. She's the one you'd normally see 'ere or our daughter Meg, but they're up-country seein' relatives, and I don't fish much this time 'o year, so I'm 'ere this week."

"Oh, I see," said Ged. "You know I've been coming here for years and never realised what a great shop this is. It's like Aladdin's cave! I've bought nearly all my Christmas presents."

"You're from Chy Gwyn, aren't you? I seen you 'ere afore. Don't you 'elp out at the pub with joinery and that?"

"Yes. I've done a bit of joinery and electrical stuff for a few people in the village over the years. I'm a maintenance engineer. I usually come in October, but my wife…" Ged caught his breath for a

307

moment, closed his eyes briefly and swallowed. "My wife was very ill, so I couldn't come this year."

"She better now, then?"

Ged took a steadying breath. "Erm, I'm afraid not. She passed away a few weeks ago."

"Oh, my!" said the man, clearly shocked. "I'm sorry to 'ere that. She were a real lady, your wife. Came in 'ere a lot. I mean, I don't know 'er by name, but I never forget a face. She sure keeps that garden smart, don't she?"

"Thanks, yes, she was a very keen gardener."

"Well, for what it's worth, I'm really sorry for your loss."

"Thanks," said Ged quietly. "See you around."

"Yeah, take care, mate; I'm Andy, by the way," he said as Ged opened the door to leave the shop. "Maybe see you in the Pub later?"

Ged found a painting-by-numbers kit and watercolour pencils at the gallery shop for Alice and a smart week-to-a-page leather-bound diary for Aunt Sophie. He bought gift bags and wrapping paper there, too. Tracy greeted him with clear delight.

"What a nice surprise to see you here, Chippy," she said. "We missed you in autumn."

"Nice to see you too, Tracy."

"You stayin' for Christmas?"

"Not sure yet – I'd like to … if I can persuade the family."

"Lovely. Maybe you'll be swimmin' in the harbour, Christmas Day, then?"

"Christmas Day? It'll be freezing!"

"Christmas tradition, Chipp. It's an annual event; Look." She went to the rack of postcards near the door and pulled out a postcard showing a black and white photograph of the little fishing harbour with around forty people in it. They weren't exactly swimming, but all were shoulder or waist-deep in the water, some wearing fancy dress outfits and all smiling and waving. 'Christmas Day Swim, Porthcovery, 1979'.

Ged was astonished. "Wow! They're a hardy bunch."

"Whaddya mean 'they'? Look, there's my Mum and little me by the ladder."

"Goodness! I didn't realise. Looks like a laugh."

"Oh, it is. Anyone can join in. It's usually a real good crowd."

"Well, I'll have to get some trunks from the harbour shop, I suppose."

He bought provisions from the little grocery store and made his way back to the house to wrap the presents. He passed the Seagull Café on the way home. It looked closed, but he noticed a sign in the window showing winter opening times. It seemed to be open from eleven until two every day except Monday and evenings from six until ten pm, Thursday to Sunday. He made a mental note to pop in there the following day for lunch.

Once the Christmas presents were wrapped and bagged up, it was almost dinner time. He was hungry and decided a pub meal was the best option. He pulled on his warmest winter coat and walking boots and headed out.

Glyn was pleased and surprised to see Ged standing at the bar.

"Evenin' Chippy, good to see yer," he said, "I missed yer in October; I was wonderin' where you'd got to. What can I get yer?"

"A pint of Guinness and your best lasagne and salad if you have any, Glyn," Ged replied as he hung his coat on the coat hooks next to the door.

"You're in luck. I made one today. What brings you 'ere this late in the year then?"

"Not the best of reasons, I'm afraid, Glyn. Marge passed away a few weeks ago, and I've come here to try and get my head together."

"Oh, Ged. That's a shock! I'm so sorry, mate. I didn't even know she were ill."

"No, neither did we 'til August. She had brain tumours, and it was an aggressive sort of cancer. She didn't even have chemotherapy. Not that it would have made much difference."

"It's a bugger, that cancer. My wife's brother had chemo last year for bowel cancer. Really nasty treatment."

"Is he okay?"

"Well, so far so good. They're monitorin' him, but it's always a worry. Sounds like it was more aggressive for Mrs B."

"Yes. We had no idea there was anything wrong until she suddenly went blind, and they discovered it was affecting her vision."

"Oh, poor woman," said Glyn with feeling, "and poor you, too. You've had a rough few months then, I take it?"

"Yeah. It's about the toughest thing I've ever had to deal with. I needed to come here just to get away and try to work out what happens next."

"Well, you know where we are if you want a bit of company, and I've plenty of work for you to help keep your mind off things if that's any use? My lad is workin' as a labourer for a maintenance company in Falmouth now, but these joinery and electrical jobs are a bit above his skills just yet."

"That's a great idea, Glyn. Make a list of what needs doing: electrical, joinery, plumbing, anything. And I'll see what I can do. I'm going to be staying here 'til the end of the first week in January."

"I'll pay you, mind."

"No need for that. You know I'm happy to help out."

"Find a seat in the bar. There's your pint. I'll get the order to the kitchen."

Ged took his pint to a table in the corner of the bar where Glyn's old Alsatian dog, Monty, was snoozing by the open fire. As Ged sat down, he came over. Ged ruffled Monty's ears and took a long gulp of his pint. He relaxed back into the cushions and looked around at the familiar pictures displayed on the walls: A frame demonstrating sailing knots, a huge old black and white photograph of a ship that was wrecked nearby, and a photo of the old lifeboat being launched. And a new picture: a hand-drawn sketch of a fisherman hauling in his catch… Ged's illustration of the dreadlock-haired fisherman. He blinked and shook his head. How had one of his sketches ended up in the pub? Ged looked for Glyn or his wife Helen, but they were both serving customers at the bar.

Helen brought Ged's lasagne to him.

"Hi, Chippy, here's your lasagne. I brought your cutlery; Glyn always forgets."

"Hi, Helen. Thanks. And before you go, can I ask something?"

"Sure."

"Where did you get that sketch?"

"Auntie Emily had it in her café, and I kinda liked it." Ged was sure he saw Helen stifle a grin. "The pirate looks like Andy, one of our reg'lars. Never heard of the artist, though. Could be a relative of yours, though, I reckon."

"Oh?"

"There can't be many G Baker's around, can there?" This time, he definitely saw a grin. "I had no idea you could draw, Chippy. Is there no end to your talents? Building bars, fixing toilets, electrical stuff and an artist to boot."

"I didn't know you were related to Emily."

"She's my Dad's sister. We were brought up in Porthleven. I only moved here when Glyn took over the pub. You know, Emily's sold loads of your sketches, Chippy. People love 'em. She's had plenty of prints done of this one and all those ones you did of Val's cat."

Ged found himself shaking his head again. "Blimey," was all he could think of to say.

***

Sarah called that evening on the mobile phone to say that they would come on Boxing Day, and Ed was planning to come before Christmas but would be in touch. Ged breathed a sigh of relief. He hadn't realised just how much he didn't want to have Christmas in Warwick until he knew he didn't have to; a knot in his stomach hinted at the guilt he felt at not wanting to be in their old family home.

***

Sharon greeted Ged with a pained expression of sympathy and a hug when he arrived at the Seagull Café the next morning.

"Sarah rang to tell me about Mrs B. I'm so sorry, Chippy. You must still be in shock."

"Thanks, Sharon," said Ged quietly.

"Can I get you a coffee? And maybe some cake?"

"Yes, please. Do you have any of that lovely carrot cake?"

"I do."

"I'll have a slice of that with a Cappuccino, in that case."

"Fair enough, my lovely, comin' right up."

There were seats outside and a pile of warm blankets, but the wind that day made it too cold for Ged to sit outside. He settled into a corner bench seat inside the café. The table was next to a window, looking over the terrace and out to sea. Sharon and Bill had made it cosy with cushions and blankets. He looked around at the pictures on the walls of the café. As usual, there was a varied range on display, and most were for sale. Bright abstracts and harbour scenes brightened up the room on this overcast day. The Café was decorated for Christmas but not in a gaudy way. There were sprigs of holly and spruce in vases on the tables. An ivy garland with occasional red baubles had been hung from the old beams around the room, and there were fat cream church candles on the three windowsills sitting amongst berried holly.

Ged unzipped his now faded pink unicorn backpack with its purple unicorn and pulled out his sketchbook. He thought the candles and holly arrangements were simple but effective and wanted to capture one of them. Once more, the unhurried, smooth style of drawing came quickly to him, and the image soon took shape on the page. A hint of the coastal scenery outside the window gave an impression of the scenery outside, but the focus was the berried holly sprigs and the candle.

Bill brought Ged's cake and coffee to the table.

"Mornin' Chippy. Good to see yeh, mate. 'Ere's your coffee an' cake," he said. "Eh, I'm sorry to 'ear 'bout the missus. I s'pose it must 'a been a shock."

"Thanks," said Ged, drawing the coffee saucer towards him. "A long, drawn-out shock, Bill, but yes. It was a total shock."

"Sharon told me Mrs B went blind."

"She did. One of the tumours was on the optic nerve. They operated, and she got some sight back, but she had other tumours too; it was aggressive and spread quickly."

"So, did she 'ave chemo then?" he asked.

"No, she decided against it. It wouldn't have helped much, and it was vanity that stopped her from having it."

"How come?"

"Didn't want her hair falling out."

"An she'd-a been throwin' up for a fortnight. If it weren't going to do much good, then not much point, I s'pose."

"Exactly. I think she made the right decision."

Bill twisted his tea towel. Ged knew this was a sign that there was something he wanted to say but didn't know how to put it or that he was thinking hard.

"Business okay, Bill?" he ventured.

"Er, yeah, not bad, mate."

"What's on your mind?"

"Well, Sharon thought I oughtn't to say anythin'."

"Bill, we've known each other too long; there's not much you can't say to me."

"Well, I was wonderin' 'ow long you're gonna be down 'ere. – cos there's summat I need your 'elp with if it's not too much trouble."

"Go on. I need a distraction."

"We need a new menu cabinet for outside. I'm not great with 'ammer and saw, and I were wonderin', well, 'opin' really, if you can make it. I'd pay you, like. Sharon was 'opin' you could do it in October, and when you din' come down, I gave it a go," explained Bill sheepishly.

"I'd love to do it," said Ged, smiling. "I've finished buying and wrapping the presents, and I'm at a loose end. It will help keep my mind off things. I'm going to do some work for Glyn at the pub, too. He's making a list. I'll have my coffee, and you can show me.

***

Ged went back to the white house for his toolbox, changed into jeans, his warm, red tartan work shirt, and jersey and went back to the café. He spent the rest of the morning rummaging in Bill and Sharon's store for suitable bits of timber, and together with Sharon and Bill, over a lunch of crab sandwiches, he drew up a plan. That afternoon, he made a trip to the builder's merchant in Helston and set to work.

That afternoon and the following day, with some help from Bill, the cabinet was complete. It had brass hinges, framed doors with glass panes and a brass latch to open them. There was space for two A4 menu sheets on the back and a little space underneath for promotions. He placed a menu folder from the café inside the box and had fixed swivelling brass catches to prevent it from moving about. The top of the box had an apex roof to allow rain to run off. Bill painted it sage green to match his window frames whilst Ged prepared the place it was to be displayed on the wall, which was uneven, so Ged created spacers to hold the box away from the wall. This offered the added advantage that it wouldn't stay wet at the back after rainy days and rot the wood.

Sharon was delighted and invited Ged to stay for dinner as a thank you. Ged wouldn't let them pay him. They ate a lamb bolognese in the café, lit by candlelight and shared a bottle of red wine that Bill had tried to give Ged in payment. They chatted amiably about food and what things the couple wanted to do with the café. As Ged took off his boots late that evening, it struck him what a good couple of days it had been. He really enjoyed being creative again, both in drawing and cabinet-making.

***

Ged worked four short days for Glyn at the pub. He replaced some of the wiring for the chillers in the cellar and repaired the three-phase wiring rig to the storehouses outside, which had been snagged by a careless lorry driver and inexpertly repaired. The toilets inside the pub needed new flushes, and he installed new taps in the kitchen. A few windows needed draught excluders to make the dining room area more cosy. There was a long list of jobs, and Ged couldn't have possibly done them all, but he spent a very happy four days working with Glyn and his son Benjamin, who was a trainee electrician. He knew what he was doing but had little confidence. Ged took him under his wing and was impressed with his work.

"You know, Ben," he said when they had finished the wiring to the store sheds, "You're better than you think. The apprentices at the factory couldn't hold a candle to your work ethic. And you're tidy too, which, trust me, is a big deal."

"Er, thanks", muttered Ben shyly.

"Seriously, you seem to really know what you're doing when it comes to electrical work. You'll make a good sparky."

The days flew by, and soon, Ged realised he would have to start thinking about getting the house ready for Christmas. He hadn't thought about what to feed everyone, and it was the 22nd of December already. Ed was due to come down that afternoon with Karen and baby Laura, and thankfully, when Ed called the evening before, he offered to do the food shopping on their way down.

Ged got a small Christmas tree through a contact of Glyn's. The gallery shop had a few sets of baubles. Glyn gave him three strings of broken multi-coloured Christmas lights, which Ged fixed easily the following evening. He spent the morning of Ed's arrival setting up the tree and pinning a string of lights around the bay window. He stood back to admire his handiwork. Next year, he thought, he would really go to town and join in with the Christmas light festival. He had so many ideas about what to do. He would decorate the eaves with a garland of holly and ivy with white bulbs through it. He would put twisted strings of white fairy lights in the bushes at the front of the garden. He would create a picture of lights to place at the top of the driveway... A present? Reindeer? He would decide later. He realised he was already planning next Christmas before this one was over.

35

Ed and Karen arrived late in the afternoon; the car was loaded with groceries, wine and Christmas gifts. There was barely enough room for Laura's little car seat. At the pub later on, Laura cooed and gurgled charmingly in her pram. A constant flow of admirers drifted in and out of the bar, stopping to admire or comment on how good she was being.

It was a different story back at the house as Karen tried to feed her and put her down to sleep. She cried every time Karen tried to put her in the cot and go back downstairs.

"She's in an unfamiliar place; she won't settle," complained Karen, yawning widely.

"Does she sleep ok in the pram?" asked Ged.

"Yeah, usually."

Ed was immediately tuned into Ged's wavelength; "We could try putting the cot from the pram inside the travel cot. I'll stay with her 'til she falls asleep. Talk to her, bore her to sleep," suggested Ed.

"Okay, anything to stop her screaming," said Karen, yawning again. "She was such a fraud in the pub; everyone thought she was an angel. She's a nightmare to get off to sleep.

"Some kids just are," said Ged. "Jamie needed Sarah or Brian to stay in the room, or he wouldn't settle."

"How long for?" asked Karen.

"Well, some nights it was ten minutes, but thirty minutes wasn't unusual."

"No, I mean, how old was he before he could settle on his own?"

"Oh," said Ged ", I think he was okay by the time he was about eighteen months."

"Eighteen months!" exclaimed Karen disbelievingly, her eyes widening. "But that's... I mean, that's a year and a half!"

"Well, if that's what it takes for peace, it's better than doing shuttle runs up and down the stairs all evening," said Ged. "If you're worn out, maybe Ed could do the evening shift."

"I guess so," said Karen uncertainly. "She's still sleeping in our room, as she has a small night feed, but she makes such a lot of noise that I'm not getting any sleep."

"Ahh, the zombie-land of early parenthood, it stinks," said Ged, hugging her.

Ed unclipped the pram cot from the frame. He took that in one hand and his beer in the other. "I'll take my beer upstairs and try singing her to sleep in the pram cot," he said, kissing Karen on her forehead.

There were five more minutes of squealing and grizzling from Laura, followed by Ed's tuneful voice, singing *some* kind of lullaby, though the words weren't familiar to Ged.

"Never opened myself this way. Life is ours; we live it our way ay ay ay," cooed Ed over the baby monitor. *"All these words, I don't just sayeee – And nothin' else matters…"*

"What's he singing?" he asked Karen.

"*Nothing else matters*, by Metallica," said Karen. He doesn't know any bedtime songs, so he just sings rock songs instead."

"Classic! I love it," said Ged, chuckling."

"Funny, isn't it," said Karen, "One of Metallica's best-known songs is a ballad about feelings. Those guys might seem hard rock, but they're all mush."

Laura, Karen and Ged were treated to a montage of *Every Little Thing She Does'* by The Police, Pink Floyd's *Wish You Were Here'* and U2's *Where the Streets Have No Name'*, finishing with James Taylor's *Classic 'Golden Moments'*. This last song brought tears to Ged's eyes. He didn't try to stop them; James Taylor was Marge's favourite singer and one of his too. They had been to three of his concerts and danced to Golden Moments at both. Ged had often sung this song to the twins and his grandchildren at bedtime.

***

317

Christmas morning was bright and sunny. Ged prepared a delicious breakfast of scrambled eggs and smoked salmon. Ed opened a bottle of Champagne to go with it. They exchanged presents as they sat around the tree. Karen was delighted. Her family had never been very imaginative with Christmas gifts and usually swapped celebrity biographies or vouchers with a chocolate bar as it was easy to wrap.

They dressed in warm clothes and went for a walk along the coast. Karen had brought a kiddie carrier backpack, which they assembled and then installed Laura. She wasn't as impressed as Ed and threw up her breakfast on the back of his neck, which, thankfully, was protected by a scarf. The weather was bright but cold, and the walk to the headland was bracing. As they returned to the village, they saw a large crowd gathered at the harbour.

"I almost forgot; it's the Christmas Day swim in the harbour!"

"What?" cried Ed, "they must be mad. It's freezing in there!"

"It's an annual event, apparently. They've been doing it for years. They get people to sponsor them and go for a swim on Christmas Day. It's for Cancer research."

"Well then. We'd better go and get our swimming stuff on, hadn't we?" said Karen.

"Who's going to look after the baby?" Ed called after her as she broke into a run.

"Trying to get out of it, eh?" mocked Karen over her shoulder. "Last one in is a wet blanket! Come on, Ged, are you with me?" she called as she ran to the house,

Ged rolled his eyes. "Go on then. I must be mad, but yes, I'll do it."

All three went into the harbour, along with about thirty locals. Sharon and Bill were there too. Sharon looked after Laura in her pram, and they cheered as Karen, followed by Ed and his father, ran into the freezing water. Ed and Karen wore T-shirts and shorts as they had no swimming things. Ged had bought trunks as promised but also wore his red tartan work shirt. He had never felt cold quite like it; the camaraderie of the other swimmers gave him courage, and he was warmed by the jovial atmosphere. People were teasing each other, laughing and shouting. Many swimmers wore fancy dress, which was soon reduced to soggy rags after being in the harbour.

Their large fluffy towels weren't enough. Bill had brought blankets from the café to wrap around their shoulders. Ged was grateful for the blankets and felt invigorated. Cold, shivering and laughing with relief, the three slopped off up the hill from the harbour in bare feet, wrapped in towels and blankets. Bill and Sharon followed with Laura in her pram, who had slept through the entire thing.

***

Karen and Ed made an unusual Christmas dinner. Ed served an avocado and prawn starter, and Karen cooked duck breasts with a delicious Madeira and cream sauce, along with parsley potatoes, Kale, and a few sprouts, as a nod to the season. After a long pause to digest, they all had some Champagne-fuelled fun in the kitchen, flambé-ing Crepes with orange and too much brandy. Ged had vanilla ice cream in the freezer, which complemented it perfectly.

Full, happy, and leaving the washing up entirely un-done, which, Ged mused would have incensed Marge, they wrapped up in warm coats, hats and scarves and left the house for another walk down to the southern end of the village, following a familiar circular route, taking them up to the headland along the coast path and back down to the village via a steep road from the school.

Back at the house with a happily snoozing Laura, they sat in comfortable companionship, watching an old black and white comedy film on TV. They missed the Queen's speech, which had previously been a hard point in the Baker family Christmases, but Ged preferred to watch highlights on the news. Throughout the day, they took turns changing nappies and keeping Laura entertained. Ged had bought some crab claws from one of the local fishermen, and they chatted over a light supper that evening after Ed had sung more rock songs to Laura.

"Dad…" ventured Ed over supper, "Have you ever considered moving down here? I mean – permanently?"

Ged paused. "I've had pipedreams about it over the years, but Mum would never have gone for it. There aren't enough jobs down here to make a decent living. Not like the factory."

Ed pursed his lips sideways. "Well, you don't have to ask Mum now, do you?" he said, his face tense and perhaps ...was that a little defiant? Karen kicked him under the table and glared at him. Ged spotted it.

"It's okay, Karen, I don't mind Ed talking straight. In fact, I prefer it to the way a lot of people go round the houses without getting to the point. Actually, Ed, if this experience has taught me anything, it's that life is short, and money doesn't buy you good health."

"So, you'd consider it?" Ed pressed. "You could earn money doing jobs for the locals. They know you're good, and you've helped them enough times for free."

"Good point, but I don't want to make any decisions after the best part of a bottle of wine. I promise I'll give it some thought. The one thing that puts me off is not seeing all of you as often. Cornwall is a long drive from London and Warwickshire."

Ed glanced at Karen. Something was being communicated between them that Ged couldn't even guess at.

"Actually, you might not see us much less if you lived here," said Karen.

"How's that possible?"

"Last month, Ed applied for a job with a power generation company based in Bristol. They are installing wind turbines and are getting into other renewable energy. They're looking for a supervisor-level fitter to be based in the South West, and as my Dad lives in Exeter, we were thinking of renting out our house in Warwick and moving in with him while we decide if it's a permanent thing. I hate my job at the council, and I don't want to go back after my maternity leave, so it all seemed to fit."

As she spoke, Ed held her hand, fingers interlaced. He looked imploringly at Ged as if he needed his blessing.

"That sounds like a great opportunity, Ed," he said. "Getting into renewables could be a smart move. Even if I don't move down here, you should go for it."

"See," said Karen, giving Ed an *'I told you so'* look. "I told you he'd be okay."

"Listen, both of you," said Ged. "You don't need a green light from me. It's your life. You live it how you choose. If you want to go for a job on the moon, go for it. I mean, of course, I'd miss you, but I wouldn't ever want you to hold back on my account. He paused and raised his empty wine glass. "It sounds like we've got something to celebrate. There's no more bubbly. How about we toast your success with a cup of tea and one of Peggy's mince pies? They're as good as her pasties!"

***

Just as Ged had predicted, Alice and Jamie were awestruck by the Christmas lights. The rest of the Baker family arrived late in the afternoon on Boxing Day. It was getting dark, and the lights were already on all over the village. The children had slept some of the way in the car, but Sarah had roused them a few miles before Porthcovery. The children leapt from the car with cries of "Oh look, that one's a Christmas Pudding!" and... "Did you see the reindeer one? Pleeeease – Can we go and see them all now, Mum?" shouted Alice.

Ged heard the shouts and pulled on his boots and jacket. He thought it would be best if he took the children for a walk along the front to see all the lights, or they would never settle. He gave Sarah a hug and kiss and winked at Brian. Ed had followed him out of the house in boots, hat and scarf.

"Shall we take these two for a walk along the prom while you unload?" suggested Ged.

"Grandad, Grandad! Have you seen all the fairy lights?" Shrieked Alice, grinning with unbridled ecstasy.

"I certainly have, Alice," said Ged, attempting to give her a hug and kiss and receiving a painful head-butt on the nose for his trouble. "Would you like to come with me and see them all?" he said, wincing and holding a hand over his nose."

"Can we go now, Grandad?" said Jamie enthusiastically before giving his Grandfather a tight hug. "Oh, look, it's Uncle Eddie," he cried and ran to hug his uncle. Ed picked up his nephew, then feigned an enormous weight and buckled at the knees, groaning in mock agony.

"Oh, no! You've grown too big; I can't lift you up any more," he wailed.

"Silly Uncle Eddie," laughed Jamie, "of course you can. If Daddy can pick me up, it's easy for you."

"Ha!" Called Brian, "that scrawny little weed? No chance! Couldn't lift a pot of tea if he tried," joked Brian over his shoulder as he lifted suitcases out of the car.

Sarah was transfixed. She simply stood with a rucksack in her hand, entirely speechless.

"They're ... so beautiful," she breathed. Her eyes pricked with tears. She was quite moved by the sight. Ged put his arm around her shoulders.

"Pretty special, isn't it?" he said.

"I...I think it's the most magical thing I've ever seen," she said, with tears welling. "The lights reflecting in the water... I feel like a little kid who's come down on Christmas morning and seen a Christmas tree for the first time."

"I know what you mean," said Ged. "I felt a bit like that when I rounded the corner coming into the village."

Ged took Alice by the hand and walked up the road, closely followed by Ed and Jamie. As they went back and forth, unloading the car, Brian and Sarah could hear the children's cries as they spotted more and more Christmas light displays, the loudest of all being Alice's exclamation of "Oh, a Mermaid! Look, Uncle Eddie, it's a mermaid and her tail is swishing."

When the tour of the lights finally came to an end, the family sat around the Christmas tree in the living room to exchange gifts. Jamie and Alice were delighted with theirs and proudly presented a box of hand-made peppermint creams to Ged and another to Karen for her and Ed.

"We didn't know what to get for Laura as she's just a baby, and babies can't have peppermint creams," said Alice in her usual no-nonsense way.

"You're right, Alice," said Karen. "She is a bit young for sweets."

"My mum made her this," said Sarah, handing a large tartan gift bag to Karen.

Karen opened the bag and pulled out a patchwork quilt of purple, blue, and green patterned fabrics.

"Wow!" said Karen. "That's incredible!" It must have taken her months!"

"As soon as she heard you had a baby, she got to work on it," said Sarah. "She makes loads of these for a charity and made one for Alice and Jamie when they were first born. It will fit a single bed. And trust me, they last for years."

"It's absolutely beautiful, Sarah; I'll write and thank her. She's so kind."

***

The family enjoyed their traditional Boxing Day meal of Boeuf Bourguignon that Ged had prepared that morning. During the meal, they raised a glass to Marge. Everyone was silent for a few moments, each with their own thoughts of how different things were going to be.

When everyone was finally mopping up gravy with hunks of fresh bread, Ed tapped his glass with his fork and pushed his chair away from the table. He stood up, clearing his throat.

"Erm, everybody, I have something I've been waiting to tell you all. We've kept it a secret until now, but as we are all together, it seems like the right time."

Ged sat back in his chair, smiling. He knew about the move to Exeter already, but of course, Sarah, Brian and the children didn't know yet.

"Despite what I've said in the past," continued Ed, glancing at Karen for a moment, who smiled broadly and nodded. "On Christmas Day, Karen asked me to marry her, and I'm pleased to announce that I said 'Yes'."

Ged sat open-mouthed for a moment, completely speechless. Sarah squealed, leapt from her seat, and gave Karen a tight hug. Both women were grinning from ear to ear. Brian stood up and went over to his brother, holding out his hand to shake. Then, he changed his mind and pulled his twin into a bear hug, slapping him enthusiastically on the back.

"So, she knows when she's on to a winner – eh Karen?" said Brian, breaking his embrace with his brother and going to give her a hug and kiss.

"She sure does," said Karen, glancing at Ed, grinning and blushing slightly.

"So, does that mean Auntie Karen will be Karen Baker, like the news lady?" said Jamie.

"Actually, Jamie," said Karen in surprise, "I hadn't thought of that, but yes. I might get a few free lunches if I book reservations with that name."

"Grandad. Can we go to go to the Lobster Pot for dinner this week?" Jamie said, totally changing the subject. "I haven't had scampi in forever."

"I don't see why not, as long as it's open. Why don't we go to the pay phone in the morning and give her a ring?"

"Er, because you've got a mobile phone, you twit," said Ed, rolling his eyes.

"Well, if you expect me to use that thing, someone is going to have to give me a lesson in how to use it. All I can do is answer it," replied Ged without any hint of embarrassment.

"Good grief, you're a senior maintenance engineer, and you can't even press a few buttons on a cell phone?" Ed shot back.

"Nope."

"Come on then. Where is it?"

"In my coat pocket."

Ed gave his father a lesson on how to make a call with a number and then explained how to put a contact in the memory of the phone and search for it. Ged fished out a piece of card from his jacket pocket and wrote down a few notes to remind him of what to do.

"Right, now… sending text messages…," said Ed.

"Er… let's leave lesson two 'til later. I'll not remember all of it otherwise. Let me practise putting in a few numbers."

Ged sat on the sofa with the phone and his small address book for half an hour, pressing buttons and grumbling occasionally when he made a mistake. He called Brian's phone twice, once as a test, the other by accident, but he soon got the hang of it.

***

Ged used the phone to make a reservation for dinner at the Lobster Pot the following day and spent a while watching the waves crash over the stone walls of the harbour in Porthleven before going in for their meal. It was a dramatic place when the tide was in and the wind got up.

Emily greeted the family in her typical effusive style.

"How lovely to see you all! Happy Christmas. So glad you could all come for dinner. I've been looking forward to seeing you all. Especially you, Mr Baker. Your drawings have been leaping off my walls all season, and they're still doing well."

"It's great to see you, Emily," said Ged, warmly clasping her hand. "Happy Christmas."

Emily took a drinks order and went to the counter. Ged looked around the café walls, and even though he knew Emily had been displaying and selling his sketches, it still gave him a start when he saw some of them in white picture frames and grey or cream mountings with 'G Baker' in neat and stylish pencil and little pieces of paper slid between the glass and the frame giving a price and carrying a title such as *'Potts in the sunshine'*.

Every wall in the café had a variety of paintings, pastels, ink drawings or sketches, and each wall had at least two of his sketches displayed somewhere upon it. He knew some of them must be prints, but he couldn't tell which ones. Seeing them on the walls made him feel like a fraud again. These were just doodles, as Marge had pointed out that summer. It seemed somehow wrong to be charging money for them.

"Look, Grandad," said Jamie, walking over to him and tugging at his sleeve, "it's Pirate Pete and here's one of the Rock-pool boys."

He led Ged over to one of the tables in the window where, just as Jamie had described, the two framed sketches were displayed, one above the other. Both had a ticket price of £25.

Ged made his way back to the table after browsing the rest of the art on the walls. He had to admit that his sketches did stand up to scrutiny when seen next to some of the other pictures. Perhaps he wasn't such a bad artist after all.

Emily had set the last of the drinks on the table when Ged returned.

"I'm so sorry to hear about Mrs Baker's passin'," she said, glancing round at the table. "Such a shock for you all. It must have been a difficult few months," she said, making eye contact with Ged and resting a hand gently on his shoulder. "It's strange to see you all here without her. Please accept my and Ron's sincere condolences."

"Thanks, Emily," said Ged as he took a long drink of his lemonade. The ice melting in the drink cooled his throat and helped to calm the lump that was forming there.

The subject was swiftly changed to Ged's sketches. Alice and Jamie took particular delight in giving Karen and Ed a tour of the gallery on the café walls, pointing out their favourites and where each of the sketches was probably drawn. They both loved them. Karen was especially taken with those of the tabby cat, Potts.

"He's got such character," she said. "What's incredible, Ged, is that you can really tell it's the same cat in each picture. That nick on his left ear, his eyebrow whiskers... and those eyes; they're so distinctive. How on earth do you do it?"

"I've absolutely no idea, Karen, to be honest. I just drew what I saw," replied Ged.

The family had a very enjoyable, simple seaside meal, chatting about the pictures and debating whether or not Ged should move there permanently. It transpired that Brian already knew about Ed's job in Exeter, and Sarah had been helping Karen and Ed to plan the renting out of Ed's small house in Warwickshire.

When the meal was almost over, Ron hobbled out of the kitchen, wiping his hands on a tea towel. He looked thinner than Ged remembered, and his bright green eyes had dark circles under them, but he smiled broadly as he approached the table.

"Nice to see you, Ron. I don't think we've spoken in a long time," said Ged as he stood and shook Ron's offered hand.

"I just wanted to say thank you for lettin' us sell your sketches. The customers really like 'em," he said to Ged. He pulled an envelope from his apron and handed it to him.

"It's you I should be thanking, Ron," said Ged, shaking him warmly by the hand. "They look so professional in those mountings and frames," he added, sitting down again and gesturing for Ron to do the same in the empty chair opposite.

"Well, they've done really well, he said as he lowered himself down gingerly, leaning on the table with one hand. My Emily waxes lyrical about 'em and I agrees with 'er. They're right, good drawin's. You should do more. We sold some of 'em five times over an' could 'ave sold more if we'd had 'em."

"I just feel like a fraud, charging money for a few doodles."

"These ain't doodles, Mr Baker," he countered with a slight frown. "They're proper art. They all tell a story. You should see some o' the crap people try to get us to sell if you'll excuse me. It's 'ard to tell 'em that they'll never make it, but I don't believe in calling a spade a gardenin' implement. If they're no good, there's no point stringin' 'em along," he explained. "When my Emily tells 'em there's no room on the wall and we don' 'ave a waitin' list, they soon bugger off. An' if they're daft enough to come back, we just tells 'em the style ain't what we're lookin' for. Now, your sketches, as it turns out, is exactly what we're lookin' for, though it'd be nice to 'ave a bit 'o colour on 'em."

"Yes, I was working on that; I'm having a go with watercolour pencils, as they seem to be easier to get the hang of than the paint and brushes," Ged responded.

"Better for the soft furnishings too – eh, Dad," quipped Ed. Sarah and Brian laughed, spluttering a mouthful of white wine before checking that Ged had seen the funny side. Thankfully, he had.

"Okay, you lot, yes I was a clumsy sod with the paint, but the crutches didn't help much, and it was a good job Sarah was around to divert unwanted attention," he said, grinning, as he winked at Sarah. "So, Ron… are you sure if I did some more, they would sell?" he said with a slight frown.

"No doubt about it. I'm sure your job up-country is a good-un, but if you don' mind me sayin', it seems a shame to waste yer talent. When yer ready, bring some more sketches – or those watercolours over, an' I'll get prints done, an' get 'em mounted and framed. You can get cards made up too for the stingy ones that don' want to buy a framed print, but I don' think you need to do that."

"Alright, perhaps I'll do some while I'm down here," said Ged with a smile, still shaking his head. He couldn't understand how anyone would pay for them, but then he couldn't understand why some people would pay thousands or even millions for some of the modern art he had seen at galleries over the years. "Oh, and Ron," he added, "the food was a masterpiece tonight. It's been too long since I've had a portion of your scampi."

"I'll second that," said Brian enthusiastically.

"We aims to please," said Ron with a smile and a nod of the head. He pushed himself up from the chair with both hands, noticeably wincing as he did so. He nodded to the rest of the family, bade them all a Merry Christmas and walked stiffly back to the kitchen. Ged watched as he hobbled back. He didn't want to embarrass him by asking what the problem might be.

As the family picked up their coats to go. Emily came to clear the table. Ged waited behind as the others took their leave and said their goodbyes and Merry Christmases to Emily.

"Thanks for a lovely meal, Emily," he said. "It was good to see Ron. I've not seen him in a very long time…er. I don't mean to pry, but is he ok? He looked in pain."

"No. He isn't, Mr B,"

"Call me Ged, please."

"He's been having prostate trouble for a while, …er, Ged. We're waiting for a date when he can go in and have his operation. We need a chef to stand in for him, or we'll have to close for a bit. I don't think I can manage on my own."

"Not serious, I hope?"

"They're removin' it. We'll have to see after that. It's an awful worry. It took me more'n a year to persuade 'im to see the doc. Oh, look at me, botherin' you with my problems," she sniffed, pulling a tissue from her apron pocket and wiping a drip from her nose. "And when you're still in mournin' for your wife. I'm so sorry for your loss," she sniffed.

"Just because I'm bereaved, it doesn't lessen the worry you must have for Ron. Putting things in perspective is one thing, but it doesn't change what you're going through. I hope the op goes well and you find someone to help you out." Ged said sincerely.

"Thanks, Mr B… I mean Ged," said Emily, wiping her reddening eyes.

Ged went back to Chy Gwyn with Karen and Ed. Laura had fallen asleep in the baby seat. In the car, Ged opened the envelope that Ron had given him. It was another cheque, this time for £200. He recoiled at the thought of his drawings selling so well, but Ron had made them look so professional with proper mountings and frames. He supposed when people were on holiday, as Marge had so eloquently espoused the previous summer, people emptied their wallets more freely than when they were at home, and £10 -£20 wasn't so bad for a souvenir of a trip to Cornwall, classier, he figured, than a fridge magnet in the shape of a Cornish pasty.

As Karen navigated smoothly around the twisting lanes, with Ed navigating, Ged ruminated over what could be a very different future. Pete's words came into his mind. *Why do we chase the money? You can't buy your health, can't take it with you when you go…'*

By the time they arrived at Chy Gwyn, Ged knew, deep in his bones, that he had always known what he wanted to do. He just had to get his act together and do it. He didn't want to waste any more time.

***

The family stayed for New Year's Eve. Brian had faith in his team in the restaurant back in London. A film director had booked out the restaurant and asked for a Thai buffet with entertainment. He was a shareholder in the restaurant and knew about Brian's mother. He wanted the staff to enjoy themselves as well as his guests and had called Brian to tell him to have a proper break with the family and leave it to the staff to prepare the party.

The children were too young to go to the pub as the party was for over 18's only, so the family had a meal and games at home and invited Bill and Sharon to join them. Brian had bought crab, lobster, mussels and some cockles from a local fisherman. He and Ged prepared a seafood feast with a bouillabaisse fish stew. They chatted amiably as they cooked. Brian had brought four new wines he was testing for the restaurant, and created some dips to try with the bread and raw vegetables. Sharon and Bill brought a delicious chocolate pudding, which they served hot with clotted cream

As it was New Year's Eve, they started the meal late at seven and dawdled over it, chatting and playing games of charades. Before it got too late and he had had too much to drink, Ged decided to share his plan with the family. He was glad that Sharon and Bill were there to hear it. He tapped his wine glass with a crab claw and stood up. Just as Ed had done a few nights ago, Ged cleared his throat before he started.

"Firstly, I'd like to say how happy I am that you all are here tonight, Sharon and Bill especially. Out of all of the people I've met over the years in this lovely village, you two have always made me feel the most welcome. I feel I can count you amongst my closest friends, and I want to raise a glass to the two of you for having such a fabulous café and making a delicious pudding. He raised his glass and looked around the table, "Sharon and Bill."

"Sharon and Bill," chorused the Bakers. Bill twisted his napkin and looked at his knees; Sharon blushed, smiling back at Ged and gave Bill a reassuring pat on the knee.

"Secondly, I want to properly welcome Karen to the Baker family. As far as I'm concerned, Karen, you're already a Baker, but I'm looking forward to making it official when you two tie the knot."

"Here, here," said Brian, raising his glass in Karen's direction. "At last, I have the sister I always dreamed of," he said, winking at Ed.

"Finally," said Ged, glancing at Brian and Ed, who both knew what he was about to say, "I've come to a decision that I hope you will all be happy with. I've decided that I would like to retire a little earlier than planned and move down to Porthcovery … erm…on a permanent basis. I may do the same as Ed and Karen and rent out the house in Warwick; God knows, my darling Marge has made it as perfect as any house could possibly be. But I really don't want to stay there. I love Porthcovery. I'll hopefully be able to earn a crust doing jobs down here, and the rent from the house will help… I'll be happy to buy your share of the house, Sarah and Brian…so, er… that's it." His cheeks flushed as he sat down, pleased to have that off his chest.

"Wow!" said Sharon, "that's a nice surprise."

"Great idea, Dad," said Sarah.

"It wasn't originally my idea; really, it was Ed's suggestion and some of the things you said, Sarah, and something my boss said the other week."

"What was that?"

"It boiled down to: 'Money can't buy your health, and you can't take it with you when you go.' I realised that Marge was the main thing keeping me in the Midlands, and I think I'll like living here."

"We'll certainly love having you live 'ere, Chippy," said Bill. "I won't have to phone a plumber or a sparky ever again!" He stood up and shook Ged warmly by the hand, grinning. Sharon had tears in her eyes. She walked around the table and gave Ged a tight hug.

"It'll be lovely to have you in the village all the time, Ged."

"So, do I get promoted from Emmet to Grockle, or what?"

"Oh, pish," said Sharon. "You'll just be 'Chippy' as far as I'm concerned. I don't go for all this 'emmet' and 'grockle' nonsense; it's offensive. We wouldn't have a living if it weren't for tourists and move-down- 'ere-ers."

Jamie looked worried, and Ged noticed that he was quiet.

"What's up, Jamie?" Ged asked him as the others began to clear the table."

"I think Nana would have liked to live here too, but she can't because she died." There were tears in his eyes.

"Actually, Jamie," said Ged gently, putting an arm around his shoulders, "I don't think she would have liked it at all. She would have had to move away from the life she knew in Warwick. I think she would have missed all the clubs and other things that she did. I have more friends down here, and that's why I want to live here."

"Will we see you as often, Grandad?"

"I've thought about that a lot. It's further to come to London, but if I'm semi-retired, I can come whenever I want. You might see even more of me than before."

"Then I'm really happy you're moving here," said Jamie, hugging him tightly.

Alice had been listening intently. She curled her arms around Ged's left arm and burrowed her face into his jumper sleeve.

"I'm glad you're going to live here, Grandad," she said. "I don't like your other house; it's too neat and tidy, and I'm not allowed to do anything."

Ged chuckled and kissed his oldest granddaughter on her head. "You know, young lady, I think you will go far. I've always liked your brand of straight-talking."

Ed organised a treasure hunt for Alice and Jamie, and the whole family joined in, trying to figure out the clues. They were all entertained when he put Laura to bed, once again, singing a medley of eighties and nineties rock songs that the others could hear on the baby monitor. Brian started a game of 'Name that tune' as Ed started each one. Bill won easily. He turned out to be quite the music buff.

The children went to bed soon after, but Sarah woke them before midnight so that they could see the New Year fireworks in the village. Ed and Brian carried the sleepy children outside, wrapped in blankets, and they sat on the garden wall to watch. Shouts and cheers could be heard from the pub as the fireworks went shooting over the calm bay from a field in the centre of the village. The reflection of the fireworks in the rippling water doubled the delight.

36

After the family left on the afternoon of New Year's Day, Ged spent a few hours on his own, tidying the house and folding up the travel cot that had offended Laura so much. Ed had shown him how to send text messages, so he practised by sending thank-you texts to Ed, Brian, and Sarah. He realised that he didn't have a number for Karen.

He fetched a pad and made a list of everyone he needed to contact. It wasn't a long list, and unsurprisingly, Annie's name appeared at the top. He had spoken with her on the phone over Christmas and shared his thoughts about moving to Cornwall. He had invited her to come for Christmas with the family, but she was volunteering at the cottage hospital.

The journey back to Warwick felt longer and gloomier than ever. Rain hammered down, and the traffic jams were endless. He sure wasn't going to miss this, he thought. Going to work and coming home to an empty home, his and Marge's home, filled him with dread. He knew he would probably have to work a month's notice and was resigned to it.

Pete was more optimistic. He helped Ged to negotiate a two-week notice period with Human Resources instead of four, arguing that Ged had not actually used up his holiday the previous year, and the two weeks allowed Pete to arrange a retirement celebration. On his last day, all of his colleagues gathered in the brew area, along with a small crowd of people from other departments who had worked with him over the years. He was quite moved by the sheer number of people who had gathered to say goodbye. He realised that the factory was where he had made the most friends over his working life. They presented him with a huge card signed by countless people and a fabulous new toolbox, paid for by a whip-round which Martin had organised. Dave had made a trophy in the workshop with a wooden plaque base and a pewter model of one of the cars they used to build at the factory mounted on it. In front of the car was a stainless-steel plate engraved with Ged's name, the dates of his tenure and an inscription: *Happy retirement, Ged. We will miss you.*

Pete made a short speech, thanking Ged for his hard work, his expertise and his friendship. Ged swallowed hard; a lump had formed in his throat. He realised he would miss the banter and the friends he had made, but he knew it was time to move on.

"Thanks, everyone," he said, forcing the lump down. "This is a perfect gift, and I'll treasure it," he said, gesturing to the toolbox and then holding up the little trophy. "Seeing you all here today makes me realise just how many friends I've made here over the years." he cleared his throat, forcing down a surge of emotion. "If you're ever in Cornwall, feel free to give me a ring and pop over to Porthcovery… especially now I've worked out how to use my blasted mobile phone!"

***

Ed came to help Ged pack the van for the move. Ged decided not to take much of the old furniture from Warwick. He had everything he needed in Porthcovery. Marge had chosen almost every item of furniture in the house, and although they were all good pieces, Ged preferred a simpler style. He thought there would be enough reminders of her in Chy Gwyn.

Annie came to help, and Karen too. They packed away all of Marge's clothes into large shopping bags and took them to a charity shop. Everything, that is, except the turquoise kimono dressing gown, which Ged gave to her with pleasure when she told him the story.

Ged took some crockery, cutlery, some cooking items, and all of the food, groceries, and spices from the kitchen, as well as cleaning products and toiletries from the bathroom. They dismantled his workbench and packed up all of his tools from the garage. In the end, they only managed to fill the Lincoln van two-thirds full. The house had been rented fully furnished to a newly married couple, the wife of whom had recently started a finance job at the factory.

Ged drove his Honda estate down to Cornwall while Annie drove the rental van. She had planned to spend a week with Ged after returning the van to a depot in Newquay.

**

After years of coming for his maintenance weeks, Ged felt immediately at home in Porthcovery. Opening the door felt as natural as putting on his favourite pair of slippers.

As January storms battered the coast. Annie and Ged spent a week helping him unpack and set up his workshop in the lean-to shed in the small yard at the back of the house. It had once been a sculptor's workshop, so there were already some handy hooks, shelves and places to keep tools. Annie was a dab hand with DIY. She helped Ged to modify his old workbench and fit it under the window. There was a power supply to the workshop, but it was in a bad state, so Annie and Ged replaced the wiring and fitted more sockets and lighting above the workbench. They painted the inside walls of the workshop with whitewash, fitted a new and more secure lock to the door and bought an outdoor storage box for the garden tools. Ged fitted shelves and hooks in the utility room to store beach things that had been previously kept in the shed.

Each day, they would finish their work early if the rain abated and go for a short walk along the coast path or take a trip out to Falmouth or to one of the beauty spots along the Helford estuary. They treated themselves to tea at the Lobster Pot midweek and enjoyed a meal at the pub. Sharon and Bill invited them to dinner one evening, and Annie really hit it off with them. They spent the evening laughing or agreeing vigorously about various subjects. In particular, their upset at how badly many older people were treated.

"People just treat older people like they're invisible, or like a farm animal, not like individuals. The older you get, the more irrelevant you become," Annie complained.

"I know exactly what you mean, said Sharon. When I go up to Helston' for shopping, the way some o' the clerks at the bank treat the older folk is disgustin.' They talk to 'em like kids. An' all of 'em could teach those young – 'uns a thing or two."

Bill joined in the rant: "I can't prove it o' course, but my Auntie Sue was abused by some of the carers at 'er first 'ome and definitely was neglected. When I moved 'er out of the first place an' into the second one in Falmouth, she 'ad bedsores. She were so thin! The new place was further away, so I didn't see 'er as often. I feet bad, but at least she were bein' looked after."

"I'm afraid it's all too common," Annie replied. "I volunteer at a hospice, and we've had many patients who end up there after having spent time at poorly run homes. One or two of the patients flinched when I came to give them medication or just to see if they wanted a chat, or a walk in the garden. They seemed terrified," she said. "It's disgusting how little dignity people are given in some places. There are lots of good ones, of course, but they are expensive places to run, and some will cut corners…"

"Auntie Sue's last place relies on volunteers to make ends meet. They were really nice. I used to go take 'er out for a trip to the coast once a week. She missed Porthcovery like mad."

***

Ged drove Annie to the station in Penzance for her trip home. She invited him to come and stay in her Cottage when the first of the holiday tenants were due to stay in Chy Gwyn in April. Sarah had stopped taking bookings, but there were at least ten that season. Ged had made arrangements to stay with Sarah and Brian for a few of those weeks, and they had planned a week in France. He would be staying with Annie for two separate weeks in the spring and autumn, and Pete had invited him to come and stay with him and Emma in North Wales for another week. He had rented a room at the pub for the other weeks. This meant that he would have to keep the house in tip-top condition for at least that first year.

While he completed the jobs on Glyn's list at the pub, other local shopkeepers and café owners began to get in touch, asking him to do various jobs before the tourist season got underway. Ged got the existing phone line reconnected at the house, as the signal to his mobile phone was non-existent in some parts of the village. They had never connected the phone before, as the aim was that the house was a getaway. Now, it was Ged's main home; he needed a phone. He decided he would put an honesty box next to it for holidaymakers that year. Sarah sent him a gift of fifty business cards with *'Chippy'* in large blue letters, *'Joinery, Electrical and General Maintenance'* underneath, a picture of a crossed hammer and spanner, and his house and mobile number on the front. She had expanded on the services he could offer on the back. The business cards were not really necessary, but Ged liked them as they made him feel more professional. Word quickly got around the village that he had moved there on a permanent basis, and most of his weekdays, for the first two months, were filled with maintenance jobs at the pub, cafés and local shops. He asked Benjamin to help him with some larger jobs and started to teach him plumbing skills. Benjamin was quiet but was a quick learner and a hard worker, and just as he had been before Christmas, he was tidy, too. Ged quickly built up a reputation and got calls from other establishments further afield. It seemed that working in an industrial setting made his skills more suitable for businesses. Many other local tradespeople seemed focused on domestic jobs or holiday properties. Not that Ged didn't get a few calls for those, but shops, pubs and farms seemed to be the mainstay. His trusty Honda estate made a great work van. With a large payload and a heavy-duty roof rack for ladders and items that wouldn't fit in the car, it suited his needs. However, after a couple of months of this kind of work, it no longer looked as pristine as it once had, and some of the narrow and bumpy tracks he had to negotiate took their toll. The scratches and dents, however, somehow made it fit in with the rough-hewn surroundings of the Cornish coast.

Weekends were spent hiking along the southwest coast path or sketching and practising with watercolours. He joined Caroline's painting class, most of whom, like him, had moved to the village from elsewhere but, unlike him, had retired completely.

As more tourists began to arrive, Bill and Sharon opened the Seagull café full-time and closed only on Monday evenings; Ged would often go there for lunch if he was working in the village, would have coffee in the morning if there was time, and use it as a place to sketch from. Bill had a little table in the corner of the covered terrace that he would reserve for Ged, who usually turned up early before the tourists arrived.

One Saturday, even though there were other customers on the terrace, Sharon made a beeline for Ged's table, looking excited.

"Hey, Chippy, I've got something for you," she said, holding up a white envelope. "It's been posted 'ere, but it's addressed to you. You'll never believe who this is from," she said eagerly… Go on, I'll give you three guesses."

"Sarah..? I've still not called her back about staying with them."

"Nope."

"Oh, I know, it's a cheque from Bob at The Feathers. He didn't have my address; that's why he hasn't paid me for the work I did on the loos in the pub." (Ged shuddered at that thought. It had been a most unpleasant job. The toilets at the pub had been troublesome for years, and the landlord's attempt at DIY had gone very wrong and landed him literally in a pile of foul-smelling unpleasantness.)

"Last guess," said Sharon.

"Er, it's the queen inviting me to tea at Buckingham Palace."

Secretly, Ged thought it might be the publisher fellow trying to get in touch, and he really didn't know if he wanted to look at it if it was.

"Nope, you lose. It's that pretty Danish bird…Inger, er Inga…"

"Rita? Rita Thorstensen?"

"Yeah… Blimey, you got a good mem'ry, 'avent you?"

"For names, not bad, actually. Phone numbers, I'm useless.

"Well, anyway. I opened it cos I weren't expectin' post for you 'ere. She wants you to get in touch. 'Er daughter 'as written a story book, an' wants you to do some pictures for it."

Ged was stunned… he was expecting this, but not from Rita, and all he could say was, "Oh." He took the letter from the envelope. He could hear Rita's tinkling Danish accent as he read the letter.

Dear Ged (Chippy)

Thank you for leaving the picture of our boat at the Seagull Café last summer. You left before we could say it. It was really nice that you remembered us. Chris had a frame made for it, and we have it in our house in Zealand.

I have sent this letter to the café because I don't know your address. Chris thinks maybe I am being cheeky. Please say no if you don't have time, but there is something we would like you to do if you can. Our daughter, Greta, is very shy and didn't come to the café for breakfast. She has won a competition in Copenhagen for a children's book she has written. Her prize is to have her book published. She really liked your drawing of the pirate, and she wrote a story about him. She started it in Porthcovery. We would be very happy if you could do some drawings for her book. Please write to tell us if this is possible. It would be a dream.

We will come back to Porthcovery this summer to windsurf. I hope we see you again.

Yours
Rita Thorstensen

Sharon kept glancing back at Ged as she served other customers as he read and clearly re-read the letter. When he finally folded it and put it back in the envelope, she came over.

"Well?" she said eagerly.

"Well, what?" said Ged.

"Are you going to illustrate Greta's book?"

"So, you read all of it then?"

"We both did. Twice… or was it three times? Oh, please say you'll do it, Chippy, your sketches are brilliant. Emily's bin tellin' me about 'em. I wish Sarah 'ad given em to me to sell. We'd be quids in."

Ged felt a sudden pang of guilt that neither he nor Sarah had thought to give his good friends the sketches to sell. Then he remembered Bill's scornful remarks about budding Rembrandts the summer before.

"Sorry, Sharon," said Ged. "You can have some sketches to sell if you want them, but if you make anything, I'm giving my share to the lifeboats. I don't want a penny. They're just doodles."

"That's pish, Ged Baker," said Sharon, her hands firmly planted on her hips. "Forgive me, Mrs B -God-rest-her-soul- might've thought they was *doodles,* but she was wrong. Them that knows better don' agree, an' that includes me, Emily, Ron, Bill, Glyn, his wife Helen and *now* Rita…An' er daughter. We can't all be wrong, can we?"

Ged really didn't have an answer to this impassioned speech and sheepishly took a gulp of his now lukewarm coffee.

"To be honest, I don' 'ave time – or the skill to get 'em mounted an' framed, otherwise I'd 'ave asked you for a few. Ron does all the ones at the Lobster Pot, so it's easier for them. Most of the artists who ask us to sell their pictures bring 'em in already mounted an' framed."

"I'll get some framed for you then," said Ged, "maybe Caroline could show me how to do it. Or I could ask Ron."

"Never mind about that… What about this young shy girl an' 'er book?"

"Okay, I need to get my head around this. I'll write to Rita, I promise, and find out what she needs."

"I should think so, too. You got some talent, an' you won't always be strong enough to be luggin' bits of timber around or fit enough to be stompin' up an' down ladders, and you know, if you want to make a livin' down 'ere, you need two jobs. You've been busy 'til now, but the café's shops and pubs won't want you in the loo with a plunger and a spanner when they got tourists around… well, not 'less it's a 'mergency.'"

***

Although it was still quite sunny, there was a fresh, northeasterly breeze. A change in the weather was on the way, judging by the speed at which the clouds were moving. Ged left the café after finishing his coffee and decided to take a longer walk to one of the lookout points along the coast. He had made a sandwich at home and had planned a long walk that day. He suspected it might not be walking weather in the week to come. When he arrived at Treleaver Point, with its whitewashed stone lookout station, he sat on the bench on the western side of the structure, sheltered from the wind and got out his sandwich and a small flask.

As he sat looking westwards along the coast, he heard a deep snort right by his ear. One of the many ponies that were often allowed to graze around the southwest coast path had clearly decided to investigate if Ged had anything or was indeed himself edible. Ged knew better than to feed the ponies. They were semi-wild. Feeding them would just make them expect food from people, and they might bite. He sat quiet and still and allowed the stocky brown pony to sniff his hair and shirt. Eventually, once the animal had satisfied itself that Ged was neither an opportunity nor a threat, it slowly wandered off down the grassy promontory to graze.

Ged quietly unzipped his backpack so as not to startle the animal, took out his sketchbook and began to sketch the pony, which began to, rather inexpertly, scratch his right ear with his hind leg. Ged silently chuckled at this totally natural but, in some way, comical act. The character of the pony began to take shape in his mind. He exaggerated his features. The shaggy mane and tail became more unkempt, the bottom became rounder, the tummy fatter, and the eyes more expressive.

He finished sketching the pony grazing and tried to capture it scratching its ear. This was very difficult to get right now that the pony was no longer doing it. He decided to bring a camera next time. He made up a scene where the pony had its nose in his backpack. He imagined he was the Yogi-bear of ponies, stealing sandwiches out of unwary hikers' *pick-er-nic* baskets, or in this case, backpacks. There were other ponies grazing around the little headland, a grey and two black ones, but 'Yogi' was different. He had more of an Exmoor appearance, with blends of tan over his body and dark brown ears, legs and muzzle. He seemed bolder than the others, too. When Ged looked up from his imagined sandwich-stealing sketch, Yogi was making friends with a family of three hikers. A girl of around thirteen was stroking and patting his neck. Yogi turned his head to sniff her backpack as she patted him.

Ged did a stick person sketch of the scene to remind him of it and studied the family discreetly. The parents looked well-off, with matching wax jackets and brown leather hiking boots. The mother held a Labrador on a short lead. She had a broad smile and laughing eyes. The father appeared thoughtful and serious, but smiled when he saw one of the ponies following his daughter, sniffing her backpack as they walked to the lookout hut. The girl seemed to have a way with horses, and one following her got a gentle scratch between the ears before the girl's mother called her to join them for their lunch in a soft, home-counties accent.

"Harriet, come along, have some lunch and don't feed the ponies, or they'll expect it and might nip," said the mother.

"They're gorgeous, aren't they, mum?" said the girl.

"Cute as buttons... in fact, that black one looks a bit like old buttons, doesn't he?"

Ged tried to sketch the scene of the girl and *'Yogi'* as he investigated her backpack from memory. He didn't include the parents but added the black pony they had dubbed *'Buttons'*, coming to investigate. The ponies took on quite a comical boldness to their investigation of the humans invading their habitat.

Large droplets of rain began to fall as Ged walked back to the village down a steep shortcut from the coast path, which took him past a pretty row of cottages. He broke into a run as the rain intensified and made it to the pub before the downpour.

"You're early, Chippy," called a grinning Glyn from behind the bar as he finished slicing lemons.

"Wind blew me here," said Ged with a wink.

"Rain washed you in, more like," Glyn said, peering out at the rain battering the harbour.

"Get us a pint of the black stuff, please, Glyn?"

"Pint of Guinness comin' up," said Glyn, cheerfully. They chatted amiably about the terrible weather forecast for the following week while Ged hung up his coat to dry near the fire and gave old Monty a fuss as he nosed his hand. He ordered a portion of Lasagne and salad and sat at the table in the corner by the fire. He opened his faded pink unicorn backpack and got out his sketch pad, turning the pages, one by one, trying to look at the sketches he had done over the last few weeks as if he were not the artist: A ginger cat, the lightness of the pencil lines hinting at its colour, prowling around the boats in dry dock by the harbour; some drawings of Monty, snoozing by the fire or befriending tourists in the pub. His favourite sketch of Monty summed up the old dog perfectly: Ben, one of the older pub goers, often sat on a stool at the end of the bar, near the fire. Once Ben was seated, Monty would walk over and lay his head on the man's lap, looking up at him as though he was the most wonderful person he had ever met.

Ged still didn't have a high opinion of his sketches, but Sharon's words came back to him: *"We can't all be wrong, can we?"* He rummaged in his pencil case for a ballpoint pen and turned to a page of his sketchbook on which he had drawn the pony's head in the corner and wrote a letter to Rita on it.

Dear Rita

It was nice to get your letter. I'm glad you liked the sketches I left with Bill and Sharon for you.

Much has happened since we met. My wife, Marge, passed away before Christmas, and I have decided to come and live in Porthcovery permanently. I am making a living doing maintenance work for the pubs, shops and restaurants here.

As you can see from these pictures, I am still sketching. If Greta would like me to do some drawings, please tell her I would be honoured to illustrate her story. Could you ask her to describe the scenes she would like me to draw? I just drew Pete the pirate; I have no idea what he was up to, so I would love to read her story and find out what he was doing. Maybe she can write another story about these cheeky ponies. The one nuzzling my hair is called 'Yogi', and the one following the girl is 'Buttons'.

So that I can remember what he looked like, please could you send a photocopy of Pete? It will help me to make him look like the same person in every picture.

I look forward to hearing from you and Greta.

With warmest regards

Ged (Chippy) Baker

Ged tore out the page with the letter and the one with the two drawings of the ponies and read over the letter once more. Helen brought his lasagne with cutlery wrapped in a napkin.

"Ooh, let's have a look, Chippy," she said, dropping her shoulder and twisting her head to better look at the sketches of the ponies. "Aah, they're so cute, those ponies, aren't they? Are those the ponies that the National Trust has got grazing on the headland?"

"Yes. This one is cheeky. He likes investigating people's picnics, so I called him Yogi."

Helen chuckled. "I really like them; cartoony but not too much. Looking at the pictures, you can imagine them being able to talk. He's a naughty one, that Yogi. Did he really do that?

"Yes, but nobody gave him anything. Maybe others before have done."

"I wish people wouldn't do that with animals. They start expecting food, and when they don't get it, some of them bite. I'm always asking punters not to give Monty any tidbits. I don't think he'd bite anyone, soft old thing, but if everyone who came in here gave him food, he'd be round as a barrel!" she said.

"I think Monty prefers fuss, anyway," replied Ged.

"That's 'cos he knows you and old Ben never give him anything, so he has to settle for a bit of a love-in with you two."

"Helen, can I ask you a favour?"

"Anything, Chippy," she said.

"I don't suppose you might have an envelope that this could go in by any chance?" he said, holding up the letter and the pony sketch he had torn from his book.

"I think I do have one or two that size. Give me a minute to serve the other two customers over there, and I'll nip to the office and have a look."

37

Julian Barker finally threw in the towel early in January. Barker-Mead and their lawyers didn't succeed in striking the long-hoped-for film deal. The bank refused an extension on the overdraft and insisted that they begin repayment of the loans. Lance Mead's parents had run out of patience with his lack of business acumen and had refused to bail them out for a third time. They had agreed to pay off any outstanding bank loans to prevent their son from being declared bankrupt. The stigma would be his ruination (as if having long lunches with his private school cronies, wining and dining Sloane rangers, going to night clubs and getting drunk every night instead of working hadn't already achieved that), but they would no longer bankroll a failing business. Julian had not hidden the predicament from the staff, most of whom had already deserted the sinking ship. However, Mike and Beth, the receptionist and administrator, remained as they had not found anywhere else to go. Julian had secured some work with his wife.

Julian, Mike and Beth went out for a farewell lunch at a nearby restaurant. On their return, a van had arrived to remove the last of the furniture that had been sold to a local business. The three assisted the van driver and his mate to manoeuvre the desks and chairs down the narrow stairs and out onto the street.

Finally, Mike, Julian, and Beth stood with their personal items in a few cardboard boxes at their feet. In Julian's office. Julian had already removed all the books from the bookshelves in the days before. The place looked twice as big now that it was empty. Outside, a car horn beeped twice.

"Well, then, I'll be off," said Beth. "Roger is picking me up, as I knew I'd have too much wine at lunch. It's been a pleasure working with you both." She kissed Julian and Mike on both cheeks, leaving a smudge of bright red lipstick on Julian's and a slightly pink one on Mike's; then she picked up her box and carefully negotiated the stairs.

She was a little wobbly in her four-inch heels, having drunk the majority of a bottle of St Emilion at lunch.

"That's that, then, Mike," said Julian, shaking Mike's hand. "Don't be a stranger. If you change your mobile number, let me know."

"Yeah, same to you, Julian," said Mike. "And if you spot any likely job openings, will you text me?"

"Sure," said Julian. Mike picked up his cardboard box of personal items, and they headed for the stairs. Julian stopped at the top and took one last look around the empty office. "It's not so hard to leave this place now, it looks like this, and there's nobody in it."

Mike didn't reply. He just wanted to get back to his flat and figure out what to do next.

***

The following week, he was back in Porthleven, in Auntie Doreen's House. She was still in Australia visiting his cousin, Greg. She said he could stay as long as he liked. She wasn't due back until the end of April, but said if he wanted to stay on a bit longer after that, she would be delighted to have some company.

Mike had decided to try and set up as a freelance agent. He had no major debts and a modest amount of savings behind him. His needs were few, especially now that Jane wasn't helping him spend his money. In fact, he had noticed, since they had split up, that his bank balance looked very healthy indeed. Jane had expensive taste when it came to restaurants. He supposed she liked to be noticed in all the right places. He had given notice on his London flat and decided to spend some of his redundancy money on a new computer and some office essentials. Auntie Doreen's spare room served well as a place to study in his twenties, and he already had his old desk, bookshelves, and bookcase, which he used when he was a student.

He called Jenny Halshaw's agent.

"Hi, Suzy,"

"Hiya, Mike, y'all right? Everything go ohh-kay at Barker's last week?" she said, her Lancashire accent always real and totally charming.

"Yeah, it was a bit sad. It sounds like Beth has got herself a job at a gym somewhere, and I was right about my guess for Julian. He is going to work for his wife at the magazine publisher. I don't think it's what he wants, but you have to pay the mortgage somehow."

"So, *are* you going to set yourself up then? Y'know, go freelance, like?"

"Well, as long as you're still with me… That's what I was calling about. I've bought a car at long last, and I've been driving around meeting up with some of my authors from Barker's – Mead over the last few weeks. Are you still ok to meet up on Thursday?"

"Can't wait. Like I said, Mike, as long as you can get me an illustrator in the next four weeks, then we're on. You know Hacker's have given me a final deadline, or they'll get James Dickie to do the illustrations. Which would be a disaster, but 'ah don't have a choice, do ah?"

"I'm going to give it one last try with this Ged Baker guy, and I'm giving a guest lecture at the art college in Falmouth, so if he still won't budge, we might have some enthusiastic budding illustrators. Could you ask Jenny if she could come? Having a famous author there will boost numbers, and they aren't going to be all that interested in boring old me, are they?"

Suzy laughed. "You're not borin', Mike. You're just a bit shy. And you'd give less of a boring impression if you get rid of them awful beige corduroy trousers. I mean, you might as well have leather patches on t'elbows o' your tweed Jacket for goodness' sake. Wear a pair of decent Levi's jeans and a white shirt with that Jacket o' yours. You'd look much more your age instead of looking like a sixty-year-old 'istory lecturer."

"Oh, you're so bossy," chided Mike.

"No… I'm right, is what I am. I know you won't go somewhere posh, so, go to Marks and Spencer's and spend some o' your redundancy on a couple of pairs o' blue jeans and a few decent white shirts."

"I do have jeans, you know."

"So, wear 'em! I swear it, Mike, I'll come round your 'ouse and nick them chords off the washing line and shred them up! They're bloody awful!"

"Okay, bossy boots." See you on Thursday.

***

Mike dropped into the Lobster Pot for his dinner that evening. Emily wasn't around, so he had a quick walk around and looked at the pictures on the walls. He noticed a new painting in acrylics of waves at the beautiful and unmistakable Kynance Cove. With no one in the restaurant and Emily and Ron nowhere to be found, Mike decided to investigate the kitchen. He found Emily there alone, filling vinegar bottles. She looked somehow older than she had when he had seen her before Christmas, but she was delighted to see him.

"Oh! Michael! You gave me a start. Back so soon? ... oh. Does that mean…?"

"Yep, I'm now part of the jobless masses, Emily," he said, grinning and giving her a hug and a peck on the cheek. "Are you open for dinner?"

"Nearly. I'm a bit behind, to be honest. Ron's in hospital, and I'm doing the cookin'. I thought when you came in you were my 'oliday lad, Chris. I've asked him to wait tables for me this week, but he can't get 'ere 'til six most days as he don't get 'ome from college 'til half-five an' 'is mum drops 'im off. He's a good lad; He reminds me o' you when you were 'is age.

Well, I'm at a loose end most of this week. Can I help?

"Oh, Michael," she laughed, "don't be daft…." Mike looked a little offended.

"Oh, you were serious… well, you're probably lookin' for a job, aren't you?"

"No. I'm going freelance. I put a few irons in the fire last week, and I'm waiting for a few of them to… well, warm up. I've no rent to pay, I've got two meetings this week, and I'm giving a talk at Falmouth College, but other than that, I'm all yours… if you want me, that is. I'm a bit rusty with the cooking and the waiting on, but I'm sure I'll soon get into the swing of it again. I suppose it's like riding a bike."

"Oh, Michael!" She cried, putting her hands in the air and then stepping over to him and hugging him tightly. "It's like all my prayers 'ave been answered. She took quite a while to release him from her hug, and when she did so, there were tears streaming down her face. She fished in her apron pocket for tissues. Mike was really concerned. Emily was like family.

"Come on. Sit down, Emily. What's up? I've never seen you like this. I'll make a cup of tea."

"Oh, it's my Ron… he took so long to go to the doc about 'is prostate. I'm so scared 'eel have cancer. I bin tryin' to 'old it together an all, but I'm scared, Michael; He's been in so much pain lately, it's been hard for him to concentrate. He's so tired every night, we hardly say a word to each other afore he crashes on the sofa with a beer at the end o' the shift."

"Oh, Emily," said Mike, frowning with concern, "I had no idea! Listen, Auntie Doreen says I can stay as long as I want. I'll do whatever I can to help, whether you want me in the kitchen or waiting on. I can collect your lad from Helston if his Mum can't bring him."

"Thanks, Michael… well, if you wouldn't mind helping me lay up the tables and then we'll get the kitchen sorted. I'll show you where everything is. Not much has changed since you were here last. Just use the coffee machine, and you'll soon get the hang of it. Young Chris is really good at it. He can teach you," she said, wiping her eyes with a napkin and then blowing her nose noisily on it.

Mike got to work. He hung up his jacket in the little utility room behind the kitchen and put on a black waiter's apron over his jeans. He didn't think the Genesis t-shirt he was wearing was really suitable, but at least it wasn't offensive.

They had a quiet night. Only twenty customers came in, altogether, mostly older couples, for a simple evening meal, plus one 16th Birthday party family group.

Chris arrived at around six-thirty and was surprised to see Mike with his apron, but soon realised that he had done this before; even if he was a little rusty, he appeared to know where everything was and had a pleasant, unfussy way with the customers.

Chris gave Mike a lesson or two on the Italian coffee machine and promised to come in early to give him a longer training session the following afternoon, so that he could be back from college early. Mike gave him his mobile phone number and Auntie Doreen's telephone number so he could call him for a lift if he needed one.

Mike worked at the café for most of the week. Suzy had agreed to meet him there to talk about plans for Jenny Halshaw's book. She was astonished to find him in an apron, taking an order from a customer near the counter when she came in. He had reserved his favourite window seat and gestured to her to take a seat there while he finished taking the order.

He disappeared into the kitchen and returned without his apron, followed by Emily, wiping her hands on a tea towel. Emily nodded to him as he went to greet Suzy.

"Hi, Suze," he said. She stood up and embraced him, pecking him on both cheeks.

"What's goin' on 'ere then? You was in an apron, takin' orders jus' then."

"I'm helping Emily out. Her husband is in hospital, and they run this place together, so she's a man down. I used to work here years ago. Do you want a coffee? I'm getting quite good at it now."

"Er, yeah, I'll 'ave a Cappuccino if you can do 'em and as I'm a mate, can I 'ave double chocolate sprinkles?"

"Oh, I don't know about that; you could lose me my job!" he said, winking. "I'll get your coffee back in a mo. If you fancy a slice of cake, I can highly recommend them. The lemon drizzle is particularly good."

"I'll come and 'ave a look," said Suzy, walking over to the counter with him. Mike cranked the handle to deliver the deliciously scented freshly ground coffee into the filter holder, packed the coffee down and fitted it into the machine just as Chris had taught him. As he did so, Suzy got a plate and helped herself to a slice of Coffee and Walnut cake from the cake stand.

"Are you havin' anything, Mike?" she asked.

"Yeah. Get me a slice of the Lemon Drizzle, would you?"

"Hey! I jus' noticed… you're wearin' jeans!"

"I thought I might be at risk if you caught me wearing my cords."

"You would 'a bin," said Suzy with a chuckle.

He made himself a pot of tea, noting what they had had on a pad next to the till. He would settle up with Emily later. He took his tray of drinks over to the table in the window.

"Before you sit down again, come and have a look," he said, beckoning Suzy to follow him. He proceeded to walk her around the café, like a guide at a gallery, pointing out all of Ged's sketches and prints on the wall. All of them were now priced at £25 each, and Emily had no trouble selling them at that price. Suzy giggled at the image of the pirate fisherman and took down the picture of the boy looking into the rock pool to have a closer look. When she saw the sketch of Potts climbing in through the window, she made a squeak in the back of her throat and took a quick intake of breath.

"It's Tiger! It's just like him. He used to do that. Came in mi' bedroom window when mum kicked him out o' the 'ouse for scratchin' the furniture."

"This one's name is Potts, and he doesn't like eating mice outside, apparently. Mike led the way back to the table in the window. He and Suzy went over the plans for the following weeks and months. Suzy was sure that Jenny would love the sketches and decided to ask her to come here from her home in Mevagissey to have a look, but they needed a plan to win Ged Baker round. What little Mike had learned from Emily confirmed that he still felt that making money from his sketching was like fraud, and he gave the money he earned from the sketches to the Lifeboat charity. He did learn from her, though, that Ged had moved down to Porthcovery after his wife passed away and was starting up a business, doing electrical work, joinery and the like with local businesses.

Suzy persuaded Jenny to come to Mike's lecture about what it takes to be an illustrator at the art college in Falmouth. He had her entire back catalogue of books, and Suzy had a few boxes of Jenny's most recent ones in the car in case any of the students wanted to buy a signed copy at the event.

They arranged to have dinner together afterwards at the Lobster Pot. Suzy called Jenny there and then on her mobile phone. She had booked a small holiday apartment in Porthleven as it was cheaper than staying in the local inn for three nights. There was a spare room, so Jenny could stay over if she wanted.

38

"Oh, go on, Bill," Sharon was calling from the terrace as Ged arrived at the seagull the following morning. "Emily needs a partner. Ron is still recovering from his operation… Or are you going to stop her having a good time?"

"I can't dance a bloody step, Sharon. Emily will end up in hospital. I mean, I'll do it if she can't find anyone else, but I'm a poor second to Ron's twinkle toes!"

"Oh, Hi, Ged," said Sharon as she spotted him coming up the steps. "Cappuccino?"

"Yes, please. Everything ok?"

"No, not really. I'm trying to persuade Bill to go to her dance class, but 'es not very enthusiastic."

"What kind of dancing?"

"She does Jive and Salsa and stuff like that, I think," Sharon called over her shoulder as she went to prepare the coffee. "They've been going for a few years, but poor old Ron can't do it; at least not for a few weeks. He had his op the other day."

"Prostate, wasn't it?" Ged said. "I used to dance quite a bit before we were married."

"Really?" said Sharon, "you never said."

"I don't suppose the subject has ever come up."

"You go to Emily's place a lot, don't you? I'd say you know 'er pretty well, don't you?"

"Well, yes…"

"Oh, go on, Ged, you'd make 'er week…especially if you know what you're doing."

"Well, it's been a few years, Sharon. And I don't know her that well."

"Come on, Chippy," Bill joined in as he came out of the kitchen with his familiar bucket of coffee. You have tea there nearly every week, an' she sells your sketches. She'd love to 'ave a decent dancin' partner. Anythin's better than my two left feet."

"Yeah, Ged, oh, please say you will?"

"Alright... honestly, you two are so *bossy*!"

Sharon and Bill high-fived each other. "I owe you one for this, Chippy," said Bill. That Cappo's on the 'ouse! 'Ave a piece of cake as well," he said, clapping Ged enthusiastically on the back, almost making him choke on his coffee.

"When is the class?"

"Tomorrow evenin'. Seven o'clock at Helston Sports Club. She closes the Lobster Pot on a Monday and has a night off, like us."

***

Sharon knocked on Ged's door at six on Monday evening.

"Wow, you scrub up nice, don't you?" she said as he opened the door. He wore his smart dark blue jeans and a black shirt with a light silver-grey tie.

"You can come in our car to Porthleven, Ged. I persuaded Bill to have a go at dancing with me. Me an' my brother used to dance a bit when I was young, an' I'd really like to try it."

Ged tied his polished brown brogues, donned his black leather jacket and followed Sharon to the car.

"Lookin' sharp, Chippy," said Bill, with a broad smile as Ged slid into the back seat.

They met Emily at the door of the Sports centre. She looked so different out of her apron. Her hair was brushed back into a ponytail, and she was wearing a little more make-up. She wore low-heeled black dancing shoes, and her knee-length purple floral skirt revealed slim, muscular calves.

Her lips were smiling, but her face was drawn with worry, and Ged guessed it was a lack of sleep. Sharon embraced her friend like a sister with a tight hug and kiss.

"Come on, Emily, let's dance our cares away. I told you I'd get you a partner, and here's the good news... It's not Bill!"

"Hi, Emily," said Ged as Sharon released Emily from her hug.

"Hello, Ged. It's nice of you to step in. Sharon says you're a dancer."

"I was. My mum taught me, but I haven't danced for a while. I might be a bit rusty."

"That's alright. I danced last week, but I'm pretty rusty, myself. Plus, it's a fairly gentle class, and you can sit out if you need a rest."

The class was what his mother would have called her 'second stagers'. Most of those attending knew the basic positions. That week, they were focusing on Jive. Poor Bill couldn't keep up. The teacher had two assistants who each took Sharon and Bill through some basic steps, whilst the rest of the class practised the steps as the teacher instructed. Ged knew the steps well. He had always liked Latin more than ballroom. The music was fast and furious, and he removed his jacket after ten minutes; he was sweating and pink-faced. He thought he would be fit from all the walking, but he hadn't done this kind of exercise for a very long time. His feet seemed to remember the steps almost automatically. Emily was a good dancer. She completely lost herself in concentration and threw herself into the first three dances; then, the whole class took a drinks break.

"You're a really good dancer, Ged," said Emily. "You said your mum taught you, but I didn't realise she was such a good teacher," she added, mopping sweat from her face with a tissue and gulping down a large glass of orange juice.

"She *was* a dance teacher, actually. She was a national Latin champion in her youth. That's where she met my Dad; They were on the competition circuit together."

"Wow! said Sharon. "A champion? So, did you compete when you were young?"

"Yes, until I was about seventeen or eighteen. I wasn't a national champion or anything, but I won a few trophies. The trouble is, unless you're absolutely the best, you can't make much money, so when I started work, I didn't have time for the top-level competitions, and it became more of a hobby. I met my wife through dancing."

"Oh," said Emily. Her smile faded. "You must miss dancing with her."

"I missed that for over thirty-odd years, Emily. We entered a few amateur competitions when we were courting, but her father didn't approve of Latin and banned it as a condition of our getting married."

"You must've really loved her to give this up," she said, gesturing around the room with a sweep of her arm. There's nothing that makes me feel more alive!"

"I did. She was the most beautiful girl I'd ever seen. I couldn't believe my luck when she agreed to marry me. We had been dancing for nearly a year before I asked her, and neither of us bargained on her father's conditions."

"What? So, did you never dance again?" said Sharon.

"Well, we did a bit of foxtrot and quickstep at weddings and parties and the like, and we did rumba at a concert once when her Dad wasn't there, but we had to be careful as word would have got back to him. He was a magistrate, and he would have been furious if he knew."

"Is he still alive?" said Bill.

"No, why?" asked Ged.

"'Cause if I were you, I'd have danced on his grave for stoppin' yer doin' somethin' you're this good at. You clearly love it. I'm just keeping up with Sharon, and I'm knackered!"

"Well, I'm going to be creaky in the morning, that's for certain."

The rest of the class went by in a blur for all concerned. Bill sat out the last two, and Sharon took a turn with Ged while Emily took a break. Ged quickly fell into step with Sharon's slower pace and led her sympathetically, giving pointers and calling out the steps to help her. For her first time, she did well and was able to keep up with the tempo of the music.

The last dance was a freestyle. The couples were encouraged to try anything, relax and enjoy themselves. Ged, once again, fell into step with Emily. She could chicken walk and do the drunken sailor, and they practised a few spins, laughed when they got their arms tangled trying a more complicated move and when the music came to an end, everyone stood and clapped each other.

Ron had prepared a fish stew ready for their return to the Lobster Pot, and they all ate in the main restaurant around a table near the kitchen. He joined them, looking rather pale.

"Thanks for stepping in, Ged," he said.

"You're welcome; I really enjoyed myself. Although I think I'm going to know about it in the morning."

"Well, when Ron gets better, you can be Shazzer's partner." Bill chipped in. "I'm not sure I'm ever goin' to get my dancin' legs."

***

Ged's prediction proved right. The following morning, although he had stretched and drunk plenty of water the night before, his legs were awfully stiff. His muscles ached more than he could remember them ever having done before. He grasped the handrail tightly as he very slowly hobbled down the stairs. Each step was agony in the front of his thighs, and his calves felt like they had been turned into saddle leather overnight. He really wanted to go dancing again, but would need to do some serious preparation for the next time. How had it come to him so easily before?

He had no pressing appointments that day and decided a hot bath, some arnica and a few gentle walks would be good. He wanted to do some work on the outside of his workshop, but rain was forecast again, so he pottered in the house, doing a little cleaning and tidying. He had decided that he would practise using his watercolours and pencils if the weather was inclement, so he spread a plastic tablecloth on the large, polished dining table in the main living room and set himself up next to the window seat to make use of the light.

He fetched the kitchen timer and set it to go off in half an hour so that he would remember to stand up and walk about frequently to stop himself from getting too stiff. He found the ticking of the little apple-shaped timer oddly soothing. He had most of his sketches stored in a large shoe box. He took them out of the box and spread them on the table. He had done many more drawings over the winter; several depicted the local fishermen maintaining their boats and nets, some of the houses and shops in the village, a cartoon-like drawing of Bill standing with his bucket of coffee in the doorway of the kitchen at the Seagull café.

He came across a few studies of the herring gulls he had done. They struck him as rather beautiful, clean-looking birds. Each had a definite character. Some were malevolent, others grumpy, and some had a haughty stance; one appeared nervous and jumpy, and another was relaxed and self-assured. One or two of the younger ones were downright funny as they figured out where they stood in the pecking order of the Porthcovery clan. He had studied them so long over a few days that he had begun to recognise individuals, not only from their wing and beak markings but also from their behaviour and habits. Certain birds favoured particular places in the village. The roof of the store behind the gift shop, the roof of the pub; there was a pair who nested in an old car tyre which had been left on a wall behind a brick store house in the yard of the pub.

Ged used these sketch studies as a foundation for that morning's creation. He continued his comical theme from the ponies the previous day. He gave the Gulls exaggerated features, depending on their character and gave each one a name. He sketched 'Bossy Brenda,' jealously guarding the roof of the gift shop, beak open, aggressively defending her territory against all comers, including the cheeky Jackdaws and sparrows. He did one version of Brenda using his watercolour pencils. There was a limit to what he could do with these, especially when it came to blending colours, but they were quick to work with. When his alarm went off, he pushed himself up from his chair, groaning at the difficulty of such a simple move. Then he fetched his watercolour box from the bookcase where he had left it weeks before, made a cup of tea and returned with his mug, a water glass and some rags.

The varying shades of grey of the gull's markings took a few attempts to perfect, but eventually, he was pleased with the effect. He repeated the technique and created four separate rough-sketch watercolours of different gulls, each more comical than the last. He finished with the skinny "Haughty Henry", who had his beak stuck up in the air as he stood beside a very fat gull eating a Cornish pasty. Ged finished off the painting with an added caption: *"The seasoning's all wrong."*

***

357

The phone suddenly trilled into life. It startled Ged as it had been so quiet in the house. He hadn't even turned the radio on that morning for the news.

"Hello?" he said.

"Hi, Ged." It was Emily. "Is there any chance you can do a job for us at the café today? I really don't want Ron doing anything, and the handyman we used to have doing things for us has retired. One of the toilets is out of action, and although the rain is keeping some visitors away, we might get busy if the weather perks up. There are a couple of other things that need doing, but they aren't urgent."

"No Problem, Emily. I'm a bit stiff from the dancing, but I'm sure I can sort it out. Do you know what the problem is with the loo?"

"Well, I'm not sure. The flush isn't flushing. You press the button, and it spits out a bit of water, but that's it."

"Okay, I have an idea what it might be. I'll have my lunch now and come and have a look in about an hour; then, I'll probably have to go to the plumber's merchant for some parts. It should be done in time for the dinner time service if they have the parts. Will that be ok?"

"That would be great. Do you have any plans for dinner?"

"None."

"Then eat here. On the house. For coming so quick."

"Thanks, I'd like that. It would be nice."

***

The job at the Lobster Pot was very straightforward. After he had finished repairing the toilet flush, Emily showed him all the other jobs she needed doing: A new mirror in the ladies' toilet, a new handle for the main door of the café, some guttering and tiles on the roof at the back of the café which had been damaged in a storm and half a dozen other jobs. Ged sat at a table at the back of the café, making notes of each of the jobs, materials he needed, and how long they were likely to take in his notebook. He called builders and plumbers merchants he knew in Helston for prices and worked out the cost of each job for Emily.

"Mug of tea and cake, Mr Baker?" said the waiter.

"Oh, thanks, yes, just put it there for now," he said, gesturing to the other side of the table. Ged looked up briefly and smiled at the waiter. He seemed familiar.

"You're new here, then?"

"I worked here a long time ago, Mr Baker." The man said. Ged stopped in his tracks.

"Mike?" blurted Ged, a questioning inflexion. "Er... Mike..."

"Anderson," finished Mike for him.

"What on earth are you doing here?"

"My new job."

"But that means..." Ged began with a look of concern.

"Yes, my publishing house went under. I was made redundant in January."

"Oh, I'm so sorry, Mike said Ged with feeling. "You said that was likely when we met."

"Mr Baker... Ged. May I call you Ged?" he said, a little uncertain.

"Yes, of course." Ged remembered his manners and stood to shake Mike's hand."

"Are you very busy? It's just that there are no customers, and I was wondering if I could have a few minutes of your time."

"Well, if Emily is ok with that, I'm just pricing these jobs up. I'm almost done. Just waiting for a call from the builder's merchant."

Emily called from the kitchen doorway: "Emily is definitely alrigh' with it. You go ahead, Michael. Shall I bring you a mug of tea?"

"I'll get it. Thanks, Emily. I need to get something from Auntie Dots." Mike replied.

Mike disappeared just as Ged's phone played its merry tune. Ged answered, nodded, said "Right" a few times, and made some notes.

Mike returned ten minutes later with a steaming mug of tea and a slice of fruit cake and sat down. He waited quietly for Ged to finish. He could see that he was reckoning something up and didn't want to disturb him. Ged shut the book and took a big gulp of tea.

"Perfect drinking temperature," he said. "Tell me – what happened? You did mention that your publishing house was in some kind of financial trouble."

"Not much to tell. When I met you, Barker-Mead were on their knees, financially."

"It's odd, but when I think of businesses going under, I'd never have thought many publishers do."

"More often than we would prefer to admit, Ged," said Mike ruefully. "Publishing isn't the glamorous business people imagine. We have to be based in London, which makes it expensive. Success hinges on hunches and gut feel. We just had a bad run of luck."

"Surely, you can get another job in publishing. I mean, you seem to know your stuff."

"I probably could, but to be honest, I didn't want to. I wanted to get out of London altogether for at least a year or so. I thought I would try going freelance as an illustrator's agent. I've come to Cornwall as... well, where else would you find such a wealth of artistic talent?"

The café door opened, its little sprung bell tinkling. Four walkers came in, windswept and more than a little damp. Mike excused himself, rose to his feet and offered them a table. Tourists then came and went all afternoon, so they didn't get a chance to speak for some time. Mike had left two books on the table. Ged flicked through them. They were both written by Jenny Halshaw. Inside the front cover, she had signed them: *To Mike, thanks for helping to bring Pumpkin to life, Love Jenny.'* As Ged had finished his estimates and needed to wait for the café to become quieter to talk to Emily about them, he settled down to read one of the books. It was an illustrated chapter book of around 80 pages about a Ginger cat who had a habit of playing with the wrong things in his owner's house. The book seemed to be aimed at children around Alice's age. There weren't so many words on a page, presumably, thought Ged, to allow kids to feel a sense of achievement at getting through the book reasonably quickly. He read the book from cover to cover in half an hour. He imagined reading it to Alice and Jamie on the sofa. The illustrations were black and white, except for the cover. They had a gentle softness about them that seemed to suit the shy but mischievous character of the cat in the story. 'Why wouldn't Mike simply ask this illustrator to do Jenny's latest book?' he wondered.

Emily came over, at last, to talk to him about the work, going over the jobs and prioritising. Ged had enough time that day to fix a new handle on the front door of the café, re-attach the gutter and slates that had come loose above the back door, and replace a mirror in the ladies. As he worked, Mike, Emily and Ron served customers into the early evening. Ged took his time over the work. His thighs were still sore, and he found himself walking even more awkwardly than Ron had done before his operation.

The last customers ambled out of the café at around eight that evening. Emily flipped over the sign and locked the door with a sigh as Mike cleared the remaining tables.

"Come and join us for dinner, Ged," said Emily. We've got a treat tonight. Ron's got a lot of seafood that we need to eat, so he's made fish stew."

"Sounds lovely, Emily, I'll tidy up here," he called. "I'll be out in a minute."

***

"So, Mike, why did you want to leave London?" asked Ged as they all wiped their bowls clean with chunks of delicious crusty bread. No one had spoken from the moment Ron put the bowls in front of them while Emily poured crisp white wine into their glasses. The food was simply too tasty for conversation.

"Yes, Michael. Why *did* you come down here?" chimed in Ron as he poured more wine into Mike's glass. "Sorry, son, I don't mean to pry, but I 'ave been wonderin'."

Mike looked a little uncertain, but the wine had loosened his tongue.

"I've wanted to get out of London ever since Jane and I split up. Probably before then, really…" His tone became earnest; "I don't see why, if you're in publishing, in these days of mobile phones, you can't be an agent or an editor wherever you feel happiest. I love books, I love art, and I love Cornwall. There's so much talent here. The landscape and the light of the south west seems to bring artistic talent out of people. I'm *glad* Jane and I broke up. I saw her on TV last night,

361

and now I'm away from the city. The things she's asking these celebrities about are so trivial. Being here gives me perspective. I mean all this celeb stuff... It's banal!" he said with passion. The others stared back at him, speechless. "At that film premiere she covered on the news last night, if you combined the talent of the three so-called celebrities she interviewed on the red carpet, you wouldn't get as much talent as you have in your little finger, Ged."

Ged waved a hand dismissively. "Nah, I just doodle on my days off," scoffed Ged.

Mike sighed and glanced at Ron and Emily. They shook their heads. Mike took a swig from his wine glass, put it down carefully, and leaned forward, resting his elbows on the table and clasping his hands in front of him. He looked directly at Ged.

"Look, Ged," I was a curator at two art galleries and an art critic for a popular art magazine. After that, I did a long stint as an art director for a children's publishing house. Are you telling me I don't know talent when I see it? If you don't want to illustrate, Ged, then that's your decision, but please don't waste your talent. I'm glad you moved down here. You seem to fix toilets and taps really well, and I'm sure the gutters will be glad of your attention, but do us all a favour and believe in yourself." Ged didn't know how to respond.

"He's right, Ged," said Emily. "Your drawin's *are really* good. Popular too, they aren't art that you have to *try* an' appreciate, like abstract artists. They have ...life and character..."

"They tell a *story*," said Mike. "That's why I wanted you to illustrate Jenny's book."

"What about this, Alex ...er. King?" asked Ged.

"Retired – Parkinson's disease. Illustrated his last book six months ago."

"Oh, 'ow sad," said Emily, kindly.

"Did he do all Jenny's books?" asked Ged.

"All but one. She did one book with a young chap, but they didn't gel," Mike replied.

"She's picky. – that's why you're strugglin' to get an illustrator, right?" said Emily.

"Well, officially, it's not my problem anymore. Her agent, Suzy, needs to find a new publisher and get a deal, and secondly, I won't be the editor or the art director."

"No, but you're still in touch with Suzy, aren't you?" said Emily, "and as Jenny did you a favour by coming to your talk at the college, surely you could help her out."

"I don't know," said Mike, shrugging his shoulders and draining his wine glass. "It all depends on which publisher she gets a deal with. Most of them have a pool of illustrators that they work with, but Jenny is famous, and yes, she is really picky with her illustrations. With her profile, she can probably have more artistic control. Suzy told me there are three or four publishers almost driving a wagonload of money to her door, but she doesn't seem interested in any of them. So, Suzy's looking for a small independent that, ideally, isn't going bust. We always tried to make sure she was happy at Barker-Mead. We got more out of our authors if we gave them a product they were happy with… "Maybe that's why we weren't so good at making a profit. We didn't chase the commercial angle enough, but then, we didn't need to with Jenny. Her books sold themselves. We had queues of kids and their parents camping out on the pavement at her last launch."

After one glass of wine, Ged began to feel sleepy. He knew he had to drive back, so he asked Ron if he could have a coffee before he went home. The coffee did sharpen his senses. He packed the last of his tools in the Honda, bid the others goodnight and headed home, promising to return to complete the remaining jobs over the next few days.

Ged worked at the Lobster Pot for another day. He finished Emily's list of jobs by mid-afternoon on the second day, but Ron had thought of a few more for the following week. Ged's legs were feeling even stiffer, and he was looking forward to having a long soak in the bath. Ron helped him load his tools into the car and gave him an envelope with cash for the work he had done.

"Thanks, Ged," he said in his usual, quiet voice.

"My pleasure, Ron. It's been a joy working here, but you know if you give me too much work, I'll have to go on a diet!"

"Oh yeah, thanks for the work and all, but I didn't mean that. I meant for taking Emily dancin' Monday evenin' there's no way I could. Will you be alrigh' ter take 'er next week?"

"Oh, you're welcome, mate. Certainly, well, that's if I can get these legs loosened up, I'll take it easier next time. I mean, my feet know what to do, but I think my legs have forgotten how much effort it takes."

"Well, I really 'precicate it, anyhow," he said, offering a hand. Ged shook it warmly.

"How's the – y'know, recovery going?" asked Ged.

"Oh, not bad, I s'pose. 'Have you got a sec? There's summat' I wan' ter show yer."

"Yeah, I'm all done here."

Ron led Ged around to a small lean-to outhouse at the back of the café. Ged had assumed it was a food store when he was repairing the guttering on it, but when Ron opened the door, he had an ah-hah moment. Ron turned on the light to reveal a brightly lit room with white-washed stone walls. In the centre of the room was a heavily built, narrow wooden table. Strewn about the table were sketches and paintings in various stages of being mounted and framed. There was a large, green cutting board at one end of the table.

"So, this is where you turn doodles into art, eh?" said Ged with a wink.

"Yeah, this is where the magic 'appens," replied Ron, grinning.

Ron took Ged briefly through each stage of the mounting and framing process, showing him how he achieved the angled edge on the inside of the mount with the special mount cutter.

"I got a bit 'o time next week. I'll show yer how it's done, an' maybe you can give me a hand with this lot if you like… One of our regular artists is a teacher at the college an' asked me to frame some of the artwork for their reception area an, I got a bit behind with it.

"I'd love to have a go, Ron," said Ged, eyes wide with interest. One of his favourite parts about the maintenance job at the car factory was learning how to use new tools.

***

Back at Chy Gwyn, he unloaded his tools from the car, put them in a wheelbarrow and wheeled them to the workshop. As he put his key in the front door, Sharon walked up the driveway with a parcel.

"This came, special delivery," she said. "It's from Denmark... Look at the postmark."

"That was quick," said Ged.

"From Greta," said Sharon. "It's her story, I know it is."

"Thanks, Sharon," said Ged, "I'd invite you in for a cuppa, but my legs are killing me from the dancing, and I'm going to get a hot bath."

Sharon chuckled... "Yeah, can't you smell the muscle rub on me? My legs are murder as well. I 'ave to get back to the café. We're really busy."

She dashed back up the road, and Ged finally got into the house, glad to be home at last.

39

Greta's book was in Danish, but Rita had handwritten a translation on lined paper. The story went that Pete the pirate had been the unluckiest fisherman in the harbour, and the other fishermen teased him for his awful catches. His luck changed when he met a talking seal who told him of some rum smugglers who were looking for crab fishermen to help them, sneaking strong rum ashore to avoid the customs men.

Unfortunately for Pete, the local fishermen to whom he was hoping to sell the rum didn't like it and preferred drinking beer, so he couldn't sell it to anyone. This meant that he had bottles of Rum in his crab pots instead of crabs, which made his catch even worse than before. His old friend, the seal, took pity on him and told him of a farm that was famous for their rum and raisin ice cream. He sold the remaining rum to them for less than he had bought it and got a job on the farm, cleaning the cowshed floor every day. It was a tough job, but his fortunes changed when he fell in love with the ice cream farmer's daughter, learned to make rum and raisin ice cream, and with his stocks in the crab pots at the bottom of the sea, they had enough rum to last the rest of their lives.

Rita provided her phone number in case Ged wanted to call and talk about anything.

She added a footnote to say that, as the story was meant to be funny, could his drawings reflect the humour? – Perhaps something got lost in the translation, Ged thought.

Greta had left a gap in the text where she wanted an illustration, and Rita had lightly pencilled a brief note if Greta wanted it to show something in particular and wrote *'your choice'* if she wanted Ged to come up with an appropriate illustration. As Ged had requested, Greta had sent a photocopy of the original drawing she had of Pete. He had only done two drawings of Pete, and he thought this one was infinitely better than the one in the café. Pete looked shiftier, his muscles more defined. Ged put the story and drawings on the bathroom stool next to the bath, lay back in the warm tub and closed his eyes to think.

***

Ged woke, shivering in a tepid bath. He emptied some water out and turned on the hot tap. Once thawed out, he dried, dressed and went downstairs for a cup of tea.

He re-read Greta's story translation and fetched his unicorn backpack, determined not to put off doing the drawings. He felt that if he put it off once, it would be all too easy to procrastinate, and he would never get it done. A promise was a promise, after all.

He read through Rita's illustration notes and created scenes which matched her basic instructions. The first note required an image of two or three crabs and a bit of seaweed in the bottom of a crab pot. Ged did this, adding the detail of all the crabs being females with small claws to further the lucklessness of poor old Pete – in his sketch, one crab had lost a claw altogether. The next instruction was to depict the other fishermen laughing at his catch. Ged realised he may have to draw them again, so he made sure they had memorable and humorous features: a large bulbous nose and dungarees on one, a bushy beard and ponytail on another and the third fisherman was tall and skinny with glasses and a striped bobble hat, rather like a grown-up version of Wally from Jamie's *'Where's Wally'* spotting books. Then, Greta wanted an image of the seal talking to Pete. Ged struggled with the proportions of the seal's head and the placement of its eye. He felt that the seal should at least have similar proportions to a real seal. He went to the bookcase in the living room to see if he could find a book that contained a picture of a seal. He found a leaflet advertising the Cornish seal sanctuary.

Ged got quite carried away with developing the pirate seal. He filled three pages of his sketchbook with light sketches of the different seals in the leaflet, seeing which ones he found easy to replicate and how he could create more of a cartoon-style caricature. He settled for giving the seal a scar over his eye and a shifty look. He chuckled to himself as the character of the pirate seal took shape.

367

Ged made another cup of tea and cooked a speedy dinner of scrambled eggs on toast. He didn't want to stop long as he felt like he was on a roll. He took the tea and a glass of Jura on ice back to the table and got back to sketching. He hummed a little made-up sea shanty as he drew.

He drew Pete's dreadlocks longer, thicker and more unkempt in each subsequent sketch. Throughout the story, Ged decided to make his stubbly chin grow into a wispy beard. He wore a red three-point scarf around his neck, and his jeans became more and more ripped to accentuate his increasing poverty. He was, however, always the best-looking of all the characters in the story, with muscular arms and legs and a twinkle in his eye.

When Ged finished his seventh illustration, he checked his watch; it was half past midnight! He really must set an alarm to stop himself from working so late. He left all of the drawings and the story on the living room table and padded off to bed.

***

The stiffness in Ged's legs had lessened slightly the following morning, although he still felt the need to hold on to the bannister rail as he hobbled stiffly down the stairs. He took his tea and two rounds of toast and marmalade to the table and got straight to work.

Outside, the rain poured down in torrents so great that the water washing down the windows was a shimmering silken fabric; the step dark clouds blocked out most of the sunlight, dulling the room, so that even though it was still morning, it felt more like late evening. Ged switched the light on over the table and laid the pictures and pages out in order, marking each drawing with a number corresponding to the page of the photocopied manuscript. He took the kitchen timer and set it for an hour each time he began to draw to make sure he remembered to get up and walk about or get a drink.

***

Three days, two sketch pads and two pencils later, he had created all the drawings plus many, many more. The only thing left to do was to recreate an image of his original Pete the Pirate sketch as a possible cover image for the book. He wanted to get this done in colour, but not too much. Pete's features needed to stand out. The painting classes with Caroline had given him enough skills to apply a background wash and bring splashes of colour to the original scene he had drawn the summer before. Pete's now familiar red and white striped t-shirt was a recurring theme, and he placed another tiny pink lobster on the gunwale of the boat at the stern. It was late in the evening. Ged left his finished watercolour to dry and picked up the phone. He had no idea if the drawings he had done would be suitable. There was only one sensible way to really find out...

Ron answered the phone at the Lobster Pot. Mike was serving customers, so Ron took a message asking him to call back.

***

The following morning, the sun finally broke through the clouds. Ged went for a long walk along the coast path. As he walked up the road, he realised that his leg muscles had finally started to feel normal. He dropped in at the Seagull café on his way home, as he hadn't seen Bill and Sharon since the dance class.

The café was packed with early spring tourists enjoying the first shy rays of sunshine in a few days. Sharon flitted from table to table, charming and serving customers. Bill was, of course, in the kitchen. He came to the doorway to greet Ged but was soon bustled back in by his turbo-charged wife with another fistful of orders for early lunches and late breakfasts.

Ged had brought a book to read. A favourite Terry Pratchett novel that he had read before, which always made him laugh. The characters leapt off the pages and ran around in Ged's head. He was so engrossed that he didn't notice a shadow cast over his coffee cup.

"Mind if we join you?" It was Mike. He had arrived with a woman Ged didn't recognise. "There are no tables free. Can we share?" Ged grinned at him, stood up and shook Mike's hand, smiling broadly.

Mike introduced the woman he had arrived with. "This is Suzy; she's Jenny Halshaw's agent."

"Nice to meet you, Suzy," Ged smiled and shook her hand, then Suzy sat down.

"I begged Mike ter bring me ter meet yer," she said in her distinctive Mancunian accent. "I'm a big fan!"

"You are?" said Ged, incredulously.

"Oh, yeah, absolutleh," Suzy replied "I love yer illustrations. I bought two o' them ones o' the tabby cat for mi kitchen. They remind me o' mi old cat, Busby."

"Well, I should say thank you, then," said Ged.

"I hope you don't mind me coming over instead of calling," said Mike. "I've been dying to bring Suzy to Porthcovery, and this is the first excuse I've had."

"Not at all," said Ged. "We couldn't have discussed what I wanted to on the phone, so it's probably just as well you're here in person."

"Okay, I'm all ears… what is it you wanted to discuss?"

Ged paused a moment and took a deep breath. "I have a confession to make…" he began. "I know I told you that I didn't want to be an illustrator, but…"

"But you've changed your mind, right?" said Suzy eagerly.

"Well, I'm not sure… I – well, I made an accidental start."

"Accidental…?" said Mike, a quizzical frown shadowing his forehead.

"I met a lady from Denmark last summer whilst I was drawing. It was here at the Seagull, actually. Her daughter won a writing competition recently, and the prize was to get her book published. She wrote the book because of that sketch I did of Pirate Pete, and she asked if I would do some illustrations for her book. Well, to get to the point… I gave it a go."

"Okay, so what's the problem?" asked Mike.

"Well, I don't know if they are any good," replied Ged. Mike and Suzy exchanged glances and raised an eyebrow each.

"Do you have the sketches with you?" said Mike.

"No, they're at my house up the road. I could go and get them, but it is a bit windy, we could have lunch, and you can come to the house.

I would offer you lunch there, but I hadn't planned for guests, and unless you want to share a small can of baked beans, one egg, a slice of ham and two slices of bread, I think lunch here would be better."

"Ok. What's good fer lunch 'ere?" Said Suzy.

"Bill's crab or club sandwiches are my personal favourite, but anything he cooks is great. Save some room in your cake stomach, though; Sharon makes the best carrot cake I've ever tasted. Even Hilary Scott from Radio 4 asked her for the recipe!"

"Well, if it's good enough for Hilary," said Mike, patting his stomach and grinning. "It's more than good enough for me; I'm starving!"

**

Back at Chy Gwyn, Mike and Suzy silently read the translation of Greta's story and then looked over Ged's illustrations, shuffling the pages around, quickly figuring out his numbering system and how each drawing fitted with the story. Suzy asked for a pair of scissors. She cut up the story and relevant illustrations, then laid the paragraphs and drawings out in order on the table and then sat quietly, holding a pencil to her lips. Ged felt as though he wasn't contributing a great deal and went into the kitchen to make some tea.

"Okay, I think we're getting somewhere… What do you think, Mike?" said Suzy, finally standing up close to him, her hand on his shoulder.

"I think," said Mike, in a low voice, leaning towards Suzy, "that Greta is a very lucky girl, and Jenny Halshaw is missing out on being the author for Ged Baker's illustrating debut."

"As it's Denmark," said Suzy in a low, conspiratorial tone, her face close to his, "we *could* keep it quiet and not mention it when we make a splash wi' Jenny's book. There's a bit of work to do 'ere an' there an' a little polishin' of the details, but what I think we 'ave 'ere is what you'd call a '*natural*'." She chuckled in her excitement. "You were right, Mike; Ged's a bloody genius!" She put her arm around Mike's shoulders and kissed him on the cheek. They looked at each other for a few moments, then Mike took Suzy's face in both his hands and kissed her fully on the lips; she wrapped her arms around him and kissed him back, but properly this time.

Ged returned to the living room to find Suzy and Mike in a deep embrace. The mugs on the tray clinked together as he stopped in his tracks. He politely cleared his throat.

"Sorry, I'll come back later; I can see I'm interrupting something," he said.

Mike and Suzy broke their embrace and stood back, holding each other's hands and each other's gaze. Without looking at Ged, Mike replied, "Only something I should have done a long time ago," said Mike, shaking his head.

"I… I thought it would never 'appen," said Suzy, uncertainly, as she gazed into Mike's face, cheeks flushed, a smile playing at the corners of her lips.

"Same here," said Mike. He couldn't stop a grin from spreading across his face. There was an awkward silence.

"Tea?" asked Ged to break the awkwardness.

"Thanks, Ged," said Mike, letting out a satisfied sigh.

"Oh, you're welcome," said Ged, handing him his mug of Tea.

"No, not for the tea…for…that."

"Eh?"

Suzy turned to face Ged. "I think what Mike means," she said, "is that, because of *you*, Mike has rediscovered his Mojo. Because of *you*, I've come to Cornwall three times in the last month and… because of *you*," here she glanced at Mike, "we have finally… finally… done what we should have done years ago." She took two steps over to Ged and kissed him on the cheek. "Thank you," she said.

"Oh. *That.*"

40

It was eight months after Suzy and Mike's visit with Ged at Chy Gwyn. Ged was in a large branch of Billingtons Bookstore in the heart of London at five o'clock in the afternoon with a severe case of writer's cramp, having completely forgotten the meaning of his own name. The effect of signing your name five hundred times in a row is that it seems to lose its meaning. (Though it had lost its meaning after about twenty.) He just scribbled his name-or a rough version of it-on autopilot as Jenny Halshaw passed him the books. She chatted briefly with fans as they asked her questions: What will she be writing next? Will there be more Pumpkin or Tiger books? Would they be made into a TV programme or a film? If Tiger was on TV, who did she think would do his voice?.. And so on.

The children also spoke to Ged, asking questions like: 'How did he get into illustrating? What should they do if they want to be an illustrator? How long had he been drawing cats? Was he Jenny's boyfriend?' He had never done anything remotely like this in his life, and it was entirely alien to him. By the end of the day, he was utterly exhausted.

***

Jenny had visited Ged in Porthcovery several times over the early summer before the tourist season really got underway, when he had to move out to make way for paying guests. Essentially, these were supposed to be working visits, but Jenny had worn down her hiking boots a little more on the coast path and had grown to love her visits to discuss the illustrations for her next book: *Tiger in Trouble'*. She would time her visits so that they could enjoy a walk before having afternoon tea at the Seagull Café. Then she and Ged would spend an hour or two at Chy Gwyn, going over Ged's sketches of *Tiger'* who bore a striking resemblance to Val's old cat Potts who, miraculously, still patrolled the café and had quickly wormed his way into Jenny's affections, as he sunned himself on Val's garden wall in full view of the café terrace.

***

"Is that it?" Ged finally said, rubbing his wrist. The bookstore staff ushered the last few remaining customers from the shop, locked the doors and pulled down the shutters.

"Until tomorrow," said Jenny kindly, putting a hand on his shoulder. "We've got another book signing in Manchester and an interview on BBC Radio Four. This is the most tiring part of being an author. I love talking to Tiger's fans, but I find it really tough if I'm honest. It's why I live where I do. In a week, it will be all over. Then it'll be on to the next project."

"That's a good point, Jenny. Where *do* you live? We meet up at The Lobster Pot and Chy Gwyn, but I've never come to your place."

"I'll only tell you if you promise to keep it a secret," whispered Jenny, looking around to check she wouldn't be overheard.

"Mum's the word," said Ged, leaning closer.

Jenny wrote down her address on a slip of paper and handed it to Ged, who took a brief look, raised his eyebrows in surprise, and then stowed it away in his top pocket.

Suzy and Mike joined them for dinner. They went over the itinerary for the next few days. Ged had never been interviewed for anything since the car factory job interview thirty years ago. Being interviewed for a radio programme, let alone a national one, filled him with dread. The train journey up to Manchester went better than he expected. Jenny had a new idea for a story and was planning it out in her notebook. She shared the concept with Ged, and they chatted about how they could bring it to life. Ged had brought his sketching things with him.

"Ah, so this is the famous Unicorn backpack," said Suzy as he unzipped his bag.

"Never leave home without it," replied Ged as he pulled out his pad and a sharp pencil.

"Don't you get teased about it?" she asked.

"I did, but I'm far too long-in-the-tooth to let it bother me. It's kind of become my mascot; it would be strange not to have it. It's the perfect size for all my sketching and art things. I'd be lost without it."

***

The radio programme interview with Kathryn Plummer went very well indeed. Kathryn asked Jenny most of the questions. Jenny was engaging and effusive with Kathryn; they had good chemistry and had clearly met several times before. Jenny read a passage from the book. Then Kathryn introduced Ged.

"We also have in the studio the illustrator of Jenny's book, Ged Baker. Welcome to the programme, Ged."

"Um. Thanks. It's nice to be here," he lied.

"So, Ged, how did you come up with the character of Tiger?" Ged was totally honest.

"I drew him long before I knew of Tiger, actually. There's an old tabby cat who lives in a cottage near a café where I was sketching in the summer. He's a real character in the village, and everybody knows him. He's always up to mischief, and he thinks he's the king of the village, so, when I read Jenny's story, old Potts, um...which is the cat in my village, sounded just like Tiger and, well, the two cats became one."

"Okay," said Kathryn, "so would you say you are a cat person, Ged?"

"Well, if you had asked me that a year ago, I would have said no, but whenever I see them, I can't help drawing them. I find them fascinating and funny animals. They do such bizarre things. I once drew a cat hunting an empty crisp packet!"

Kathryn gave Ged a thumbs up as her producer made a winding-up signal with her hands and counted the seconds down. "Well, thanks to Ged Baker and Jenny Halshaw. Author and illustrator of the latest in

Jenny's series of early reader novels, *'Tiger the Troublesome Tabby'*. I'm sure my kids will love it."

Ged removed his headphones and breathed a sigh of relief. Mike and Suzy met him at the door of the studio.

"Can you both come to the foyer? There are quite a few people at the radio station who want a signed copy, and it's rare that we get the author and illustrator together, so it's a great publicity opportunity." Ged and Jenny obediently followed their agents to the foyer and sat behind a table that had been hastily placed there. A sizeable queue of people were waiting with books in their hands, waiting for them to be signed. A few members of the public had heard that Jenny would be there and wanted to get her autograph on a book or buy a signed copy. Suzy made sure that there were plenty of copies available wherever they went, and she had a thick cash purse and a credit card machine to facilitate proceedings.

Ged really didn't fancy going to the big bookshop in the centre of Manchester, but he had signed up for it, and it was the last appointment of the day. The queue outside the shop was immense, and his wrist began to ache after only half an hour of book signing. Jenny showed him a trick during a coffee break; she had figured out a way to sign with her left hand. Ged practised a few times with his left hand and managed a barely legible 'G Baker', but at least it would mean that if his hand got too tired, it was a possible solution.

One child had brought some drawings to show Ged, as well as the book to sign. She had copied his drawing of Tiger under an ironing basket. She had done a pretty good job, too.

"That's absolutely brilliant!" said Ged. "How old are you?"

"Nine," said the girl shyly.

"Well, it looks like you'll soon put me out of a job. Do you draw other things, too?"

"Sometimes horses, but cats are my favourite. How can I get into drawing other things, Mr Baker?"

"Erm, well, I suppose, just sit down somewhere comfortable next time you're out and about and just look around you. See what catches your eye."

"Will you sign my drawing?"

"Hmm. You sign it first. Here's a pen, yes, that's it, then I'll write something by it and sign my name, agreed?"

The girl signed her name, "Carol Langton", and Ged wrote a short message next to her signature. *This is a lovely drawing, Carol; keep your eyes open and a pencil handy wherever you go; best wishes, Ged Baker.'* The girl skipped off to her father and showed him the drawing.

It was a long four days of travelling, signing, smiling and trying to stay chirpy. Jenny and Ged were exhausted by the end. They finished off in London at another bookseller late on Thursday evening. Afterwards, Ged drove over to Sarah and Brian's House. He had invited Mike, Jenny and Suzy to eat at Brian's restaurant the following evening, where they planned to celebrate the end of their first promotion week. Ged was glad to see the grandchildren, although he was conscious that he wasn't much of a fun grandad as he was so tired. He gave each of the children a signed copy of Jenny's book, and after dinner, he curled up on the sofa with them and read it to them as a bedtime story. Alice and Jamie were excited to see their Grandad's name on the front of the book and his pictures of old Potts as the illustrations, and couldn't wait to take their copies to school to show their teachers and friends.

"Are you going to do another one, Grandad?" asked Jamie.

"It certainly looks like it, Jamie. We were talking on the train going to and from Manchester about another book that Jenny has planned."

"What is it about Grandad? Is it another one about Tiger?" asked Alice.

"Actually, Alice. I have to keep it a secret. Even the publishers don't know yet, so I can't say, but as soon as I can. I promise I'll tell you."

The children were terribly frustrated that he couldn't tell them about the next book. That would be something to really show off about at school.

***

"Dad. Do you have a mobile phone number for Mike?" called Sarah after the children had gone to school the following morning.

"Yes, Sarah, why?"

"I've got Emily on the phone. She needs to get in touch with him urgently."

"Oh. Okay, hang on, love." Ged got Mike's business card out of his wallet and went to the phone.

"Hi Emily, It's Ged. Everything ok?

"Hi, Ged. No, it's awful… Ron's been taken ill—Ee's in 'ospital in Truro. I'm going to have to close the café… unless Mike can come back," she said. She sounded nasal from crying.

"Okay, Emily. I'm due to see him in an hour, where they are staying. I'll go early and give him a message that you called. Do you have his mobile number?"

Emily read out the number she had for Mike, and it was correct, but she said that she kept getting an answering machine. Ged tried to reassure her, but it was clear that there wasn't much he could do from London. He needed to get to Mike.

***

Ged went immediately to the hotel where Jenny was staying. Mike was staying in Suzy's flat in London and hadn't arrived, but Jenny was able to call Suzy and speak to her just before they set off for the meeting. By the time Suzy and Mike arrived, they had sketched out a rough plan. Suzy and Jenny would do the remaining promotional appointments with Ged. Mike would go back to Cornwall immediately. It would make things tricky, though, as Mike had travelled with Suzy and didn't have his car.

Ged offered to drive Mike back to Cornwall and help at the café unless his presence was absolutely necessary at the promotions. Mike and Suzy agreed that it wasn't vital for Ged to attend, but it would have been preferable.

Four hours later, after a hasty and apologetic departure from Sarah and Brian's house, he and Mike were crossing the River Tamar in Ged's trusty Honda estate. He left a letter for Alice and Jamie, each with an explanation about Ron and a promise to return as soon as he could.

Mike knew how to cook in Ron's kitchen and could manage most of the dishes on the menu. He chatted to Ged on the way about what they could do between them. Ged would act as commis' chef and learn to wait tables and work the coffee machine – after all, how hard could it be? They called Chris, the young local waiter. Emily had called his mother, so he knew about Ron. He had roped in Sam, a friend of his who sometimes helped out on a Saturday.

**

When they reached Porthleven, it was almost three in the afternoon. Emily prepared cakes and pastries and bought all the fresh food for the weekend. Another fish delivery would be arriving soon. She looked pale, red-eyed and flustered.

"I'm going to Truro in an hour. Thanks for offerin' to help out, Ged; I can't tell you how grateful I am that you both came. I really thought I was goin' to 'ave to close the café.

"Are you sure you are ok to drive, Emily?" asked Ged. "If Chris and Nick are coming to wait on tonight, I could take you to Truro Hospital. I've been there before."

"Let's see how we get on with the preparation for tonight. I might just take you up on that. I've a splitting 'ead, and I 'ates drivin'. I 'aven't been to Truro 'ospital in years," she said.

Mike was efficient and capable in Ron's small kitchen. He instructed Ged on how he wanted him to prepare vegetables for a bouillabaisse and other dishes; then, he stacked plates into a warming oven ready for the evening. Whilst Ged washed the items they had used and mopped the kitchen floor, Mike checked the booking diary with Emily. Between the three of them, they rearranged and laid up tables for that evening's first four bookings. Ged inflated some birthday balloons with a helium tank and tied ribbons to them for the birthday party table. Emily and Mike agreed on which dishes to put on the specials board and what to take off. With Ron away, they needed to keep it simple, opting for Bouillabaisse, mussels and a vegetarian lasagne that Ron had made the previous day. They were ready for the evening when Chris and his friend Sam arrived.

The two teens were equally as proficient in the restaurant as Mike was in the kitchen. They made sure the coffee machine was full of coffee beans and counted the float with Emily.

Emily was less nervous than she expected about leaving her beloved restaurant in the hands of Mike, Chris and Nick. On balance, it would have been worse having a rookie like Ged serving on a Friday evening, so she was glad that he was driving her to Truro.

On the way to the hospital, she described what had happened that morning. Ron had woken up with a terrible stomach ache and a raging temperature. He was in too much pain to go to the doctor. His GP had decided to send a paramedic, who immediately called for an ambulance.

"He was speaking in riddles and making no sense." She said. "He'd start a sentence and then trail off, forgetting what he'd said. The paramedic thought he might 'ave a urinary infection, but she said she was concerned about 'is stomach as well. Since ten thirty this morning, I've 'ad no word of Ron. I phoned the 'ospital three times during the day to find out more. All they said was that he'd arrived safely, 'bin sedated to manage the pain and was undergoin' tests."

Ged didn't speculate what might be happening, but it didn't sound good. He tried to help Emily remain positive. They drove in silence for a few miles. Ged decided to change the subject.

"I didn't know Mike was a chef as well as a waiter," he said, conversationally.

"Well, all those years working for Ron and me, Michael made himself useful wherever 'ee was needed. We could always trust 'im; 'e could turn 'is 'and to just about anythin'. O' course, he won't 'ave the speed o' Ron and a few of the dishes 'ave been scratched off the board. I just hope he doesn't get any stroppy customers tonight. You know how some people get to expect things, and when we don't 'ave them, well, some of 'em can be a bit awkward, like."

"A bit like a production manager in a car factory, really... You've been fixing the press for ten years, and then one day, you tell them you can't magic a Japanese part for a two-million-pound press out of thin air, and they get all sniffy with you."

***

380

Emily asked the receptionist at the hospital for directions to the ward number she had been told Ron was in. Ged went with her, following blue lines taped to the floor. When they arrived, Ron was lying in his hospital bed, slightly propped up on pillows, staring straight ahead blankly. He had a drip, and several machines were beeping. Emily went to Ron's side and held his hand. He slowly turned his head to look at her and smiled weakly.

"Hello, my love," said Emily.

"Hi," he replied in a near whisper.

"'Ow's the pain?" ventured Emily.

"Oh... not too bad, I s'pose." He replied. "Better tomorrow, so they tell me."

"What's happening tomorrow?"

"More flowers," said Ron. Emily glanced at Ged and shrugged.

"Shall I see if there's anyone who knows what's going on with him?" offered Ged.

"Oh, would you, Ged, Luvvy?" I don' think ee does."

Ged and Emily chatted to Ron about the Lobster Pot and how it was in good hands with Mike, Chris and Sam that evening. Ron seemed to understand one minute, and then he would say something about flowers or cars that made no sense. He seemed to be struggling to find the right words for most things. He asked Emily to pass the frame. She looked around for something that he might be referring to. Ged watched his eyes as he asked again. His eyes went to the table over his bed, which only had a few pieces of paper and a plastic cup of water with a straw in it. Ron pursed his lips as he asked for the frame again.

"Try giving him the glass of water. I think whatever is wrong is affecting his ability to find the right words. I've seen this before when my mum had a urinary infection.

Emily reached over and took the cup. She looked at Ron questioningly, and he nodded, reaching his hand out.

"Blimey, well done, Ged. I'd never 'ave guessed that.

The doctor came on his rounds and spoke briefly to Ron, checking his temperature and pulse, and then she spoke directly to Emily.

"You are Mrs Leather, I trust?"

"Yes, Doctor. Can you tell me what's goin' on?"

"Okay, well, a couple of things, actually. Your husband has quite a bad urinary infection. You may have noticed some difficulties with cognition and language. That's entirely normal in these situations. He is on strong antibiotics. We will only know if they're helping by tomorrow morning. Ideally, we would wait, but we are also concerned about a mass in his stomach. Once the antibiotics have taken effect, we would like to do a biopsy. If the antibiotics are having an effect, we will do that tomorrow afternoon. You are welcome to visit tomorrow, but it is likely that Mr Leather will be very heavily sedated as we will do the biopsy under general anaesthetic."

"Oh, okay, so am I best not to come tomorrow?"

"It's entirely up to you, Mrs Leather, but I gather you have to come quite a distance."

"Yes, we're on the Lizard."

"Well, of course, you are welcome to come, but I don't think you'll get much out of him tomorrow evening."

"Can someone call me, or is there a number I can call to find out 'ow he is?"

"I will ask my secretary to call you tomorrow evening when we have more information, but if you wish to get in touch, her number is on this card," he said, handing her a plain business card.

***

Ged went over every day to help out at the Lobster Pot, even if there didn't seem to be anything he needed to do. He wanted to keep an eye on Emily and would find little mending jobs to pass the time. He fixed the door of the walk-in refrigerator. Emily and Ron had to lift the door every time they wanted to open or close it and had learned to put up with it. After it was fixed, Emily kept making excuses to open the door and shut it again just to feel the easy click of the latch. Each time she would say, "I can't believe we've been puttin' up with it all that time, an' it only took you fifteen minutes to sort it."

"It's easy when you know how this kind of thing is put together. You might save a bit on electricity with that fixed, too, as the seal on it may not have been perfectly sound," said Ged as he worked on the gas burners on the big stainless steel gas stove, decarbonising them. When he had finished with the massive hob, it gleamed!

He was paid with delicious lunches, pots of tea, cups of frothy coffee and as much cake as he could manage. Sometimes, when there was not much to do, he would sit at the window and sketch the comings and goings of the busy little harbour village. Late in the afternoon, he helped Emily and Mike to get ready for opening time, preparing vegetables for that evening's stew, curry or soup, laying up tables, cleaning floors, ensuring there was water and a fresh flower in each of the little vases on the tables or filling salt, pepper or vinegar pots. He found the work varied and satisfying. He was impressed by both Emily and Mike taking the complexity of running a restaurant largely in their stride. Neither of them got flustered, and there was a place for everything, so very little was mislaid.

Each afternoon, Ged drove Emily to Truro Hospital. Ron had responded to the antibiotics; a biopsy of the mass in his stomach was taken, but he was in intensive care. The infection had affected his heart, and his body was struggling to cope.

Emily was taken completely by surprise at the alien-ness of the intensive care unit with its machines, tubes and wires, hissing, clicking, and beeping. She rarely wanted to stay very long, but couldn't bear not going and visiting Ron.

Ged encouraged her to talk to Ron as though he were awake. He had heard that people in comas often can hear what is going on in the room, so Emily would tell him which dishes Mike was doing for specials, which paintings and pictures had been sold that day, stories and anecdotes of interesting customers and any gossip she had heard in the village, which Ron had always been keen to hear. She stroked Ron's hair, kissed him on the lips, and whispered. "I love you, my lovely man," before leaving with Ged, a fresh tissue grasped in her fist, ready for the gentle stream that would come once she got in the car for the journey home.

The doctors and Ron's two ICU nurses were kind and attentive, but Ged got the distinct impression that they didn't hold out much hope for Ron's recovery. Time would tell, they said, whenever Emily asked about Ron's progress.

**

This visiting arrangement worked well for around two weeks; then, one Tuesday evening, just after Ged, Mike, and Emily had finished their usual late dinner in the back of the restaurant, the phone rang. Mike answered. A grave expression shadowed his normally relaxed features. He called Emily to the phone.

"It's for you...." He took a breath. "It's the hospital." Ged's heart sank into his boots.

Emily picked up the receiver with a shaking hand, giving Mike a look of pleading blended with abject fear.

"H-hello... Emily Leather here," she said as steadily as she could manage. "No," a sharp and shuddering intake of breath... "No, no, no." she sobbed. "When?.... Should I, should I come?.... Oh..." she trailed off and then dropped the receiver. Her legs buckled. Mike managed to catch her as the receiver clattered to the floor. Ged went to help.

"Will you talk to the hospital, please, Ged," he said. Ged picked up the receiver.

"Hello? Are you still there? Yes, understandably, she's not taken the news at all well."

"Post mortem? Oh, I see, so it will be a while before we can make arrangements. Yes, I understand. Can you keep his effects until then? Oh, yes... I suppose he was taken in urgently. So, he has no personal items except for his clothes? We will arrange for them to be collected. Yes, okay, and thank you."

Mike supported Emily and took her upstairs. Ged made a pot of tea and poured Emily a large sherry, taking them both into the small parlour sitting room above the café. Emily sat on the sofa with her head in her hands, rocking backwards and forwards, unable to say anything except "No, no, no.... Not my Ron. Not now."

Mike sat beside her, his arm around her shoulders. Ged laid the tea tray on the table, and Emily looked up at him. Her tear-stained face had aged her ten years in just a few minutes. Her grief was palpable. He sat on the sofa on her other side, put his hand on hers and handed her first a fresh tissue and then the glass of sherry.

"Here, have some of this. It might help you sleep a little." She took the glass silently and sipped it.

***

Over the next few weeks, Ged helped Emily to make funeral arrangements for Ron. Mike kept the café ticking over. On the day of the funeral, the local Church was packed with people from all over The Lizard. The café was closed, and a local community hall hosted the funeral reception and wake. Over a hundred people came to pay their respects. Flowers kept arriving at the café with messages of gratitude and love.

After the funeral, Ged suggested that she might take some time off, perhaps visit her cousin up-country, or get away for a little while, but she didn't want to leave the café. She went into a kind of numb autopilot mode. She served, prepared food, took orders efficiently as always, and was polite with the customers, but Mike and Ged both agreed she had lost her passion.

On many afternoons, at quiet times when there were no customers around, Mike, Chris, or Ged would find her sitting at a table in the café with a cold cup of coffee in front of her, staring into space, twirling her wedding and engagement rings absent-mindedly. On other days, she cried herself to exhaustion and simply didn't have the energy to come downstairs for the lunchtime shift. They would find her fast asleep on the sofa in the parlour, holding her favourite framed photo of a very young Ron and herself raising a glass at the door to the café. The picture had been taken on the day they opened the Lobster Pot; they were both grinning from ear to ear. Ron wasn't looking at the camera but at Emily, an expression of absolute adoration on his face.

Mike kept things going, and on most weekends, Suzy would join him, working in the café. She turned out to be a wonder with the barista coffee machine, teaching herself to create patterns in the frothed milk, which the customers loved. She had always baked as a teenager and began baking cakes early in the morning to serve in the café, which took the pressure off Emily and meant that they didn't have to buy them in. Auntie Dot had returned from Australia a month before Ron's death. She got up early and baked with Suzy on Saturdays in her tiny kitchen. She taught her to bake deliciously light Cornish buttermilk scones, as she had once done for Emily years before.

Auntie Dot often took Emily out for short walks along the coast. They had been friends for decades. Emily seemed to be able to face the evening serving a little better when she had been out for one of Auntie Dot's walks, but a light had gone from her eyes.

***

Artists sometimes came to the Lobster Pot with their work; some were regular exhibitors. Ged had spent several days with Ron when it was too wet to do some of his planned jobs outside, learning to mount and frame artwork. He found it fiddly at first, scrapping several mounts initially, but soon got the hang of creating the neat internal corners. It took a week or two to get hold of all the materials he needed, but soon he had got everything together and had mastered the technique. Mike made the decisions as to what was good enough and what wasn't, which paintings or sketches to get extra prints of and where to display them in the café.

The weeks rolled by, and it was soon the June half-term holiday, almost their busiest time of year. Mike was working in the kitchen permanently, and Emily had agreed to take on an extra helper for him, as she and Ron often did during the tourist season. Every day was relentlessly busy, and although Emily was starting to have a little more energy, she would take herself off for longer and longer walks, sometimes not showing up for the start of the evening shift, leaving Mike, Chris and Sam to get on with the business of running the busy restaurant.

Over the summer season, Ged stayed in one of the guest rooms at the pub during weeks when Chy Gwyn was rented to paying guests. He took a trip up to the Cotswolds to see Annie, and they met up with

Jed-number-two and his wife, Barbara, for a delightful cheese and wine evening and spent another evening with Annie's other friends at the pub quiz. They took walks along the River Windrush and had lunches at Hattie's.

Annie encouraged Ged to draw. They would occasionally reminisce about Marge. On those occasions, it became even more apparent to Ged that Annie and Marge had led quite separate lives as girls and young women. Annie was very different to her big sister. She had always felt that she had two left feet when it came to dancing and had a very different approach to gardening than her father and Marge, preferring to allow her garden to grow fairly rampant with perennials, fruit bushes and old roses. She allowed wild flowers that her father would have called weeds to take over in her garden. This attracted a variety of buzzing and rustling wildlife. She would pull the grass and dandelions from her small patio only enough that she could set up her little wrought-iron table and chairs. By far, the most remarkable difference between Annie and her elder sister that stood out to Ged was her acceptance of other people. She rarely, if ever, offered an opinion about someone unless it was a positive one. In stark contrast to Marge and their parents, she simply allowed people to be themselves. She had no opinion about what others should or shouldn't do or how they ought to behave. Ged guessed that either her grandmama must have instilled this in her, or perhaps she disliked it so much in her family that she was determined not to be judgmental herself.

On the summer visit, Ged was restless. He telephoned the Lobster Pot every day before the lunch time, sitting to see how Emily was doing. Invariably, it would be Mike or Suzy who answered the telephone, and he would ask after Emily. He always got the same answer… "Oh, she's okay, nothing new, keeping busy." Ged talked with Annie about her:

"I just wish I could do something to help her. She just isn't the same. It's like part of her has died."

"That's because it has," said Annie simply.

"Why don't I feel the same way about Marge?"

"Because you two didn't run a restaurant together every day of your lives. You had other interests. Plus, everyone is different, Ged.

You really can't compare how you responded to your bereavement with anyone else. We all feel how we feel, and feeling guilty about not being sad enough is a waste of energy."

"I do wonder if I should feel more upset than I do, but I suppose life has been so busy since I moved down to Porthcovery."

"It's the best thing you've ever done," said Annie.

41

August 1999

It was the last two weeks of the children's summer holidays. Ged had written to Alice and Jamie over the spring and summer, sending them postcards and letters illustrated with scenes from around Porthleven and the busy harbour there. The children sometimes wrote back. Jamie sent him a story he had written about Christopher Columbus, and Ged wrote back with some cartoon drawings. Alice wrote a card and sent one to Jenny Halshaw, thanking her for the book and asking if she was writing about Tiger again, suggesting that she could write a story about Purple Unicorns and ponies that fairies could ride. Jenny replied and promised to meet her when she came to Porthcovery in the school holidays.

This started a correspondence between them that would last a lifetime. Jenny wrote back to Alice every time she got a letter or card, encouraging her to write her own stories about the purple unicorns.

Brian and Sarah drove down a little earlier than usual, and the children were wide awake when they arrived, leaping out of the car and rushing to the house to find Ged. The door of the house was locked. Despite rapping on the door and ringing the new doorbell that Ged had installed, there was no sign of him. There was hope, though, as the old Honda was parked in the driveway.

"Where's Grandad?" Jamie whined.

"Grandad is here!" called Ged, walking down the road with a large paper bag in his hands. "I guessed you might be hungry, so I brought provisions," he grinned.

"What is it?" asked Alice.

"Five of Peggy's best," he said to her, giving her a one-armed hug and kissing the top of her head. "So, how's my biggest granddaughter then?"

"Hungry," said Alice. "But not for long."

"Have you got any tomato ketchup, Grandad?" said Jamie.

"Bought three bottles last week to prepare for your arrival," said Ged, hugging his Grandson.

"Hmmm, may have to pop out for more by Wednesday," said Brian ruefully, "they're both completely addicted."

"It's lunchtime, Dad," said Sarah, "Peggy's usually sold out by now."

"She has started making two batches. Now it's high season, and a friend is helping her. She's really busy since she started selling cakes, tea, and coffee last summer. I ordered these so they would be warm when you got here. I know it's only half past four, but I thought you might be hungry."

The family were soon sitting out in the garden, sinking their teeth into delicious Cornish pasties and washing them down with mugs of tea. Sarah took a look around.

"Something has changed, but I can't put my finger on it."

"Well, Mum isn't here, moaning about something," said Brian.

"Brian, that's not nice," said Ged, sternly. "Especially now we know it was the tumours talking."

"Oh, come on, Dad. She was always grumpy on the first day of the holiday, long before she became ill."

"I still don't want you rubbishing your Mum."

"Sorry, Dad. It does feel different here without her. And it doesn't look the same. Have you done much to the garden?"

"Erm, except pay the gardener to cut the grass, I've done absolutely nothing. I expect I should have pruned the roses, but I wouldn't know where to start. And those flowers that are growing on the border. I've not seen them before. I don't know where they've come from."

"I think Mum used to pull them out," said Sarah, "they're a weed."

"Isn't a weed simply a plant that is somewhere you don't want it to be?" said Ged.

"I guess so."

"Well, I'm happy for them to be there, so they aren't a weed anymore," said Ged ", so no need to do the weeding," with a wink. Sarah grinned back.

"Would you like me to have a go at the garden?" she offered.

"There's no need, but if you want to potter, feel free," he said, "and don't pull those blue weeds out; I like them."

"Let's have a look at the workshop, Dad." Said Brian. "I can't wait to see what else you've done."

Ged took the family around to the little yard to the side of Chy Gwyn and unlocked the Workshop door. Ged had filled the holes in the render, and the whole lean-to building was now whitewashed inside and out. The workbench was set up under the window with a long fluorescent tube over it and a long-necked spot lamp. Ged had made a shadow board for many of his tools, the floor was swept clean, and there was a neat stack of picture frames in a large cardboard box on the workbench with some discarded mounts in another.

"You're framing your own artwork now, are you?" said Sarah.

"And others too... Since Ron passed away, I've been roped in to help. He showed me how to do it months ago...." Ged trailed off.

"Dad? Are you ok?" said Sarah.

"Mmm. I just thought it was... well, you'll think I'm being silly, but it's as though somehow, he knew..."

"Maybe he did, and he wanted to make sure Emily would be looked after."

"Mmm..."

"How is Emily?" asked Sarah.

"Not good, to be honest. It has really hit her hard. She and Ron have run the Lobster Pot for twenty-five years, and they spent nearly every day together. She's lost half of herself."

"I guess you, of all people, can connect with how she feels. Your own grief must still be pretty raw."

"Actually, no. I don't feel like that, and seeing Emily so completely bereft and heartbroken kind of makes me feel guilty that I don't feel that way. I was married to Marge for over thirty years, so I feel like I ought to feel sadder than I do."

"Everyone responds differently, Dad. I think you hit the nail on the head with what you said about Emily. She and Ron have never known what it's like to have separate lives. I mean, Mum had all her groups, her garden and the crossword. You rubbed along pretty well as a couple, but you didn't do all that much *'together'*, did you?"

"I wasn't allowed to. If I so much as touched a pair of secateurs, Marge would have had a fit! I wasn't interested in flowers. To me, they're just nice-looking vegetables; I mean, they make a place look nice, but I'm not really interested in them. She didn't like me cooking with her. I just got under her feet. She was happy for me to cook on my own, but we wouldn't cook together. Decorating this place, now that was where we made a good team – decorating, but we didn't do anything together: She picked the colour of the paint or the wallpaper, and I got it on the walls properly; she would choose the kitchen cabinets, and I'd build them. We always seemed to agree on where things needed to go."

"What about the dancing?" said Sarah.

"Ahh, dancing… dancing was the only thing we ever really did together and that git, James Cookson, put a stop to that. The twins were our greatest connection; we had very similar ideas about how they should be brought up. We were united on that."

"You don't need to feel guilty for feeling the way you do. We just feel what we feel."

"And I suppose she was more – well, even more judgemental in recent years, which I can't deny has had an impact on us as a couple."

"Well, that's hardly surprising… and your way of coping with the loss seems to have been to throw yourself into your work. Loads of people cope with bereavement that way… I was a bit concerned about you moving down here. I kind of thought you were running away to get away from the memory of Marge, but I think your heart has been down here a lot longer than that, hasn't it?"

"Definitely, Sarah, love. I can't tell you how right I feel here. I feel more at home than I've ever felt anywhere in my life. I'm treated like one of the family. I don't feel like a stranger from Warwick. It's like I was always meant to be here. It's like finding the missing bit of sky in a jigsaw you've had for years. I feel like, at last, I just fit in here."

"I'm so pleased, Dad," Sarah said, regarding Ged, her eyes sincere. "You look happier than you have looked for years, and that's an odd thing when you're so recently bereaved."

"I couldn't agree more, Sarah; it's so strange to feel so happy and settled after such a dreadful year. There's something else… I wanted to thank you."

"Thank me?"

"Well, when I found out you'd gone behind my back and given Emily those sketches, I have to admit, I was a bit surprised, but if you hadn't gone behind my back, Mike wouldn't have spotted the sketches, and I wouldn't be stood here – a published illustrator, would I?

***

That summer, the Bakers had the most typical of summer holidays: French cricket on the beach, picnics, bodyboarding, sand-casting and long walks along the coast path, rediscovering favourite secret coves, eating ice cream and Cornish cream teas. On the second Monday of their holiday, Bill and Sharon treated the family to a private family meal at the Seagull café behind closed doors. Bill and Sharon wanted to try a few new recipes on the family, especially Bill, who wanted to offer more continental and vegetarian options. The two chefs sat at one end of the table with Ged listening in and extensively trying the new wines that Bill was thinking of offering as an evening drink. They even tried a few new children's options on Jamie and Alice, who were happy to oblige. Bill's Spaghetti Alla Carbonara and Spaghetti Al Aioli went down particularly well with the family. Brian made a few suggestions, and Sharon engaged Sarah and the children in a game of Animal charades, which seemed noisier than Charades were supposed to be but was later voted the highlight of the week by Jamie and Alice, especially their mother's charade of a giraffe after three glasses of wine.

Alice spent rainy days drawing with Ged and writing her story. True to her word, Jenny Halshaw came to visit the family on one of their beach days. She brought her grandsons, who were visiting. They were similar in age to Jamie and had a wonderful day, bodyboarding and playing cricket, while Alice, painfully shy at first, got to know Jenny, who had brought her a few of her earlier books and read one or two of them to her. Jenny read Alice's unicorn story and then helped her to plan out how she might edit and improve it. She did a number of creative writing workshops in schools. So she knew how to be sensitive, gentle and kind with her feedback, helping to bring out the best of Alice's writing and encouraging her not to be afraid to edit out the parts that didn't make it flow or might seem irrelevant to a reader. "Show, don't tell, Alice," she repeated over and over.

When they parted after an al fresco fish and chip supper, sitting on the harbour wall, Jenny promised to keep writing to Alice and asked her to send the story when it was finished. She knew of a number of Children's writing competitions she could enter if she wanted to.

Ged occasionally went over to Porthleven to see how Emily, Mike and the others were managing at the Lobster Pot and took the family to eat there twice a week over the fortnight. Mike took the opportunity to ask Brian to come into the kitchen to advise him on any equipment that might need refurbishing and how to maintain a few of the pieces of equipment he was less familiar with. Brian was happy to help and could see that Mike was managing the kitchen really well for a newbie, though he remembered that Ron had taught him how to manage the kitchen when he was a teenager. Sarah was worried about Emily. She hardly spoke at all. As it had been a year since Sarah had seen her, it was a shock to see her looking so old, and she thought she had lost a lot of weight too.

Sarah managed to get her on her own on the second evening.

"Hey, Emily. You know, I never really thanked you properly for selling Dad's sketches. It's really given him a whole new lease of life."

"Oh, no problem, Sarah Dear. I s'pose it's something positive since the loss of Mrs B."

"Yes. I suppose. Listen, Emily, I don't mean to intrude, but I can see that losing Ron has been a terrible thing for you. Have you – er been to see anyone about it?"

"See anyone?" asked Emily. "Who would I see?"

"Well, I know of at least two things you could look for," said Sarah. "If you have a branch of *Relate* near here, they do bereavement counselling, and there are also *'Cruise'* counsellors. My brother died of a heart attack when I was in my teens. We had a Cruise counsellor, and she was really helpful."

"How?"

"Well, I suppose the only way I can describe it was like – the pain didn't go away, but the counselling helped me to… well, I suppose it helped me bear it better… and figure out how to move on. Talking to my counsellor was easier than talking to my Mum and Dad. She wasn't involved. My parents were grief-stricken, too, so it was really hard for them to support me. And besides, she was trained to do it." Emily sniffed and took out a tissue; she wiped her eyes and paused for a few moments.

"If I did want to find someone, 'ow might I go about it?"

"Well, there's a national register of Cruise counsellors and Relate is actually a couples counselling charity, but they also do grief counselling. Your doctor will probably be able to put you in touch with them or maybe the Citizens' Advice Bureau. I'd be happy to help you find your nearest person. I think you'd be surprised how many of your neighbours have done the same thing."

"Thanks. I'll think about it. I just don't feel complete anymore. Having no Ron is like having no right arm and left leg… even what I 'ave doesn't work."

"I can totally understand. You've been together all these years, and you're hardly ever apart; you're one whole unit, and now half of that is gone. I can't imagine how awful that must feel. I know Dad is really concerned for you; we all are." Emily's eyes were reddening.

"Oh, I'm sorry, Emily," Sarah began, "I didn't mean to…"

"No, it's alright, dear. Ged an' Mike, Suzy, Chris, young Sam an' Dot 'ave all been a tower o' strength. I don't know how I would've managed without 'em. I will think about what you said. I'm sorry for your loss 'o your brother too."

"Yeah, I miss him still. I wish the kids could have met him. He was such a clown; he would have had them laughing like mad." Tears pricked the corners of Sarah's eyes, too. The two women embraced briefly, too long, and they would have been sobbing.

All too soon, the family holiday was over, and Ged was standing on the coast road, waving as the family drove homeward. He had thoroughly enjoyed having them all over to stay. The children still energised him, and he loved seeing how they were changing and growing up. The house seemed empty without them. The last group of rental visitors were due to arrive the following day, and Ged was going to stay at the pub for another week. Glyn had a long list of small end-of-season jobs for him to do, so he knew he would be busy.

***

The day after she spoke with Sarah, Emily went for one of her long walks with Dot.

"Dot, I think I need some 'elp. I mean a different sort of 'elp to what you, Mike and Ged 'ave been doin'. Do you know anyone who does... bereavement counsellin'?"

"Yes, my Lovely, I was thinkin' of suggestin' it. There is someone in Helston, I think. My neighbour said she was marvellous. Cruise or some such name. I'll give her a call when we get back and let you know."

***

Since the family visit, Ged had managed to get back into drawing and was busy mounting some of his own sketches and some paintings by a local artist. This time, the frames were destined for the Seagull café. Ged had continued his watercolour classes and had done a couple of surprise commissions for Bill and Sharon. One of Sharon, carrying plates of cake to a couple of ladies – who looked remarkably like Marge and Hilary Scott – sitting together at a table and another of Bill standing proudly in his usual position at the door of the kitchen with his bucket of coffee. The paintings were in a cartoon style, but the resemblance was remarkable. Ged had put them together with a collection of paintings and illustrations that he and Mike had chosen from the art students at Falmouth. Half of them were to go on the walls of the Lobster Pot, and the other half would be exhibited at the Seagull café.

Ged popped into the house to have a rest. He had been standing doing the frames and mounts for almost two hours, and his legs and back were stiff. As he sat down, the doorbell rang. He wasn't expecting anyone... perhaps it's the post lady, he thought.

Emily stood on the doorstep in a bright pink coat and a pair of blue jeans. Her hair was tied back into a ponytail, and she looked ready for walking.

"Well, are you going to invite me in then?" she said.

"Sorry, Emily," Ged shook himself out of his surprise at finding Emily on his doorstep without warning. "I wasn't expecting anyone. It's great to see you. I just made tea; do you want some?"

"That would be nice," She said. "You know, I 'aven't been to Porthcovery in years. Ron and I would always go up country if we had a day off. I did come here with Dot in the winter, and we'd come here for days out when I was a little girl. We'd come for an ice cream on Sundays after church."

"The ice cream is heavenly, isn't it? Was it always Mawgan's?"

"Oh, yes. I always had Strawberry when I was a girl." Emily took off her coat and hung it on a chair by the dining table. She went over to the large window seat while Ged went to make her a cup of tea.

Ged came to join her with their mugs of tea. "Er, do you want a biscuit? I'm afraid they're only ginger nuts," he said, handing her the mug.

"Oh, no thanks, just tea is fine."

"So, Emily," he said, "to what do I owe this surprise visit?"

"Well, I think I've come to ask your ...well, your advice, I suppose. I have a bit of a decision to make, and I'm not sure how to go about making it."

"I'm honoured that you would ask my advice, Emily. What's the issue?"

"I've tried to carry on as before at the Lobster Pot without Ron for three months now, and I just can't do it. Without Ron, it just ain't the same. Don't get me wrong, Mike is doing a great job. In fact, he and Suzy have added new things to the menu, and the customers love 'em. The restaurant is as busy as it's ever been. I just feel...empty."

"I understand, Emily. It must be so tough. You and Ron were like one person. Losing him and so suddenly like that must be like losing part of yourself."

"Oh, I knew you'd understand," said Emily. She looked at him with an almost pleading expression. "It really is, but then you would know. It's not so long since Mrs B passed, is it?"

"Well, no, but it's been different for me. Marge and I led quite separate lives, in a way. I mean, I'm sad that she's gone, but I don't feel torn apart like I suppose you must." Emily's eyes were glassy. Ged placed his free hand on hers. He was so fond of this lovely, kind and sweet woman. His heart ached with sorrow for her. He had a strong and sudden urge to take her in his arms and hold her, if that could take some of her pain away.

"So," Emily said, taking both hands to her mug and sipping her tea. She paused to look out at the bay; it was a calm and peaceful day; the sea was almost mirror-smooth, and the sun sparkled on the tiny ripples. "So," she repeated, "I've been seeing this lady in Helston. She's a cruise counsellor. She's been wonderful, 'elpin' me get through all this over Ron."

"That's great, Emily," said Ged. "So, do you feel any better for it?"

"Certainly. It's like your lovely girl Sarah told me: it doesn't take the pain away, but it helps me bear it. It's like puttin' a bandage on a bad leg. It still 'urts but I can get on with my day a bit better. Think a little bit clearer if you get my drift."

"Oh, did Sarah suggest it? I do seem to recall she had a lot of help when her brother died. I know those were tough times for her."

"Well, yes, an' I asked Dot too. She put me on to Frances – Frankie, they call 'er. Turns out quite a few of my neighbours have been to see 'er over the years, an' she 'as quite a reputation," explained Emily. "She's so patient and kind, y'know, doesn't rush yer or tell yer to 'snap out of it' or tell yer those lies like *it'll get better with time*'. 'cause I know it won't. She just 'elps you to work out 'ow you're gonna get through the next few days, then the next few weeks after that, then your first few months and even look ahead to the first few *years* after the loss. Y'know, so you start to realise that there is a future, a different one, but a future nonetheless."

"Sounds like a wise woman," said Ged sincerely.

"Yeah, well, it's got me thinkin', y'know, 'bout the future an' all. I went to see our solicitor in Falmouth, an' then our accountant. Ron always was a prudent chap. An' neither of us were great spenders. The Lobster Pot 'as always done a good turnover over the years, but that's the thing with runnin' a place like that, you get used to workin' all the time an' you never get round to spendin' much."

"Uh-huh?"

"Ron' 'ad a tidy sum put by, and I got a good pension. I'm sixty this year, so I reckon I'm gonna retire."

"I see," said Ged, smiling. "Seems like a good plan to me. It's exactly what I did after Marge passed. I mean, I keep busy doing jobs, but I'm essentially retired. I do as much or as little as I want to, and I only work for people I like. I've got the rental income from the old house in Warwick, I'll get a pension from my last job, and my needs are fairly modest. I have to admit, Emily, I haven't felt so settled and happy in a very, very long time."

"The only problem is," Emily continued, "If I sell the Lobster Pot, then I won't 'ave anywhere to live. Well, unless the owners want to rent me the flat above the restaurant. And I really would rather not be there with someone else runnin' the place. I'd be interferin' all the time, and it's a constant reminder that Ron's not there anymore."

"Have you told Mike about your plans?" asked Ged.

"Not yet. You're the first person I told, well, after Frankie, that is."

Ged sipped his tea and looked out to the bay. A cormorant had settled on a rock a few metres out to sea and was warming its wings in the sunshine. He took another slug of his now lukewarm tea and took a deep breath.

"Emily, do you think Mike might like to take over the restaurant?" Ged suggested. "He could either buy it off you or maybe run it as a manager while you still own it. You could still be involved... I really think it might be worth asking him. I've seen how brilliantly Suzy and Mike work together; they really are naturals. And Mike told me that he's never been happier than when he's working at the Lobster Pot, both now and as a young man."

"Well, there's no one I'd rather sell it to, that's for sure, but...."
Emily's voice began to falter, and tears began to well in her eyes. "I've never lived anywhere else, and I really don't know where I'm goin' ter go if I leave the Lobster Pot. I really want to be somewhere else. I've got no family elsewhere. All my relatives are gone. Ron is all I 'ad...

her voice cracked, and she bowed her head. A tear splashed into her tea mug, and her shoulders began to shake.

Ged grabbed some tissues from the box on the table and handed them to her, taking her empty mug away. He shuffled up next to her and put both his arms around her. She fell into his arms, her head against his chest and sobbed freely. Ged simply held her, gently rocking her.

"Oh, Emily, you're such a lovely person," he murmured. "Ron was a lucky man, and you were lucky to have him, too. Getting to know you two has been one of the best parts of moving down here for me."

Emily's sobs gradually slowed, and she held the tissues to her eyes.

"I just don't want to go back there anymore, Ged," she said. "Every tile, every glass and cup, our bed, even the loo makes me think of how he's not there with me and how much I miss him. The pain is physical, really physical, and I can't get away from it."

Ged gently sat her up and held her shoulders so that she had to look at him with her reddened, puffy eyes. He took a breath. "I have two spare rooms. Come and stay here," he said. "Stay as long as you like. Call it a holiday. I bet Mike and Suzy will be fine, and if they aren't, you're only a phone call away. They might not have the place running like clockwork without you, but I'm sure they can muddle through with a bit of help from Chris and his mate."

"Really? You mean it?" whispered Emily, her eyes met his in an almost pleading expression.

"Really."

"I need to talk to Mike and Suzy. What if they don't want to run the place?"

"Well, there's only one way to find out. Come on, let's go for a walk up to the headland. I need a walk, and you came dressed for one, so let's not waste this lovely weather."

42

June 2000

Ged put down his pencil and surveyed the latest set of illustrations he had produced. Tiger was becoming bolder and even more 'Cat about town,' but he had a new problem to deal with. Scamp was a lively and chaotic canine addition to Tiger's family. Jenny's latest story introduced him as a new and likely long-term addition to her Tiger series of children's books. Ged had spent the last week drawing different styles and breeds of dogs that might suit the character. The dining table was covered in sketches of a wide variety of dogs. He was leaning towards a medium-sized scruffy black mongrel with bright eyes.

Emily waved to Ged as he arrived at the Seagull Café for his ten-thirty coffee break. She disappeared inside the café for a few moments, returning with a mug of tea and a cappuccino, then glanced at Sharon, who nodded to her and smiled. Emily took off her apron and hung it on the back of a chair on the verandah, joining Ged at his table.

"So, do you have to go to the book festival?" she asked.

"It's not essential, but the publishers are really keen for Jenny and I to do Hay-on-Wye. It's supposed to be the highlight of the book year. They want us both there on the first day together, at the very least. Jenny is doing a reading, and I'm doing a sketching workshop or two in the main marquee on the first day. I'll be back in a couple of days."

Emily reached her hand across the table and held his hand for a moment.

"You're going to miss dance class, and I'll be on my own for the first time in Chy Gwyn."

"Well, why not invite Sharon and Bill over for a bit of company?"

"I'll ask Sharon. It's not a bad idea."

"You could watch that film you fell asleep in front of last night. I think you only saw the first fifteen minutes before you nodded off."

"Oh, Yes. I did want to see it, but I was just so tired. How long will it take you to get to Hay-on-Whatever?"

"Quite a long time, according to Suzy. She's driving us there."

"There's another festival I'd like to take you to, Emily, but I don't want to go as an illustrator. It's called the 'Just-So' festival. I always loved the *Just So* stories. I'm thinking of taking Jamie and Alice. We can hire a big tent there for the whole family."

"It sounds exciting. I've never been to a festival before. What's it like?"

"I'm just about to find out when I go to Hay-on-Wye. I've never been to one either," said Ged, grinning.

"Life has been quite an adventure since I moved in with you."

"I thought it was supposed to be temporary," said Ged with a wink.

"Oh, it is. Just until I get a better offer," Emily quipped back and drank the remainder of her tea. Sharon walked past with some sandwiches. "The boss here is a bit of a dragon. I'd better get back to work."

THE END

Epilogue

Ged Baker went on to illustrate over forty children's books with Jenny Halshaw and another sixty books with other authors in Britain and Scandinavia. He wrote a few of his own children's books, too. The most popular of these was a fairy tale involving a purple flying unicorn.

Ged and Emily finally had a marriage ceremony (of sorts) at their tenth Hay-on-Wye festival in a large Yurt decorated with coloured flags... With cats printed on them.

About the Author

Fi Miles was born in Cheshire and has written stories all her life. Since her first trip to the Lizard, she has been an unabashed Cornwall fanatic. Years of hiking along the Southwest coast path, finding hidden coves and getting to know many creative, friendly and inspiring people who make their living in this beautiful part of the British Isles has given her a deep love for the area and its inhabitants.

She began writing more seriously after having her children and writing many stories for them. She was inspired to write a novel about the residents of a beautiful and exclusive nursing home located on one of her favourite hikes along the coast path. Wondering who those residents may be and how they afforded a place at such a home gave birth to a wealth of interesting characters, one of which was Ged Baker.